MY *Unlikely* SAINT
ACT 1. BOOK I.

By CC Carlquist

My Unlikely Saint is a work of fiction. Street names and locations have been stage-managed. Any errors in this story are of my own making. Veteran Minnesotans who see a resemblance to actual people and events, I assure you, it's a coincidence.

ISBN-13: 978-1468199499
ISBN-10: 1468199498

Thank you Rob, Elaine, and Suzy for what you said.

A special thanks to Eleanor Brekke and Muriel Krusemark, my
partisans long ago.

And Sammy, custodian of seclusion.
Only you know where you are.

CHAPTERS

PART I

1. Toni Padua
Anthony, the Patron Saint of Lost Things

Standing next to her at the front desk already checked in and settled in with no business other than to locate an open bar in the hotel, I could hear every word she said. Something about the woman's demeanor kept me from interrupting with my menial drivel. That the person she was seeking was not registered seemed obvious to me. Bart behind the desk strained to hear over the hotel ruckus. She asked would he please try a different spelling? Ac maybe? Es? Each time he checked, she'd duck her head as if her troubles might be airborne. Our eyes met once. The pan-beige smear under one eye barely concealed the purple crescent. I smiled kindly and looked away. Could he check the first name? Claire? Bart offered her the desk phone instead. She shook her head and ran a hand through her hair, soot black with the unmistakable dull luster of a dye job. Bart waited, his customer service smile on hold. She glanced down at the boy standing beside her. His blue parka was zippered to his chin. His unruly hair needed a comb. I resisted the urge to brush it out of his eyes. I could have, because he stood still as a sentry with his hands clasped behind his back. Odd behavior for a kindergarten kid. But what did I know?

The woman pulled a curled-up photo from her coat pocket and smoothed it flat for Bart to see. "She's thin and blonde and looks like Dusty Springfield."

Bart leaned in for a closer look. "Dusty who?"

I headed into the lobby in search of a bar, pub, lounge, maybe a canteen. The lobby served as midway for the Romance Writers Conference: tables and kiosks loaded with cliché-a-day calendars, promo mugs and clip-on mini lights, Nooks next to the books. And record attendance this fall, these divas of the heart, amongst whom a dozen possible Dusty Springfields were trolling for the buzz and a glimpse of Nora Roberts.

Ah, there. The concierge. Busy on his laptop.

"Excuse me, sir." Keys clicked, then the mouse. "Ahmm, I know it's early…" I lowered my voice, "…but is there a–"

"Stonehenge. Follow the green vine carpet, take a right at the Saxon swords."

"–bar open somewhere?"

"Through the double doors," he added. His eyes hadn't left the screen. Didn't need to. He'd suffered it all before, a thousand times ten. Someone needed to tell Mr. Snappy here that this was a hotel — a midday cocktail didn't mean a thing. I'd had a testy morning, that's all. His cell phone rang. He felt around for it. I followed the green vine carpet.

I missed the Saxon swords, but the double doors were open. The lounge was empty, no more than a nightlight behind the bar. I considered the mini-fridge up in my room, the *discreet* mini-fridge up in my room, and turned to go, but a shadow pop-up in the nightlight caught my eye. It was all I needed to cross what was now red vine carpet and take a stool. I dropped my backpack and settled in next to a faux marble pillar at the corner of the bar. The shadow popped back up in front of me like a Jack-in-the-Box, stormy hair and all, but minus the happy face. BOB was satin-stitched to his porter jacket.

"How about a martini?" I chirped. Still smarting from the concierge's whiz-bang appraisal of my deflated self, albeit correct, I added, "No fuss. On the rocks is fine. Stoli, if you got it."

Bob pulled a long-stemmed glass from the rack and shoveled it full of ice. He twisted the lid off a jar of olives, set the jar down, and tossed a curled-up lemon rind into my glass. Not even a programmed hello.

I slumped against the faux marble pillar, which scrunched like Styrofoam, and focused on the four tiers of liquor bottles aligned in a single-minded manner; clear graded to amber, a swatch of watermelon, a slash of lime, medicinal and untouched. Grappa. Ouzo. Kümmel. Kümmel was caraway seeds.

"Who drinks Kümmel?" I asked, favorably conversational.

Bob turned away to find the vodka. It'd been a turn-down-day so far, so this blatant incivility should have meant nothing. Plainly, it stung. I swiped a cocktail napkin from the tray, dabbed at my eyes and sniveled, dabbed again, then folded my arms and peeked around to see who might have witnessed my pathetic display of self-pity.

She had.

I hadn't noticed her against the wall, L-shaped bar that it was. Her black hair, pale face, and mottled sweater blended like calico with the rag-rolled stucco wall. She wore the posture of a parochial schoolteacher, and tidy with her overcoat arranged on the stool next to her as if that seat were taken. Eyes with a halfway Asian slant appraised me without sentiment. She took a sip of her drink, the glass wrapped in a cocktail napkin, a rather matronly idiosyncrasy, I thought, not knowing at the time that she never left fingerprints.

My eyes had adjusted to the dark, which wasn't so dark after all, and I saw right away why the bar was called Stonehenge. On the wall to my left, knights on horses rode into the Highlands, or some such place, where baby clouds floated up onto the pocked ceiling tiles, crossed the room and floated down into the ladies-in-waiting, who, seemingly unaware of the departing horsemen, were gathering roses. A curious incongruity separated the people from their landscape. The people, rendered flat and stretched like faded Modiglianis, had been stuck into scenery painted by the Norman Rockwell Club, who should have stopped with their crazy brushes, but had gone on and converted the entrance into dungeon doors, striated stones and all. A wacky side exit, similarly painted, cut through the ladies-in-waiting. Equally peculiar, the old-timey tables and knobby chairs conjured up a Sam Shepard western, not Canterbury. And not one lunch straggler. The schoolteacher and I were Bob's only customers.

Back behind the bar, steam gathered like a galactic nebula in the middle of which stood Bartender Bob. With his stormy hair and smooth, flat face, he could be the man from Mars come up out of the mist to mix my drink. He poured the vermouth, then the vodka (which didn't look like Stoli) into a cocktail shaker, capped it and shook the life out of it — after I'd told him not to fuss. The man from Mars. That would explain it: this offense to good sense of a bar was a prop, a cunning distraction, a cover for some red planet experiment — romance writers drugged and transported into a parallel world. Or Canada.

And a fitting end it would be, having stumbled out of university with a degree in history, having spent the last decade writing uber-zealous romance novels, and at long last, mercifully terminated in a human species recruiting station disguised as a castle disguised as a bar. Modigliani knights in a Norman Rockwell landscape. Martian paintings.

What cooked behind the bar continued to steam. Space Bartender Bob poured the soylent solution into my glass and set the potion in front of me, spun around to the register and slipped on a pair of Oakley knockoffs and tapped his secret codes onto a keyless pad that could double as a rocket-launcher. The mirror detailed his peevish face, which might better explain the empty bar. He'd not said one word to me.

Sure, I could lose a few pounds or ten (twenty if we go for svelte). But I'm not an ugly Betty. Maybe more like a plain Betty in a prairie Nordic sort of way. Straight nose. Straight teeth. Straight hair forever clipped up having more to do with an unsightly tsunami at ear level than any sense of style; its forever black color accentuated my forever pale face — even more so in dark rooms. Years ago in a South Dakota beer hall, a tequila-soaked bass player told me that my eyes reminded him of sun-bleached brownstone. Obviously, I've hung onto that snippet. How many calories in a martini?

The concierge, the snappy one who'd given me directions to Stonehenge, appeared at the bar, helped himself to a pineapple chunk, glanced at me, but, having never laid eyes on me before in his life, gave no sign of recognition. Should I have tipped him? That was so vague anymore.

Space Bartender Bob kicked a door shut and my steamy space station disappeared. He leaned into the bar and talked to the concierge. They talked like they were dating.

Martian bar.

I turned my attention to the schoolteacher. Her narrow eyes fixed on mine. She held her napkin-wrapped glass like a knick-knack, but did not take a drink. Having all but emptied my martini in two swallows, I conveniently drew the assumption that she might welcome conversation.

"I'm a romance writer," I said.

"Why would you write something you know nothing about?"

What do you say to that? Crap, she might have flat-out diagnosed my problem in one simple sentence. Did she know me?

"You're too young to know those stories," she added.

I opened my mouth to protest, but lacked the passion to explain myself. My eyes welled up again. I pulled at the cocktail napkins and sent a stack floating to the floor. That brought Bartender Bob. He swiped them up and stuffed them in the trashcan. Before he could punish me with attitude, the woman pointed to her drink and said with a nod towards me, "And another for her. Make it Stoli this time." She talked like the boss.

Too depressed and lightheaded to protest both her preposterous criticism of my choice of genre and what amounted to a twelve-dollar pour of alcohol, I mumbled, "I'm not sure what I'm going to do."

"Crime," she said.

I snorted a laugh, then considered my lack of accomplishment, which translated to lack of money; next step would be the soup kitchen and those black plastic bags and cardboard boxes, campfires in the alley — tumbled to homeless. If it weren't for my convenient and loving commitment to cat-sit

Mystery Man, my mother's orange tabby, while my parents kicked around Florida nine months out of the year, I might very well be homeless.

"Crime," I huffed. "It just might come to that." Having swilled down an entire martini, I felt bold aiming my finger at Bartender Bob. "Stick 'em up and give me all your Kümmel." He turned up his nose and set the fresh martini next to my smudged-up glass, which I jerked closer, a good half-drop clotted to that lemon rind. The schoolteacher wrapped a fresh napkin around her glass and took a polite sip.

"On second thought," I said. "Nobody pays cash anymore. Banks have all the money. And armed guards, too." I sighed, dramatic. "That leaves convenience stores."

Her mien suggested critical interest or reserved disbelief. Maybe both. Maybe she was entertained by my antics. Then my brain cleared and I shook my head. "Sorry. It's been one of those mornings." I kicked my backpack, which contained three hundred and five pages of *Love is a French Verb* schlepped to the Romance Writers Conference on the off chance that my assigned agent, having read the first fifteen pages, would beg to see the entire novel. I would snap open my pack and present her with a perfectly typed manuscript. No such thing had happened. At the end of the fifteenth page of my perfectly typed, first fifteen pages, she'd written that both characters and storyline needed a wee bit less swoon.

"You're suggesting I write crime instead of romance. Right? Crap. I know less about crime than I know about romance."

"Crime is mechanics," she said. "Romance is lunacy, only clear in hindsight, years too late."

"That never stopped anybody." Which brought to mind my older sister, almost forty, who'd recently married a pinched-faced dentist from Taiwan because she wanted a baby. They'd flown to Reno, but not before she'd signed a prenup. I gave it two years.

"You bite down knowing full well there's a thumbtack hidden in the bonbons, and one day it up and–"

"Rob a bank and you'll know right quick if there's a thumbtack. A Kimber 1911 is precise. A box of chocolates is not."

"But that's exactly my point. Chocolate is like romance. It's vague. You can make it up as you go along. Who cares how many chocolates are in the box? Crime is precise. I can't do precise. Dave — he's a guy from up home, but that's another story — anyway, Dave read this book where the guy pulls out a revolver and flicks off the safety. Uh-uh. Not with that gun he didn't. Dave still laughs about that."

"Like dropping a magazine out of your revolver."

"Only an accountant can work that kind of detail." I captured the re-hydrated lemon rind from the bottom of my glass. I spit it back. "And, anyway, there isn't a crime that hasn't been hacked to death in the pulps. Money laundering, murder, smarmy cons — flat out, worn out." I slid my empty, finger-smudged glass an arm's length down the bar. "There are no new stories."

"I can tell you a story."

I didn't roll my eyes, but I thought it. Everyone had a story. Everyone believed their experience to be so extraordinary they should write a book. When they told you what was so extraordinary, you could nod off in ten different languages. It was always the same damn story. There are more storytellers than there are stories. I was sitting in a hotel full of storytellers. The world was full of us. But the schoolteacher had bought me a twelve-dollar pour. Schooled in manners, the least I could do was act interested, listen a minute, ask a few questions. *Be polite, Jenn.*

"What kind of story?"

"True crime."

"True crime," I repeated with my best, good-natured look. "True, huh?"

"It's my story."

Even worse. Another victim. Victim, schmicktim. There should be a victim genre. Or would that be Memoirs? I glanced at my watch. Forty minutes until my Writing Romantic Memoirs class. Two martinis and no food, not even a peanut — I might not make it. I stifled a yawn and said, "Why don't you write your own story? Everybody's writing memoirs."

She spoke in an offhanded manner, almost a shrug, although her shoulders remained taut. "I'm not a writer and you need a story."

I needed something; that it was her story I needed was doubtful. Add a twelve-dollar martini to the social equation: "Your story, huh?"

"My story, yes."

Husband? Brother? Boyfriend? Some criminal misfit without any swoon and she had the goods on him? But why would she tell me? Why would I get involved? Find myself peering through the peephole one day at some B-movie guy named Mugsy. Then what? Drop that magazine out of my revolver.

"How soon before some creep comes asking how I came upon this incriminating and confidential information?" I sounded light-headed, not to mention disingenuous, but I couldn't stop myself. I tapped my head. "Crazies."

She appeared to be considering my fatuous inquiry. Then she said, "I don't believe that will be a concern. Those who hire me, I do not call them by their names."

That took a second. "Hire you?"

"We were all a bunch of phantoms."

I lowered my voice. "You're the criminal?"

"You would write that in the past tense. I'm working one last contract, then I'm done with this nasty business. Unfortunately, the job has become impossibly complicated. The pieces don't link. And I work alone, so I'm quite at a disadvantage, which is why I'm sitting here in this ghastly place."

"I thought you were a schoolteacher."

"I wish I were."

It might have been her deliberate tone, the calm assuredness that brought me and my martini around the faux marble pillar to her leg of the bar. The entire conversation seemed odd, so odd that maybe, just maybe, it had wheels. This from a man, I would have dashed out the dungeon doors. I settled on a stool, her coat between us, with time enough to figure out if this was a ruse.

"What sort of impossible job? Can you talk about it? What you're in the middle of?"

"I'm not in the middle," she said, fingering her pendant, a Celtic cross or something, thick and silver, some high-energy metal.

I waited, vaguely aware that my curiosity had slipped out of balance with its antidote, caution.

"I'm on the outside."

"Well, then..." I flicked my hand. "...walk away. Who would know?"

"Not a soul."

I nodded as if that made sense and reached in my bag for my notebook and my Sony VOR cassette recorder. "I'm at a writing conference here in the hotel. We could set this up like an interview. Did you read *Interview with the Vampire*?"

"No."

"Anne Rice wrote it. The pithy twist was that the vampire told a hellish story about life as a vampire. Hellish didn't matter. In the end the boy goes looking for the rogue that will change him into a vampire."

"How does the boy know where to find this maker of vampires?"

"He figured it out from the tapes. The vampire had inadvertently told him, never dreaming the boy would want his terrible life. Having lived so long as a vampire, he'd forgotten that people don't want to die." I pushed the tape recorder towards her.

"We could start with your background. How you got started. Maybe a crime or something. Then I can see if I, ahmm…" not sure how to describe our improbable relationship, I suggested, "…if I might interview you."

"A crime or something," she repeated. She folded her arms as if considering, then said, "That seems undeniably reasonable. I am compromised; therefore, I am no longer honor bound." Her dark eyes met my brownstones. Up close, I could see she wasn't Asian. "Yes. I will tell my story."

I punched RECORD. "This is voice-activated."

"My name is Toni Padua." She spelled it for me and glanced over at my notebook. I wrote it down.

"Padua is a town in Italy. Toni is short for Anthony, Anthony of Padua, the Patron Saint of Lost Things and Missing People. Saint scholars consider Anthony to be one of the greatest teachers of all times. He is also the Patron Saint of Barren Women. I haven't a notion how he garnered that accolade."

"So you were named after a saint?"

"Yes, but not that one." She held up a hand. "It will make sense later. I will begin with my mother."

"That sounds right," I said and almost added, "for a criminal."

"She might have had something to do with things. Then, again, maybe not."

Or was this indifference? Don't criminals blame everything on their mothers or some big-breasted woman figure? Even without the criminal element, the neutrality of indifference seemed unlikely in any mother-daughter relationship, most certainly not in storytelling. Some sound psychological blather and a virgin observation would be essential for the story. My best friend Penny, her dad was a psychologist in the Minnesota Education system. He'd help me with the blather. The virgin observation would need to come as an epiphany.

"My mother," Toni said, "got banished from the Order of the Sisters of St. Bibiana because she refused to give up her illegitimate child."

"Whoa. Your mother was a nun?"

"That is correct. She spent the rest of her unacknowledged life doing penance by caring for the sick in the name of the Holy Roman Catholic Church and the freight load of saints who ride with it. She worked at the prison. Every crazed and ruined lunatic who made it to the infirmary on my mother's watch got canonized and sent back to his cell with the name of a saint tattooed on his soul. My mother referred to her sinners by their martyrs' names that she cataloged in her head like favorite recipes. I can still hear her, raptured to the heavens, always the heavens. 'God Praise, Saint John of Capistrano has come home.' God praise, was right. Her good Saint John killed a bank guard in Duluth and skipped back into prison, his retirement secure.

"Growing up, I spent time at the prison while my mother worked. Prisons weren't as locked down and litigious back then. She considered it a valuable life lesson, my helping out, not to mention charitable. Young and dumb, I had an eye for the mean James Deans who made their way into prison like it was some kind of casting call. Always in need of a patch job, these boys provided my mother the opportunity to save them." Toni shut her eyes, her thin lips pressed tight. I waited. She opened her eyes and said primly, "Of course, I knew all along her true life's mission was to get back on the good side of God the Father. My mother's narcissistically righteous life was hatched out of one miscue." She tapped her Celtic cross. "Me."

Her face, fixed like a mask, gave no clue to the nature of her reality. Cocktail in hand, the napkin stuck like paper maché, she brought it to her lips, but set it down untouched. "And like my mother ... I, too, got a miscue."

"A miscued what?"

"Start. A miscued start. They come easy when you're young. You already know that, don't you?"

I already knew that.

She peeled the napkin from her glass and replaced it with a dry one. "One night while pouring drinks at the Triangle Bar on the West Bank of the University of Minnesota, I met the only man north of Miami who drank pineapple Daiquiris. He told me he was an accountant for a large corporation downtown St. Paul. I told him I was an actress playing the role of a bartender forced by the evil universe to pay off a worthless degree in theater. I detailed for him, with a modicum of pride, my expertise in costume and make-up. The next two months he drank his Daiquiris on my shift.

"I could spot him at the door. His whiteness was clearly out of step with the West Bank hippie culture back in the day. He'd come wearing the same beige, checkered leisure jacket and tan pants hiked up over sloppy fat. Squinty eyes, fat face, hair too thin for a comb-over. You know the look. But if you tip well, social gaffes are overlooked. He was a shy guy, my Pineapple Daiquiri, and seemed interested in me, but not in a wolfish way. Then one day he asked if I might like to capitalize on my theater expertise, make some money, pay off the evil universe. Behind in my college loans, behind in my rent, desperate for daylight, what could I say?

"One week later at precisely ten-fifteen A.M. Central Standard Time, I marched into his high rise office disguised as a rent-a-cop and arrested him, handcuffs and all. I read him his rights and escorted him out the door and down the elevator to the garage. From the trunk of his blue Ford Pinto, he handed me a Donaldson's shopping bag, which contained a trench coat that covered my uniform and enough money to pay off my college loans, the back-rent on my apartment, and then some. I'd never seen so much cash. I dropped my wig and hat into the bag, fluffed my hair, walked up the ramp to daylight and caught the University Avenue metro home. I never saw him again.

"Of course I suspected something not quite right about our mini pageant, but I didn't know how much not right until I read in the newspaper that a great sum of money had gone missing from said company and said accountant's blue Ford Pinto had been found in the parking garage right where I'd left him. Seems they'd been on to him, but slow to move. I believe his hoked-up arrest bought him flight-time by confusing the issue. And much to law enforcement's dismay, and to my surprise, nobody could describe the officer who'd arrested him. I thought about that for a long time."

"Nobody noticed you?" My eyes flicked to Bartender Bob who was slicing fruit. "I know the feeling."

"They were his associates, his friends. All eyes stuck on him or the floor, embarrassed for him. Nanny cameras didn't exist. In the mind's eye, I was a uniform. That's all. Not a thing about me memorable. A face like mine was part of his plan."

I squinted at her in search of a mole or a dimple, a defining crease between the brows, something that flagged her. Neither her thin lips nor her strong chin seemed noteworthy enough for memory. The narrow eyes were an earmark, for sure, but her overall semblance appeared downright ordinary. She could be glamorous made-up at one of those celebrity photo salons or quite homish with a hangover. She turned and faced the liquor bottles. Her dark hair, pulled into a chignon, underscored a profile as unremarkable as a store mannequin.

I pointed to her hair. "That's a wig?"

She pulled a wisp at her ear and wound it around her finger. "Every so often I think about my Pineapple Daiquiri. I call him that because, come to find out, nobody, including me, knew his real name. Imagine that. No one knew his real name. And then he was gone. I hope he found his Venus rising. He was my only mentor. He showed me how to employ my expensive skills." She took a sip from her napkin-wrapped glass. I remembered my martini and did likewise.

"In my mother's honor," she said, "I continue her celebration of the saints. Cataloged by patronage, these glorious martyrs are my identities. It is how I've kept my business organized. It is how I know in any given situation, at any given moment, and without hesitation who's addressing me."

My Sony VOR clicked off. "I've got cassettes in my room," I said, fully prepared to skip Memoirs.

She glanced at a thin silver watch on her wrist. "I will come again at six."

Book signings were scheduled for six, but I couldn't remember who was signing. "Six is good," I said.

She reached in her coat pocket and pulled out a bill. Holding it by her fingertips, she tossed it on the bar like a dirty tissue. It was a fifty-dollar bill.

"What's your name?"

"Jennifer," I said, momentarily taken aback that we'd talked like co-conspirators and my identity had not yet been considered. I'd forgotten to say my name. And she hadn't asked. My nonentity status had worsened. "Sands," I said, needing to be remembered. "Jennifer Sands."

"Jennifer," she said with a tic of a smile that went no further than the corner of her mouth. Missed, if you'd blinked. "I'd know your age within three years without ever laying eyes on you."

"Yeah," I said wretchedly. "The Jennifer Years."

She stood up from her stool and bent primly, knees together, and retrieved her pocketbook from the footrest. She straightened and said, "Also known as The Bee Gee Years."

"There are a bunch of us out there. For sure."

"That could be an asset."

Clarification anticipated. None came.

She draped her coat over her arm. "What's your middle name?"

"Allison. Jennifer Allison Sands."

Half turned to go, she said, "I will call you Jas." She nodded once, as if pleased with herself.

"Okay," I said, not sure what to add to that. I watched her disappear through the dungeon doors with her perfect posture, tight as the knot in her hair.

Jas. With an s, of course. I was as far from jazzy as I was from being a published romance writer. Jas could be my city name. Nobody back home would call me Jas. People didn't listen to Jazz in towns like mine. Jazz was city music. I closed my notebook and stared at my name, big and monkey-bold, scrawled across the cover. She'd known all along.

Bob removed her glass and the fifty-dollar bill. He raised an interrogatory eyebrow at me.

I pointed to her glass. "What was she drinking?"

"Water."

2. Alex Edessa
Alexius, the Patron Saint of Beggars

One thing was certain: I wasn't a memoir writer. Maybe in twenty years, when I had something to remember. Nobody writes about my kind of childhood. Boo Radley, Almira Gulcho, Fagin — none of them lived in my town. No one owned the Baskerville hounds. My father was an accountant who came home every night at six, except during tax season. My mother worked mornings at Anderson Florist. They danced to the one-hit-wonders of The Sixties on the jukebox in the basement. They didn't drink, at least not in front of me. Even more boring, I graduated high school without a delinquency. I got grounded a couple of times for curfew violations, and TP'd somebody's yard once and lost my allowance for a month. My childhood lacked literary color. No one put the dark on me.

I did not return to Memoirs after the break, but spent the rest of the afternoon in my room with a nap to shake off the booze and a shower to wake up. I played and replayed the tape I'd labeled TONI#1. Listening to that cool, judicial voice, I was unable to determine true or false. But why would she waste her time fabricating some bizarre story? What would be the point of that? I would meet her at six like she'd said. Raised in the rural Midwest by third-generation American Legionnaires, when it came to age, showing respect trumped common sense, and she outranked me by a good twenty years.

She seemed like a nice enough lady.

Parked on the same stool where she'd left me, I had a power view of Stonehenge: a table of unattended soda pop tweens, a table of lushed-up romance writers, two business men at the bar working their laptops, and one woman done up like a realtor. But maybe not a realtor — her fawn brown suit and washable silk blouse suggested more than Open House and a yard sign. Perfectly blunt-cut, chestnut hair with salon highlights argued banker-lawyer, pulling a salary my history major would never generate. Throw in a brass nameplate.

Washed out from my two-martini lunch, I stifled a yawn. Two sips of Stoli would straighten me out. I cleared my throat. Twice. Apparently not loud enough. Bartender Bob lolled at the register, busy in a notebook, done with me and my glass of ice water served up without a word. He probably had a day job writing for *Popular Mechanics*. I decided to call the hotel and ask them to ring the bar, give Bartender Bob my drink order on the phone. I dug around in my bag for my cell phone, but that social crutch was not to be found. Last seen in my room. If I ran to fetch it, I might miss her. Or not. She might not come at all. Changed her mind. Her crazy mind.

I settled in to wait.

A chichi blonde Dusty Springfield joined the romance writers at their table reminding me of the woman at the reservation desk and her ill-fated hunt for … I'd already forgotten the name. Probably her agent. That would make perfect sense. But there'd been that sad little boy, so still. Something unmanageable had been kicked at the two of them. I wondered if I could have helped. Why hadn't I asked?

Claire. Yeah, that was it.

About to admit that Toni Padua had gone back to the asylum, I let go an indignant sigh. The banker-lawyer lady glanced at me with notable blue eyes. I sent her a "sisters in wait" nod and took a sip of my water capturing an ice pellet in my mouth. She returned the nod and took a sip of her drink. And there it was. The napkin-wrapped glass. I choked on my ice.

"Toni?" I sputtered and patted my chest. She'd been there the whole time.

Drink in hand, she slid off the stool and with a long, fashionable stride as authentic as Toni Padua's short, prim steps earlier, she rounded the faux marble pillar.

"I'm Alex," she said, energizing the dead air that, up until that moment, I hadn't noticed. She set her drink down, hooked her purse on the backrest and slid onto the stool. "Alex Edessa by way of Alexius, the Patron Saint of Beggars. Born rich in Rome, he dropped the glam and moved to Syria where he lived a penniless life championing the homeless. There was a brief period in the history of the almighty, rich-beyond-righteous Catholic Church when street poverty didn't exclude one from sainthood."

"Isn't sainthood about miracles?"

"Money is miracles."

No way was this the same woman. "Your eyes."

"My eyes," she said.

We all knew that *Teen Magazine* trick: brown shadow in the crease, highlighter on the arch; but Toni Padua's Asian eyes had not been transformed to Caucasian contour with the swipe of a shadow wand. And Toni's nose had been narrow. Or was that the other *Teen Magazine* trick: Cover Girl Umber up the sides, *voila!* the Roman nose? And the chin ... diminished? Lips plumped? Squinting, close enough to kiss, I could distinguish her natural lip line, spot-on, which meant that Toni Padua's lips had been in-lined with white pencil. I studied the altered face. A box of creams and wands and humongous patience — yes, this was possible. Except for the eyes.

This was not Toni Padua.

"Indeed," she said, as if reading my thoughts.

"I'd have sat here all night and we could have talked about loans and the sub-prime. I wouldn't have known."

Alex had a feathery laugh, more like a thought than a sound. She held up her napkin-wrapped drink. "But you have keen observation."

"Not a lot of people do that napkin thing. Is that water again?"

She smiled, as if pleased with my research. "This is Pernod. Toni Padua doesn't drink alcohol."

I chuckled at what I assumed was good humor.

Her mouth slid into an easy smile with perfect teeth reminding me that Toni Padua hadn't smiled, much less laughed aloud. The woman's entire demeanor was changed. Completely. Alex Edessa presented herself as a relaxed and congenial businesswoman. Toni Padua had been a stiff and proper schoolmarm.

"How did you learn to do this?" I reached into my bag for my recorder.

"Like I said, when I got my worthless degree in theater, I specialized in theater make-up. It seemed prudent at the time, like a musician knowing how to tune pianos or a history major knowing how to lay bricks."

I set the recorder on the bar and punched RECORD.

She leaned towards it and spoke: "I own fourteen ventilated, lace-front, human hair wigs. I carry more tinted contact lenses than Pearle. My inherited eyes are pale which allows me to change color and not look like a spice junky out of *Dune*. I use eyeglasses, too — nonprescription, I'm proud to say, although lately I've added reading glasses to the mix. Throw in professionally crafted theater teeth: European country, Hollywood perfect, and a rather unfortunate overbite. Designed and fit to flawless in Gothenburg, Sweden. My teeth are my most expensive props. I also wear single, double, or triple caps — plumpers, we call them — that broaden my cheekbones or add girth to my jaw or a new curve to my mouth. The theater holds a heap of trade secrets, and I have a few of my own. Both Toni Padua and Therese List — that's Therese of Lisieux, the Patron Saint of Florists — wear a thin band under their wigs fixed with tiny combs and a spot of glue." She pulled the skin back at her temples. Her eyes narrowed.

"I knew it! That's Toni Padua. But is that reliable? Combs and glue?"

"It's good for a couple hours. The strip can also come up over the head for a junior face lift." She positioned her fingers at her temples, pushed upwards and lost ten years.

I said, "Get that in the big chains, you'd make a fortune."

"Every time you smiled you'd peek in the mirror to see if anything had slipped."

"Toni never smiled."

"You're a good witness." She took a sip of Pernod and surveyed the room. Her new blue eyes with their redesigned lids seemed to register everything with pointed patience, including me. I didn't know it, but at that point in our relationship, she knew all she needed to know about me.

"I kinda see the mechanics, even in the dark here."

"Nobody gets in my daylight face. And winter is best, when coats and parkas are standard fare, and most importantly, gloves are in season."

"How many of these saints do you have?"

"They come and go. Some stay for years because their employment is steady. These veterans have their own voices, handwriting styles, facial tics, their own scents. Toni smelled like Ivory soap." Alex waved her wrist and I caught a scent both spicy and musky like fresh cut wood. "This is vetiver."

I wrote that down, plus the detail that Toni Padua's thin, silver watch had been exchanged for a brown leather band.

Alex settled in on the stool. "So, my bonny biographer, where were we?"

"Pineapple Daiquiri and the police officer disguise job."

"Ah, yes. The directive from Pineapple Daiquiri was to play the role of the arresting officer as if you truly are the arresting officer, as if that is all you have ever been, and that is all you will ever be. Pineapple pulled a stack of business cards from his pocket and told me that if the arrest got botched, I was to laugh and sing out, 'Happy Birthday from Lenny!' Then announce that I'd just started a freelance party joke company and this was my first job.

Pineapple said, 'I'll laugh with you. We'll all laugh. You'll undo the handcuffs and I'll go back to my office. You pass out these cards and disappear.' The business cards read Party Joke Company.

"Was I the arresting officer type? Hardly. But I became one. I studied cops on TV, stalked them on the streets, followed them into city hall. I carried on as if some coveted award lay on the table. Understand, Jas, that the change in personality is equally important to the change in costume. And always, always, always stay within the cliché. Blonde hair and ruffles. Black hair and leather. Never draw attention. And never, never, never, no matter how tempting, send out extremes like *Mrs. Doubtfire* or *The Princess Bride*. Casts and molds, foaming sponge gelatin and alginate make magnificent disguises, but a major overhaul like that does not hold up under fluorescence. People notice. Not to mention peeling off your face in the backseat of a police car. You betcha. Opens one up to troublesome questions."

"Toni Padua had…" I tweaked my chin.

"Yes, Toni had chin."

"I like yours better. Your chin. Alex's chin, I mean."

"Good-looking is never the goal, no matter how tempting. Well-groomed and clean are not priorities. Marty Bethany — Martha, the Patron Saint of Cooks — is a mess with her stringy brown hair and slept-in clothes, skin blotched with tanning gels."

"Why so many saints?"

"To spread the risk. You can't find someone if you don't know who it is you're looking for."

"Who's looking for you?"

"Someone's always looking. And it's never the Prize Patrol." Alex sat with one arm propped on the bar. She watched the romance writers squeeze past a blustery couple blocking the dungeon doors. Her eyes moved to a fat man in a workout suit flushed and radiant from the free-with-your-room mini gym. He joined the two businessmen at the bar.

"Is somebody looking for you here?"

"Not as Alex Edessa."

I wondered how she could be so sure. "You said ... or I guess I should say that Toni said ... anyway, Toni said earlier that she'd been compromised."

"Yes, the contract is a landmine. I don't do domestic. But two years ago I did. On the cheap. You'd think I'd learn, but here I am again, sitting on another landmine."

"What happened two years ago?"

"I kidnapped a kid." She met my astonished look with a nod. "Domestic is always a landmine."

The woman had kidnapped somebody's child, and the breadth of her regret was that it'd been domestic.

She said, "You look somewhat scandalized."

"That blows. Kidnapping."

"Maybe this is where you start the story. Jolt them on the first page."

"Kidnapping is not so cool. People who kidnap children are not likeable characters. We'll need to come up with some heartfelt reason why you kidnapped somebody's child. Maybe start with your own childhood. Or maybe the regret factor. Redemption is crucial here." I shook my head. "Kidnapping, that's a soul stealer. It must have cost–"

"I lost money, that's a fact."

"What I meant–"

"The snatch was out of Canada," she continued unabated. "Gas, food, lodging. Cha-ching. But I felt sorry for the mother, a beleaguered angel, poor dear, what with the boy's father one fork short of the devil. And here I am again, one base short of a ballgame." She chuckled at her verbal caprice, then frowned and said, "This new contract is loaded with tricks, and I can't figure out who's oiling the rim."

"This new contract is another kidnapping?"

"It is."

"Screw the rim. Go to the police. Tell them what you know." The look on her face suggested I might have just told her to get a racing tip from the pope. "Quite frankly, Alex Edessa, Patron Saint of Beggars, readers will not identify with you."

"I wouldn't expect you to make me a soccer mom, but can we get somewhere in between? People can't relate to their goldarn neighbors, but they expect familial vibes from some *ignis fatuus* in a dime novel? Ridiculous." She stopped, eyebrows raised. "I should give a talk at your writing conference."

"You'd need to know about writing."

She shrugged. "I know someone who writes river guides."

"I doubt very much that redemption has ever come up in a river guide."

"Redemption."

"That's the key," I said. "Oprah's beat the trash out of it. Agents love it."

"Well, there then. I must be redeemed. And you're the one to do it."

Redemption would throw the story into the fantasy genre. This interview was sliding out of my comfort zone. Was this even the same woman from earlier? Maybe I'd beg off, excuse myself. I tried to remember who was signing books in the lobby.

She must have sensed my faltering. "Or don't redeem me. Redemption doesn't happen in real life. People would be forced to admit that they'd misread the tealeaves, that they hadn't understood the instructions, or they'd misjudged the miles. To admit error, you must wriggle back and resurrect some inset moral code you'd learned in catechism but long since abandoned. Few people concede those things."

"People do that on a daily basis."

She raised an eyebrow. "Are we talking about the same thing here?"

"Redemption."

"What exactly is that?"

"Atonement," I said. "Make amends. Saved. Redeemed."

"Store coupons." She grinned.

I frowned.

"Say we have this criminal," I said, not sure who or what I was defending, but provoked beyond good sense to explain the favorable moral code necessary for redemption, "and he's bad to the bone, but he goes out and risks capture to save someone's life. That'd be redemption."

She snorted. "When in real damn time has that ever happened? Name me one real person you know, a friend of a friend, anybody anywhere, who's atoned for their mischief."

I didn't know any Hester Prynnes or Raskolnikovs. Unable to produce a real-life kite runner, I said, "Sometimes criminals find God in prison and they–"

"Oh, stop. Those outlaws are making the best of a bad situation. Otherwise they'd have found God on the schoolyard instead of the prison yard."

"Redemption, more often than not, is private. Neither the transgression nor the atonement ever makes the neighborhood gossip circuit. It's small, personal things you atone for on a daily basis."

"What, my dear, did you atone for today?"

"Okay, not every day, but you know what I mean. Maybe your confessing, I mean, your telling your story is your redemption."

She sobered. "I never intended to tell my story."

"What made you change your mind?"

"The boy."

I liked Alex better than Toni, but reminded myself that this was the same person. I would need to meet the real person. I needed tenor with the real person, or all I'd have was a voice on tape. Two voices on tape, neither of which was the mainsail. I checked the recorder, just in case, and promised myself a new microchip miniature once I got my bills paid. Or a job. Or some Pineapple Daiquiri walked into my life. How likely was that?

"Tuesday," she said. "My downslide started Tuesday, before I even took this damn contract. We were riding down Hennepin, Kerby and me, in his jet black, right-off-the-rack Lexus ES 300 discussing my being arrested for breaking and entering and who he can press to make it go away."

I picked up my pen.

She spelled the name. "K-E-R-B-Y."

"Who's Kerby?"

"My lawyer." She smiled fondly. "He's the only one who calls me by my name. We went to high school together."

An accomplice? At the very least, an associate. I'd track him down. Find him on some lawyer list, in the phone book, Google. "Does Kerby know about the saints?"

"Nobody knows my file system."

"For the record, can you clarify this file system?" I repositioned the tape recorder again. I couldn't stop fussing with it.

"It's simple. Each client knows a saint. No two clients know the same saint. If my mother had been a gemologist instead of a nun, you would be talking to Crystal instead of Alex. I'd be organized by jewels, not saints. Opal, Ruby, Amber."

"Turquoise?"

"Turk for short."

"My mother is a gardener," I said. "Flora actually radiates personality, you know. I could be Rose or Daisy. Marigold Mary."

"Your last name could be the color you associate with the flower. Mary Gold. Rose White."

"Rose White," I repeated. "That is so metrically stark. I could like that. Speaking of disguises, what do you do when you're handcuffed in the backseat of a patrol car?"

"I'm not dressed as Wonder Woman or Wendy the Witch. My costumes are street clothes. With a couple swipes of my hand, I'm back at base. Or close enough. Wigs and make-up are everyday attire. I'd swallow my plumpers if I had to. Demolition is nothing more than knocking down blocks. Assemblage is the real operation. Assemblage and control of all the parts. Control of something as simple as a smile." She demonstrated a quarter moon smile. "That was Brigid Ireland." She tightened it. "That's Angela Folly." She smiled again as Alex. I had never considered the many possible muscle contractions and their varying chi, much less pointedly managing them.

"The Risorius muscle draws the angle of the mouth sideways. Learn to manipulate that muscle. There are books that show how to tighten your facial muscles for a cheap face-lift. I've expanded that."

"How do you keep it all straight? As in what muscle maneuver belongs to what saint?"

"Toni Padua's trademarks could not be confused with Brigid Ireland's."

I would meet Brigid Ireland soon enough, and that statement would prove true.

"I'd show up somewhere in the wrong wig."

"Four saints are the most I've ever worked at one time. Too much motion can compromise a job. Just recently Barbara Dios, the Patron Saint of Architects, had business in Wayzata. That same day Cecil, Cecilia, the Patron Saint of Music, had a contract in Medina. Barbara drove across town to St. Paul and changed into Cecil, then drove all the way back to Medina. What could have taken two hours took all day."

Such a major production — the elaborate camouflage and the complicated timing. Except for the kidnapping, she didn't seem criminal enough to warrant such obsessive coverage. Most criminals use aliases of some kind, but what a crazy application, commandeering the saints for her dirty work. Her mother a nun.

Nutcase?

"Your mother was a nun, and you are the polar opposite."

"Truth be known, I enjoy the saints and the church and all the chaff that comes with it. I appreciate that 'Sin on Saturday, Saved on Sunday' way of life. I appreciate the pragmatic sanction of Christianity and hang close to the simplicity of self-service in the name of God the Father, that old wild goose."

I blurted a laugh. "You've transformed these holy do-gooders into criminals."

"The favorable intersection of crime and philanthropy is not a comfortable notion for the truly God-fearing. But few people are truly God-fearing. I can count on one hand the truists I've met. Most who claim to live by The Word have their own interpretation of what the words mean. I told Father Robel once that religion was like five different versions from five different eyewitnesses who all saw the same accident. Each believes earnestly in his own experience. Father Robel said matter-of-factly, 'God is not everything we've come to depend on him for. Never was.'"

"Father Robel?"

"Father Robel is a peppery old gladiator and an ambitious fundraiser over at St. Vitus. He knows me as Zita, the Patron Saint of Maids and Lost Keys. Young Zita from Lucca cleaned houses, helped criminals and poor people, performed miracles. Four hundred years later she got sainted, for all the good that did her back when she was scrubbing her knuckles raw. Father Robel is a living saint, a holy man, but also a practical man. He questions things, and sometimes he has issues that need tooling. About twice a year I get paid to clean the vicarage, although I've never seen the inside of that French-splendid chateau du tithe."

"You do work for the church?"

"Which Father Robel forgives. After he forgives himself, of course. Forgiveness abounds in Christianity, which certainly suits my lifestyle better than that New Age crap where bad deeds boomerang back at you. You'd have to be a saint to live like that."

That this might not be the same woman from earlier nagged at me. Alex Edessa seemed years younger than Toni Padua and appreciably more cheerful. Maybe Toni and Alex were friends and this was a ruse. I couldn't shake the uneasy notion that I might spot Toni Padua and friends gathered around a table watching us. Typical. Me, outside the joke, pranked by "Girls Behaving Badly." But the room had emptied. The men at the bar were gone, their places wiped clean. Bob vamoosed.

"Were you ever married? Have kids? Mow a lawn? Clean a cat box?"

It took a minute for her to answer. "You see this guy at the diner with his kids and their greasy faces, hamburger wrappers and French fries flying around, and you wonder what your life would be like if you'd married the likes of him. I'd have grandkids now. You can't help but wonder these things."

"Did you ever consider a different career?"

"Keep yourself off the floor once you've slipped."

"Becoming a criminal was out of your control?" I scoffed.

"You can decide that when you write my redemption chapter."

"What do you do on holidays? Like Christmas."

"Christmas is my busiest season, like retail."

"Who are you?"

"That's not important."

"I want to know."

"I know you do."

3. Alex Edessa

Heroines do not kidnap children for money. A heroine who murdered for money would be an easier sell. And why would this flimflam saboteur of saints tell me, Miss Anybody, about it? The whole thing was sounding like somebody too long on Pernod. Was she setting me up for some kind of scam? I reached down and felt my purse.

"Tell me about your identities. How do you get them?"

"A timely question, indeed. My identities were established long before the internet, back when moving numbers involved Wite-Out and laminate, back when fifty bucks on Lowry got you credentials clean enough for social security. I haven't established an identity that carries paper in fifteen years. No need to."

It was a satisfactory enough explanation. Identity theft was sleazy and so easy it had become a crime without aptitude. No swank. Lower than robbing convenience stores. And I didn't have the savvy to write about something as plebeian as identity theft and create an appealing identity thief all in the same story. There I was again, centered on an appealing character. I didn't need an appealing character. This was True Crime. Just the facts, ma'am.

"About this breaking and entering thing. This lawyer guy from your high school bailed you out of jail? What was that about?"

"Broder Circle, yeah. We're driving down Hennepin, Kerdy and me."

"Wait. I think I wrote Kerby with a B." I scanned my notes. "You just said Kerdy with a D."

"It's K-E-R-B-Y. Kerby with a B."

"Earwax, I guess."

"B's and D's are phonetically muddy. And I've got my Hollywood teeth installed." She tapped her front tooth. "Anyway, I'm explaining about the wrong address this dildo Matzo gave me."

"Matzo? As in matzo ball?"

"He's an Eastern Bloc, displaced, alien outlaw." She folded her arms on the bar, seemingly annoyed. "Can't get a green card, and there he is, camped on Jug's desk like some backyard butch. He's got this thick yellow tablet, arm up around top. You know how people write upside down like this?" She demonstrated. "All hunched over, mouth skewed-up like some dim-wit first grader, one little number at a time, one little letter at a time, like he's drawing stickmen, for God's sake. You want to jump up and yank the damn pen right out of his stubby fingers. I should have." She shuddered. "How do you say dyslexic in Russian?"

"They might not have that in Russia. Is Matzo part of the breaking and entering job?"

"He *is* the breaking and entering job. A nothing job. So easy it was laughable, if it'd been somebody other than me with a Glock 17 stuck to my thoracic five in the middle of the night in the middle of the room in a subdivision designed by communists. You've seen those places with the same square front yards, the same putty plastic siding, the same worthless front porch and cut-rate bay windows, and the same identical damn floor plan. The back room of Three-SIXTY-FIVE Broder Circle was an office that contained my target file cabinet. The owner of that complicated cabinet was in Hong Kong. The back room of Three-FIFTY-SIX Broder Circle was a bedroom. The owner was in bed. I could have been shot.

"The reason I wasn't shot was because the man in charge of the Glock, mid-fifties respectful, didn't have the bristle to shoot a mid-life woman in black chiffon, even though he had every right to do just that. I feigned drunk in search of an old boyfriend. I swore the front door was unlocked and called up some tears for him. He called up the police for me." She took a sip of her Pernod, then said with a kind of reflective resignation, "These past few years I've been broad-sided with the disheartening evidence of my diminished powers of persuasion. Ten years ago that man would have fixed me a drink." She appraised my face with the eye of a salon technician mining for pores. "Coming your way faster than you can say facelift."

Not that fast, I thought, but rolled my eyes at that rank injustice and steered her back to Broder Circle. "So the police came?"

"The police came and charged me with breaking and entering because of the small and very expensive case of proprietary lock picks in my black satin clutch. Lucky me, I wasn't carrying. I own a gun, but never carry, which has always worked in my favor. Truth be known, I'm not fierce enough to use a gun, which might appear contradictory for someone in my trade. But, then again, maybe not; I fulfill my obligations with meticulous planning. There is no call for antediluvian violence. I've never seen brass knuckles in real time. The only slice I make with a knife is through a hunk of cheese. I couldn't roundhouse my way out of a KinderCare. Those long-legged, collagen-lipped Hollywood babes who can dropkick a Suma wrestler into retribution and not break a sweat are such fun and as unlikely as Harry Potter. I keep a can of pepper spray in my purse and run like hell. Black Betty stays under the bed."

"Black Betty?"

"That's a period expression, my dear, before your time."

"You own a gun, but you've never shot anybody?"

"I'd liked to have shot Matzo, but it would have been for trifle. Broder Circle was the last job I'll ever do for those corkheads. Jug's in jail for grand larceny and his idiot brother-in-law can't run a vacuum cleaner. Poor Jug. It doesn't look good for him. I hate that he went down. Never argued a fee. Oh, he'll talk. They all talk." She shrugged. "Doesn't matter. Jug knows me as Terry Avella, Teresa of Avila, the Patron Saint of Headaches."

"There's a saint for headaches?"

"There's a saint for everything: cabinetmakers, candlestick makers, perfume makers, mountaineers, lighthouse keepers. Name it, it's sainted. I'm peeved about Terry Avella with her cruel headaches, forced into early retirement. She carried good ID, which included a Wisconsin driver's license that worked in the system, a BP card, a graduation diploma, a library card, a fishing license, and a major merchant card. She walked with a limp. She had nice handwriting. A bastardized Snell Roundhand."

I wrote "Snell Roundhand" in my notebook to look up later. "So, let me get this straight: Terry Avella and her headaches got retired because she was Jug's contact?"

"When the man goes down, his saint retires. In Jug's circle of misfits, I am Terry Avella. That's all he knows."

"Jug doesn't know who you really are."

"My business revolves around that one point. I cannot be compromised."

"You sound pretty certain about that."

"Several years ago Cathy Senna, that's Catherine of Siena, the patron Saint of Fire Prevention, was working a surveillance job from a barstool over in St. Paul when in walks Jug and sits down next to her. The Patron Saint of Fire almost choked on a chicken wing. The Twins were on the tube. Jug's a baseball nut. They sat through three innings together, not a blink of recognition. Cathy has muted red hair and she's plump, looks nothing at all like Terry Avella; but, still, you'd think, after three innings." Alex sighed. "And now he's finished, and Matzo Ball Stroganoff, key gripper, day tripper, gets promoted. I take one lousy job from that migrant and get arrested. It was my own damn fault feeling sorry for his sorry ass."

"Is the Broder Circle arrest connected to the kidnapping?"

"Without Matzo and Broder Circle I wouldn't have been on Hennepin Avenue. It is most fortuitous that I be on Hennepin, Kerby and me."

I tapped on the tape recorder. "Hennepin it is."

"Traffic has slowed to a crawl. I don't have Kerby's attention. He cranes his neck. There's someone on the sidewalk.

He draws on his words, 'over there.' I look in the direction he's pointing and know exactly who he's pointing to.

"'Sammy's dead,' I say. 'Not a fact,' he says. I remind him that twenty years ago they found Sammy's abandoned car in Iowa. He says, 'But they didn't find Sammy.' I say, 'It's been too long, for God's sake. The man's dead.'

"Kerby and I argue like that, our eyes on the tall man with the Jack Sprat bent, hands punched high in the pockets of his blue windbreaker. His thin, gray hair is clearly not an obsession. Sammy would look like that.

"Kerby says, 'He's the right age to show up. You got to come back to your roots. It's human nature.'

"Kerby's a believer. He believes that everybody's goal is to be class president, first on the list, at the front of the line, and anything less than enthusiasm is juvenile impertinence; those of us stuck in the back row or lost on the sidelines will eventually figure this out. You'd think that twenty-five years in the legal system would have rubbed him wary. Uh-uh. Not Kerby. What Kerby doesn't understand is that it's not a matter of choice for some of us, this lack of appreciation for the swell of humanity. DNA, that twisted, double-strand, jokester slideshow of chromosome hell, is why some of us are not front-line enthusiasts. It was never there for us. Never will be. Kerby was born with front-line DNA, so he can hardly be blamed for his exasperating goodwill. He's actually kind of fun to be around — not that day.

"We catch up with the blue windbreaker. My window slides down. Kerby yells across me, 'Sammy! Hey Sammy!' I squench back, he's that loud. People look. But not the man who could be Sammy. He makes a military turn up Eighth Street, a one-way not in our favor. 'Louie Louie' by the Kingsmen filters out of a pick-up truck in the curb lane. *Away I gotta go now.* Something about the beat, something spoiled and saved and long gone all at the same time. Put the blues on you in ten notes or less."

I said, "My parents have that on the jukebox."

"Jukebox?"

"Uh-huh. In the basement. They dance."

"Sober?"

"Afraid so. They've won contests."

She was quiet for a moment, then said, "How do you get there? I wonder." She sounded genuinely curious and somewhat sad.

"Whatever it is," I said, "it skips a generation. They're also eight handicaps on the golf course, both of them. They've won tournaments."

She studied me a moment. "Had a lot of free time on your hands, did you?"

"My sister, she's ten years older, taught me to tie my shoes and brush my teeth, which is probably why we're distant now. We were both accidents." Not prepared to discuss my parent's childrearing skills or their charmed life, I prompted, "So Kerby thinks the blue windbreaker is your classmate, but you think he's dead?"

"It makes sense, because I could never figure out what Sammy was running from. But every five years or so, Kerby reports a sighting, Jack Sprat's ghost."

"What's Sammy's role in the kidnapping?" The tape recorder clicked off. I dug in my bag for a cassette.

"He's the clown on the bicycle, the crow on the fencepost, the cloud shaped like Jesus." She watched me label and load ALEX#2.

I punched RECORD and said, "Sammy's on the sidewalk."

"And Kerby's hyped. He honks three quick ones. Louie-Louie rolls forward. Kerby shoots in behind him, stomps the brake, and pushes at me. 'Catch him!' he yells, 'It's Sammy! I swear!' I am incredulous. You can imagine. He says, 'It's him! Quick! We're gonna lose him.' The tall man clearly did *not* want dialogue, but Kerby will have none of that. He leans across me and shoves my door open. It scrapes the curb. Brand new car.

"Thanks to Matzo Ball, I'm compromised and need my lawyer. I pull myself out of the car and the door releases from the sidewalk. I slam it hard and smile at the streak of black paint on the curb. Kerby guns it through a light that's past pardonable. Exhaust from a metro bus whooshes at me.

"Indian Summer, that last vestige of clemency and decency, blew out faster than it blew in. Having bargained for one more day before triple fleece, the people on the sidewalk hunch up in their Indian Summer jackets. The exhaust, hot grease, and ice particles in the Hennepin Avenue corridor elicit a gut reflex no stronger than humdrum. Hands in my pockets, tired and put upon, I trudge up Eighth where the man who could be Sammy is nowhere in sight. I cozy up to a tobacco shop window and watch clerk Khomeini count cigars. He glances at me with the look of somebody I don't want to know. I move again, chasing Sammy, who was lost twenty years ago.

"I stop in front of a small Euro café. The window is fogged. I consider for a moment that Sammy might have ducked inside. So what if he did? It's none of my business. If Sammy wanted to be found, he'd call. People go missing for reasons that are nobody's business but their own. A more timely consideration is that I'm freezing my ass off. It'll be ten minutes before Kerby gets back around. I enter the cafe. The only business is a table of women drinking specialty coffees. I head down the pine-paneled hallway to the restrooms. The doors to both toilets are propped open, freshly scrubbed and empty.

"A waitress balancing a tray of dirty dishes bumps through a set of swinging doors, and I catch a glimpse of stainless steel. Sammy, one time philosopher, defender of liberty, now a short-order cook downtown Minneapolis? Might as well check it out. I burst through the door and lurch to the center of the kitchen for a three-sixty view. With my best astonished look I say, 'Oops! Wrong door for me, I tell ya.' I yammer on like I just caught on how to knit. The waitress glances up from her dishes. A cook in a pirate scarf stops scraping the grill and shoots me a critical eye. I back out of the kitchen, draw into my coat and exit the café. No one will remember me.

"Look around you out there, Jas, and you'll see that people in motion have a small circle of awareness, and unless somebody outside their circle stands on his head or dresses like Lady Gaga, the rest of humanity is nothing more than background noise. This self-absorption of the human race lightens my load. I skirt around these circles like a clerk with a clipboard. A bonus perk of this human awareness deficit is that I can scan the swarm and know who's working a deal. He's the one focused outside his circle. He's studying the landscape. If your eyes lock, it is both alarming and unnerving. If it's a rogue woman, you better be good. They are not easily charmed."

"If it's a woman, what then? Look away?"

"That would mark you. I've only been picked out once. A former client of mine, now dead, his girlfriend, Missy Golden, was hunting Saint Julia Hosta. Julia had collected a delinquent debt out of Missy's apartment. Two days later I had the bad luck to be on the street as Barbara Dios, a saint who's close in appearance to Julia, and there came Missy, less than thirty feet, eyes locked on me like a sugar doughnut. Caught with a knee-jerk 'Oh-shit!' on my face, and too late to unlock, I waved and yelled, 'Hey Marge!' and scurried towards her with a cuckoo shimmy-shimmy and my best smiley face, aggressively festive. Missy Golden cut through four lanes of traffic to escape the nutcase. Julia got retired.

"Always remember, Jas, if somebody appears interested in what's going on outside his personal self, there could very well be a crime in progress."

"That would not have crossed my mind. Julia was another saint?"

"Julia Hosta from Julian the Hospitaler. Now there's a saint for you. Saint Julian killed his parents, was forgiven, and became the Patron Saint of Hotelkeepers and Travelers. Think the murdering Menendez brothers will get a crack at sainthood? Say in about four hundred years?"

"It sounds like a possibility."

"They will need to tithe."

Her expression changed, reflective. "I'd been considering, even before my current crisis, that I might be too old for this business anymore. Truth be known, in many ways my work has gotten easier. The older a woman gets, the less visible she is. Slipping in and out of places required a great deal of cunning when I was young and cute. Except for this sloppy Matzo job — which I can only attribute to diminished estrogen — my unrighteous career has that one less complication. Over the years, I have worked hard to be invisible. Now I truly am. But isn't that how a career progresses? The longer one works at a discipline, the easier it becomes and the greater the rewards, which balances and tempers the gnawing anxiety that accompanies the loss of possibilities. I've more than tripled my income since I rolled into middle-age."

"You've certainly put your multifarious talents to work."

"Talent? No. I simply found a slot to slip into. With the simple act of mindfulness, I am rich beyond my qualification, beyond what Darwin would have allocated the likes of me. I'm an example of how people acquire more than their birth-intrinsic share without winning the lottery."

"And you are self-deprecating."

"Not at all. Unlike the rest of you pundits and scholars, I truly appreciate the fact that most people are smarter than I am. Consequently, I underestimate no one. High IQs underestimate everyone. That's why they get caught."

"Oh, please. Most people wouldn't have a speck of sense, much less the chutzpah, to carry on like a damsel in distress with a gun in their back in some strange house in the middle of the night." I flicked my hand. "Add theater to the equation."

"Theater. Mercy. If I'd hung on to that mirage, I would have ended up homeless. Frankly, I consider myself a student of that old robber baron, steelmeister, keeper of the coin, Andrew Carnegie. I might even posses the mutant gene that got John D. Rockefeller Standard Oil and Jay Gould Western Union — Christian pilgrims, those two. Where would civilization be without their guile?"

And there it was again, the only marker that would follow from saint to saint: that tic at the corner of her mouth, the prelude to the smile that never came.

4. Brigid Ireland
Brigid, the Patron Saint of Fugitives
SATURDAY

We'd agreed to meet at Stonehenge again, which was where I sat, slow-sipping a martini in an honest effort to make it last longer than my usual throw-down. Not to mention provoking another alcohol-on-an-empty-stomach episode. Faux-cheese mini-crackers out of the vending machine would not save me. I envisioned my roast chicken plate served to an empty seat at the awards banquet. My mouth watered. Maybe Alex and I would grab something later.

Meanwhile, determined to spot her before she revealed herself, I worked by the process of elimination. That bumped the four distinctly masculine suits at the bar. Then there was the man in the fisherman's sweater with the Fabio hair, double debonair. I entertained the idea that he might be the real Fabio, a mini surprise at the Romance Writers Convention. How likely was that? Bartender Bob set a glass of white wine in front of him. Fabio took a sip. Bob waited. Fabio's cell phone rang. Bob twirled away to polish a glass.

A shriek at the double dungeon doors got my attention. Three miniature hooligans spiked up on fructose were wrestling with a woman who was trying to get them into their coats. One of them plunked down on the red vine carpet and howled. Alex wouldn't go that far to fool me. At a table in the corner, two couples chatted with the amiable stiffness of prom dates. Scratch them. Near the side door, four colorful women in stylish activewear, hot out of the free-with-your-room mini-gym, treated themselves to patio cocktails. They looked too old to be Alex. I reminded myself that I wasn't looking for Alex. The lady facing the wall was swathed in bulky pastel; the pale strip of fat that separated sweatshirt from stretch pants could not be engineered anywhere but Hollywood. A better bet would be the skinny brunette in the yellow tank top, Toni Padua dipped in tanning gel. She worked her glass with gnarled and knuckled fingers. No way could my criminal pull off arthritis to the armpits. The third woman, a tubby silver-blonde wearing a gold lamé baseball hat was talking like an auctioneer. No amount of packing the plumpers could produce those cheeks and go nonstop. The fourth woman, a pallid brunette in a red t-shirt, sipped her cocktail through a straw. I watched, encouraged, until she belted out a laugh, clutched her glass with a bare-handed chokehold and threw it back happy-hour shooter style. Not one napkin-wrap among the foursome, even though that fastidiousness might come natural to that age group. Nor did I believe my criminal chummed around.

My best bet sat alone at a table mid-center reading a paperback. Her no-nonsense black sweater could have come out of Toni Padua's closet same as the trench coat on the adjacent chair. I willed her to look at me. She didn't. But she could be casing me over her Franzen glasses. If I had her life, I would be casing me. What's to say I hadn't called the police? For all she knew, all five faces at the bar were waiting for her to approach me; well, maybe not Fabio in the fisherman's sweater, who picked up his glass of wine and walked coolly out the dungeon doors like some Edmund Fitzgerald down from Superior for a debonair weekend. Bob watched while pretending not to. That left four policemen. Drinking on the job? The paperback lady turned a page and took a sip from her bottled water. How long would we play this game?

We. We who?

What I needed was a base name. Without Alex-Toni's real name, my saint would confuse the reader. My saint? It sounded right. I wrote that down. My Saint.

A newcomer strolled up to the bar, male on the soft side with a cratered face and fat lips. She could do that with theater make-up. He caught me staring and twinkled his eyes at me. I looked away.

A perky lady in gray sweats carrying a plum-colored coat entered through the side dungeon door. Her short blonde hair was stylishly tousled and anchored with a pink headband. She stopped at the table of exercise queens. They listened to her talk. All of them laughed. The silver-blonde in the lamé hat pulled out a chair. I refocused on the lady reading the paperback novel, the best candidate for My Saint. Any minute now she would acknowledge me, and I would be looking straight at her when she did. Five more minutes, I'd approach her. I took a sip of my martini. Bob had tossed in an olive. Must have run out of dried-up fruit rinds.

I had inquired at the front desk about an extended stay, but discovered that the new non-conference triple rate was not in my budget. I would have to find something cheap if I thought I could get a story out of this criminal. So far, I didn't have anything that resembled a story; nor was I convinced that one was forthcoming. But I couldn't ignore what she'd told me, what she was planning, this kidnapping. Then again, the woman might be nothing more than some crackpot out from Lake Street. Or some bored housewife from Chaska, who at this very moment was home baking tater tot casserole while I waited at the castle. Lady in waiting. The paperback reader looked up from her book and took a sip of water. Her eyes dropped back to her book. And I reviewed the steps necessary to teach writing at a junior college. Sorely lacking in that detour from reality was the money for grad school. Details. The paperback lady smiled and turned the page — chick-lit, for sure. Nothing else was funny anymore. Maybe Nora Ephron. Eyes glued on the best candidate for My Saint, I didn't notice the blonde exercise lady in the gray sweats and the pink headband until she was standing next to me.

"There are those jobs I can't do anymore," she said with billowy energy, "now that young and cute has come and gone. I was young and cute when Eddie Valentine bulleted through the ice into Big Lake on his snowmobile. I knew he was going down, although I didn't acknowledge my liability until long after he was dead."

I fumbled for my tape recorder, slapped it on the bar and punched RECORD.

She leaned away from it. "This might be misconstrued as a confession."

"For my ears only," I said. "It's reference, not forensics."

"Forensics, ha! Once reserved for the pocket-pal crowd. No more, honey. 'Cold Case Files' and 'CSI' are magnets for the mainstream. And I'm not happy about that. What saves the likes of me is that these contemporary crime hunters are such perfect darlings. Never mind being technically fictionalized past the point of fatigue, they're on it like feeder fish with their microscopes, telescopes, proctoscopes."

"I could just take notes."

"They'll never find me." She flipped her hand in dismissal, suddenly distracted. I followed her eyes to the exercise women who were gathering their belongings from the table.

I pointed my pen at them. "Who are they?"

"I have no idea."

"But you acted–"

"Acted." She held up a finger. "There you have it. I saw an opportunity to fool you." The exercise women waved at My Saint and exited the dungeon doors.

"Who are you tonight?"

"Brigid Ireland — Brigid, the Patron Saint of Fugitives." She spelled Brigid for me. "No T, no E." She fluffed her hair. "She's aged decently. Think?"

"I like her hair."

"It used to be long and flowy, but those days are history. Long and flowy hair on a seasoned face is memorable and not in a good way." She draped the plum-colored coat on the stool next to the stucco wall.

Brigid radiated energy, a vitamin woman with buxom breasts and ample hips. Fifteen to twenty pounds heavier than Alex Edessa, thirty pounds on Toni Padua, the extra weight did not look like bad padding or too many sweaters. Her fashionable knuckle-length sleeves covered hands that would be too thin for her girth. Dental plumpers fattened her cheeks. Full, red lips suggested some kind of irritant. Her nose seemed upturned, but it was more an attitude that played off pink headbands and breathlessness. Brigid held a permanent, on-the-verge-of-a-laugh smile. Toni, Alex, Brigid — none of their varied expressions were inherited; however, I believed I could distinguish the baseline features, not because they resembled Alex Edessa or Toni Padua, but because I had seen them before.

"How'd you know I hadn't called the cops?"

"I can tell a dick from a dork a mile away."

Bob stood before us. I ignored him, determined to stretch my martini into the next hour. Brigid ordered vodka and water.

It registered that her voice was changed. And she talked fast, unlike Alex with her easy rhythm or Toni with her careful talk.

"Your voice sounds different again. How do you keep that going?"

"You could stand on one leg for fifteen minutes if your life depended on it. Most people I see for less than ten."

"I couldn't stand on one leg for one minute. Nor could I hold a voice shift for five."

"You don't have a worthless degree in theater."

"I've got a worthless degree in history."

She chuckled. "What year did Lincoln say the Gettysburg?"

"That didn't stick."

"Isn't that something a history major would know?"

"A history major teaching history."

"What else can history majors do? How many history teachers can the market bear? And how the hell do the rest of you earn a living?"

I wished I'd had an answer, an answer that meant I'd thought it through, thought about possibilities and consequences and had made intelligent decisions regarding my future. I shrugged. "Crime. We'll all do crime."

"Then you might as well go to law school."

I forced a laugh. "So what about this Valentine who bulleted through the ice?"

"Eddie Valentine was a restaurateur, a moneyman, a busy man, out of control. Eddie needed relocating. Rumor had it that he'd had little Jimi Waller killed for holding up a full house to his three kings, among other things. I was contracted through Ronnie the Roach — yes, the man truly is a cliché. He owns a fence company in Richfield, three or four drycleaners, a bank. Or two."

"Does Eddie Valentine connect to the kidnapping?"

"No. But he's got a case file if you need verification. It's also one of my first jobs."

"The start of an illustrious career."

"And remembered fondly. Roach set me up with a man named Zen, who smiled all the while he was explaining my role — small, but vital, he told me — in the Valentine operation. I was to get Eddie to his cabin on Big Lake. Zen handed me a down payment of one thousand dollars wrapped in Santa Claus paper tied with curly red ribbon. He kissed me on the cheek. His lips were chapped. I never saw him again. I don't know what outfit he worked for. I don't ask when it comes from the Roach."

Eddie Valentine was not his real name, I was sure, and too long ago for Google. More like the library archives. I wrote drowning, snowmobile, winter, and early seventies in my notebook.

"January I got myself hired as a waitress at one of Eddie's restaurants, Valentine's on Nicollet, a dark grotto hideaway. Eddie spent a good deal of time in the back room doing bidness. If you know what bidness matters, men like Eddie are easy.

"Eddie's full-time mistress was feisty-famous for slinging all the wine glasses over the bar one night. Eddie liked them feisty. Feisty and not too bright. Therefore, I became feisty and not too bright, which called for a little method acting and non-filtered Camels. Those who claim the first seven years of life make the man don't understand the tools of reinvention. Pair a costume with a non-filtered Camel and *voila!* you're reinvented."

I added, "Don't forget that worthless degree in theater."

She laughed heartily. "Two weeks later I played a bimbo at Eddie's cabin on Big Lake. The entire subterfuge was easy, because Eddie didn't report his whereabouts. 'Nobody's goddamn bidness,' he'd say; although, I'd heard that his wife knew all about his bidness. But Mrs. Valentine was at the age when social floozies are looked upon as a kind of reprieve."

"Not in my marriage, never."

"Of course not. It's as cold in the cabin as it is outside. We stand around the stove smoking Camels and drinking cheap brandy, waiting for the place to thaw. Eddie blabs on about Eddie's LeRoy Neiman collection, Eddie's powerboat on Mille Lacs, Eddie's lynx coat — 'shot 'em myself,' — Eddie's gold chains, Eddie's gold teeth." Brigid shuddered, remembering. "He grabs my crotch — you know the type. But there will be no bidness by the stove. Uh-uh. I demand a hot shower and steer him to the bathroom, all the while helping him out of his buckskin briefs. Now how revolting is that? I herd him into the shower to lather-up while I go replenish our drinks. Kiss, kiss. Back in a sec. Asshole. I crank up the music, grab my overnight bag, and even though I had not removed my gloves, except to undress Eddie, I do a triple-check for fingerprints. Satisfied, I flick the porch light twice and escape out the front door with my brandy glass full of cigarette butts to a car parked a quarter-mile down the road, which I drive back to Minneapolis and abandon in the Zebra Lot at Southdale Mall. Final payment was in the glove box."

"That's it? You weren't chased? No shots fired? We could use a little action. For the story, you know. And a little more sex than a crotch grab and buckskin briefs."

"You can add that."

"How much was in the glove box?"

"Two grand."

"Plus a grand from Zen with the chapped lips? You were paid three thousand dollars to get somebody to a cabin?"

"That's cheap. Consider the trespass. I should have asked for more, but I was young and lacked credentials. You're thinking they could have found some whore, paid her a hundred bucks."

"That's exactly what I was thinking."

"Discretion is obsolete; therefore, it is priceless. I am discreet. I am priceless."

"Nobody suspected you."

"You can suspect all you want. If the alibis and the assholes don't match up, your suspicions are worthless. The police found Eddie's car parked at Castle Royale, which was a restaurant before its time in the Mississippi caves over in St. Paul. The next week at Valentine's I told a VIP customer to go to hell and got myself fired. I never cashed that pitiful paycheck, and Bill Gates was still picking zits, so my bogus social security number never showed."

"Why such a production? Why didn't they just take him out back and shoot him?"

"Class I crime is so finely orchestrated that nobody knows it happened. You'll never read about it in the papers or see it on the news or on the crime channels. It'll never be a cold case. It simply and matter-of-factly cannot be seen. Bodies in the alley is bad business, not to mention bad manners."

"Above the law."

"The law doesn't have anything to do with it."

"People you've worked for are in jail."

"The not-so-bright," she said derisively, "are knocked off the board early. Darwin, you know. I'm still standing because none of those not-so-brights knew my identity."

"This elaborate disguise is all about covering your arse."

"What else would it be about? Meeting and greeting my mother's broken saints, I got a full understanding of lock-down. Not to go there, I signed onto Eddie Valentine's exit contract as a different person. Why would I put my own face out there? The only thing that Roach said about Eddie's demise was that there'd been a back-up plan."

"You were an accessory to a murder."

"An accessory," she said with an inappropriately quixotic smile, "is a rare and irreplaceable jewel."

"Did your lawyer, this Kerby guy, know about Eddie Valentine?"

"I hadn't seen Kerby since high school. I met up with him several years later when a badly timed bar melee landed me in jail. Now there's a learning experience, I tell you."

"What'd you learn?"

"That a front-plan with no back-plan gets you lock-down. And there I stood, face pressed against the bars, weighing my options when who walks by but my man Kerby. Imagine my surprise. Imagine his surprise. I looked a wreck. He calls me by my name. My cellmate for the last eight hours, a gal named Rosaline, thinks my name is Lucy. Lucy is the Patron Saint of Sore Eyes."

"Sore eyes?"

"Don't get me started." Brigid's eyes glistened, merry. You couldn't help but feel happy with the Brigid saint.

"Rosaline blurts out, 'I thought your name was Lucy.' Kerby raises an eyebrow and puts a funny little grin on his face. I ask if he can get me out. Holding that grin, he says, 'What'd you do?' I tell him that somebody told the cops I'd kicked off a brawl over at The Cascade Nine. Now he is truly surprised. I tell him I saw the crazy chick shoving everybody around. Blonde bitch. I grab a clump of my hair and say, 'Does this look blonde?' His grin widens. He says, 'Wait here.' I yell after him, 'Still the joker!' He turns, walking backwards, and says, 'Luu-cy.' That was the start of our arrangement."

"What was the Cascade Nine about?"

"Lance out of Fridley paid me to create a diversion at midnight. Two men up from St. Louis used the opportunity to collect a package."

"A person?"

"I have no idea. Hell, I barely got my blonde wig stuffed into the back of a speaker on the bandstand before the police arrived. Twenty-one people went to jail, including me. And if Kerby didn't come back, I'd be sitting there with Rosaline waiting on some court-appointed lawyer. There was nobody coming for Rosaline."

"Did you stay friends with this Rosaline?" My Saint's inscrutable solitude was both curious and unsettling. Any associate I could track down would be a bonus.

"The only thing Rosaline and I had in common was that we were members of The Arrested Club. You, too, can be a member. The prereq is need and a lack of resources. Rosaline had taken advantage of a situation with the good intention of righting things as soon as she got square."

"Is that what happened to you"

"I never had good intentions. I never had bad intentions. Rosaline had two kids to feed. Then she got membership. Have you ever been convicted of a crime other than a traffic violation? How do you answer that question and get a job that feeds the babies? Unless she gets a full identity change, her arrest will follow her to the grave — worse now than ever in a world logged on to Intelius. I hope she invested wisely."

"What was she arrested for?"

"She put on the red light."

"Sting?"

"Stung. Two hours later I'm released. A case of mistaken identity."

The backlit liquor bottles glinted in the Saturday night light. Private conversations, clinking glassware, city faces sculpted by candlelight, DJ Shadow's moody electronics: together they spawned a sexy energy strong enough to temper the wacky castle and its medieval warp. Anything was possible. I nibbled at my olive.

"You've got information that the police would die for. Would you ever turn state's evidence?"

"The day Bob Dylan moves back to Hibbing."

"That's not going to happen."

She slapped her hand on the bar. "Then that's settled." She waved her empty glass at Bartender Bob and pointed at mine.

I'd have smoked a cigarette if someone had given me one. I was that far out of my sensibility range.

5. Brigid Ireland

"Tell me about your lawyer."

"We trade, Kerby and me. What I need from him is information: sealed records, depositions, applications, land grabs, stuff that JoAnn Public has no right to know and can't find on the internet since the government forced the good stuff back underground. Kerby sometimes gets attitude about the risks he takes. He has his eye on the governor's chair, but lacks the physical prowess to wrestle his way to it."

"On the Jesse Ventura highway?"

Brigid Ireland had an easy, complementary laugh, the kind of laugh that gets you thinking you might be smartly entertaining after all. I knew better, but was tempted all the same.

"What do you do for Kerby?"

"Like Father Robel, Kerby understands that sometimes things need steering. He's Robin Hood with a Lexus. He employs street services not available at the office. The information I've dug up for him over the years has made him a formidable opponent in the justice system."

"Street services? Sounds risky for a law abiding lawyer."

"He knows I'll never turn on him. I may be a criminal, but I'm an honorable one."

"Oh, please. You're about to snatch somebody's kid."

"If I don't do it, somebody else will. Business will move on without me. And like any other self-employed person, I worry about business. Sometimes I get the creepy feeling that the world is about to become selfless. Which would put me in the dumpster. Then I snap out of it. My business *is* the dumpster business. As long as there are people, there will always be a load of crap needing to be dumped."

"Other than your stint as a bartender, you've never had a real job?"

"Sometimes it's necessary to get hired to fill a contract. A big corporation means a background check, which is complicated to engineer, and risky. It's easier to bring out my pest control shirt or my Motley Maids uniform and stay in motion with a clipboard or a pesticide canister. Now if the conduit is a no-background-check, disposable job, I'm an easy hire. My longest run was an antique shop over on Grand Avenue. Roach contracted me to monitor the flower shop across the street. Seems there were too many customers carrying briefcases and no bouquets. After that business settled, I could have stayed on with the walnut trunks and the deco glass and the marvelous rosewood clocks. The owner was thrilled to pay me cash. No FICA, no payroll. But some shithead detective traced Jamie Lester to the store. That's James the Less, the Patron Saint of Druggists and Mad Hatters. Mr. Detective dropped in one day. I'd used the phone to call Jamie's employer, whose phone, come to find out, had been tapped. I told the detective that customers use the phone all the time. He pulled out a grainy photo of a feathered blonde with a toothy mouth. There was no mistaking Jamie's unique, rural look. That was all I needed to get gone."

"What does Kerby think you do for a living?"

"Rascal jobs like hiring out as a clerk or a housekeeper or a chauffeur to infiltrate people's lives for information. He understands public relations work with paranoid executives and wayward CEOs. I even told him about collecting that four-year-old out of Canada."

"Kidnapped," I countered.

"You might call that chapter, Crossing the Rainy. It took three weeks to snatch that kid. Domestic, uh-uh. Not only does the pay suck, they want to write you a check." She pointed to herself. "A check? Right-o-la. Lance in Fridley contracted the job. Lance knows me as Clare Assett by way of Clare Assisi, Patron Saint of Television. That's Clare without the i."

Claire was the name the woman at the front desk had been seeking. Clare? Could the woman have been looking for My Saint? No. She'd have asked for Toni Padua, that being My Saint's identity at the time. No one would just come in off the street unannounced looking for My Saint not knowing her time-appropriate name.

"Clare farmed the job to an expert in retrieval, another saint, of course. When you meet Clare you'll see that she would not be up to a kidnapping. Uh-uh. She told Lance she knew someone who could grab the kid and disappear like sugar in water. That was all he needed to know."

Clare Assett was one of My Saint's aliases but Brigid talked about her as if she were a different person. And this 'expert in retrieval' as yet a third person. But they were all one and the same person. Was this a modern-day Sybil?

Brigid was talking about the kidnapping, the crux of the story. I needed to pay attention.

"I've known Lance for twenty years. He's my most significant employer, which is why I took that loser job. I almost lost myself. It was the closest I ever got to the maelstrom. I could have ended up in the Rainy. I underestimated the job and had to improvise, which is something I don't do well. I'm not a fast thinker. I need time and space up front to work out every detail every way possible. I wish I'd had the good sense to drop it. There was no ransom, none of that kidnapping regalia. This was nothing more than the mother repossessing what the father stole. The tribulation here is that he will kill her if he finds her. Such violence, domestic."

"So this was more like a rescue than a kidnapping?"

"You could spin it that way. These last two years, I've felt compelled to check on that kid."

"You keep in touch?"

"From a distance. I don't believe he'd recognize my polymorphous self. Although this boy was uncannily observant."

"Listen to yourself. You have feelings. Maybe even conscience."

Brigid smiled, but not with me, more like at me.

I blurted, "Oh, crap, just imagine what you could have done with your life."

"And what might that have been?"

"Surely to God something other than what you do. You lack introspection. That's protective."

"Protective of what? History being what it is, I could be sainted someday."

"You will need to tithe." That got a laugh.

"Frankly," she said, sobering, "I'm not the pariah I was twenty years ago. Times are moving in my favor. I'm more confident operating in today's monotonous, global desperation than when I started this business. To stand out nowadays, pierced and tattooed kids with green hair show their butt cracks, eat truckloads of hotdogs on MTV, prance around on stage in their underwear. Why such garish extremes? Because all the good stuff has been taken, and no one can figure out a way to make anything special out of what's left. How much more square could Josef Albers paint a square?"

She appeared distracted. She was speaking to me, but her eyes were on the double dungeon doors. A gray-haired woman wearing a long black coat stood in the doorway. The woman seemed to be looking for someone, or possibly wondering what kind of kooky bar she'd wandered into. She sat down at a table near the door. Brigid took a sip of her drink and focused on me.

"How much more glass can you slap on the Tower Glory? That leaves us with tasteless sex, rabid slashers, gay guys chasing straight guys on cable TV — everyone a rebel in their own mind's eye. Me? I've done jobs that have been seditious, lawless, subversive, oftentimes sad, and sometimes funny. Some I wouldn't do again. Now there's introspection for you. Ha! Hindsight and maturity, the keepers of regret. I did those jobs for money, not to be a rebel. Rebel, schmebel. Such a silly notion, to fool yourself like that. I can't afford to fool myself. My business is fooling others. Deception is much more forgiving than self-deception. Self-deception will land you in jail."

I would replay this diatribe later. Distracted or not, what she'd said sounded too reasonable, too coherent. Or was I having some kind of Patricia Hurst moment? The tape recorder shut off. She'd moved back into the shadows. I followed her eyes.

"That man is out of context," she said. "The one at the bar with the sheaf of dark hair."

The man was unremarkable except for the thick sweep of hair that shaded one eye. Late-thirties, his puffy jacket half zipped, decent jaw-line, he could be a "Sex and the City" walk-on.

Brigid said, "Breezed in like this was some Nicollet hotspot."

The man caught me staring. "Oops," I said.

"Men are easy. Do Lolita."

"Lolita? I'm not good at that babe stuff." I tried to remember what exactly Lolita did. "He keeps looking over here," I said. "He's got that five o'clock shadow going. I can like that."

"Brush your hair back."

I brushed at my ear. "Why did I do that?"

"It tells him he stands a chance. A woman always touches her hair if the man has a chance. She's not aware of it, much less its implication. If a man eyes a woman and she doesn't touch or straighten her hair, even the most flimsy brush-back at the neck…" Brigid demonstrated. "…he knows she's not interested."

"I've never heard that."

"Of course you haven't. You're a romance writer. Now that you know that little detail, you'll catch yourself."

"I don't know this because I'm a romance writer?"

"I suppose if you wrote about the mechanics of romance, it would bore the socks off everybody. On the other hand, the mechanics of crime are center target — once you block the psychobabble."

"You lost me there."

"The psychology as to why someone commits a crime is asinine. Criminals behind bars make it up as they go along, accumulating points for cigarettes. They have no idea regarding the psychology behind their crimes, much less possess the ability to articulate to some fool in a white coat without words put in their mouths. You think they lie on their cots at night and think about apology? They don't have a rat's ass of a notion why they robbed the convenience store other than they needed money. Unless there's a glitch in the DNA strip, which could yield a Ted Bundy psychopath, crime is nothing more than a need for things one cannot buy. If it's revenge or hate or jealousy or any other impassioned affectation that causes someone to kill — that someone kills only once to shake a problem that has no resolution. Once they've eliminated the problem there's no reason to repeat the crime. Remember Claudine Longet?" She chuckled at my puzzled look. "Before your time. Claudine sang French songs, married Andy Williams, and shot Spider Sabich in Aspen, Colorado. That was 1976. She never shot anybody again. No reason to."

"Who was Spider Sabich?"

"A famous skier. He dumped her. He was her one and only kill. She was acquitted. It was an accident."

"So if they're not Jeffery Dahmer psycho or Claudine Longet scorned, it's about money."

"There is nothing else to pin it on. The person who kills for kicks or repletion is insane."

"A truly insane person wouldn't know enough to hide his tracks."

"If you think Ted Bundy and Jeffrey Dahmer were sane, you've read too many psychobabble books." She watched the man with the sheaf of black hair without watching him. No darting eyes or stealthy stares.

"Do you know that man?"

Humorously scathing would best describe her look. "Some men are not for knowing. He's a poser." She stood up and yanked her sweatpants straight.

"You're leaving?"

"I have to kill someone."

I laughed. "Are you coming back?"

"Tomorrow. Six o'clock. I'll take you to dinner."

I watched her walk to the dungeon doors and turn in the direction of the lobby. The grey-haired woman in the black coat stood up from the table and followed. Coincidence? Brigid hadn't acknowledged her. I watched the man with the sheaf of hair reach into his pocket and pull out his wallet. Had she creatively misdirected my attention to this frown face? Was I making something out of nothing? What I needed to consider was how to pay our bar tab. Crap. I could be sitting financially unfettered at a banquet table for twelve, plumped up on chicken with mushroom sauce and mango cream pie.

The man with the hair opened his wallet and pulled out a bill. His eyes cut to Brigid's plum-colored coat. She'd forgotten it. She'd remember when she stepped outside. The man stared at it for a moment, then back at the dungeon doors, then at the coat again. Bartender Bob swooped in and chatted him up. I wondered what Bob could be chatting about, having not said one word to me.

Even though it was early for a Saturday night, Stonehenge had thinned to a dime. I could catch the Poetry Open Mike in the auditorium. Maybe I'd roam the lobby. Check out the displays. Buy a rhyming dictionary or a cliché-a-day calendar. Catch a glimpse of Fabio. I kept glancing at the door, hoping Brigid would come back for her coat. And me.

When I picked up my tape recorder to put it in my bag, a folded-up fifty-dollar bill popped out from under it. I hadn't seen her do that. Add sleight of hand to the performance.

Frown Face put his change back in his wallet and picked up his beer. He was heading in my direction. I ran my hand through my hair, then cursed myself for doing that. Had I always done that? His frowning face was smiling when he rounded the faux marble pillar, and not so tall up close.

"Can I buy you two a drink?"

I made a point to glance around me. "Are you seeing double?" That got me the chilly eye.

He flicked a hand at Brigid's plum-colored coat. "What about your friend?"

"She had to leave."

He glanced around the bar, back at the coat, then back at me. "She looked familiar. Like someone I went to school with."

I estimated a fifteen-year age difference.

"What's her name?"

"Brigid."

"Bridget."

"No E. No T."

"I don't remember any Brigids. What's her last name?"

"Ireland."

"Say where she was going?" His eyes locked on her empty, napkin-less glass.

"Nope."

He picked it up and held it to the light, then set it down. "Chipped rim."

It didn't look chipped.

He seemed both perplexed and irked. "She a friend of yours?"

"I just met her. She's up from Des Moines for the writers conference."

"She a writer?"

"So am I."

He focused on me as if I were part of the conversation. "What do you write?"

"Romance."

He was about to ask me something. My name? Nora Roberts was on the tip of my tongue. He finished his beer in three swallows, set the bottle down and said, "Hope that works out for you," and walked out of the bar leaving behind the scent of copper pennies.

6. Angela Folly
Angela of Foligno, the Patron Saint of Temptation
SUNDAY

I tossed the empty dime bottle of complimentary lavender lotion into the wastebasket, clipped up my hair, and pulled on Friday's khaki pants and maroon turtleneck. I'd loitered as long as legal in my four-star hotel room; but not to be wasteful, I gulped down the last two cups of complimentary coffee while I scanned my complimentary newspaper. It was checkout time.

A couple miles down the freeway I stumbled upon a no-star motel two months shy of the wrecking ball. The spooky man behind the desk handed me a tarnished brass key. No key-cards here, uh-uh. He should have provided a battering ram. With a hard shoulder shove and a reverse flick of the key, the door released. Stale, suffocating air gagged me blue. I pulled open the drapes to let in the light of day and quickly closed them. Ceiling to floor brown and orange Rorschach stains did not need the light of day. I was keenly aware that I had not checked into the Ritz, but this was flat out border town.

Eager to get out the door, I stumbled over my red Travelpro. I considered hauling it back to my car and searching for a one-star. Not at this price. I shut the door and scurried to the car. Before driving off, I pulled Brigid's plum-colored coat from the backseat and switched it with my mill coat. Tailored to fit Brigid's padded self, the soft cotton coat with its topstitched pockets and real darts fit me like high couture. I slipped the tarnished room key into the breast pocket.

I drove to The Mall of America, which seemed like a decent place to kill some time, but instead, proved dispiriting — shopping without money being about as much fun as driving without wheels. I bought a miniature box of factory fudge, settled in under a giant ficus tree and watched the Sunday shoppers come streaming in with their Saturday bags filled with buyer's remorse.

A coiffed blonde plunked down at an adjacent table and installed her Kmart bag between her feet. Mall of America sans Kmart, a three-month-old Macy's return would be my guess. She looked like Dusty Springfield with a hangover, which reminded me of the woman and her sentry boy at the hotel, especially the boy. I was no expert, for sure, but I didn't believe kids stood that still with their boy-jaws set like beat cops. What's more, unhappy or sad or sick kids whined and pulled on their mothers' coats. What would freeze a child? Some dreadful awareness? Fear? I wished I'd said something.

A scruffy man wearing a baggy crocheted hat skulked past my ficus tree. Our eyes locked for a moment. If My Saint was correct, peering outside his circle like that, he was up to something. I lost sight of him in the crowd. Keen on finding another criminal in Sunday's congregation, I challenged every face, but no one met my eyes or anyone else's eyes outside their immediate circles, which was a good thing, I concluded, meaning that no one was prepping to blow up the place. After a half-hour of grinding carnival machinery, juvenile hysteria, ambitious parents, and texting teens with more nose rings than a Botswana medicine man, the only eyes I'd caught aimed outside 'the circle of self' had been glassy and unfocused. The self-absorption of the human race with the never-ending inflow of self-absorbing technology had rocketed off past Pavonis Mons. Earthlings would text an extraterrestrial before they would ever look one in the eye or shake its hand. How long would a body sit dead under a ficus tree? Until somebody stuck a SALE sign on it. Gloomy, if you stayed on that too long. I didn't.

I tossed the empty fudge box and retreated to my car. Too much sugar and caffeine had me both jittery and tired; surface streets seemed prudent. And lucky, because I happened upon a library in Bloomington that would serve as my afternoon holding station.

Prowling the aisles of a library or a bookstore always fanned an edgy awareness in me. It's as if the words were seeping out off the pages and generating small electrical chatter within the air molecules that, without fail, recharged my dull brain. A book, like a plant, is a life form with its own unique vibration culled from its creator. That very vibration constitutes its soul. I would, if I could, hole up in a library surrounded by these paper souls and their divining energy.

I'd once contemplated a degree in library science, but the health of that science was looking more and more tenuous what with the internet, the Nooks and the Kindles, ADD, and the twelve-hour workday. Mr. and Mrs. Sands would be thrilled if I shelved books. They'd be more thrilled if I would "just go out and find a job in some lovely office" (the industry didn't matter, provided there were benefits). My mother would add, "and work your way up to head secretary." She still called them secretaries. What the Sands refused to believe is that I could earn more money waiting tables than I could loading spreadsheets on my way up the ladder to Head Secretary.

Penny, my fretful friend, was always telling me to write historical romance. Didn't I have a degree in history?

Truth: I didn't care a crap about history. The ignominious secret I would die with was that I'd majored in history because J.H. majored in history. I'd met J.H. my first year of college. For three years we dissected the past over coffee and creamers. Then J.H. took his diploma, moved back to Jersey and entered law school.

Dear Jenn, without you, history would have been such a bore... Sincerely, J.H.

Sincerely? We'd had sex!

The fact that he tore through more creamers than I did should have told me something. I'd aced my senior year because I'd needed to keep my mind off this unseemly error in judgment, after which I moved back to hometown Dave and resumed our low-energy relationship. Dave worked for a landscape company and would be relocating to Fargo to open a lawn and garden satellite. He'd asked what I thought of Fargo. I'd told him it'd brought the Coen brothers to the table.

Alone at a table perusing Ann Rule's *Without Pity*, it didn't take me too many pages to realize I was in the wrong book. My Saint would never be in the same book with Ann Rule's sociopaths and psychopaths whose crimes were heartless and evil, senseless. What's more, no money changed hands. When it came to crime, was money the measure of sanity?

...

Seated on the exact same stool three days in a row, I ordered the exact same martini from the exact same Jack-in-the-Box, who took my order as if he'd never seen me before in his life. Bob plunked the drink down in front of me and hustled back to his scratch-off lottery tickets. How would he be acting if I were Nora Roberts, the world's most famous Romance writer, drinking martinis at his bar? That he knew what she looked like was doubtful. Once she signed the check, she'd be properly famous, but too late to ask after her agent.

Just for grins (because My Saint would trick me again), I set about scoping the bar with my new Ann Rule investigative eye; and there he stood, the man with the hair. Cripes. He raised his beer bottle to acknowledge my seeing him. Who was he? He jerked his head to flick the hair out of his eyes and glanced at the dungeon doors, then back at me, then at Brigid's coat. Having no idea what she'd look like, how would I warn her? One elbow on the bar, he watched the room, which wasn't much to watch.

Stonehenge was pitifully empty: the man with the hair, an older woman drinking what looked like a cup of coffee at the far end of the bar, two tables of Sunday stragglers, and my ever-faithful self. My eyes moved back to the coffee drinker. She looked like the woman who'd followed My Saint out the dungeon doors. Or maybe not. The hair was different. Last night the woman's hair had been straight. The coffee drinker's curled hair was parted on one side, pulled flat across her forehead and anchored with a clip a la Eva Braun. A hotel guest, for sure. My eyes moved to the man with the sheaf of hair, who was something more than a hotel guest. *Out of context.* Stalker. Killer. Maybe I'd read too much crime at the library, all the pretty girls with names like Donna and Lori. Pretty Midwest girls. Innocent. Hopeless. Dead.

"Jennifer Sands?"

I let out a yelp, hand to my chest. The concierge, the snappy one, looked clearly put out. Up close I could read his nametag. Bill? A hotel hoax, for sure: Bart, Bob, and now Bill. I stared at him. His broad, turgid face dovetailed the Modigliani horse butts on the wall behind him. Martian.

"You have a phone call in the lobby." He turned and headed towards the dungeon doors.

Who'd be calling me in the lobby? I grabbed my purse and slid off the stool and caught up with him at the doors, but he quickened his pace keeping two steps ahead on the green vine carpet. At the desk, he indicated a phone. I picked up the receiver. He punched line three, waited a moment, then marched off without a word. "Hey, thanks," I yelled after him. Should I have tipped him? I picked up the receiver.

"Jas," the voice said.

"Brigid?"

"Hang up the phone and walk out the front door. Get in your car and drive to your motel."

"But, I–"

"Quick."

"Your coat's in the bar. I'll have to–"

"Leave it. It's not my coat."

"Whose coat–"

"If you go back in there he'll follow you."

I whispered, "I haven't paid–"

"Bob's owes you. Get out of there. Now." She hung up.

I fast-walked through the lobby that a few hours ago had been the heart's bazaar of the romance convention. Cleared out. Cleaned out. Polyvinyl settees and giant rhododendrons slipped back into place as if it'd never happened. Late afternoon check-ins, mostly business, rolled their luggage over the vine carpeting heading to the elevators. Two women from housekeeping coaxed their overloaded utility cart through a Staff Only door. The snappy concierge was nowhere in sight. Bart was not at the front desk. I pushed out through the revolving door at the same time a woman and a boy, both awkwardly wedged into the same partition, pushed in. If they were not the mother and her sentry son from Friday, they were related. I hesitated. The moving door hit my heels, and I stumbled out into air so cold I gasped, Mother Mary, and caught the door back into the lobby, dogged to retrieve that plum-colored coat, which immediately felt like a bad idea what with Bartender Bob, the man with the sheaf of hair, and Concierge Bill, every last one of them stressing me stupid. I loved that plum-colored coat. *If you go back in there, he'll follow you.* I circled back out into the bitter cold and bolted to my car, my maroon turtleneck a sieve for frost, all the while digging in my bag for car keys, and, like the damsel in distress, fumbled them, dropped and kicked them, and snatched them up again, jangled them around and nicked the paint before I fit the key into the lock. I jumped in with a wrought-up yelp, slammed the door and hit the lock half-expecting a sheaf of black hair to pop in front of my windshield. That didn't happen, but I screamed anyway. I jammed the keys into the ignition. The car started on the first try. It hadn't set that long.

I yanked my coat from the backseat and wrestled myself into it. The satin lining felt like aluminum foil. I fisted my hands to stop the shaking and stared at the hotel entrance expecting to see Bob run out waving my bar tab. A family exited, huddled together, and disappeared into the dark. No one else was on the move.

Why was I running? The easy answer was that I'd walked out on my bar tab. The more likely answer hinged on the man with the sheaf of hair and my association with the woman he was hunting. Does she owe him money? Any second now, he will come out the door hunting me and my Midwest girl self. *Get out of there. Now.* I shoved into reverse, floored it, and smacked into the car behind me. I lurched forward again, but stomped the brake in time.

"Holy crap, get a hold of yourself!"

I stretched around to see what I'd hit which turned out to be a U-haul truck with a rumpled license plate. Hell, they're all rumpled. Seeing no one who might have borne witness, I inched back out and aimed for the frontage road that would take me to the freeway.

Go to your motel, she'd said. I hadn't told her I'd moved to a motel. We hadn't discussed sleeping arrangements, hers or mine. What was I missing?

I stood outside my no-star motel room and dug around in my purse even though I knew damn well I'd left the no-star brass key in the pocket of the plum-colored coat. Was the name of the motel on that key? The man with the sheaf of hair could be on his way, plum coat in tow. He'd had his eye on it. I leaned against the door. It opened and I stumbled in, catching myself on the corner of the bed for the second time that day. The woman holding the door wore dark jeans and a green army parka. A khaki colored stocking hat concealed her hair. If I'd been anywhere other than eye level with my red Travelpro, I would have figured I'd fallen into the wrong room.

"Brigid?"

"Angela Folly. Angela of Foligno, the Patron Saint of Temptation. Call me Angie." With her black gloved hands she pushed the door shut.

"Well, hell." I pulled myself up. "How'd you get in here? Crap, the lock's probably easier to pick. And why are you here? And that guy at the bar last night with the hair–"

"At the bar again."

"And he's looking for you. So why am I the one who's out of breath? This is the height of paranoia. I'm a romance writer, for gawd's sake! I ran out on my bar tab."

Angela Folly's green eyes fixed on me. "You got the makings of a criminal." Her droopy eyelids suggested fatigue or boredom. Maybe pushed down with hidden weights? Was that possible?

"Yeah, well. Look, Angie, Toni, Brigid, Alex, whatever your name is, I don't know about this you and me and a story makes three. Things are funking up." I squinted at her. "How'd you know he was at the bar?"

"I saw him when I passed with my luggage trolley."

"Luggage trolley?"

"What name did he call me?"

I stared at her, uncomprehending. "Last night he didn't know your name. I didn't talk to him tonight. You were staying at that hotel? This keeps getting better." I flopped onto the bed. It felt like I'd landed on the floor. "The key to this room is in the plum colored coat."

She nodded, as if considering, then heaved the desk chair in front of the mirror and motioned for me to sit. She removed her gloves and reached deep inside a leather bag the size of a mailman's pouch. She pulled out a soft case, unzipped it and held up an ash blonde wig, chin-length and straight. "He won't be looking for blonde."

"So he is looking."

"I told you, someone's always looking." She combed the wig with her fingers.

"Nobody's looking for me."

"Except in the course of looking for me."

That I had gotten myself attached to somebody's trouble was fairly certain. But I was not yet vested. Get up off this army cot and walk out the door. I'd be home in two hours with enough time to delete a wee bit of swoon out of *Love is a French Verb*. I'd call Dave and we'd...

I pulled up off the bed. "So now what?"

She nodded once, as if something had been decided, and said, "Dinner. You must be starving."

"Dinner?" I shrieked. "We're being hunted."

She held up the wig. "Then let's get you recast."

With a half-crazed smile on my face, but admittedly intrigued (hungry and near broke), I plunked down in front of the mirror. She wound my hair and twisted it tight while stretching a black nylon cap onto my head. That took the smile off my face.

"You got too much hair," she said, tucking strays.

"Ouch!" I said and really meant it. I stared at my reflection. I could swim at the Y with my sausage-skin head. She shimmied the blonde wig down over the cap. Tiny combs bit my scalp. I touched my new hair. It felt creepy real, someone else's hair. Someone else's expensive hair. She brushed the bangs to minimize my black eyebrows and feathered the sides forward. I had never been blonde. It wasn't a bad thing.

"You can admire later. Let's go." She held my red Travelpro in her, once again, gloved hands, her mailman's pouch over her shoulder.

"But I paid for this room."

"But you no longer have the key. I have a place you can stay."

Anything would be better than this. I picked up my purse and the backpack that contained *Love is a French Verb* and almost dropped it down again and kicked it under the bed. I didn't, of course. I heaved it onto my shoulder. It weighed more than a dead cow. I slammed the door behind me — let him wrestle with the lock — and hurried after her. This new Angie saint had a slouch to her walk.

Four cars littered the parking lot, one up on blocks. We headed towards a black sedan that looked like a taxicab.

I said, "I wonder what he's driving."

"A green SUV. Ford."

"How do you know that?"

"I saw him leave the hotel last night." She unlocked the trunk and hoisted my suitcase inside.

"I thought you went off to kill somebody." I sounded bitchy, but I wanted her to know that I remembered things. And saw things. "Who was that woman who followed you out of Stonehenge?"

"A woman followed me?"

"Black coat? Gray hair? She was sitting by the door. She looked … foreign sorta."

Her perplexed frown told me I was, indeed, an enthusiast of fabrication. "How does one look foreign?"

I shrugged. "It's more intuitive than visual. You watched her come into Stonehenge last night."

"I watch everybody, but I shouldn't be that obvious. Lettin' my guard down around you, I guess."

Was I flattered? Yes. "I'm not sure, but she might have been at the bar again tonight."

"Probably a lost romance writer."

"I told the man with the hair that you were a romance writer."

"I like that."

"He smelled like copper pennies."

We exited off I-494 onto Highway 12 and turned onto a frontage road. Two more turns brought us into the parking lot of a restaurant called Lords. A kid with his hands in his pockets, his nose buried in a winter scarf, watched us drive past.

"I never valet," she said, slowing down at the row of favored cars with their valet tickets tucked under the wipers.

"It could snow any minute."

"My mother's favorite sermon was that snow was cleansing like Jesus Christ. She would open the white prayer book to the page with the three hearts. The black heart represented mortal sin and a life in hell, the spotted heart was venial sin and would get you to purgatory, the empty heart was your snow-white ticket to heaven. I rather like that Porsche Boxster."

"I'll take the white Mercedes."

"Mother would say, 'Which heart will you take with you when you die?' She always answered her own question. 'The snow white heart, of course.' One day I took a crayon to it."

We parked in the back row with the Fords and the Buicks and scurried to the restaurant in night air too cold for October. It occurred to me that her attention to that line of Mercedes and Porsches might be business and not a passing interest, and just as I opened my mouth to inquire, the shivering kid leapt out of the key shack and pulled open the restaurant door and we stepped into a room so bright it stopped me dumb. I squinted at the white tile floor, glossy white walls, and the row of white enamel cabriolet chairs. A stylish, gray-haired woman wearing a white blouse with a white tie peeked out of a window and offered to check our coats. Angie told her no. Good. Except for my blonde head, my chassis was chilled. I clasped my coat tight and followed Angie through a white metal door into what could have been the bottom of a coalmine. We'd gone from shine to blind. The governing light came from the amber lamps on the tables. A smoldering fireplace added a ruddy glow. An outlying backlit bar gave off light like the moon. Nowadays, restaurants, even the nice ones, were lit up like cafeterias. Much to do with litigation, for sure, because it certainly wasn't inviting. In contrast, Lords was a night stage of shadows and clinking glasses, the flick of an eye both quickening and covert, the beast *en croute*. I shivered in a good way.

A commanding angel wearing a short, strapless dress of white feathers materialized out of the dark. Angie held up two fingers. The angel said, "Mind the steps," and motioned us to follow. Six pin-lights down, we crossed the room and slid into a u-shaped booth of smooth, black leather. A brass lamp cast an amber glow.

Angie eased off her hat and stuffed it in her pocket. Her mousy brown hair was chop-cut to her shoulders, a tad stringy. She pulled out of her parka and let it crumple up behind her. A tight, long-sleeved, black t-shirt affirmed her slender frame, light years from Brigid's chubby self in her bulky sweats. From every angle, this woman transfigured into something different. But I sensed a rhythm now. I just might recognize her on the street. Nobody else would. Nobody else had seen her multiple selves close-up and in such a short timeframe.

The waiter placed two silver cocktail discs on the table and told us that his name was Darren and he would be our server. My Saint leaned forward, extended her hand and introduced herself as Angela. This reverse etiquette being out of rote, he faltered, but held his expert smile. She kept hold of his hand while she introduced me as her daughter, Rose White, up from Mankato.

"Glad to meet you," I chirped. It seemed appropriate given the circumstance.

My Saint released Darren's hand and, except for the caring smile pasted on her face, settled back into Angie mode. While Darren said the specials, I watched the angel hostess seat a pretty couple bedecked in matching white cable sweaters and blue jeans. The woman had Carrie Bradshaw hair; the man favored George Stephanopoulos. I imagined they'd checked their London Fogs at the white entrance. Who were these people? What kind of lives did they live that allowed them white cable sweaters, skinny jeans, and Sunday dinners at Lords. Frye boots kicking around under the table.

Darren asked what we'd like to drink. It seemed like a Turner Classic Movie kind of night. I ordered a whiskey sour cocktail. Angie ordered a Jack Daniels and Coke.

"Very nice," Darren said.

I pushed RECORD on my Sony and said, "We rode over here in something that could have once been a taxi cab. Do you own it?"

The amber light caught her contact lenses and her eyes turned to emeralds. "It's back-up. I used my gofer car at Broder Circle and had to dump it."

"Do you have a car registered in any of your names?"

"That'd give me tag, tail and trace issues. Unencumbered transportation is a challenge. Only one saint has the necessary plastic for Avis or Hertz, but the small, private fly-by-nights will take cash for collateral without fuss. I'm always prowling for purchase."

Darren delivered our drinks and placed a black, oversized book next to each of us. LORDS in bold silver letters glinted off the cover. I rubbed the polished, sans serif S. It was metal.

"How do you get these cars?"

"Luck. Last year I found a fifteen-year-old Chevy in the classifieds. To avoid the legal bullshit, I gave the farmer cash plus an additional four-hundred to let me drive it a couple of days, see if I liked it. If I didn't like it, he'd keep the four-hundred. If I liked the car, we'd do the paperwork. Some of those old guys still do business on a handshake. Two days later I called him and told him I'd totaled it, send the paperwork and keep all the money. I drove it another nine months. Would have driven it longer, but I'd torched a boathouse on Minnetonka, spotted a tail, and had to ditch it."

"What about license plates?"

"I've got dealer tags and lost tag plates and out-of-state plates where the numbers track to addresses where nobody's home in unfamiliar towns like Moline, Caruthersville, Natchez. A map on the dashboard covers the vehicle ID." She pushed at her sleeve and peered at the round white face of a watch on a black leather band. I wondered how many watches she owned.

My eyes had adjusted to the lighting. In fact, I could see just fine. I watched a man wearing khakis and a dark sports jacket cross the room with the smooth style of a British spy, Sean Connery in his anthropology years. He sat down at a table next to a giant palm and adjusted his chair to escape its magnificent and annoying fronds. A waiter followed with a cocktail.

"What was that about? Torching a boathouse?"

"The boathouse is not significant enough to be interesting. It was contracted through Bill Soderholm, my first official contractor." She smiled with affection. "You'll want to know how I met Billy."

"Yes, I'd like to know that, how you get your contacts. Like if your Roach guy doesn't know Jug and Jug doesn't know Lance and nobody knows Zen, how does that work? You don't advertise in the Yellow Pages." I edged the tape recorder closer to her.

"Back at the Triangle Bar it didn't enter my mind that I'd ever do any more Pineapple Daiquiri police-pageants. Especially after I'd discovered he'd embezzled a fortune from his employer, skipped town, and I'd helped. That was unsettling." She glanced at me. "It really was."

"Not unsettling enough to go to the police."

She sighed. "Thanks to Pineapple, I was out of debt. Bartending paid the rent. I'd earned a mini reputation as a capable make-up artist in the neighborhood theaters. I operated under the juvenile notion that I was climbing life's proverbial ladder. I trifled around in that poverty because I was young. It didn't take long to see that I didn't have what it took to play the angles and make a living in the glut. Not naturally enduring or effusive, I couldn't get on the A list.

"Then Billy shows up at the Triangle and hands me a card, which I recognize as the Party Joke Company card with the same damn bogus phone number. A man in Brisbane had given it to him. I say to him, 'Brisbane?'

"He says, 'Australia.' Like I didn't know that. Somebody had drawn a triangle on the back of the card. Curious beyond control, I ask him to describe the man who'd given him the card. I add, 'I mighta seen him in here.'

"Billy gathers the image, then says, 'Weight-lifter type, dark complexion, black wiry hair.'" Angie focused her sleepy eyes on me. "You remember how fat and beige my Pineapple Daiquiri was?"

"And bald," I added.

"A comb-over roly-poly, yes. I tell Billy he's got the wrong bartender. He's perplexed. He says, 'I could have sworn ... oh, well.' He glances around, glances at his watch, and settles on a stool and says, 'I'm here. Give me your best Scotch neato.' Billy talks like that. Neato.

"I set a Black in front of him and make change from his twenty, hoping he's a one drink kind of guy. I'm uneasy about him. I wonder how he came by the Party Joke Company card. There'll always be some gumshoe hunting Pineapple. I get an order for margaritas. I pour the tequila and the triple sec into the blender along with a stream of simple syrup, then lemon juice. A tick of raw egg white gives it a plush layer of foam. This was back before salmonella and lawyers, of course. I salt the rims, squeeze the limes and pour. Billy watches like I might be performing some magic trick. His eyes follow the waitress to a table of John Lennon types.

"He says, 'I don't know how they drink those sissy things and look themselves in the mirror.' He lowers his voice and adds, 'You know, I wondered about the guy who gave me the card.' He gives a nod to the Party Joke Company card in the ashtray. 'Odd sort. Was drinking pineapple Daiquiris.'

"I say to Billy, 'You're looking for Therese List.' It just popped into my head, that saint thing. Saint Therese, my mother's favorite saint. My first saint."

I injected: "Therese of Lisieux, the Patron Saint of Florists, not to be confused with Teresa of Avila, the Patron Saint of

Headaches." And there it was again, that tic at the corner of her mouth, that slip of self. Then it was gone.

She said, "Billy hands me his business card. He's a building contractor. Now how vague is that? I say to him, 'I'll have Terry call you.'

"It happened that fast."

My spy guy under the palm took a sip of his drink and leaned forward, elbows extended, shoulders slumped. Weary looking. I would call him My Spy. Maybe write him into the story. The waiter brought him another cocktail. I wondered what he was drinking. Something dark. I wrote Rum and Coke in my notebook.

I said to Angie, "Tell me about the boy. The one you kidnapped out of Canada."

Angie had a way of sighing, as if operating in some low energy sphere where there wasn't enough oxygen. The mood was infectious. I stifled a yawn. My eyes drifted back to My Spy. He took a long swallow from his Rum and Coke. I noted that Angie had barely touched her Jack and Coke, my whiskey sour near empty.

"The boy's name is Bentley Graas. Bender, for short. Cute kid. Wednesday I was on my way to Burnsville to dump the Broder Circle car and figured, what the hell, I'll drive by the boy's house. I hadn't done that in awhile. I pull in down the street behind a pick-up truck. The line-up of ranch houses is one long pastel smear; but not anywhere near the sheer duplication of Broder Circle. That brings Matzo Ball to mind, and I process that disaster until I've had quite enough of it. I'm about to turn the key when a sedan pulls into the driveway and Fanny Graas climbs out."

"Fanny is the boy's mother?"

"Yes. And I see immediately she's got issues, because her natural blonde hair is dyed black. Bender comes around from the passenger side, his parka open and askew. Fanny pulls out a couple bags of groceries and hands him a six-pack of Squirt or Mellow

Yellow, something yellow. The porch lights come on and the front door opens. It's Lil, the grandmother, in a jogging suit. I've never seen her in anything but one of those stretchy, mid-life cover-ups. The fact that she is a mere ten years older than I am is not lost on me. Bender hands her the six-pack and gives her a boy-hug and disappears into the house. Lil wrote Lance a check for two grand, which he converted to cash for me. I took a loss. It was my own damn fault taking the job, and I blame that, too, on waning estrogen."

"It's been two years since the kidnapping and you still check on the boy. You bonded."

"You could write it like that." Angie's sleepy eyes traveled the room passing over My Spy. She frowned, but it didn't mean anything to me at the time. "Lil follows Bender into the house. Fanny stops and turns around. She stares in my direction with the alertness of a hunted animal."

I said, "Dave says that deer can hear a gun cock a mile away."

"And catch the stench of copper pennies."

7. Angie Folly

"Fanny fast-walks up the sidewalk. She opens the door and stops, takes one last look around, backs in and slams it shut. I can almost hear the locks click."

"She thinks her crazy husband is out there?"

"She knows he's out there."

"He's threatened to kill her and the police have not been notified? What am I missing?"

Angie half-yawned, half-sighed. "Laddie Ogren. You're missing Laddie Ogren, the husband. The police mean nothing to him."

"I don't understand."

"I know you don't."

"Can't somebody talk to him?"

"He's a well-equipped psychopath."

"There are organizations that help women. Hide them."

"Fanny can hide herself."

"Obviously not so good."

Somebody needed to throw this Fanny woman a safety net. And what might that be? A court order? A restraining order? What do the Laddie Ogrens of the world think about restraining orders? I said, "This is why I've never written crime or mysteries or thrillers. I don't understand the Laddie Ogrens of the world. How do they get so crazy mean? He was somebody's little boy once."

"No, he wasn't."

"Well, of course he was. Everybody was somebody's little something once."

"Maybe you should write fantasy." Angie closed her menu and added, "It's a good thing Toni Padua isn't here. She's vegetarian."

Darren drifted past our table. Angie motioned him over. I ordered the porterhouse. I could have eaten the Lord's cut, max meat, but called up some self-control and ordered the Lady's cut.

Angie ordered wild mushroom polenta and substituted a side of French fries for the salad. Once again Darren told us what fine choices we'd made.

I said, "Your story needs to be True Crime. The advantage of True Crime is that readers don't expect to identify with the central character."

"But I'd like readers to identify with me. Write me so readers identify."

"That'd be like asking Ann Rule to get her readers to identify with Ted Bundy."

Angie frowned at the comparison.

"You know what I mean," I said, conciliatory. "See, Ann Rule writes nonfiction. Nobody has to identify with anybody. A character could be so far off the floor he floats and it wouldn't matter because it's nonfiction. Same with memoirs. There's one where a homeless couple in New York own oil rights in Texas."

"That's not possible?" Her gaze shifted to the man under the palm.

"Not where I come from." I waited for her full attention.

She spoke, distracted: "If the world can identify with Harry Potter, they can identify with me."

I snorted. "Harry Potter is fantasy. And even if he wasn't, the kid is endearing. So far, you've told me nothing endearing."

"Well, hell, throw in some pink. Have me plant wildflowers at roadside rest stops. Give me a chocolate lab named Hershey. You're a romance writer. Write something fetchy."

"Fetchy," I repeated. What I needed was a paragraph or two that resembled everyday life. "How about a boyfriend? A little romance to spice things up."

Her eyes met mine, but I sensed a lack of focus. "Write me a mean James Dean. Have him do me wrong."

So much for romance.

The waiter set a basket of bread on the table. So as not to lunge at it like a refugee, I paged through my afternoon's research on criminals.

"About your story as nonfiction," I said trying out a professional mien, "a significant point is that Ann Rule wrote about Ted Bundy, Jack Stolle, Charles Campbell quite some time after they were caught and punished."

"That aces it then. Fiction, it is. And you make me enduring."

"Just because it's fiction, doesn't mean you can make things up."

"You lost me there."

My recorder stopped. I fished in my bag for a fresh cassette.

Angie said, "I'll use the restrooms while you do that." She slid out of the booth and headed towards the hostess desk, skipped up the steps, and disappeared into the dark. I released the cassette, wrote Angie#1 on it, and popped in a fresh one. I stirred my cocktail. My Spy was reading his menu. The handsome couple in the white cable sweaters clinked their glasses together and laughed. Too many minutes for a restroom break had passed. I wondered what my financial obligation might be if Angie didn't return, but there she came, out of the dark and down the steps. She slid into the booth. Cold spilled off her as if she'd been outside. Maybe the toilets were outhouses.

She said, "What you need, Jas, is some hands-on street experience."

"Bail is not in the budget." I waited, tapping my pencil on my notepad. "Okay then, enough about bail. Is there any more to chasing Sammy down Eighth? We're stalled in the coffee shop."

"The coffee shop."

"Kerby pushed you out of the car. Sammy wasn't in the coffee shop."

She stared at the amber lamp as if remembering. After a long moment, she released a slow breath, almost a whistle, seemingly refocused. "In my business I work the sidelines. And there I stood on the sidelines freezing my ass off. Kerby must have run into roadwork on Seventh. He'll be disappointed. He's always been chasing Sammy.

"An omelet-colored Plymouth is headed down Eighth. A man in the backseat has his bare elbow out the window like it's Miami or something. Not only that, he's wearing sunglasses. I'm keenly aware that I'm not an attention grabber in my gray fleece coat and black sweatpants, but he's staring straight at me. I turn away and find myself facing the window of a rare and antique bookstore. The glass mirrors the Plymouth as it trawls past and I recognize the fool in the sunglasses. Barney's boys out of Golden Valley.

"Barney Katz is my most volatile employer. He keeps a stable of trigger-happy chunk punks who melt down in the cuffs with nothing more than a dirty look. I know of two jobbers in prison by way of Barney blunders. Barney knows me as Gert Nivels — Gertrude of Nivelles, the Patron Saint of Cats. Gert wears a blonde braid wrapped around her head that agrees with paisley skirts and Birkenstocks. Barney wears rings on all his fingers and keeps a white Persian cat named Blofeld. Need I say more? He pays the full tab up front plus an additional high-risk assessment fee. When I've finished a Barney job, I pack up and move."

I reached under the napkin that covered the bread and helped myself to a fat bun, tore it in half and slathered butter on both sides. The warm bread was orgasmic. I couldn't chew fast enough. "You rent by the month?"

"Boarding houses and motels, yes. Apartments, no. Too transient. Many times I've felt it prudent to disappear, but I've never jumped rent. I pay the balance in cash. Expensive? Damn straight. It's part of my overhead, a necessary security. The fewer people chasing me, the better."

I buttered up a second roll. "I'm guessing you've never seen a Welcome Wagon."

"If I'm careful to the point of being ridiculous, it's because I have no safety net. Nobody comes looking if I don't get home for supper. Every roaming eye, pulled shade and puffed newspaper is a threat. A couple years back, some detective latched onto Cathy Senna."

"Catherine of Siena," I interjected. "Patron Saint of Fire Prevention. Overweight with strawberry blonde hair."

"You pay attention."

"Writers do that."

"You're an odd lot."

I took that as a compliment. "How'd you know he was onto you?"

"If something out of rhythm gets in your space you feel it. Pay attention to that, Jas. People have resources, inherent skills they don't tap. The dick had taken up residence in Cathy's parking lot. Just for grins, I decided to test my skills. When I left my apartment as Alex or Gert or Terry, he stayed behind the newspaper in his green Toyota. But when Cathy Senna came out, the puffed newspaper dropped six inches. I moved out."

"Didn't he take notice when the moving van pulled in?"

"No vans. Two carloads in two different cars loaded by two different saints. No saints on active duty ever drive the same car. I don't know if Mr. Detective with the green Toyota figured it out. I never did know who put him onto me, or why. Doesn't matter. Most of those guys are history majors. No offense."

"None taken."

"Now if Kinsey Millhone ever got on my case, I'd have to retire everybody. We'd be the *S is for Saints* sequel. Kinsey would tag me and not even Kerby could fix it."

"It's *S is for Silence* and it's already on the discount shelves."

"That was fast."

"Not in this world." We'd drifted again. It was easy to drift. I said, "Kerby pushed you out to chase after Sammy, and this omelet-colored car drives by."

"Barney's boys. Yes." Tired as she seemed, she never rubbed her eyes or her forehead. No chin propped on her hand. Not to smear her make-up? The woman had discipline going. "The jerk in the sunglasses didn't recognize me because he knows me as Gert."

"Gertrude of Nivelles, Patron Saint of Cats," I injected, more to get the story moving than to flaunt recall.

"Yes. I don't look like Gert, but I'm feeling uneasy. I escape into the bookstore. Bells over the door, three of them, tinkle." She turned and looked straight at My Spy. When she turned back, I sensed an ill-defined alertness, a change in the air.

"And there he is, his blue windbreaker drawn tight like a bib. He holds an open book close to his face reading over the top of a pair of super-sized glasses that sit low on his nose, which means he's nearsighted in need of bifocals. He closes the book and sets it down and picks up another and pages through it, snaps it shut and shoves it back into its slot. His long fingers wander the spines. He pulls a black hardbound.

"Pedestal signs label each table, but there is no sign on Sammy's table. I pass the Animals table and stop at Fiction. So many authors, so little time. *Tales of the City.* I love that title, but have never read the book. Was that Somerset Maupin or Armistead Maugham?"

"Armistead Maupin."

"Is that a man?"

"Yes."

"You can't take gender pitch for granted anymore."

I chuckled.

"I move to the Political Science table. The title *White Men Can't Jump* gives me pause. I'd like to page through it and see what that means, but my hands stay in my pockets. I read a good bit, but never used books or library books. The absorbency of book paper is one step up from paper towel, like handling somebody's dirty tissue."

I was about to suggest latex gloves, but she said, "What's the matter? I'm a writer's dream. What good are all those people checking out library books? Don't you need to sell them?"

"People who've never heard of you might read your book if they can check it out for free. Then they buy your next one."

"There is that possibility." She looked amused without the smile.

"Libraries buy books." I sounded defensive. Of what, I wasn't sure. I wasn't published.

She checked her watch again. "If a sure passport was as easy to get as a library card, all the saints would be international. Francis, the Patron Saint of Authors, is the only saint with a foolproof passport. She speaks with a quasi-British accent and says things like 'indubitably' and 'to whom do I speak?' If she didn't have such a profitable employer, we'd all move to London. The streaks and stains in those library books? You gotta hope it's food."

"That's reason enough to buy an e-reader."

"Maybe I will." She glanced again in the direction of My Spy, then, using her spoon, fished out several ice cubes from her water glass and stirred them into her Jack and Coke. "I'm thinking this man is too old to be Sammy, then I remember how old I am, and I'm momentarily chafed at that hapless contradiction in my mind's eye. His head jerks up and he adjusts his glasses and blinks; his eyes drop back down to the book. His mouth stretches into a quick ghoulish wow-ah which allows his glasses to slide back down. This man's got history with glasses. Sammy wore glasses."

"Why didn't you just walk over and ask him?"

"The story would be over." She peeked again at her watch. "Sammy and I read philosophy. We were the only two people in that little farm town deficient enough for Nietzsche. We both owned *The Portable Nietzsche*, a thick, lavender-colored paperback. Our English teacher, Mr. Ives, had warned of the difficulty translating, most translators sacrificing meaning for style, or prose for ideas in search of the *übermensch*. The ultimate goal, according to Mr. Ives, was to read *Zarathustra* in German. Our goal was to read it in English."

Along with Angie's stepped-up energy, her slow talk had also quickened.

"School nights at the bowling alley, Sammy and I discussed the dark *Geist*. What we read was enough to convince us that the unfeeling, inanimate universe was alive and well and living on the prairie, disguised and gussied up by the Lutherans. That's what we thought. Sammy and I had our own version of the heartland. Do you have a best friend?"

"Penny," I said. "You'd like her. She slides into bases."

She seemed to consider that, then said, "At the back of the store, grandma hovers over the Good-housekeeping table. At the counter, a Nordic woman in a white cable sweater with a stack of books for purchase watches the clerk as he records each title into a spiral bound notebook. The clerk is an heirloom blonde, mid-thirties dressed in Seattle flannel and baggy jeans. He's clumsy with the calculator. I move to the Nature table. A book on oceans catches my eye. I love oceans. Sailing without a net. There is no one to catch you in the southern basin. Who the hell do you sue for your troubles? Not for everybody, that freedom."

I followed her eyes to My Spy under the palm. Was Angie intrigued? Does she know him? She fished a bun out of the breadbasket and set it on her plate.

"I look like myself that day. If that was Sammy, he would have recognized me and smiled that lopsided grin and said, 'Life is like a river.' That was our class motto. Sammy's idea."

"Life is like a river?" I chuckled. "That's a cliché."

"Who says that?"

"George Washington on the Potomac. Seriously, why didn't you just introduce yourself?"

"That's not how you approach someone who's chosen to disappear. Apostates renounce for reasons that have everything and nothing to do with their people. Sammy would have no idea which camp I was in. He turns a page, seemingly devoted. I stretch for a book out of reach and strain to see what he's reading, but I can't decipher the silver type beneath his bony fingers.

"His eyes move to the door. I turn just in time to catch the omelet-colored Plymouth glide by again. I notice that the grunge clerk is eyeing the door. Experience tells me that laissez-faire is in progress here beyond that with the Nordic woman at the register. Sammy turns the pages in the black book, but his eyes are on the door. The clerk's eyes dart from the door to Sammy and back to the door. I half-expect one of Barney's boys to burst in. I turn back to Sammy just in time to see him slip the book into the front pocket of his blue windbreaker. I am momentarily shocked.

"Although I wouldn't put it past him to glom a book. Sammy was a socialist." Angie picked at her watch, turning it on her wrist, smoothing the leather band. "The man who could be Sammy moves towards the door. His expression is oddly aloof. The bells jingle as it opens and shuts. I half expect the clerk to take off after him and grab him by the blue windbreaker. But the lady at the register clears her throat and the clerk gets back to business.

"Sammy moves off down the street. Should I follow him? Kerby would say yes, but I can't come up with a reason to do that. I walk over to the table where he'd stood. The books are German. I had two years of that huckster language and have forgotten everything, which is fine. What's the point of German nowadays?

"There's nothing more to be done in the bookstore. The bells announce my departure. The wind bites like January. I step back into the alcove and it catches my eye, the black hardcover with the silver title propped against the brick. I can see the grunge clerk through the window bagging books for the very patient lady in the white cable sweater. I snatch the book and slip it into my pocket. I don't know German anymore, but I know this book: *Also Sprach Zarathustra*. I step out to the sidewalk. There's no sign of the blue windbreaker, but lo and behold, down the street in front of Khomeini's tobacco shop sits the omelet-colored Plymouth and here come two of Barney's boys carrying coffee cups. In the other direction, Kerby's Lexus crosses Nicollet. One more loop won't hurt him; I can't resist this.

"Traffic stops. I jog across the street and duck into the alley behind a dumpster. I yank a pale blue stocking cap from my pocket and pull it down over my ears and tuck my hair. I slide out of my coat, turn it inside out and jerk it back on."

Angie stopped talking. Something in the dining room caught her eye. But maybe not, because she said, "Have you ever noticed how much colder it feels in an alley? It's the combination of transience and filth." She looked at me. "A chilly mix, don't you think?"

I nodded, willing her to stay focused. Although Angela Folly acted consummately distracted, it did seem as though we were moving towards a plot point.

I prompted, "You've turned your coat inside out."

"Yes. I am now wearing a black coat. My blue hat covers my hair. I pull a pair of black-framed glasses out of my pocket. The bows are so cold it feels like I've slit my temples. I yank on my gloves. The black Lexus moves down Eighth with Kerby on the phone. The Nordic lady exits the store carrying a shopping bag in each hand and stops to adjust her grip. The grunge clerk flies out the door and plows into her causing her to drop her bags and catch herself on the railing. He picks up her bags and hands them to her and shoos her off, then paces the sidewalk in front of the store looking like he's lost something. He stops and fixes his hands on his hips. I can't hear him, but I know from the forward jerk of his head and the flash of his front teeth that he's just said the F word. He says it again and goes back inside.

"Barney's boys reach the bookstore and stop outside and fidget around like a couple of jerks waiting to mooch a cigarette. The one with the sunglasses spits on the sidewalk barely missing a baby stroller. The woman lashes at him. He shrugs like a horse that just dropped his load. I'm beginning to think this is going nowhere when his pal nods towards the door and they go inside. My guess is they're not looking for Armistead Maupin. Traffic stops. Traffic starts. They exit the store. Whatever their business was, it was quick. They head back to the omelet-colored Plymouth and walk past it and disappear around the corner.

"Traffic stops and I sprint across the street and into the bookstore. Grandma, glasses on her nose, ambles towards the front of the store, but stops at the Nature table and picks up my book on oceans. It has a catchy cover.

"The clerk is not behind the counter. I snoop around and notice that the back door is unlatched and propped open with a book. I'm curious to see what book deserves this fate, but the ragtime music distracts me. The backbeat snaps, fugal and faint. It's not music. It's the uneven clickety clackity ching of a typewriter, an old Remington or something. Nobody types on manuals anymore, but someone is, and quite expediently. I follow the sound to the counter. The wall to my left is a ceiling to floor bookcase. To my right is a bulletin board thick with old play sheets and announcements. The wastebasket is empty except for two cups of coffee sitting upright. I'm surprised those two losers didn't just sling 'em in there like most people do, splattering coffee that dribbles out the bottom of the bag all the way to the dumpster. I step behind the counter for a closer look at a ten-year-old poster advertising *Macbeth* at the Guthrie. The wall of books swings towards me. I jump back outside the counter. The clerk slips out from behind it. His cubbyhole clearly shares a wall with the toilet, a rogue space I'd failed to notice. He asks if he can help me. He's not smiling."

Angie glanced again at My Spy under the palm. What was it about the man under the palm? She rolled her arm so her watch was visible.

I said to her, "Is there a meter running?"

"Huh? No. Our food is taking awhile."

"Now that you mention it."

"I tell Grunge that I was curious who was typing on an old manual. He says, 'Now you know.' I ask if he has *Thus Spoke Zarathustra* in German. Attitude changes to scrutiny. With my blue cap, black coat and glasses, he doesn't recognize me from earlier, so I wonder if this particular book, the one I have in my pocket, means something to him. He comes around the counter and heads towards the table where the man who could be Sammy had been standing. I follow.

"'Had it,' he says. He squints at me, then at my coat pockets, then crosses his arms and steps into my space. Me and Grunge are eye to eye and I'm not liking his eyes. He says, '*Die Elster stiehlt, so gut sie schwatzt.*'

"Not all my German is lost. That's an idiom I remember: The magpie steals as well as it chatters. The stolen book suddenly feels large in my pocket. I tell him that I don't speak German. It would be a gift for my dentist.

"He smiles, showing too much teeth, and I get my ass out of there. I'm walking fast towards Nicollet. The black Lexus is coming down Eighth again with Kerby still on his phone. I yank off my cap and glasses, shove them into my pockets ... and wave." Angie's speech had become halting, as if she were reading ahead of the script. "He pulls to the curb. The warm leather seat..." she repositioned the bun on her bread plate, "...feels soft as bread dough."

"Are you okay?"

"Kerby hasn't noticed..." Angie's eyes narrowed into a hard stare, "...that my gray coat has turned black." She fell silent. I cleared my throat. She said, "I see someone I know," grabbed her drink, and slid out of the booth and walked off. Gone was the Angie slouch; back was the Alex Edessa stride, right over to My Spy. They shook hands.

Well, damn.

Had I been prescient singling him out? And why had she acted like she'd just spotted him that very moment? I wrote 'questionable chain of recognition' in my notebook. If she knew My Spy, he had to be dirty. I watched. They talked amiably. Until she set her drink down on his table, leaned towards him and peered at his collar, jumped back, grabbed his napkin and swatted the back of his neck. My Spy jerked forward, batting at his collar. He leapt out of his chair knocking it over, shedding his jacket to the floor. Angie stomped on it. He fluttered his arms as if shaking off numbness. Angie grabbed his drink and handed it to him. He threw it back in one gulp, ice cubes tumbling down his white shirt, and steadied himself on the table. The angel hostess and a busboy and what looked like the manager converged. Angie pointed at the palm tree, then squatted to the floor. I could no longer see her, but when she stood up, she handed the manager a wad of tissue or something. The manager shined his pocket light on it, then tossed it in the bus tray. My Spy sat down and the angel hostess inspected his neck. She shook her head, picked up his jacket and headed across the room. The party followed her to another table where she pulled out a chair. My Spy dropped into it. Angie talked to him. Comforting words? That would be interesting. She patted his arm, and he grasped her hand with both of his. She nodded towards me. He stared in my direction for a millisecond then released her hand. Across the room back at the palm, two busboys were examining the fronds with a roadwork beacon.

Angie slid into the booth. "Spider," she said. "Must have come in with the boat."

"Eeech." I glanced around me for a potted palm. "Did they find it?"

"I smashed it into the rug."

"You might have saved his life." I tucked both legs up off the floor. "Who is he?"

"Roland Keach. He owns a bank or two." And without the usual prompting, she began her story exactly where she'd left off, talking with the untroubled cadence of somebody who'd just come in from a garden tour. "Kerby and me, we're driving past the bookstore. Grandma exits, empty-handed, negotiating the steps. The clerk is on her heels but doesn't knock her down, just stands there like a mini-Viking with his hands on his hips and his hunter eyes.

"With one hand on his phone, Kerby manages to activate his blinker, but the bumper cars in cell phone hell won't cut him a break. I glance back at the bookstore. Mini-Viking is still on the steps."

After what seemed like time enough to butcher the herd, Darren delivered. My steak smelled divine. I could have stuck my face in it. He asked Angie if she'd like another Jack and Coke. Angie said she'd prefer a Miller, no glass. Darren complemented her good taste.

While I shamelessly carved and chewed, Angie regarded her food like an annoyance that might not be dealt with today. She began talking about the bookstore again. I'd mistakenly assumed that chapter was finished. It had seemed that way.

"I pull the book from my pocket and page through it. My eye is drawn to spots of recognition in the dense, foreign text: *gute, liebe, Sonne. Sonne* means Sun. I try to remember the last time I saw the sun. I stare at the face in the wing mirror that nobody knows and turn away to the gray sky that pushes downward, and I'm not liking how I can't shrug it off anymore. I shut the book.

Also Sprach Zarathustra shines like silver off the black cover."
Angie picked up a fork and speared a mushroom.

"Kerby says into his phone, 'I'll handle it. I know
someone.' He signs off and jostles the phone into a widget holder
screwed to the dashboard and says to me, 'Your breaking and
entering on Broder Circle didn't happen. Thanks to good Judge
Wilkerson.'" Angie laid down her fork with the mushroom
attached and bit off a corner of bread. Rather than chew it, she
worked it around in her mouth like old people do. I scooped up a
forkful of hash browns. "Thanks to the good judge, Terry Avela
never existed. Teresa of Avila, Patron Saint of Headaches, dead
over 400 years is dead again."

"That's amazing," I said. "You walked away from a break-
in totally unscathed."

"I'm too old for scathing. Kerby crosses the bridge to the
East Bank where my car is parked. He hasn't asked about Sammy.
I know from his phone conversation that he's got a more pressing
issue, an issue that involves me. I know this from experience.
Kerby's about to tally my ticket.

"His fingers tap the steering wheel. He's tallying. I wait.
We're almost to Dinkytown when he gives me his eyebrow shrug
and says, 'How about some rearranging and filing over in St.
Paul?' He's tallied. I look out the window at the sky. It's dropped
another shade of gray. We are in that colorless time before the
snows.

"I say to him, 'Files? You've got to be kidding? You just
sprung me for files.'

"He gives me his Kerby grin and says, 'What files?'

"Kerby's not understanding my lack of enthusiasm.
Pillaging files is a horse and buggy industry. Somebody wants
information nowadays they hack a hard drive.

"'What I need,' he says, 'is from the good old-fashioned
file cabinet days.' Some days he can read my mind.

"I say, 'Subpoena it.'

"He says, 'Not an option.' He's turned on his you-owe-me voice. 'This case cannot see daylight. And it won't when the resistance knows we have locations, dates, and signatures.' Kerby gives me his quirky little smile again. I can't resist that man. But the thought of a stink job without pay sticks on me like lint on wool. That very moment I'd have shot Matzo in the balls if he'd been within range.

"Kerby drops me in Dinkytown to pick up my car. I'm as cold as a snowflake on an ice cube. There's a Caribou Coffee up the street and I ramp up on a double shot while I contemplate the bookstore. It nags at me and I can't make it stop. Even though it's rush hour crazy and out of my way, I am compelled to take another look."

Angie's eyes cut to My Spy and stayed on him while she talked. "I'm stopped on Hennepin, but I can see up Eighth. Police are everywhere. A jaywalker tells me there's been a murder at the bookstore."

"Holy crap!" I said. "The German guy? That's why the back door was open, wasn't it? Barney's boys went in and opened it. Someone came through the backdoor and shot the clerk."

"Strangled," she said. "He was strangled."

"Scary stuff. Geez. You could have been in the store when it happened." I followed her eyes to Roland Keach, who was forking it in with the resolve of someone who had suddenly been given a deadline. I said, "Your banker looks ill."

"He actually looks good. He just had triple bypass. Even so, I expect he'll order dessert. Some things never change." She pulled on her sleeve and checked her watch.

I wondered how things would have turned out if years ago she'd caught a break. She possessed enough steel to discover a new color band, a higher decibel, a way to make fuel out of crabgrass, something, anything meaningful to life on earth. I decided to try a Barbara Walters question:

"When it's all over and done with, what might be your greatest regret?"

She didn't hesitate. "To have died a wasted death."

"Wasted death?" Silly me. I'd been thinking wasted life. "Wasted death like crashed in a car chase? Bullet in the head kind of wasted death?"

"No." Her eyes moved to Roland Keach. The waiter removed a long and narrow black book from his table and disappeared. "Dead, ahead of your time from a contradictory disease like cancer or a heart attack. That's a wasted death."

She crossed her silverware on her plate, finished, English style. I'd never seen anyone do that out on the prairie. She'd barely touched her food. I'd never seen anyone on the prairie do that either.

Roland Keach's waiter was back with a tulip bowl piled high with ice cream topped with a dark sauce and what looked like a dome of whipped cream.

Angie mumbled something that sounded like freaking A's, took a deep breath and settled back into the booth.

"Let me tell you about Genny Ross."

8. Angie as Genny Ross
Genesius, the Patron Saint of Actors

"You won't meet Genny Ross, but she's important to the story. That's Genesius, the Patron Saint of Actors." Angie peered over at my notes and added, "Genny with an e."

I scratched out i and wrote e.

"Strips of flattened cardboard lead to an old pitch pine desk where Genny sits facing Mr. Dean. The desktop is bare except for Genny's gloves and a brass banker's lamp that casts Mr. Dean in green shadow. His dark flannel shirt and Scotch plaid sweater vest give him a neighborly look. The top of his head is bald. His nose is round, but not bulbous. His eyes are the color of night. It wouldn't matter if they were the color of day. They reveal nothing. He has the presence of a large animal."

Angie stopped talking while Darren served me a fresh whiskey sour. He glanced at Angie's beer bottle. She shook her head.

"Genny is wearing a black wool gabardine pants suit with a long-sleeved, white linen shirt. Heavy starch. The ruby cufflinks are fake, but who would know? They shine like red stars. Her glossy black hair, the most expensive wig in the world, is blunt cut with short Piccadilly bangs." Angie finger-snipped across her forehead to illustrate how short that would be. "Her face is quite white except for her tabloid-red lips. She wears a Marilyn mole. Her press-on, red fingernails are not cupcake long, no, but sensible, enabling dexterity with the rolling papers she's just pulled from her purse." Angie examined her trimmed, unpainted fingernails. She noticed my attention and folded them away and said, "Calvin Klein four-inch heels add muscle to her Gaelic look."

I added the name Mr. Dean to my contractor list. "I'm assuming Mr. Dean is another fine citizen making up the rules as he goes along?"

"Even more so than the others. But a lovely man all the same. He pays like Daddy Warbucks. I recently flew to Minot and got a room at the Days Inn registered as Marty Bethany. That's Martha, the Patron Saint of Cooks. I made four strategically timed phone calls off a script sheet, flew back the next day. He paid five grand."

"Five grand for one night in Minot?"

"Plus expenses."

I gave her what was becoming my chronic look of disbelief.

She said, "Sometimes all I am is a monkey wrench."

"An expensive monkey wrench. Mr. Dean is obviously loaded, why isn't this meeting taking place in some penthouse with an oriental rug instead of an empty room with a cardboard runner?"

"That's my Mr. Dean. He dresses like a yardman. His cars have vinyl seats. He loves his macaroni and cheese."

"Oh, please. Rich people fill their toilet bowls with flower petals to make toileting a joyful experience. They can't help themselves."

"They don't get away with murder. You might write him like a Godfather. He'd appreciate that, such a sublime sense of himself, Mr. Dean, my punctilious wizard."

Angie had settled back into her worn-out mode, the spider energy dissipated. Her eyes drifted to Roland Keach, who, as if sensing scrutiny, looked up from his business with the ice cream tulip bowl. Their eyes locked. What passed between them was indiscernible, a recognition of agencies, business at a distance. I couldn't say for sure because my sense of it vanished, but I got the feeling that My Saint had somehow upped him, and he knew it. He adjusted his shoulders, jutting his chin to stretch his neck. I wondered who would break the gaze. Angie did. Her eyes slid to the amber lamp.

She said, "Mr. Dean stretches his neck in his flannel collar…"

I glanced back at Roland Keach who had just stretched his neck in his white collar. Kevin Spacey in *The Usual Suspects* popped into my head. Kevin Spacey with his fictitious answers to the detective's questions inspired by paraphernalia on the detective's bulletin board and the bric-a-brac on his desk. Keyser Soze answers. Or was I seeing something where nothing was? I needed to pay attention.

"…and says to her, 'I need something special done.' Genny pulls a tobacco pouch from her black leather Cleo and Patik shoulder bag and lays it on the desk, all the while careful not to touch anything." Angie held out a hand, fingers splayed, and said, "And that includes Mr. Dean's desktop."

"I couldn't keep that up," I said.

"It's like wiping your feet when you come in out of the rain. Once you know to do that and you understand the consequences of not doing it, you wipe your feet even when it's not raining."

"Well, maybe."

"Genny finds her French cigarette papers and folds back the flap. Genny's got attitude when she says to Mr. Dean, 'Everything and everybody is special nowadays. The only people who see it otherwise majored in one of the sciences, most likely biology.' She pulls two slips from the pack of papers and says to Mr. Dean, 'Twenty years ago these cost thirty-nine cents.' Genny holds up the pack. 'Two bucks.'"

I followed Angie's eyes back to Roland Keach who was rubbing both arms simultaneously as if suffering a systemic itch. She said, "Mr. Dean spends his life watching. He possesses the hypersensitivity of the deaf. Genny makes a point not to lock eyes with him when he talks, always busying herself with some minor task like working a hangnail, worrying a loose thread, fishing in her purse for that lost girl-thing. When it's time for eye-contact, she gives him a sweeping, occupied glance." Angie turned to me and demonstrated: her eyes skimmed across me. "Casual, but seeing everything."

I nodded.

"That cigarette comment breaks the strain. Mr. Dean is an ace poker player with a wall of trophies to prove it. Most of his opponents wear sunglasses. Mr. Dean doesn't wear sunglasses. He feels it's unsportsmanlike. But without sunglasses, time becomes a nerve fuck under his unremitting stare. Genny's going to defuse his dominance by rolling a cigarette. Genny no more rolls her own cigarettes than she fills her own teeth." Angie's eyes flicked back to Roland Keach and stayed there. She stopped talking as if she'd lost her place.

"And?" I prompted.

"Umm … yes. Mr. Dean is sixty and looks it. But sixty is good." She pointed a finger at me. "You're young, Jas, and that's great fun, but youth is treacherous when you live outside the rules. I don't work for young men. Even when I was young I understood what the combination of the lack of innate experience and unvarnished ego could do to me."

I asked, "Have you ever worked for a woman?"

"No," she said without hesitation. "It is unlikely that would ever come up. Lil and Fanny contracted through Lance in Fridley. No way would I have considered the job if they'd somehow got to me directly. Women cannot concept consequence in relation to the whole malefaction unless it concerns family. Estrogen is a black hole in my business."

I made a note to query her frequent condemnation of estrogen. Too much or too little of it, neither sounded flattering. Or maybe it was, but not in a criminal context.

"Genny licks the glue strip on one of the papers and sticks it to the other. She looks up at Mr. Dean, half-expectant, half-impatient, and says, 'What's so special?' She opens the pouch, pinches a clump of silage and spreads it across the square. See how this sideshow muddies the water?"

I nodded. Even more fascinating than her distraction tactics was her shift between saints. When Angie spoke as Genny, her sleepiness changed to a sharp reserve, which included a subtle eastern accent — no Beantown without the R, but definitely not from Minnesota, more like the transitional accent people take on having lived in a region for a couple decades or three. My Saint's ability to switch between characters quickly and evenly was ... was what? Schizophrenic?

"You're switching back and forth between these saints, how do you keep it going?"

"Diligence. Indefatigable practice. My characters don't just..." she snapped her fingers, "...pop up for lunch. They require precise preparation and total concentration. It's a full-time job."

I silently disagreed. I believed she slipped in and out of saints as easily as her underwear. It was happening right in front of me. Angie to Genny to Angie and back. Which seemed outrageously complicated at this point in our relationship, but I didn't say that.

Darren offered a dessert menu, which was a long and narrow version of the dinner menu with its black cover and silver type. Sammy's stolen Zarathustra — black cover, silver type. Roland Keach's ice cream sundae was not on the menu.

"Mr. Dean leans forward in the chair and crosses his arms, elbows extended — a tall, aggressive pose, and nicely done, considering he had a stroke a couple years back that left him with a droopy left arm. He says to Genny, 'You can buy a Lamborghini.'" Angie rubbed her fingers together, the international sign for money. "Abandon that at the mall."

I said, "Pricey drop."

"The fact that Genny thinks that's an idiotic notion doesn't show on her face. She moistens the glue strip with the tip of her tongue and asks again what's so special about this job. Mr. Dean throws his punch line: 'What I need is for you to nab a kid.'"

"Whoa." I held up my hand. "Mr. Dean contracted this kidnapping job you can't figure out?"

"That is correct."

"Does he know you have experience?"

Angie considered for a moment. "My contractors don't collaborate. And Genny, sitting there rolling herself a cigarette doesn't care, because she doesn't do domestic. She explains that to Mr. Dean as she works the paper into a cylinder, thumbs rolling upward, packing, tightening the load. Mr. Dean's hands are as still as Genny's are busy. She presses with both thumbs, twists each end to a point, then holds the blunt up for inspection.

"Mr. Dean says, 'I need you to do this for me, Genny.' He pulls a bent-up, metal ashtray from a drawer and slides it towards her, then clamps his hand back onto his limp left arm and says, 'Okay. Forget Lamborghini. You can retire, quit the penny-anny, lock-picking shit.'"

"He's referring to Broder Circle? Contracted through Matzo? Is that something Mr. Dean would know about?"

"That is not something he would know. Mr. Dean knows nothing about Matzo Ball. This is Minnesota and we've got the Russians, but my employers are not the mob, those worthless clowns, all of 'em jumping at the same hoop. None of the people I work for got rich by doing the 'Vinnie from Brooklyn' walk. Mr. Dean did prison once. But that was thirty-six years ago."

"Thirty-six," I repeated. Not an estimate like thirty or thirty-five. Something significant had happened thirty-six years ago that involved Mr. Dean. My Saint would have been in high school. Her mother worked at a prison.

Correctly interpreting my thoughts, she said, "My mother sainted him."

"So you and Mr. Dean go way back."

"Way back." She nodded. "Mr. Dean's surprise lock-picking remark is equivalent to a fireball. Genny starts to sweat. She resists the urge to wipe her palms on her pants." Angie fell silent again, as if she were rethinking Mr. Dean in present time, then said, "Was it a good guess? Poking and hoping? Maybe. Or Matzo mouth? I don't think so. The file job on Broder Circle was never completed. Jug's target file is still in the back room of 365 Broder Circle. And believe me, Jug knows how and why that job went south. I paid him a visit and pressed that yellow page from Matzo's yellow tablet to the glass. I'd circled Matzo's pubescent 356 Broder Circle in red marker. I gave Jug my Gestapo eye, turned and walked out, surprising myself by remembering to limp. Terry Avella limps, you remember."

I hadn't remembered. Keeping the saints straight as they multiplied was complicated. Maybe I could find a handy pocketbook guide for saints, like birds and seashells.

Angie rubbed the face of her watch and glanced at Roland Keach, who picked up his napkin and patted his forehead. What if he had been bitten? And the poison was percolating in his bloodstream. I wondered if he could drive.

The storybook couple in the white cable sweaters stood up to leave. The woman collected her leather bag from under the table, set it on the chair and reached inside for something.

Angie said, "Genny picks her purse off the floor and searches for a match. She's thinking she doesn't want this job and reminds Mr. Dean again that she doesn't do domestic, but he won't acknowledge that and rambles on about the mother being crazy and how the father has taken it upon himself to save his son.

"Mr. Dean huffs, 'The damn fool knew the situation. Got too comfortable and some shark slipped in and snatched the kid. Now I gotta get him back.'

"Genny can't find her matches and acts like she might be considering saving her cigarette for a later date, a way-later date, when out of nowhere, Mr. Dean stretches across the desk and flicks a lighter. The movement is swift. She is surprised at the flaming Zippo in his left hand. She leans forward and grabs the light and says, 'Therapy kicking in?'

"He flicks it shut. He'd been saving that left hand move. Just like him to do that. His face is blank. Genny leans back in the chair and draws on the cigarette. Not being a smoker, she feels nauseous. She says, 'Where is this kid?'

"He doesn't answer. He won't say anymore until she commits. That's how it is. Nobody knows anything. Even after you're on board, you know only what's necessary — careful in hyperbole."

Angie stopped talking and motioned for Darren, who appeared genuinely interested in our happiness. Bartender Bob wouldn't last a full shift at Lords. While Angie complimented Darren on the food and his excellent service, I considered the empty table where the woman in the white cable sweater had picked her bag off the floor and searched inside, perfectly synchronized with Genny Ross picking her bag off the floor to search for matches. And the Nordic woman Angie described in the bookstore had worn a white cable sweater.

Darren left with another drink order. I was throwing back whiskey sours like lemonade. I wasn't driving.

Angie yawned and said, "Genny draws off her cigarette and exhales with a cough. She really didn't need to cough, but she does, and it's quite timely. Coughing covers a merry-go-round of reactions. In the art of deceit, it is prudent to establish early during benign interaction the necessity of a cough."

I said, "In other words, it's too late to start coughing after the roof has caved."

"And the roof is not firmly attached here, and Genny is asking herself why she's even considering this lunatic job. That question is answered when Mr. Dean says, 'Two hundred.'"

"Two hundred thousand?"

"But Genny has caught an edgy vibe. She asks, 'What's the catch?'

"Mr. Dean says, 'Half now. Half when the job's done.'

"Genny says, 'I don't do halves.'

"Mr. Dean's good arm drops to his side and surfaces with a briefcase, which he launches onto the desk and pushes in front of her. His left hand stays locked at a dislocated angle. He says, 'I always ask, don't I?'

"Genny plucks her smoldering cigarette from the ashtray and taps it to release the ash. She rolls it between her fingers. Her sculptured nails look rich. Two hundred thousand dollars rich. But the job sounds like a screamer. And, frankly, when you spell it out in longhand, two hundred thousand isn't really all that nesty. One of those Hilton sisters could burn through that in an afternoon."

"That's one hell of a payday," I said. "I can't believe someone would pay that much."

Angie pointed at me. "You need street experience."

"Bring it on," I said and caught that wisp of a smile.

"Mr. Dean picks up on Genny's hesitation and says, 'You're getting old, Genny.' Genny's dismayed at that comment and points her eyes at his baldhead. He blocks a grimace. Her eyes drop to the briefcase. If she puts a hand on it, she's committed. There are no papers to sign. No lawyers, no notary. Word is law. Unbreakable word, like it used to be long ago with regular folks. Nowadays, top-shelf criminals are the only people who work on word alone. Imagine that. There are more people with lawyers than there are people with doctors. Even the homeless have lawyers.

"Genny's thinking that she did it once, that kid thing, getting the Graas boy out of Canada. But real time experience tells her to stand up and walk. If she commits, there's no way out, except Brisbane.

"Mr. Dean says, 'Technology left you behind, Genny. You're a dinosaur.' He's calling *me* a dinosaur."

"He was goading you. What'd Genny say to that?"

"She says, simply and matter-of-factly, 'Juvenile hackers are a dime a dozen, and unless one of them can kidnap the kid on his keyboard, you're paying me.' That shut him up. Genny eyes him through a haze of smoke and asks, 'How old is this kid?' Mr. Dean tells her six. She's repulsed. She'd been thinking three, four max. Six-year-olds have watched too much television and have ideas like street monkeys. She carps, 'A six-year-old boy? That's not like snatching a baby from a stroller, you know. Have you ever heard of McCully Culligan? Or McCally Callihan? Little shit, whatever his name was.'

"Left hand slack on the desk, Mr. Dean shoves the briefcase closer, reaches over it and snaps it open. 'No halves,' he says. 'Four up front.'

"Genny's lips form an O which melts into a K. She touches the money, honor bound, and is confident that the Father of Evolution is doing the old proverbial rollover in his grave. Along with Rockefeller and Carnegie. Mr. Dean leans back in his chair. His eyes have never left her."

In my notebook I crossed out 2 and wrote 4, and added Roland Keach, the banker, into the equation. Four hundred thousand illicit dollars would be something to discuss with your illicit banker. Roland Keach probably owns Laundromats and garbage trucks. I wondered what his take would be. Money laundering right here in Lords.

I said, "I knew I was nervous for some good reason."

"You're nervous?" She looked genuinely surprised.

"I've been nervous ever since I met you." I let go a chittery little laugh and snapped my pen on my notepad. I looked back at her in time to catch, once again, the accidental smile.

"Genny takes a drag from her cigarette and asks where is this kid? Mr. Dean tells her Burnsville." Angie waited to see if I'd connected the dots.

"Bentley Ogren? The same kid you kidnapped out of Canada two years ago? How could that be?"

"That's exactly what Genny's thinking. She coughs out a puff of smoke and pats her chest, picks up the tobacco pouch and glares at it. Still coughing, she shakes the bag and manages to say, 'What the hell is this shit?'" Angie coughed and patted her chest, demonstrating how Genny had deflected Mr. Dean's perfect vision. "See how useful 'the cough' can be? Thank God Genny had the good sense to have it going."

I said, "I would have peed my pants."

"Not allowed at Mr. Dean's desk. He says to Genny, 'I'd think you were smoking marijuana there if I didn't know better.' He says this with obvious disdain, and rightfully so. Nobody does drugs. Well, maybe Barney's boys.

"Genny is holding the blunt between her thumb and forefinger. Still hacking away, she says, 'Cuban trash. That asshole, Harry.'" Angie glanced at me and said, "Genny doesn't know any Harrys."

"Deflect?"

"Deflect. Genny's hoping that it might be some other kid snatched from his father, some other kid living out in Burnsville. Big suburb, Burnsville.

"Genny's eyes take in the wall behind Mr. Dean. She gets a trusty feeling that there's a camera somewhere. She pats her chest again and positions her cigarette so that it will burn out in the ashtray. Her foot jiggles. She stops it, even though he can't see under the desk. But, then again, every nook and cranny could be tracking body language. To be looked at later.

"Kinesics," Angie said. "That's what it's called, the study of body language. I remember a girl from catechism, sat with her legs crossed at the ankles, angled off to one side, which is supposedly the sign of an orderly mind, which didn't fit, because she had fruit for brains. Turns out she went to charm school."

"Obviously not a science to be counted on. Honestly, I'm lost here. I'm not following this new coincidence."

"Neither is Genny. The defining question is still out there, even though, at this point in time, it's too late to ask it. She's touched the money. And frankly, she already knows the answer. But she asks it anyway: 'Where was this kid two years ago when he was snatched from his father?'

"Mr. Dean says, 'Canada.'"

"I would have fallen off the chair."

"Genny almost does. She folds her hands and anchors them on the desk. It's where they need to be, up front and still, although they are damp and weak. Mr. Dean pulls a picture from the drawer and pushes it to her. It's black and white, taken with a long-range lens. A boy is holding a six-pack by one can. An older woman stands in the doorway of an unremarkable ranch house. A third person is reaching into the backseat of a car. If the camera had been pointed twenty degrees left, my car would have been in the frame.

"Genny stares at the picture longer than necessary because her brain is screaming for oxygen. Mr. Dean slides another one across the desk and says, 'That's the mother.' It's a studio shot of Fanny, Laddie, and Bender when they were all named Ogren. Fanny's hair is blonde. Laddie looks mean even when he's smiling. Bender looks like a two year old. Mr. Dean adds a third photo. 'This is the boy now.' Five kids stand at the back of an SUV filled with camping gear. Bender is circled with black marker. Mr. Dean says, 'The mother's name is Fanny Ogren. She changed it back to Graas.' Mr. Dean has no reason to mention his client's name, the boy's father, Laddie Ogren, Crazy O. But I know him.

"Two years ago when Lance contracted me to get Bender out of Canada, I tracked Laddie down in Winnipeg. I needed to get a feel for him, a sense about him. There was no introduction, no words spoken, but I learned his fury. I caught up with him walking down Osborne, yanked on his sleeve and chirped, 'Petie? Is that you?' He whirled around on me so fast I had to catch myself from falling. His hair was black and lusterless and flat to his head like a

Labrador retriever. His cold, crystalline eyes stopped me dead. His mouth twisted open showing me two pebbled paths of mercury fillings. He hissed. Then strode off down the street. Not one word. I've never been hissed at. It is an odd thing to be hissed at."

"Whew." I fanned my face for emphasis.

"He's the devil come to earth."

The busboy topped our water glasses. My head itched. I prodded with my pen point so as not to skew the wig.

"Genny picks up her bag and positions it on her lap, opens the flap and sets about transferring packs of one-hundred dollar bills from the briefcase."

"Four-hundred thousand dollars fit into your bag?"

"Phfft, I could have taken another four. Mr. Dean says, 'I won't see you again on this matter, Genny Ross...' An interesting thing here: he leaves Genny's name with an upward inflection, almost a question, like he hasn't finished the sentence.

"Genny latches the bag and stands up from the table. Her legs don't hold. She plunks back down on the chair and leans over and fumbles with one of her Calvin Kleins — another deflect, the shoe thing — all the while forcing blood to her brain. She grumbles and stands again and rocks her shoe as if she's adjusting something. Satisfied, she jerks on her gloves and hoists the bag to her shoulder.

"Mr. Dean finishes his sentence: '...or whatever your name is.'

"Luckily her gloved hand is propped on the desk or she might have flat out folded. She shoots him a look, like she thinks he might be losing his mind, all the while willing her ankles to be strong. She straightens and turns and walks to the door. The sound of heels on cardboard in the empty room unnerves her. She thinks she's heard the slide of a semi-automatic, but she's not sure, what with the cardboard and the scuffing heels. She doesn't hesitate at the door, but at the same time she tries not to act like a dog needing to pee. The door opens without a trick and she slips through. Her heels strike the painted wood. She stops at the top of seven steep steps. It could just as well be seventy steps and her on stilts. Wind chimes somewhere to her right rustle like tangled-up glass. She stands there because she is unable to move her legs. A FOR SALE sign is staked in the front yard. She pretends for a moment that she is a well-heeled realtor standing on the porch with her newly listed property, reminding herself to stop and pick-up a pot roast on the way home." Angie knitted her brow. "Do people still eat pot roast?'"

"No one calls it pot roast."

I imagined My Saint alone at the top of the steps with nowhere to go, commissioned by this card shark to kidnap the boy she'd once saved and return him to a man she'd described as the devil. Balanced by the weight of four hundred thousand dollars.

Angie said, "More and more it seems I can't escape what I've become. My big bag of money feels like stones. I should have slung it back through the window and run like hell. But if the scene stays neutral and your data is undefined, you stick with the plan.

"A woman in a long coat and sneakers, pulled by a galloping retriever, flies past on the sidewalk. She looks exhausted. I'd like to know her kind of exhaustion. I'd like to be her. I'd like to be anybody other than Genny Ross. A man in a smazzy, razzy polo sweater jogs by with a designer dog on a designer leash. It's the evening parade of dogs. Across the street a fat man with one of those mop dogs is taking a briefing from a woman tugging on a cocker spaniel that's pulling in the opposite direction. She talks and gesticulates at the fat man. He trots away with one arm extended mid-leash like a Eukanuba show handler. She yells after him. The cocker spaniel does his business on the sidewalk. She scoops it. A van for a locksmith is parked to the right, a white Infinity behind it, a black SUV with tinted windows up the street. Genny's rented-for-the-day Jaguar is fifty yards away. It could be in Tucson, it's that far. Cold as it is, she would step out of her Calvin Kleins and descend in her stocking feet, but she knows he's watching. She looks in the direction of the wind chimes, and there it is up in the corner, a small surveillance camera peering down on her like a holy eye, and that's her cue. This is theater, and she's on stage. This is Genny Ross here, and Genny doesn't whimper.

"Genny Ross, Patron Saint of Actors, smiles for the camera, then steps quickly and carefully down the steps one rubber ankle at a time. She cringes all the way down because she is fully prepared for Mr. Dean to open the door and call her name." Angie tapped her chest. "*My* name. And I am fully prepared not to turn around. Lucky for Genny, Mr. Dean doesn't show any more cards."

"He doesn't have to," I said. "He's just given you four-hundred thousand dollars to kidnap Bender from Fanny Graas and he knows you're not Genny Ross and he has a semi-automatic that he can work with one hand."

"That man could lock and load a rifle with his teeth. Down on the sidewalk Genny steps aside to let the designer dog race past in the other direction, designer leash trailing sans designer handler. She clutches her moneybag and heel-toes it to her designer car."

"I think this kidnapping is bigger than you. You and Genny and all of you."

"My reality is," she said, "if I don't grab the kid, someone else will, and I won't know one way or another, because I'll be at the bottom of Lake Superior, which, by the way, is 1,333 feet at its deepest point. Double cross, double dare, double, double, toil and trouble. Is this assignment random? What is the Laddie Ogren-Mr. Dean connection?"

"Sounds like Laddie Ogren hired a professional to get his son back."

"Laddie Ogren is his own professional."

"Editors don't like a lot of coincidence."

"The world has become too small anymore for there not to be coincidence." She nudged her sleeve up for another annoying peek at her watch. "I tell myself that I don't have a dog in the fight.

Grab the kid from Fanny, drop him off with Mr. Dean, buy a Lamborghini."

"I don't believe you'll do that."

"Buy a Lamborghini?"

"Kidnap Fanny's son."

"Hell, if I were a true businessman, I'd grab him, hang around a few days, then commission to kidnap him back. But what am I thinking? That'd be crazy. The Graas contingency has no money."

We both watched Roland Keach stand up and walk out of the restaurant, sufficiently steady, considering he'd had several drinks and a spider bite. Angie twisted around and searched the dining room, spotted Darren and caught his eye. She mimicked signing a check. He nodded. She sat back and said, "Genny is miles from Colfax before she starts to breathe. The Jag is due back in the morning. Clare Assett rented it; Clare will return it, and the car company will drop her at the Mall of America where she will flag a cab home. This is not complicated, just time consuming."

Claire again. Something about that.

"It was time to check the Edina Post Office. I rent four different post office boxes under four different names. I check them twice a week. The Edina box is under the name Lunchbox Catering.

"I file though the stack of restaurant supply junk mail and find a brown envelope stamped SAME DAY DELIVERY from Fridley Freight. It contains a brochure on refrigerated delivery applicable to the food business. That brochure means that Lance needs to see me."

"Why doesn't he just call?"

"My number changes more frequently than he calls. It's too late in the day to transform Genny into Clare and get to Fridley. Lance can wait till morning. I stop for gas and dump the mail into a trashcan. Roach once told me that a man got tracked to his home by a tiny transmitter stuck into the spine of a glossy cigar magazine marked Sample Issue. At that very moment I get a fanciful notion that I should get out the chamois and oil up Black Betty."

Left eye shut, she pointed her finger at the table where Roland Keach had been sitting. She jerked her hand as if she'd fired a gun, which caused me to flinch, because there was something about that common playground mimicry — bang, bang — some deadly control that transcended both the hobbyist and the Hollywood movie crowd who'd never fired a gun in their lives. It was as if she truly understood the weight of metal and had a fastidious familiarity with recoil. I thought about that a moment, then said, "You said you never use a gun."

She hesitated, as if considering her position, whatever that was. "I've been a cog in the wheel of surreptitious enterprise, sometimes innocently, sometimes not so innocently, but I've never triggered anybody." She focused on my eyes and asked, "Do you know which eye is dominant?"

I didn't know what she was talking about.

"Hold up your finger and align it with that painting by the fireplace. Look straight at it. Never mind that you're seeing double. Close your left eye. If your fingertip stays with the painting, you have a dominant right eye."

I held up my finger and focused on an elaborately framed painting illuminated by a brass picture lamp. "It doesn't stick," I said. "It jumps way off." I closed my right eye. "But my left eye sticks." And indeed, it stuck. Stuck on a cream-colored automobile circa 1950 collector's edition, what might be described as an omelet-colored Plymouth.

"You're left-eye dominant," she said. "But you're right-handed. You'll have to allow for that."

"That's good to know," I said.

Darren set a silver tray containing six foil-wrapped chocolates on our table. There was no ticket. Roland Keach had paid our tab.

"Lovely man," Angie said and pulled a fifty-dollar bill from her pocket and laid it on the tray. I wondered if Lords was hiring.

I wrote Penny's dad's name (ace psychologist) in my notebook below the names of Genny, Angie, Brigid, Alex, and Toni. He would give me a professional take on multiple personalities. What take that might be, I had no idea.

When I looked up, her droopy eyes were on me. She said, "Names like Sybil and Eve have made their way into your notes. You want to explain everything, make it something more than it is. I can save you that. I am neither a multiple personality, a schizophrenic, a manic-depressive, bipolar, or whatever else there is on the plate. I may be Angie one day and Toni the next, but I can get to home plate in the time it takes someone to say, 'You have the right to remain silent.' I admit to estrogen issues, but it's nothing crazy."

"You are not the average bear."

She spoke with the lassitude of someone tired of explaining. "I am average in every way. My motor skills are average, my appearance is average, my IQ is average, my needs are the same as yours. The difference between you and me is that I have, with the simple act of mindfulness, made a damn good living being average."

My brow creased. Too young to believe I was average, I said, "The average person couldn't be you. No way."

Her smile lingered on the low side of amusement, like somebody watching pets do tricks. She knew me then; but she, herself, remained a cipher. It would take another year for me to realize that the insight I needed for her character was not in Penny's dad's book of rules.

"How did you get to be you? The reader will want to know."

"I had a worthless degree in theater and a shitload of bills. Pineapple Daiquiri sat down at my bar. I got membership in the Arrested Club. What are you doing tomorrow?"

9. Louise Marille
Louise de Marillac, the Patron Saint of Social Workers
MONDAY

The drive from Lords to my new lodging took longer than it should have. The entrance ramp to the freeway was blocked. A white Mercedes had met the concrete retaining wall, spun around, and met it again. And again, from the looks of it. Posterity zero, save for the chrome SL500 logo that winked at the flashing strobes like a daft beauty queen undaunted by her scrap metal host and dour audience.

"I wonder how many people were in the car."

"One," she said brusquely. "There's only one ambulance. Clearly an accident."

I winced at her asperity.

She added, "There's only one car involved."

I wondered if alcohol had been a factor. Having thrown back a pitcher of whiskey sours, I was in no position to judge, grateful not to be driving. Angie was remarkably sober after only two bites of food and one Jack Daniels, and how many beers? I'd lost count. I'd been focused on our story along with the evening's curios of spiders, white cable sweaters, black books with silver type, omelet-colored cars. Throw in all the checks and the moves bandied about with indefinable undertones. Heck, the entire evening seemed to have been orchestrated by this run-down, distracted Angie saint, our dinner more like a reconnaissance mission than an interview. A reconnaissance mission that had nothing to do with me. Us. The story. I got the sudden notion that My Saint had lost interest.

"You're serious about writing this book, aren't you?"

Her eyes didn't leave the road. "Make a plan. Study it so intently and thoroughly that you dream it. It's not yours until you dream it."

"I don't remember my dreams."

"You sleep right through them."

I had nothing to add to that. Nor had she answered my question. Fearing the wrong answer, I didn't ask it again. I wanted this story. Needed this story?

Exiting onto Excelsior Boulevard, we turned towards St. Louis Park where My Saint had a one-month rental at a motel called American Inn. I could spend the night or the rest of the month. Whatever worked. I asked where she was staying. She didn't say, but went on to explain how she always kept two places, oftentimes in the same building using two different aliases. She favored mega-complexes with non-human, main entrance security. Sometimes she lived in a hotel. Two hotels.

"Tell me I have high overhead."

"You have high overhead."

Ahead to our right, Miracle Mile shopping mall came into view. Drawn to retail like a dame to diamonds, my eye was drawn to a shop window radiating light so crazy it would be visible from space. As we passed by, I spotted the giant Christmas spruce buried under the million twinkling lights.

Angie saw it too, and said, "It's not even Halloween yet, for Christ's sake."

"But doesn't that put you in the mood? Gather around, drink spiced wine, sing Christmas carols."

"That would depress the hell out of me."

My room at the one-star American Inn faced an outside walkway that overhung the parking lot. Barely large enough for the furniture, the room held an unctuous odor like dirty hair. The mammoth TV was not a good sign: large equaled loud. And no mini-toiletries. Not even a mini-fridge. Who's complaining? I wondered what the nightly rate was. More than I could afford this close into the city.

I wrenched off my blonde wig and the accompanying skullcap and rubbed my head with delirious relief. I plunked down on a mattress twenty percent thicker than my no-star mattress out on the freeway, only to jump up again and fold the bedspread in half, the underside being geographically more hygienic than the topside with its unidentifiable floral and its milky sheen and loose threads. I wondered if My Saint had ever slept in this room. There could be hairs, fibers, sloughed skin, all that trace evidence ambitious technicians examine under microscopes and blue lights. Ample slough, I was sure, but not hers. Then, again, so what if it was her slough? Like finding a house key in the park. Useless without the address. I contemplated the semi-shag carpet. She'd had the room for a month, which meant it had been out of rotation for two weeks. With no new slough to eat, vagrant plankton should be dead by now. I slipped out of my shoes, but kept my socks on.

Somebody in the next room sneezed. We were separated by particleboard. Thank you very much they weren't watching a rerun of *Fast and Furious*. I folded my jeans and sweater, pulled on my Paul Bunyan nightshirt and turned off the lamp, and I don't know why I peeked out the window, but I did. At the far end of the parking lot, a dark-colored SUV with orange fog lights idled under the lamppost. I could hear somebody climbing the stairs. I flattened myself against the wall. The footsteps stopped outside my door, moved on, then faded. I shoved the writing desk in front of the door, waited a beat, and peeked out again. The SUV was gone.

If the man from Stonehenge had somehow followed me here … followed me here from where? Even if he had somehow found this place through some chain of discovery vis-à-vis My Saint, he wouldn't have recognized me, not in my blonde wig. Maybe I'd hang onto it, wear it until I left town.

...

Serene and competent would best describe how I felt behind the wheel of the Lincoln AARP-mobile. In spite of the car's big-fellow size, it moved like a skater on ice. Maybe someday I'd own one, but in real time, I was chauffeuring Louise Marille, Louise de Marillac, Patron Saint of Social Workers, to a storage warehouse off Shepard Road in St. Paul where she planned to pinch a file for the lawyer she called Kerby.

It would be informative for me, she'd said, to accompany her on a job. Having never been arrested, not even a parking ticket, I'd expressed my concerns, but she'd assured me the operation was so benign that she'd considered simply walking in and asking the caretaker for the file. I'd taken comfort in the fact that a bona fide lawyer had contracted the operation, a bona fide lawyer who had his eye on the governor's chair.

"We're winging this," she said. "The resistance is clear-cut and autonomous. It's also a freakin' free job." Inside Louise's soft-leather briefcase, rolled up in a prop magazine called *Stadtleute* (City People, she'd told me when I'd inquired), was a stainless steel crate opener. An aluminum box cutter fit neatly into one of the side pockets.

My Saint, as Louise Marille, was a freelance writer for a boutique publishing company out of Chicago that specialized in coffee table books. Her assignment was working warehouse districts — 'working' in the sense that these buildings actually housed wares, which seemed light-years more interesting than the condominium-restaurant playgrounds that had eaten the narrative out of the old buildings that had once lined America's urban riverbanks.

Unlike the run-down, lackluster Angela Folly from Lords, Louise Marille had a vivacious, youthful energy that curbed her age. It was also the first time I'd seen My Saint in the daylight. She'd been blessed with a youthful face, but there was no hiding the first phase crow's feet and slackening jaw line. She had that cinnamon-girl thing going good with freckles tapped onto her sienna tinted make-up. Add a pair of rust-colored eyes seen through horn-rimmed glasses with diamonds on the points. A red velvet cloche battened down a burly, auburn wig. Her long coat was a patchwork of multi-colored velvet squares a.k.a. Stevie Nicks in her Lindsey Buckingham days. My Saint's most flamboyant costume, she'd explained, which meant she would be remembered by her attire, not by the color of her eyes or the shape of her chin. By the time anyone figured out that there was no coffee table book, nor would there ever be a coffee table book, the only shape left in the mind's eye would be a carnival coat.

"She could not pick me out of a line-up."

"You must have a warehouse full of costumes."

"Contraire. I carry very little baggage. With two suitcases of mix and match, I can swing from Ann Taylor office to Elizabeth Ashley garden party to Patti Smith Soho." She flicked a curly truss off her neck with a gloved hand. Except for the bling-blang colored stones and gold hearts at her wrists, the black nylon gloves were streamlined and criminally functional.

A scent like nothing dreamed up wafted into the front seat.

"What is that smell?"

"Frangipani."

"Where on this dying planet do you find Frangipani?" I knew about Frangipani, genus *Plumeria*, the honest smell of summer wind and sunshine. A lifetime of flowers for an ounce of essence. Pricey drops.

"I have an island connection."

Having seen chauffeurs in the movies, when we got to the warehouse, I jumped out and opened her door. She appreciated that and said as much. Louise seemed to float as she walked. I followed like a slug in my mill coat, gray pants and black pumps, drab as brume if not for my blonde wig and the floral print scarf she'd tied artistically around my neck. We climbed the steps to the entrance and pulled at the steel bar on the glass door. It didn't open. Louise pushed a button on the metal frame.

"Once we get inside," she said, "don't touch anything. It's hideous, this human compulsion to touch everything."

The door buzzed like a prison gate. We stepped into a small, pine-paneled reception room. The girl behind the pine-paneled reception desk waved and covered her mouth with a napkin as she chewed. I returned the wave. Louise pulled a card from her briefcase and laid it on the desk. The girl swallowed before she should have, patted her chest, and threw back a slug of Pepsi. "You're the writer," she gasped, wiping her hands on a crumpled napkin.

"Call me Louie," Louise Marille purred.

The girl stood up, came around the desk, and shook our hands. Mid-twenties with rusty blonde hair, she wore a black turtleneck sweater and baggy jeans stuffed inside a pair of purple cowboy boots. Her name was Heather, the office manager. She explained that the boss was in International Falls for the day (we already knew that), but she could show us around. She'd love it if we chose her building to represent the Twin Cities in *Working Warehouses*. She smiled when she talked. She had the bearing of someone who hummed a lot. I liked her.

Louise dipped her head towards me. "This is my assistant, Rose White."

"I love your name," Heather gushed. "We're both flowers. Pizza anyone?" She pulled the box towards us. The pepperonis had been picked off leaving rubbery, white craters over the remains. We shook our heads.

"That's an awesome coat," she said to Louise. "Where'd you get it?"

"A boutique in Deerfield."

"Up by Hibbing?"

"Down by Chicago."

"Oh, ya. Duh." She pulled a spiral bound notebook from the stacked trays, flipped it open and said, "This is our sign-in book. We don't sell a mailing list or anything like that." Louise ignored the available junk pen and pulled out a Montblanc. She wrote left-handed, which surprised me. She handed me her pen. I signed as Rose White and used ditto marks in the address column under her post office box in Deerfield, Illinois. I wondered if she knew the correct zip code or just pulled one out of her cloche. Details like that send criminals to prison. I memorized the number.

Heather clapped her hands and said, "Cool. I'll show you around."

"Divine," Louise murmured.

The expressions on our faces were nothing short of awe as Heather explained the company's storage business, which was specifically archival in industries such as forestry and mining. I held my Sony VOR towards her. She took to it immediately. A natural ham. Louise Marille focused on the halls and walls. On the ride over, she had told me that she didn't intend to come back after-hours, but just in case, we were to note all doorways and windows and any kind of wiring, cables, and cameras. From what I could see, surveillance was either lacking or well hidden. A half-hour later we were back at the front desk with more details about the warehouse than anybody would ever want out of a coffee table book.

Heather made a sweeping gesture that encompassed the building and said, "So what do you think? Are we in the book?"

Louise pulled a long sigh. "We're only halfway through eliminations."

Heather frowned.

Louise stretched her arm and glanced at her watch. I recognized Toni Padua's thin, silver band. She said, "At the back of the building we passed what looked like an elevator under repair. What's upstairs?"

"The really old stuff like before I was born. Nobody goes up there."

Louise said, "In other words, the real goods, what warehouses were built for, exactly what I'm looking for. Could we get a shot of the river from up there?"

Heather clapped her hands. "Oh, my gosh, it's a fab view. It's against the rules, people going up there, but I must show you."

"The Mississippi from a warehouse window could make a stunning cover." Louise turned to me with a swish of her Stevie Nicks coat. "Rose, what do you think? A Mississippi vista?"

"We should have brought Vincent." I said to Heather, "He's our photographer."

"If there's a book cover up there," Louise said, "we'll fly him back."

"Okay, wow!" Heather clapped her hands again. "It's a deal. We gotta go outside to get up there. Follow me." Midway down the hallway she unlocked a steel door. "Stay back. The dogs are fierce." She opened the door a crack, stuck her head out and whistled.

"Dogs," Louise mumbled. "On a fucking free job."

Heather slammed the door shut. I took a step back at the fierce barking. The door shook from the pounding paws. "*Du komma. Sitt,*" she yelled. "*Ja tack.*" Paws stopped. Silence. She counted to ten, then slowly opened the door. What had sounded like a pack of savage wolves turned out to be three Dobermans. "*Ja tack,*" she ordered. The dogs backed down the steps to the ground. "You gotta talk Swedish or they attack. The boss talks to them, but these are the only words I know. Keeps them down. Don't make any sudden moves."

Ja tack.

We followed her along the dirt path that led to the staircase. The dogs trailed behind gurgling and grumbling. My heels felt hot, even though they would have gone for my neck. Heather was explaining her new apartment in walking distance to St. Kate's. She just got a raise and no longer needed a roommate. Louise acted interested. I concentrated on the dogs, for all the good that would have done had something tripped their guard.

"Here we are," Heather said pointing to a staircase that looked like it'd been Elmered to the brick like a wall-hanging, and seriously pitched. And no railing. Each rusted, iron step was the size of a Chinese take-out menu.

"One person at a time," Heather said. "I'll go first. The locks are tricky. Be careful coming up. They'd dock my pay."

"What about the Swedes down here?" I called after her.

"They're decoded. They won't attack without the command."

I wondered what the command was, but now was not the time to ask. Heather leaned into the brick wall as she climbed. The stairway shimmied with each step.

Louise muttered, "Kerby dies."

At the top of the steps Heather pulled a ring of keys from her back pocket and unlocked two locks, then dialed a combination that released a tractor-sized chain that was anchored to the brick. She pushed open the door, stepped inside, peeked out and yelled, "C'mon."

The steps floated under my feet. I pinched the bricks for purchase, as if that might save me were this oxidized debris to suddenly detach. I'll admit to elevator issues, not so much small space syndrome, more like machinery, but give me a stalled elevator any day over a free-floating stairwell with Swedish guard dogs below. The dogs rustled. I slid my foot to the next step and on up. At the top, I breathed again and glanced down. Louise was already half-way up. Geez! I bolted through the door into a room the size of a gymnasium. Dusty and creaky, the hardwood floor had once been a basketball court. Milky lowlight filtered through weathered windows the size of topsails. Stacked crates, five to ten deep and labeled with months and years, covered two walls.

Louise breezed in and headed straight to a window. She set her briefcase down and gazed at the river.

Heather joined her. "It'd make an awesome cover."

Louise said, "If you stare long enough you can see old man river out there. Mystical, flowing, rolling along." Heather nodded, entranced by My Saint's feed-clip of river buzzwords. Louise let go an extravagant sigh. "All waterfront buildings have a vibration that is unique, but this one ... this one feels phantasmagorical."

"Magical, yes," Heather gushed. "I've heard noises up here."

Phantasmagorical? The place was as still and dull as a tombstone. I caught the private tug at the corner of Louise Marille's mouth.

Except for that ephemeral twitch of a smile, My Saint had no habit of gestures. All those involuntary tics and tacks that are innately part of us, rooted in our parasympathetic nervous system, the very history that defines us, were remarkably absent in this woman. What contrary electricity powered her nervous system? I couldn't imagine, but I was taking notes.

A measured look filtered through her glasses and she turned suddenly — oh, could she swirl that coat! — and raised her hands in a priestly offering. With eyes aflutter, she glided like a puffed-up ballerina into the middle of the room. She stopped and tilted her head, as if catching a whiff of perfume. My Saint was on stage to win. Swedish guard dogs and triple locks — there was no coming back after dark.

Her palms faced upwards. "Something happened in this very room."

Heather pumped her fist. "I knew it! Those noises."

Louise beckoned. "Shut your eyes, girls. Come. Lift the air."

Eyes half shut, I extended my arms, palms upwards. Heather did likewise. I sensed an amiable guilelessness about her and wished that she'd been some bitchy crone instead.

While Heather stood with her eyes squeezed shut, Louise spoke her hypnotics and studied the crates. "A coolness of spirit has settled upon us." I saw her point of focus: JUNE 1985 edged in midway to the top.

Heather nodded her head. "Yes, I think it has. I think I'm feeling it."

Louise whirled again, arms fully outstretched. "This is the place. This very room. In *your* warehouse, Heather. It's here."

Heather opened her eyes. "What's here?"

Louise stopped her slide and glide at the foot of the crates, bent over and brushed off the top of a box, plunked herself down and took a deep breath as if she were suddenly exhausted.

Heather said, "Can you know what happened here?"

Louise held up two fingers like a benediction and said with more than a little drama, "Something damn interesting." She waved her benediction at the crates behind her. "There is history here. History is information to be uncovered."

Heather shook her head. "Not in these crates. Uh-uh. That's business. Secured business."

Louise cooed, "The answer lies within."

I was tempted to add, '…the heart of all mankind, Charlie Brown.' I didn't. I was enjoying myself. I entertained the idea that I, too, could do this. Call myself Rose White, pull a caper. How hard would that be? I was in the middle of a hands-on, live lesson. And liking it. The glitch in my reverie was that I was not acquainted with anybody who needed information they couldn't google.

"This room," Louise said, "hides the story behind the entire district, maybe the whole damn city. Fetch my briefcase, Rose. I must write quickly."

I fetched her briefcase and said to Heather, who had taken on a dubious frown, "Let's you and I go down and call the St. Paul Historical Society and see what they have on this warehouse."

"I can't leave anybody up here. It's against the rules."

Louise shut her eyes again as if listening for ghosts. She opened her eyes with a contented look. "This *is* the book, Rose, and I must capture it here and now." She pulled the notebook from her briefcase and slapped it open. Montblanc to the page, she wrote with one hand while summoning spirits with the other. "Don't fade on me now," she sang out.

I whispered to Heather, "Let's call The Historical Society. Get something going here. She'll be fine up here by herself. What could happen to her?"

"That's not what I'm worried about." Heather looked at me, then at Louise. Louise scribbled, her head cocked as if she were taking dictation. Shameless dramatics. She could have been a romance writer.

"She needs space."

Heather contemplated the crates and boxes. "I suppose it'd be okay this one time. For the book and all. Who will ever know?"

I felt the color of guilt rush to my face. I turned and headed towards the door. Heather glanced once more at Louise, then tiptoed after me. Louise Marille's left-handed pen wriggled across the page.

"You first," I said to Heather. "The dogs. Uh-uh."

She stepped out. The iron staircase pounded and quivered against the wall with each purple-booted step. I glanced once more at Louise, already climbing the crates, box cutters in hand.

If she'd told me this story, I'd have questioned its authenticity, but having just witnessed ... well, what could I say? She'd just pilfered a warehouse.

Safely back on Shepard Road, Louise said, "Good job, Jas, with the Historical Society. We didn't have to kill her."

I frowned into the rear-view mirror.

"That's a joke," she said and offered me a powdered doughnut from a white bakery bag, which was exactly what I needed.

10. Clare Assett
Clare of Assisi, the Patron Saint of Television

We caught Lafayette south to the Mall of America where I hired a cab to haul me back to the no-star motel on the freeway to retrieve my car. Lucky me, it was right where I'd left it, wheels intact. I had enough time before meeting Clare Assett to stop off at the library. Three articles in the archives tracked dead Eddie Valentine. The first article reported his disappearance. Two weeks later he was still missing. Eight months later his body was pulled out of Forest Lake (she'd said Big Lake). He'd broken through the ice ... popular restaurateur ... accidental drowning. I had never considered how large and encompassing the word 'accident' could be. The universe in a word.

I moved on to Minnesota lawyers and looked up Kerby, but not so lucky there. *B's and D's are phonetically muddy*. I looked up Kerdy. Nothing there either. In all possibility, it wasn't his real name. Maybe Kerby was his first name. Too many possibilities.

The zip code for Deerfield, Illinois, was spot on.

Looking forward to a long shower and maybe even a nap before dinner, I stood up to leave. A discarded newspaper on the adjacent table caught my eye. The sidebar read: Roland Keach, Twin Cities Businessman, Fatal Car Wreck.

My Spy from Lords. Holy crap. Obviously tacked on one hour before press, the report was brief disclosing few details. The man had bought us dinner. Just last night. *Clearly an accident*. Or had Angela Folly engineered the crash? If so, I'd been part of it. My ears grew hot. Face, too. Feeling irrationally guilty, I set the paper down and looked around me for suspicious behavior — everyone a potential saint. In a nearby chair, a man wearing blue jeans hid behind a newspaper that did not conceal his sizeable clump of hair. The thug from Stonehenge. I watched until he turned the page. Crap. He was a she. I fast-walked to the exit and bolted through the doors into a parking lot that seemed eerily calm.

A quick scan of the landscape begat no solitary hedge-trimmer, lone telephone repairman, or green SUV with tinted windows going nowhere. A dutiful grandpa with an armload of books wobbled towards the entrance followed by a woman pushing a stroller.

I scrambled to my car and sped away. I had to admit that I felt oddly deflated by the lack of drama. Just in case, I kept one eye on my rearview mirror, even though the only tail I could have spotted would have had flashing red lights.

Had Roland Keach's removal been the whole point of our dinner at Lords? How'd she do it? By planting a spider? That hardly seemed likely. I played the scene back in my head: Swat back of neck. Grab napkin. Swat collar. Staff converges with flashlights. She'd picked-up his cocktail and handed it to him. With all the commotion, she could have dropped in a poison.

She would have left fingerprints on his glass. Would she break that rule? No. She didn't have to. There'd been a cocktail napkin stuck to the bottom. She'd picked up the glass using the napkin. No fingerprints. No rogue spider. She'd checked her watch all night long like a relay coach. He needed to make it off the property. The autopsy needed to focus on bad arteries. If he died at the table, the autopsy would focus on spider venom. Forensics would have found her poison.

Another sticky fact was that she'd seen him at his table long before she'd announced *I see someone I know*. I could be wrong about that. People don't necessarily focus when their eyes wander. And there'd been that slow crawl past the valet cars on our way to park. She'd chosen the Porsche Boxster. I'd chosen the white Mercedes, Roland Keach's white Mercedes. Her telling about the three hearts in the prayer book. My attention scattered.

Why would she kill her banker?

...

Louise Marille, patron saint of social workers, had metamorphosed into Clare Assett, stolen from Clare Fiumi of Assisi, the Patron Saint of Television, another turgid story of poverty and miracles. I never did ask what Clare Fiumi of Assisi circa 1200 A.D. had to do with television, and Clare Assett didn't say. But when Clare Assett entered the Granite City Brew Pub, I recognized My Saint immediately. She hurried to the table. Clare had a swingy way of walking.

"Clare..." I said with a deliberate glance at my notes, "...Assett?"

"Don't you just have the eyes of Jove," she said with more than a hint of The South.

"Spot you a mile away," I said, impressed with myself and I must admit, full of risky knowledge.

She draped her camel-colored coat over the chair and sat down. Her costume was straight out of a 1960s high school yearbook: a navy blue with white polka dot blouse and its reverse white bow with navy dots; matching navy slacks; poufy, blonde hair; Easter bunny blue eyes capped with matching shadow; rosy cheeks and rosy lips. Not the kidnapping type was how Angie had described Clare. More like one of my mother's 'serve up the coffee' secretaries fifty years ago.

I asked, "Did you see the paper today?"

Her face saddened. "You refer to dear, sweet Roland. Roland was one of the good guys."

"He was your banker?"

"He helped Angie with her finances."

"He helped Angie," I repeated. "And Angie just happened to be at Lords the same night as Roland Keach."

"Roland owns part of Lords. Discreetly, of course. Which is why he didn't fuss about that silly spider. Can you imagine if that had been a regular customer? Sued and shut down, slam bam."

She had an explanation for everything. I said, "I wonder if they ever found Itsy Bitsy."

"The spider? Probably not. It's too darn dark in that place. I'm sure it came right out of that toxic palm." She walked her fingertips on the table. "They do that, you know. Crawl out months off the boat. You don't suppose that spider took a bite, do you?"

Our waitress Brianna dropped off a basket of breadsticks. I fished one out and took a bite. "It's an odd coincidence."

"What is?"

"All of it. You're there. He's there. The spider's there. He dies. Your Nordic lady in the bookstore wears a white cable sweater same as that catchy couple two tables away from us."

She cocked her head, a perplexed look. "Everybody in Minnesota owns a white cable sweater. Then, again, it's got Charlie Dickens written all over it." She winked.

"What?"

"Charles Dickens, the master of coincidence."

She proceeded to tell me that her least favorite character was Uriah Heep. Her least favorite novel was *The Pickwick Papers*. I didn't know a single soul who'd ever read *The Pickwick Papers*, much less remembered enough to critique the darn thing. Most times My Saint seemed like some space traveler, then I find out she'd read more Charles Dickens than anyone I know including myself. People who read Dickens don't kill their bankers.

She glanced at her watch, a gold bracelet. "Is October too late for a Tom Collins?" She rummaged through her purse and pulled out a compact, flipped it open, and powdered her nose. With her right hand.

"You're right-handed?"

"I'm right-handed. Louise Marille is left-handed. Both Louise and Theresa List are left-handed, but Theresa has nicer penmanship." She angled the mirror and pushed on a tooth.

I said, "Today at the warehouse, that was kind of fun."

She snapped her compact shut. "Honey, crime and fun go together like angels and potato chips."

All of Clare's words carried an extra syllable. I wanted to tell her that she could speak normal in front of me. This camouflage business was no longer necessary. But I didn't. And she probably couldn't. Her entire existence depended on deception. She dropped her compact into her purse.

"Today could have been testy what with the dogs and all, and I don't speak a nick of Swedish. Thanks to your getting Heather down the stairs…" she winked again, reminding me of my complicity, "…I don't have to go back and inspect the wiring or rotor the toilets or some darn thing that would just make you want to jump up and shout."

"I consider myself merely embedded," I said, needing to clarify my involvement.

"Embedded," she repeated. I caught that smile-tic.

"And I think I have your lawyer's name spelled wrong. He's not in any list that I could find." I turned the condiment tray hoping to find some powdered parmesan to sprinkle on my breadstick.

"Kerby's insulated. A most complicated man."

"Insulated? I thought he had his eye on the governor's chair?" No parmesan. Not even the green can. Like I needed cheese.

"Not by way of his law practice. Goodness, no." Clare's southern drawl was tempered by a tightness at the mouth Holly Hunter style, debutant divine. When she talked, her lips barely moved.

"Brigid said you had TMJ."

"Such a nuisance."

"Have you seen a dentist?" I asked intending sarcasm.

"No dentist. I massage the pressure points." She rubbed at a spot midway between the top of her ear and the end of her eyebrow. "And here." She moved her finger in front of her ear. "You can feel an indent. Open your mouth a tad; the points are easy to find. Behind your earlobe, too, there's a little hollow. Just ease the bone back into position. Now you know what to do if you ever get TMJ."

"But do *you* actually have TMJ?"

"Didn't I just say that?"

Weary of the game, I let it slide and prompted her back to the story. "You have Mr. Dean's contract to kidnap Bentley Ogren and a message from Lance."

"Yes. Lance is my most significant contractor. After Genny took Mr. Dean's contract to grab Bender, she'd stopped by the post office and found the refrigerated freight message meaning Lance needed to see her. You remember Lance contracted two years ago to get Bender out of Canada away from Laddie Ogren."

I wanted to ask her how she could look Lance in the eye knowing she was about to undo the very kid-nabbing he'd contracted, but she kept talking, and I wanted to stay on track.

"Lance is as small as Mr. Dean is big. Parked behind his desk, the first thing out of his mouth is, 'Remember Canada?' He sees I am surprised by that question. He just doesn't know how surprised." She pointed at herself and said Holly Hunter style, "I'm at an utter loss for words what with the mention of Canada."

Clare had drama going.

"I'm sitting on a straight-back, worn velour, what might have once been a fiery red chair in the smallest office an owner of a large trucking company could possibly have and still do business. It's also the messiest office an owner of a large trucking company could have and still do business. Papers, receipt books, accounting books, tablets, white envelopes, brown envelopes, stacks of envelopes bound with rubber bands piled everywhere. There's a half-eaten doughnut on top of a stack of ledger books. He's got six TVs mounted to the wall so he can watch CNN, Fox, and the networks all at the same time.

"Lance says to me, 'We've got a problem. Lil called. Fanny needs to hook up with that Nicky girl of yours, the one who got Bentley Ogren out of Canada.'"

Pen poised over my notebook, I said, "Fanny is the boy's mother and Nicky is another saint."

"Yes. That's Nicky with a y."

Brianna zoomed past, backed up, and chirped, "The ravioli wafers are super," and zoomed away with two orders for ravioli wafers. Having woofed down a basket of breadsticks, what's another plate of carbs?

"Lance studies the mess of papers in front of him. I stare out the only window in the room. It faces a cinderblock wall. A gray, muted light is all the window will allow. It's depressing light that steals the color from your eyes. He gathers the papers and shoves them into an open drawer and slams it shut, leans forward and says, 'Someone is after the kid.'"

"Whoa," I said to Clare. "Stop right there."

Clare clapped her hands. "See what a mess this is? Lance is contracting me to hide the very kid Mr. Dean has contracted me to kidnap."

"I'd say there was crossover in your business. These two men know each other."

"No. Lance doesn't know Genny." Clare fluffed her hair. "Mr. Dean doesn't know Clare."

"Your secret identities may not be as secret as you think."

"Mr. Dean might have a clue. But not Lance. Uh-uh." She peered into the empty breadbasket.

"Sorry," I said, seriously doubting she would have eaten a breadstick.

"The little office is suddenly hot. I want to jump up and throw open the window, but it's holding decades of paint. Lance tells me that Fanny went hysterical. She's got a safe place he can go, but she can't take him there, because she's being watched. Lil's being watched. Lance says to me, 'Your Nicky will have to do it.' He's talking like we're already in agreement.

"I tell Lance that I'll have to find Nicky first. He gives me a forthright look and says, 'Ask would she do that for two grand?'"

Clare's eyes slid to mine. "Sure as shootin' you know what I'm thinking."

"You're thinking there's a three-hundred and ninety-eight thousand dollar difference between Mr. Dean's and Lance's contracts.

"See how this whole thing has gone wrong?"

I held up my hand. "Let me get this straight. These last four days you and I have been writing a book, pilfering a warehouse, eating powdered doughnuts, and walking around like there's not four hundred thousand Mr. Dean dollars in your pocket. You got the money on Thursday. Today's Monday. For all you know, the game's over. Mr. Dean's thugs could have already nabbed Bender. Laddie Ogren and Bentley Ogren might be snug in Canada this very minute." I squinted my eyes at her. "Mr. Dean will want a refund, won't he?"

"There is so much commotion right now, I can't think straight." She let go a dramatic sigh. "I'm too confused to do anything at all. I simply cannot return that money."

Tara. That's where I was. This wasn't the Granite Pub. This was Tara. Missing was the hand to the forehead and the fiddle-de-de. It all sounded so cockeyed and it certainly wasn't funny, but I laughed. She waited, unfazed by my derisive outburst.

"For the record," I said, sobering, "if you died tomorrow, who would get your money?"

"The holy Roman Catholic Church. They'll saint me for it."

Crazy mama.

"So, as it stands…" I tapped the tape recorder with my pen, "…you've been paid to snatch this boy from his mother and deliver him to card shark Mr. Dean who turns him over to bad dad Laddie Ogren who has the boy's mother on his hit list. Then Lance comes along and wants to pay you two grand to hide this boy somewhere safe from bad dad Laddie O."

Brianna set two over-sized plates of cheese ravioli in front of us. The pasta squares were as big and thick as bankers' wallets and smelled divine. I forked a steamy square. The cheese oozed out like hot lava. Suffering from breadstick overload, I could wait until it cooled.

I set my fork down and focused on Clare. "Fanny and her son," I said softly, "are in danger and you're the only one who can help them."

"Lordy, lordy, domestic. I've kicked myself silly for taking Lance's contract two years ago, so I darn sure knew better than to take Mr. Dean's contract. It's the same damn job in reverse."

"What happened in Canada? You never said." I tried again with the hot cheese and scorched the roof of my mouth.

"I'd scored a part time job at Bender's school. On soccer day I sprinkled capsicum in his uniform. He scratched and cried with the itch. I'd known that the school nurse would be at an all-day seminar. Regulations dictate ER without her. And there I was, the available driver, and off we went. When we got to my rented car, I whipped out the aloe oil and a change of clothes. All the way to the border, I called the school with progress reports: ER is slammed, problematic allergy, condition improved, back within the hour, back within the next hour, blah, blah. About the time we hit Fort Frances, Laddie Ogren was experiencing a mental episode.

"It took me three weeks to get next to that kid and four failed set-ups. The blasted job was a loss."

"You're not seriously going to take that kid from his mother?"

"I'm making up a loss. That's what any successful business mister would do."

"I don't believe you."

Clare picked at her pasta, arranging the squares on her plate, spreading them out like people do who don't like their food, but won't offend the hostess. She'd done the same at Lords. I had never seen her eat more than two bites. Skinny bitch.

"Lance set up a lunch for Fanny and me. The café has a nice layout. You can notice anyone who seems a little too interested in what might could be a mother and daughter having lunch."

Might could be?

"The self-absorbed soup and salad crowd suits me. Their faces belong in the malls. Except for Fanny. She's beautiful. She's wearing khaki pants and a white turtleneck sweater. Her black jacket is folded on her lap. With her hair tied back, high cheekbones and no make-up, she could be a kind and favored kindergarten teacher who never raises her voice. Then she goes and twirls around on the barstool and shouts at the hostess, 'Whoa, Christie! We're ready!' Startled the livin' daylights out of me. I do declare."

I would remember Clare as the affected saint.

Her fingers flitted over her polka dot bow. "I order a grilled cheese sandwich. Fanny orders a cheeseburger. We both order tea. I'd simply kill for a beer, but Fanny doesn't drink. Laddie Ogren drinks. One time he showed up drunk and broke her arm. Fanny assures me that Bender is safe for the time being. I don't know how she can believe that.

"I stress the complications of bringing Nicky to the surface, but Fanny is undeterred and tells me that Bender wouldn't trust anybody but Nicky. She smiles fondly, like mothers do, and adds that when Bender got back from Canada he'd roll his eyes and tell about the cap with the curls that Nicky had made him wear. It was a wig, of course, not a cap. He told his mother they'd gone fishing. Nicky and Bender crossed the Rainy, bait and tackle in the boat, but no fishing."

Clare forked a ravioli and raised it to her mouth, then set it back down on her plate. "I drop my tea bag into my pot of hot water and listen to Fanny talk. The waitress sets our food on the table. My sandwich is all toasted and buttery. I take a bite. It's got bonus bacon. Fanny dips a potato fry into a side of mayonnaise and tells me somebody's tailing her. I ask if she knows who that might be. She says, 'It's not Laddie. He wouldn't follow. He'd just up and shoot me.' Fanny takes a sip of water and goes on in her animated way telling me she thinks that Laddie's father is involved and that he's an ace poker player. She says, 'You know the kind of person who's always watching you? Like he's in a constant state of analysis and memorization? I don't know how he plays cards. He had a stroke a few years back so his left arm is useless.'"

"Wait." I held up my hand to Clare. "Is she talking about Mr. Dean?"

"Small world, huh? Fanny goes on to tell me that when Mr. Dean finally faced the fact that his son couldn't hold the reins on a dog sled, he'd sent him out of the country. Called him a loose cannon."

"Mr. Dean is Laddie Ogren's father?"

"It all makes sense now, doesn't it?"

"You've been withholding information." I swallowed a forkful of ravioli. "And, regardless of what you might think, I'd call this crossover. Big time crossover. What are the chances of Lance and Mr. Dean, two criminals, contracting you on the same job? That's over the top. They've got to know each other."

"Impossible." Clare brooded a moment. I thought she might be rethinking the ethics of her kidnapping contract. She wasn't. She said, "Talk about unlikely confederates, Fanny and me. I fiddle with my teapot, my throat constricted, my nerves turned against me. I open the lid and remove the teabag way too soon. I'm drinking what tastes like hot dishwater."

"Forget the teabag. Somebody is playing you here."

"That sure in toots gives me the jitters. You know, I had this dream last night. Genny was at that house with Mr. Dean. She bent over to fix her shoe and saw his feet under the desk, but they weren't feet. They were hooves."

I stared at her a moment, then said, "Here's my trick advice, Miss Clare: call the cops."

"The cops," she said, smoothing her polka dot bow. "The cops are the answer to everything, aren't they? Fact is they're seldom the answer to anything. There are citizens out there, you know, who pay more in taxes in one year than most people pay in a lifetime; calling the cops wouldn't cross their minds."

"What do they do?"

"Handle it."

"It sounds like everybody's handling here is about to blow. Now would be the time for you to do the right thing."

"The right thing," she said, looking like she was considering what that might be. The possibility that My Saint and I were talking about the same 'right thing' was unlikely.

"The right thing," she said again. "How do so many people with the same basic needs disagree on what the right thing might be? But that's a discussion for the Nietzsche crowd, silly freaks. The other day I saw a bumper sticker that read What Would Nietzsche Do? Two blocks down the street was What Would Jesus Do? Yesterday I spotted What Would Mother Do? I'm not sure what that one meant. I, personally, would be inclined to do what my father did. Skip. Skip to my Lou."

"Your mother never told you who your father was?"

"I was at her bedside when she died. I asked one last time. She shut her eyes and said, 'You were conceived like the Christ Child.' I don't know how to forget that. The room was very warm and dim with that pale winter light. A priest stood by the bed reading last rites in Latin. All the while across the hall a radio was playing real low, 'Gimme Shelter.' The Stones, mind you, in a Catholic hospital. Just a shot away.

"Going through her things I found her papers from the convent and took a trip to the Basilica of Bibiana. No one remembered my mother. There was no record that she had ever been there. There was no record that I had been born. There or anywhere."

"You were born in the convent?"

Clare nodded. "And Mother Superior was geriatric enough to remember it."

"You had your mother's papers."

"I was told that the documents were not from Bibiana. Amen."

"Can you get a lawyer or something?"

"I might could, but I no longer see the point. According to the Basilica of Bibiana, I don't exist. There is no record of my being born. That has served me well."

"Where's Bibiana?"

"Up past Grand Forks."

The busboy collected our plates, including Clare's rearranged ravioli. I made a note to google Bibiana. And a priest named Father Robel and a church called St. Vitus. Fact and fiction mottled. Lance, Mr. Dean, Laddie Ogren, Fanny Graas, Bentley Graas-Ogren, Lil, Sammy, Kerby — who were these people? The only two things I knew for certain: My Saint's banker was dead and a wily man with thick hair who smelled like copper pennies was hunting her.

Clare retied her polka dot bow and continued with her story. "Discovering that Mr. Dean is Laddie Ogren's father makes me choke on my tea. Fanny expresses concern. I fan my face and tell her, 'I come from the South. We drink it iced.'" Clare pronounced it ahhst.

"Fanny tells me she hates ahhst tea. She's finished her fries and turns her plate so the cheeseburger faces her. She calibrates it with her fingers and takes a bite. It's unbearably thick. My jaw aches. Juice runs down the side of her mouth. She dabs at it with her napkin and asks do I think Nicky will help her. She wishes she had more money. Her eyes tear up, but she blinks them dry. I put the tea bag back in the little steel pot and try for a second chance. Second chance. Shoot. I'm starring in my own darn rerun. Fanny tells me about an Oriental rug she could put on eBay."

Brianna laid our check on the table. Clare said, "Thank you, sweetie." She had that southern thing down good. "Fanny is telling me that she's kept her natural blonde hair dyed black. She asks had I ever heard of such a thing? A natural blonde dying her hair black? She's asking *me* that. Me." Clare chuckled and brushed at her hair. "I adore Fanny. The first time I ever met her she said I looked like Dusty Springfield." Clare tilted her head. "Think?"

"Fanny said that? Fanny Graas?" *...search again for any Claire at all ... thin and blonde and looks like Dusty Springfield.*

"My God," I said. "That was her. At the hotel. Fanny and Bender. Minutes before I met you in Stonehenge. I stood right next to her at the front desk. She was looking for somebody named Claire. She told the reservations guy that this Claire person looked like Dusty Springfield. She had a photo." I put my hand to my head, stupefied. "You weren't registered as Clare Assett, were you?"

Her face had lost all but the festive color. I could actually see the flat pan make-up on her skin and the stroke of her rose-colored blush. My Saint's glowing Clare disguise had metamorphosed into the flat, spooky face of a painted mime with blue frost eyelids.

"I was registered as Genny Ross," the mime said.

"The boy stood still as a soldier." I let that sink in, then added, "And I won't swear to it, but I think they were coming through the door on Sunday as I was running out." I wished I'd paid more attention, offered to help, something; although, knowing now that the woman had been Fanny Graas, would she have accepted help from me or from anybody?

I could have tried.

Then, as if the sun had risen and a new day had dawned, Clare drawled, "Well, I wonder what that was all about. Fanny knows to call me."

I shook my head. "She didn't have a phone, the phone where your ever-changing number was probably stored."

Clare talked as though nothing had changed. But it had. Her slow, southern speech had quickened. Her accent sounded contrived, her mannerisms no longer jived. Clare Assett wasn't a belle anymore. My Saint had lost focus; Clare of Assisi, the Patron Saint of Television, was running in second place. I watched, fascinated, as My Saint struggled for control.

She said, "Fanny has eaten half her grill cheese sandwich."

"I thought Fanny was eating a cheeseburger."

Clare blinked, but did not counter. "Fanny nibbles on her pickle. My food is cold and I am no longer hungry. I pour my tea again. It's lukewarm and tastes like twigs. No second chance." Clare stared, unfocused, as she talked. "I move my plate aside. Fanny reaches over and lifts that mangled sandwich and double wraps it in a napkin. A little piece of bacon gets left behind. She plucks it up and stuffs it back in the sandwich and says to me, rather abstractly, I recall: 'He's found me. I suppose I can be blonde again.'"

Clare added with a chilling detachment, "I don't know if there's time enough for Fanny to be blonde."

I shivered. "What does that mean?"

Clare drew a slow breath. Brianna flew by but didn't stop.

"My God, Clare," I said. "What's the matter with you? If that was Fanny at the hotel, and I think it was, she was afraid, really afraid."

"If Laddie Ogren is in town, she has reason to be afraid. Although she isn't whining or crying about it. She's tough, Fanny is. Even though I avoid social interaction, I do recognize character when I see it." Her speech had slowed again.

"You haven't talked to her, have you?"

"She did not show up at work today." Clare pushed up her polka dot sleeve and looked at her watch.

"You don't know where she is? And you're just getting around to telling me this? You keep holding back on me."

"I don't want to get ahead of the story."

"The story? That's crazy! What in God's name might be happening to this woman and her son while we sit here in carbohydrate hell chattering about ahhst tea? Call the police! I'll call the police." I yanked open my bag and dug for my cell phone.

"Lil would have done that if there were even the remotest possibility they could help."

"Have you spoken to this Lil person?"

"I have no idea where that woman might be."

"What, might I ask, are you planning to do?"

"What I was fixin' to do doesn't matter anymore." Clare glanced over at my notepad. I'd accumulated a half-page of notes. She said, "Now might be a good time to redeem me."

"Are you freaking crazy?"

She jutted her lower lip. But it was bad theater. She'd recovered her southern style, but this was no longer Clare Assett. This was somebody trying to act like Clare Assett. If that made sense.

Her obvious difficulty emboldened me. I jabbed my finger at her. "You. You're the villain in the story. Clare, Alex, Toni, or whatever your name is. You've been playing Fanny to get to Bender so you can snatch him for Mr. Dean, who it turns out, surprise, surprise, is the father of her devil husband. Because of all your saint names and saint faces, Fanny couldn't find you. You had a chance to help them. You're a mess. And you have no conscience."

She gave me a hurt look, jutted lip and all — believable this time, coupled with an elaborate sigh. Clare Assett was up and running again. Had my calling her out brought her back to the control board?

"Well," she said, pulling three syllables out of the word, "if you're not going to redeem me…"

"Like I said, redemption isn't necessary in the crime genre. The criminal gets caught and goes to prison. Kerpow!"

"Well," she drawled again. "That simply won't work."

"Wha-ay-el," I mimicked. "That *is* the way it works."

"You think I am not sentient. I beg to differ. Better yet..." she stabbed her finger at my notebook, "...sum it up in one simple sentence: The good saint doesn't rob little old ladies."

"You killed Eddie Valentine."

"He was whistling when I left him."

I leaned towards her, eyes narrowed. "Who contracted the hit on Roland Keach?"

"What hit?"

"Roland Keach at Lords. Your banker. Your dead banker. Who hired you to kill him?"

She stared at me, an indefinable expression on her face. "His death was heart related. My gosh, I don't think there was any funny business there."

My Saint would never admit liability. Maybe in twenty years, but not with the evidence reposed and available for autopsy.

We sat in silence and watched the host escort a family of four to a table in the center of the room. The mother shook her head and pointed to a large cozy booth by the window. The host scooped up the menus and headed towards the booth. The family of four followed.

Clare said, "You'd think they'd know to do that by now."

I muttered, "They always fill the crappy tables first."

I considered ducking into the restroom and calling the police. What would I tell them? Not only did I not know if a real crime had been committed, I didn't know if a real crime was going to be committed. Or I could take my tapes straight to the cops. Let them decide.

No names. No locations. No dates. They'd think I was the crazy one.

Clare took a sip of water and patted the corners of her mouth with her tissue. "I need you to drive the car tomorrow night."

I folded my arms. "I don't think I can do that." Crazy Momma had taken on a melody in my head. J.J. Cale on carbs.

Clare continued talking as if I hadn't spoken. "Be at Lake Calhoun. Seven o'clock. By the canoe racks on Excelsior Boulevard." She pulled a tiny, brown bottle out of her purse and twisted the cap. A heavy, rose scent powered out, as if you'd put your face in a pink bouquet. She dabbed once behind each ear.

"What's that?" I said.

"Geranium."

I wrote geranium next to Clare's name in my notebook. "What scent does Nicky Myer wear?"

"Sweat."

I smacked my notebook shut and jammed the pen into the ring binder. "I can't redeem you. Any of you."

"Writers can write whatever they want."

"No, they can't write whatever they want. Wherever did you get that notion? You know someone who writes river guides. Give me a basic break."

"I what?"

"You know someone who writes river guides."

"I said that?"

"Your words d.b.a. Alex Edessa."

She dropped the geranium vial into her purse. "It's frightful cold this time of year. The sun down so early you'd think this was Canada."

"It almost is."

"Bundle up."

"You're going to waltz in, grab the boy and bring him to Mr. Dean. What do you need me for?"

"Six-year-olds can be so difficult."

"That's another reason I can't redeem you. You show no remorse."

"Write me some remorse."

What I wanted was for her to do the right thing: give the money back to Mr. Dean and go to the police and get Laddie Ogren arrested and put away. Or not go to the police; just help Fanny and the boy disappear.

I didn't want another hands-on experience. The warehouse with the Swedish guard dogs was enough, thank you very much. I couldn't afford to be a member of The Arrested Club. But with the thought that I might help Fanny Graas coupled with the fact that I knew too much to declare ignorance, I caved. Maybe there wasn't a damn thing I could have done back at the hotel for the woman and her sentinel son, but a black dot stained my heart because I hadn't even tried.

Atonement.

I would meet her at the canoes. If ditzy Clare Assett was the core saint in charge of this infrastructure, Fanny and Bender were doomed. The story wasn't falling out like a good story should. I pulled my pen from the notebook and said, "I can't write your story the way it's headed."

She closed the flap on her purse. "The book won't work out then. Seemed like a good idea at the time."

That stopped me. Not only did her flippancy regarding our hours of interviewing surprise me, it maddened me. "This isn't a river guide. It's real life. If you'd do the right thing for once in *your* life, everything could work out. For real this time. A good ending." I clicked my pen.

"Honey, we haven't even got to the good part." She stood up and pulled her coat from the chair. "Nicky Myer will pick you up by the canoes at seven. She'll be driving a black Saturn with tinted windows. She's from the hood."

I snorted and flipped my pen into the air. It landed on the condiment tray. "From the hood? Good Christ! Would that be the neighborhood or the car hood?"

I wanted to fly at her and shake her into sanity, but I didn't, I couldn't. Instead, I retrieved my pen from the condiments and snapped it on my notebook and said crisply, "What, pray tell, is Nicky Myer the patron saint of?"

"Nicholas of Myra is the Patron Saint of Children." She bent down and picked up her purse. "Toodle-do."

I watched her stride out of the restaurant. Gone was Clare's swingy way of walking.

Nothing would make me miss this kidnapping.

River guides. Phfft!

11. Copper Pennies

The American Inn parking lot was a half-car shy of a full house. One-nighters, I figured: traveling salespeople, itinerant blue-collars, migrating Canadians. Without painted guide lines, parking was a free-for-all. I squeezed in between a decal plastered station wagon and a spiced-up Oldsmobile. Door dings were not an issue with these folks. Me neither. I opened my door into an air-brushed hockey puck and squeezed out into the refrigerator-wet night air. Was there a reason I kept on in this icebox when right this minute it was cocktail time in Arizona? Red and green salsas, pink margaritas, open firepots, Camelback Mountain backlit by the red sun. Maybe after I got published, I'd move there. At the rate I was going that might coincide with retirement.

I hoisted my bag to my shoulder and headed towards the stairs where I caught sight of an open doorway and a row of loaded vending machines. The idea of some chocolate covered confetti lightened my gloom. I was raking the bottom of my handbag for the necessary change when the thug from Stonehenge vaulted out from under the stairs, grabbed my arm and yanked me into the snack room. I screamed and whacked him with my bag. He got me with a full body hijack up against the ice machine, his hand clamped over my mouth. With one arm twisted behind my back, a feeble slap at his padded jacket was all I had. Close up and personal, he'd angled himself to prevent a knee in the groin. The man had experience.

"I'm looking for Toni Padua," he said, partly blinded by the sheaf of hair. He'd just eaten a mint. His face was newly shaved, smooth like beige suede. He released his hand from my mouth.

My second scream was no more than a quack. His hand came back so hard my teeth moved. The toxic-sweet stink confirmed him a smoker who had recently washed his hands with soap. I tried to bite, but couldn't move my jaw.

"No, no, Jennifer Sands. Shhhh. I'm not here to hurt you. I'm a private detective. Okay?"

I nodded agreement because I needed air. We stared at each other. His brown eyes looked undisturbed, nothing dazed or furtive. And he had pulled me into the fluorescent limelight in full view of the parking lot instead of throwing me under the steps.

"Shush?"

I nodded, and he slowly released his hand from my mouth leaving me gasping for air. He backed off, both hands up in submission. "I mean you no harm, but I need your help, Miss Sands."

My eyes flicked to the parking lot. Surely to God there was one person out there not glued to the shopping channel. I took a small step sideways as if I might skirt around him. He let me, although he remained posed and ready to tackle. He'd come this far. I'd have made a run for it, but I was certain this was about My Saint, not me.

"What do you want?" I blurted.

He flicked the hair out of his eyes and reached inside his jacket, pulled out a leather ID packet and flipped it open. Incensed from his attack, I grabbed it out of his hand. He seemed taken aback by my aggression. As well he should. I was fully aware of the availability of badge stock. I angled it to the light and tightened my grip to stop the trembles. It wasn't a star or anything metal. More like a driver's license with his photo. It looked real enough, but then I'd never seen a real badge, much less a fake one.

"Martin Micks," I rasped. "You've had two prior opportunities to properly introduce yourself."

He plucked his ID out of my hand and slipped it back in his jacket. "I didn't want to chase after you again. Run out like that last night."

"You look like a thug."

"Sorry. Some days I shave twice. I got a snapshot here." When he opened his jacket to pull out the photo, I caught a glimpse of a leather shoulder strap followed by a whiff of copper pennies. He handed me the picture. "You know this woman."

I recognized My Saint in a disguise I'd not yet seen, snapped from a distance of about twenty feet.

Martin Micks said, "Her name is Toni Padua."

The photo was as far from the prim schoolteacher with the Asian eyes as a photo could be. This guy was way off track.

"I got three files on my desk. The cases are not related except that a woman was sighted in all three. From the eyewitness accounts and the photos we have, the assumption is that the three women are in no way related. I disagree."

"Maybe there's a club. A club of women who oversee the low-life, keep them checked. How about that?"

"A club of women?" He snorted. "There's no such animal. Women in crime work alone. Or there's some man pulling the strings. Believe me, history has never chronicled a coven of Mafiettas." He acknowledged my frown. "The kid thing, you know."

"No. No, I don't know."

He scheeshed me. "Look, in spite of all your book clubs and sewing clubs and sister hugs, at the core you don't trust each other. I've seen your so-called sisterhood in action. Plenty."

"You know nothing about sisterhood," I said, for lack of a better response.

"What I do know is that this woman works alone using different aliases and disguises. And you had drinks with her Saturday night at the Stonehenge Lounge. You called her Brigid Ireland. That's not her name."

I studied the picture in my hand. Brigid had said that her hair had once been long and permed. This could be a young Brigid Ireland. Or not.

"How old is this picture?"

"About ten years, I suspect."

More like twenty, I thought. "Where did the name Toni Padua come from?"

"Toni Padua signed in at a hospital holding facility impersonating a parole officer. She paid a visit to a sociopath whose lawyers had engineered an insanity plea. But that's another story."

"You have her on video impersonating a parole officer?" This was getting better.

"She was wearing a hat. She never looked up."

"Sounds like a sure thing, you betcha."

He grimaced.

This man had information. This man, who had nearly rearranged my teeth, possessed bona fide facts. I added a smat of empathy to my face.

"Last night you got a phone call in the hotel lobby." He stopped as if expecting me to confirm that. Did he know I'd skipped on my bar tab?

"I attended a writers conference in that very hotel. I had a room at that very hotel. I drank martinis in the hotel bar." If he brought up the delinquent bar tab, I'd act surprised. Leave it to a romance writer to forget she'd already checked out. Such scatterbrains.

"Who called you at the hotel?"

Was I obligated to answer these questions? Discovering he was a detective, one might think that I would have hugged him around the neck and confessed everything, elicited his help, and straightened out this kidnapping mess. Instead, I felt protective. And resentful at the intrusion. But, at the same time, curious as all hell; not to mention that a newfound conflict in My Saint's story, a literary tension, so to speak, was standing right here in front of me.

"My mother called," I said and shoved the picture back at him. It fell to the floor.

"I can find out, you know."

"Find out then."

"You do understand that you and I are on the same team here, don't you?" He picked the photo off the floor and wiped it on his jeans.

"Team?"

"This woman is dangerous. I've had a line on her for a long time, but I don't have a name. She's got to have been fingerprinted along the way. But so far, I'm curbed."

"Why didn't you take that bar glass Saturday night for DNA?"

"The glass was clean." He pulled out another picture. I almost smiled at the red haired, slightly overweight woman in a parking lot outside what looked like an apartment building. It had to be Cathy Senna, Catherine of Siena, the Patron Saint of Fire. Martin Micks had been the detective in the green Toyota reading the newspaper. My Saint had recognized him at Stonehenge.

I handed it back. "Don't know her."

"You could come down to the station and answer these questions."

This man had nothing on me, not even the ditched bar tab. Suddenly emboldened, I held out my hands. "So cuff me."

"Look, lady…"

Nor did he have the authority to take me anywhere. I wondered just what kind of detective-investigator person he really was. Maybe rogue. Maybe Mr. Dean had hired him to keep an eye on his money, which was the real reason he was trailing My Saint. The man wasn't being straight with me. But neither was My Saint. How did I get to be such a forthright clod? Something to do with my parents and trustiness, for sure. Throw in the American Legion.

I folded my arms and said, "Maybe I'm her accomplice."

He snorted and said with more than a little disparagement, "Yeah, right."

Was I that homespun?

"Pay attention, Ms. Sands–"

"No, you pay attention, Mr. Detective or whatever you are. She told me at the bar that her name was Brigid Ireland. That's all I know. Now I need to wash my hair." I turned towards the door. He grabbed my arm.

"Pay attention, Ms. Sands. She's dark, that one. She'll get you into something you won't be able to laugh off. My strong advice to you is to go home."

I jerked my arm away.

"Jennifer Sands," he said, suddenly weary. "I can't tell you all the things she's done."

"Throw one out for grins."

"Money laundering."

"Oh, please. I know a cliché when I hear one."

He processed that, then said, "She broke into the Democratic campaign headquarters and stole the files."

"It was tapes. Not files." I pointed at his pocket where he'd deposited the photos. "And if she'd broken into anybody's headquarters, you would never have known it."

"Ah, ha! You do know her!" His head bobbed like he'd won something. "See, there's always evidence left at a crime scene. Always. Except when there's not. When there's not, I know she was there — identified by the absence. Sometimes she leaves false clues that we chase down, debunk 'em, and then we're back at base again with a mucked-up crime scene." The detective moved to the snack machine, dug in his pants pocket, and pulled out a handful of change. "Did she mention Faber Elliot?"

"Who's Faber Elliot?"

"Faber Elliot," he said, picking though his change, "had possession of ten key acres of Mississippi riverbank. Old Faber wanted it preserved. Then he jumped off the Washington Avenue Bridge. Family claimed he was a happy man. An environmental savior." He deposited his change back in his pocket.

"So?"

"Old Faber was last seen alive dining with a nondescript woman at Lords — that's a restaurant west of town. Faber was not a jumper. What's her name? What name did she give you?"

I looked down at my wrist and rubbed where he'd twisted it. "I told you. She said her name was Brigid Ireland. We chatted. End of story."

"What name was she using Sunday when she called you at the bar?"

Martin Micks would have spoken to the snippy concierge. Phone records would net him a phone booth or a pay-as-you-go phone. I was clear. "My phone was dead. My mother called the hotel."

"Must have been bad news. Rush out like that."

"I didn't *rush* out like that. Listen, Mr. Micks, what it sounds like to me is if you don't nab a suspect within the hour, you pin it on" —I flipped my hand towards his pocket again— "this phantom." I wondered if he knew Roland Keach or Laddie Ogren. Did he know Laddie Ogren was in town? I was tempted to ask.

"Do you have my plum-colored coat?"

"Forensics has it."

I tapped my chest. "That's my coat. I want it back."

He tapped the back of his neck. "The label. It's not sold anywhere local."

"I bought it at a yard sale."

He pulled out a business card and flicked it into a two-fingered hold. "Girls like yourself," he said shaking his head, "I've seen it. Time and again you come to the city–"

"The city? Stop it already. That city is New York, Chicago, or LA. Not Minneapolis, for Christ's sake!"

"Go home." He shoved his business card at me.

I snatched it out of his fingers and crushed it in my fist and folded my arms. "And you're not a cop."

His eyes narrowed. "I was with homicide when I started with her and I work her files through the department."

He did not have the authority to arrest me. Could he hold me until the real cops came? I wasn't sure.

He brushed his hair aside, dipped into his pocket again and pulled out his change. He separated the quarters, dropped them into the coin slot and pulled a knob. Thud. He plucked a candy bar out of the trough and handed it to me, a Snickers bar, which I unwittingly accepted. He adjusted his jacket and yanked it taut. I caught another whiff of copper pennies. He headed towards the door and stopped, surveyed the parking lot and said, "Just what *are* you doing here?"

"Sleep," I snapped. "I sleep here."

He gave me a peddler's grin and disappeared out the door.

I jammed his card into my pocket and swiped at the front of my jacket to excise his imprint. That was the closest I'd ever gotten to a man and not kissed him. Or at least danced. I grabbed my bag off the floor and raced outside just in time to see him open the door to an SUV, green under the lamplight.

I yelled across the parking lot, "I'm a romance writer. That's all."

12. Nicky Myer
Nicholas of Myra, the Patron Saint of Children
TUESDAY

Huddled between two dumpsters in the North Beach parking lot, I watched for Nicky Myer's black Saturn. I was early, as usual. I hated that about myself. Being on time had become a waste of time. Meetings kowtowed to latecomers, issues on hold until everyone was seated; the later you arrived the less of your own personal time got wasted. Pity the poor sap who'd tripped in early, clearly damned. That'd be me.

The frigid wind off Lake Calhoun snapped at my coat. I stomped my feet to keep warm. Just as I was feeling a polar scream coming on, some crazy kook wearing a wetsuit-shorts outfit sprinted past. Lake Calhoun was one of those lakes where the sidewalk around it followed the water's edge. Regular people could run its two-mile circumference without stumbling through somebody's backyard gnome collection. I watched the crazy kook, christened with each whoosh of a wave, disappear down the shoreline — probably ran his reptilian self into the water.

At seven o'clock to the minute, just when I had registered the fact that my enthusiasm for unlawful activity was, indeed, reckless, a sporty-looking car pulled in, circled the parking lot and pointed its headlights at my dumpsters. I stepped into the light and waved. The car rolled forward and stopped. I opened the passenger door to the last refrain of "Sergeant Pepper's Lonely Hearts Club Band."

Nicky Myer was slouched behind the wheel, not lazy, more like a dormant circuit. She wore jeans and a black leather jacket. Her dark hair was chop-cropped short, what I could see of it under the baseball hat, its curved brim warping her sunken cheeks and eyes into sepulchral shadows — not at all what I'd expected from the Patron Saint of Children. I'd been thinking Mary Tyler Moore in a tam.

"You're Nicky Myer," I said, reminiscent of Scrooge meeting the funereal ghost of Christmas Future.

"Where's your car?" Her voice was low and toneless. She was chewing gum.

"I took a cab." I waited for her to ask why. She didn't. Half-expecting her to floor it and screech out of the parking lot like some "Girls Gone Bad," who-can-be-the-baddest-bitch on late-night TV, I braced myself. She shifted into drive and we crept out of the parking lot as if we were driving on ice. At the stoplight, she dialed the music loud, another Beatles song I'd never understood, Mr. Kite and the show tonight. We turned right on red and headed towards Lake Street without the lakes.

I liked Hennepin and Lake. The neighborhood attracted enough of the young and half-way-there crowd to support the trendy boutiques, a significant bookstore, and a gourmet grocer. The restaurants looked invested, their styling clientele displayed in their Soho windows, ready and waiting for a nod from some tasty travels show. But no more than a dozen cartwheels on down Lake Street, the neighborhood lost its place. Nicollet-Lyndale came crawling in, dragging along its nail salons and pawnshops, thrift stores, tax returns and bail bondsmen. Focaccia to Wonder Bread.

Mr. Kite and his calliope wound down at Lyndale. Nicky Myer turned off the radio.

"Thank you," I said.

"No one sings like that anymore."

"Zippy died with The Bee Gees. The Jennifer years." That garnered the start of a smile. Having her attention, I blurted, "Last night that man from Stonehenge tackled me in the snack room at the motel." I repeated word for word my encounter with Martin Micks and how he'd threatened to cuff me and take me downtown. I'd meant to sound casual, but came off breathless instead. Nicky Myer did not seem surprised. If she was concerned that he had Toni Padua's name and young Brigid Ireland's picture in his pocket, she didn't show it.

"Didn't I tell you Brigid was cute? Back in the day."

I huffed, impatient with her nonchalance. I'd been mugged, for gawd's sake. "Do you know this Martin Micks?"

"He comes from a long line of Pinkertons."

"He said you were a criminal."

"He's onto something."

"He's been onto you for years. He won't stop, you know."

"We're a persecuted people." Her eyes worked the road and the mirrors. She glanced at my scowling face and said, "Oh, stop. It was exciting and you know it."

"Exciting? You're kidding, of course."

"You told him to cuff you. I like that."

"I was pretty sure he couldn't."

"You have a fine sense of humor, Jas."

I thought about that for a moment. I'd always considered myself too serious, even when I drank, even more so when I drank, constantly chided by Dave or Penny to 'lighten up.' Shoot, compared to this Nicky Myer saint, I was a real ham.

"He said you might be responsible for Faber Elliot falling off a bridge."

"Never heard of him."

"Faber Elliot was last seen alive having dinner at Lords with a woman nobody can properly describe. That's a Charlie Dickens short if I ever saw one."

She turned the radio back on, bringing up an advertisement for Lasik surgery. Obviously, Faber Elliot was off limits. Maybe all she'd done was get him to the bridge. Somebody else shoved him off? She shoved him off? Maybe Faber freaking jumped. Who would ever know? His death would never be resolved … how sad was that? Or was it? If Faber Elliot's file stayed open, he would end up in the cold case storage room. Fifty years from now people would be dabbling into his life. He would be resurrected on some cold case TV program; meanwhile, the solved cases were filed away in molding boxes three floors below the basement and flat out forgotten. Why would anybody want their murder solved? Long live Faber.

I said, "So, you're not worried about this Martin Micks detective-investigator guy?"

She turned the radio off. "He'll never touch me. With or without your help."

Caught off-guard and peeved at the suggestion, I said, "I'd never tell anything. Certainly not to that man. He had me in an arm-lock, one of those locks. He bought me a Snickers bar."

That smallest of smiles tipped the corner of her mouth again, which I incorrectly interpreted at the time.

She was way ahead of me.

Several blocks north on Nicollet, she pulled to the curb in front of a restaurant that, from the looks of it, one might consider off-limits. The storefront window, coated black and etched with dancing gold martini glasses, was something out of a Dick Tracy comic book. Dine In or Take Out. I wondered what they served.

"Wait here," she said and exited the car.

Okay.

I turned in my seat and watched her walk away down Nicollet. Full-framed in tight jeans, she was thinner than I'd previously thought. At the same height, I had thirty pounds on her. She hadn't said where she was going and I couldn't see if she'd entered the NetSupermarket on the corner or ducked down Eighteenth. I sat back to wait.

A dozen people wrapped in colored robes and headscarves walked by on the sidewalk, their dark faces animated, laughing and talking their way down Nicollet. Some Latino type, hands in his pockets, stepped out of the shadows and swooped towards me. I flicked the lock. He moved like a swimmer, his arms scooping and arcing, all the way down the street and out of sight. Nor had Nicky Myer said how long she'd be gone. Two minutes? Two hours?

This whole situation, so uncomfortably vague, sweet Mary, what was I doing?

Across the street six teenage boys in their cargo jackets and oversized pants hunkered in the parking lot outside a Family Dollar Store. Two of them sat on the hood of an old Ford. Too young to be unsupervised at night, too cold for hanging out, they could very well be setting up to rob the place. They had enough cargo pockets between them to hide an arsenal of weapons. I wondered if after the robbery I could describe anything relevant to the police. I counted the boys: seven, not six, the kind of boys who grow up to drive cheap sports cars with tinted windows. One of them pushed at the car's fender with his big sneakered foot. The car wobbled. I was glad it wasn't my car they were messing with. The robbery might make the morning paper. Mesmerized, I let out a screech at the hard rap on my window. It was Nicky Myer.

"Geez." I unlocked and opened the door and peered up at her.

Hands in her pockets, she peered down at me. "You okay?"

"You scared the crap out of me." Seated low, I could see she was wearing those ankle-high, shiny rubber shoes that trendy gardeners wear.

"You drive," she said and handed me the keys.

I pulled myself up and out and walked around the front of the car with my eyes on the robbers at the Dollar Store and my hand on the cell phone in my pocket. A white van with an official looking logo (I could read the word RECREATION) on the side panel pulled into the parking lot and honked. A fat black woman exited the passenger door and slid the side panel wide open. My Dollar Store robbers loped to the van like a pack of puppies and piled in. A man carrying a paper cup exited the store and waved to the woman. One of the boys stuck his head out of the van and yelled something at the man. The man waved at him. The woman chortled and flapped her hand at the boy and slid the door shut and got back in the front seat. The man got into the Ford. The two vehicles disappeared down Nicollet.

"Bite me," I said.

We continued up Nicollet to Groveland and headed towards Loring Park. Nicky Myer informed me that she expected to find Bender and Fanny, but had no idea who else might be present and how things would fall out. I was to watch the apartment door. The door was glass, so I would have a clear view. When I saw her coming back down the hallway, I would be ready to drive.

"If it's Fanny by herself, do what she says."

"Where will you be?"

"Launching plan B."

Practiced as she was, I got a feel of something different. Fleeting as it was, I interpreted it as some hybrid form of fear. Then again, that might have been my sentiment, not hers. Nuances are better defined with time and familiarity, like married people or close siblings, people who have history together. I wondered how much time we had left, she and I, together. It crossed my mind at that moment that I might never see her again. I was at a loss to explain my sadness.

The one and only available space on Oak Grove was next to a No Parking sign. She said in her toneless voice, "Keep the engine running. There'll be no fumbling with the car keys." Delivered with a straight face. Did she know I was a fumbler?

I asked if we would be delivering Bentley Graas to Mr. Dean Ogren. She said, "We're past that." I took that as a positive. Halfway out of the car, she added, "That detective. You have his card?"

"Martin Micks? But I thought–"

"Ten minutes," she said. "Start counting." She slammed the door.

"He thinks I left town," I yelled after her.

Cars rolled by like dark tanks. A man and a woman in matching trench coats scampered across the street and disappeared into the dark for a night at the orchestra. Maybe not the orchestra. Not on Tuesday. If this were my story, it would be Saturday night with a drizzling rain, neon reflecting in the pooling water, swirls of street steam rising out of the grates. The couple would be holding hands.

But it wasn't my story. I was the get-away driver. I told myself that once we had the boy in the car, I would take a stand. What stand that would be, I didn't know. I drummed my fingers on the steering wheel.

To the left of the apartment building a sub-street neighborhood grocery no bigger than a one-car garage was open for business. A woman approached the store pushing a shopping cart piled high with … with what? She clearly lacked shopper posture. The cart was her home. How many hits did she take before she reached the street? She pulled a blanket from the bottom rack and arranged it over her cart before she entered the store. The cap A in the neon Native American Spirit sign flickered. I wondered how long till it flickered out. One hour? Ten years? Where do the homeless go in the winter? Maybe when I got home I'd put in an application at the hospital. Steady paycheck. Health insurance. No crime in that. The opportunity to marry for money had never presented itself. Where do they get those shopping carts? I ought to be pumping out resumes instead of romance novels.

"And here I sit," I said out loud, "in all possibility, involved in some crime. I am the dumbest person I know." I stared at my assigned focal point.

Six minutes to go. Calling the detective seemed more prudent than calling 911. But what if Laddie Ogren was in the apartment? My Saint didn't have a gun. There'd be no time for poisons and spiders. Hypothesizing the scenario agitated me. Screw the detective. I'd flat out call 911. The police would come, their sirens wailing. How would I explain what I was doing parked outside the scene of the crime?

What crime?

I ejected the CD that was in the tape deck. Expecting to find a Beatles label, I found a TDK disk instead. Somebody had compiled a music mix for her. Who? I held it to the streetlight. Except for a small smear along one edge, it was clean of fingerprints. Would there be DNA in that smear? Resisting the urge to slip it into my pocket, I wiped the smear off on my pants and slipped the disk back into the player. The glove box was empty.

Across the street a tall man in dark clothing trotted up the apartment steps, opened the door and disappeared down the hallway. A black sedan pulled in front of the building blocking my view. The driver looked straight at me. I pulled my hair forward all the while watching out the corner of my eye. No one got out of the car. No one got in. The car rolled forward. I imagined that my observations and reactions showed caution and astuteness and more than a little savvy. A patrol car trolled past. I stared after it.

Research. I would tell them I was doing research.

Three rainbow-haired punksters walked by the bag lady's shopping cart not giving it a second glance — already knowing she had nothing worth stealing? My eyes flicked back to the apartment door. That same tall man was coming back down the hallway towing a young boy. The boy scuttled along in a contrary posture, his parka hanging open. His knit hat was lopsided on his head covering one eye. The man shouldered the door open and bounded down the steps, pulling the kid with him. On the sidewalk the boy lurched away and darted back up the steps to the door. The man grabbed him by the jacket and scooped him up and carried him off down the street. Movement at the target apartment brought me back just in time to see Nicky Myer push open the glass door with both gloved hands. She was alone. Mr. Dean would not be happy. I glanced at the clock. Nine minutes had passed. She bounded to the sidewalk and was across the street and into the car in the amount of time it took me to sigh with relief. I reached for the headlights, but she put a hand up and said, "Duck your head till that car passes." She pulled her cap down and slid low in the seat. I ducked my head, but not before I caught the flash of deflected headlights.

"Who was that?"

"Don't know. But nobody drives that slow."

"I think they've been by a couple times."

She twisted around and watched the fading taillights, then slumped back into the seat.

Head still ducked, I brushed a loose lock behind my ear enabling me to watch her while we talked. "Where's Bender?"

She stayed slumped.

"What happened?"

"Hell had already come and gone."

"Hell? Where's Fanny?" One of twenty questions.

"Fanny's gone." She glared at the dashboard. For a moment I thought she might cry. She did no such thing. I couldn't imagine that happening. I don't know what I would have done. Hugged her? A pat on the shoulder? Everything will be fine in the morning? Obviously, she didn't have a delivery for Mr. Dean. Four hundred thousand dollars later. She'd have to return the money. I really didn't care. What I wanted to hear was that Fanny Graas and Bentley Ogren were on the bus to Marfa, Texas, or some such place, disguised as artists on the desert, never to be found by the likes of Laddie Ogren, who was on his way to Canada, defeated, but grateful to be dealing with third-world weapons' customers instead of pissing off My Saint.

"Fanny's gone?" I repeated. "Where?"

"If I knew that…" She exhaled a fierce breath, bent over, pulled a foot onto her knee and ripped a strip of duct tape from the sole of her rubber garden shoe. No one would be tracking those soles.

"What about the boy?"

She shook her head, then rolled her neck, stretching her shoulders.

Like questioning a freaking teenager. "Should we call that detective? Or the police?"

She glanced out at the street, then back at me. "And tell them what?"

"That a woman is missing. A child is missing." I dug in my pocket and pulled out my cell phone. "Let's call the detective. You told me to call him."

"That was if nobody came out. Well, I'm out." She ripped the duct tape off the other shoe and crumpled both pieces in her hand. "I fucking told her I'd handle it." Her fist tightened around the duct tape. "No one fucking listens." She shook her fist. "Nobody can follow the simplest goddamn instructions."

We were silent for a moment. I said, "So it didn't work out then? The kidnapping?"

She released a breath. "It didn't work out."

Thank you Jesus, I said to myself.

She reached over the back seat and pulled up a Target shopping bag. "I need you to do one more thing for me tonight."

Desperate to stay involved in an affair that appeared to be over, I said, "Sure, anything."

She pulled the handles apart and angled the shopping bag towards me. Inside was a briefcase, a very old briefcase with fat snap locks. "I need this delivered to a house in Edina between nine and ten o'clock tonight. Ring the doorbell. When you hear the speaker engage, identify yourself as Barbara. That's all you need to say. The door will open. An old man will be sitting in a wheelchair. Hand him the shopping bag. He'll hand you an envelope. Take it and leave."

"Barbara as in Barbara Dios, Patron Saint of Architects? Is Mr. Dean's money in that briefcase?"

"It's empty."

"Empty. This isn't risky business?"

"I'm afraid not."

She gave me directions to the house. "It's a Tudor surrounded by those evergreen trees that look like a plumber's brush.

"What should I do with the envelope?"

"Take it and go."

She removed her gloves and pulled a plastic vial from her pocket, unscrewed one end, leaned over, popped out a contact lens, eased it into the bowl and capped the vial, turned the vial and did the same with the second lens. She stuffed the vial into her pocket, pulled on her gloves and adjusted her hat. "Let's find you a cab at one of the hotels over by the convention center. I got a train to catch."

"A train? A train to where?"

"It's a figure of speech."

I switched on the headlights, engaged the transmission, and headed into downtown. She shut her eyes and dropped into a meditative focus that felt dark and enraged. Nicky Myer was sinister. Angela Folly was shifty. Both of them so unlike southern Clare Assett and cheery Brigid Ireland. Then there was sober Toni Padua and professional Alex Edessa. Not to forget quirky Louise Marille. I understood why the police couldn't see this woman. How do you chase a notion? How had Mr. Detective figured it out?

I said, "That detective? You know him, don't you? You recognized him Saturday night at Stonehenge."

Her eyes remained closed as she talked. "He locked on Barbara Dios one night, years ago. He was poking around for some risky information and snagged her over on Lake Street, dragged her into some cop-infested diner, and bought her a cup of coffee. Barbara pulled a switcheroo in the loo and was out and down the street before the coffee cooled. He was young then."

I smiled, smug. The detective had been duped.

I was driving suspiciously slow because I needed to pay attention. But the real reason for my lack of scurry was that I had a gnawing feeling that there really was a train, and it was leaving the station.

"I saw a man come out of the apartment tonight. He could have been your Sammy guy. He was carrying a child, a boy, I think, who acted very upset."

"The place is full of families. It smelled like gravy. Did you ever eat gravy bread?"

I made a face. "I don't think so."

"Poor people's supper."

She had steered the conversation away from Fanny and the boy. Not to be rerouted, I said, "The boy wore a parka like the sentry boy at the hotel."

"It's parka weather."

"If you hadn't come out when you did, I would have called 911. For all I knew, Laddie Ogren could have been in there."

"Laddie Ogren had already come and gone."

"How do you know?"

"He marks his territory."

"What if he'd been there when you—"

"He'd have killed me." She straightened in the seat and punched the radio on. "Suzie Q" swarmed out of the speaker, six notes replicate. Songs like that aren't hatched in sunlight and fresh air. She turned up the volume. End of questions.

I turned off LaSalle onto Eleventh and spotted the string of cabs that were minding the Holiday Inn. I pulled in front of a fire hydrant. I was getting the hang of city parking.

We got out. Before she took the driver's seat, she reached over and stuffed a handful of bills into my coat pocket. I pulled out six folded-up twenty-dollar bills.

"That's way too much," I protested.

"We don't know that now, do we?" She slid into the car and shut the door.

"Wait. Where are you going?" I enunciated the words so she would hear me through the glass and over "Suzie Q," which she'd tweaked even louder.

She lowered the window halfway and peered up at me from under the brim of her hat. I stared, speechless, at eyes the color of polished steel, like something dreamed up. I'd seen eyes that color one time in my life about ten years ago in a pizza parlor in St. Cloud. I'd been sitting twenty feet from the man. Twenty feet away I could see his eyes, eyes like a snow dog. You don't forget eyes like that. Take your breath away.

She reached over and lowered the volume. "Suzie Q" faded.

She looked up at me again and said, almost cheerful, "I got some business over in St. Paul." Her dark mood had vanished.

"I could help."

"I need you to deliver that briefcase." Her silver eyes flicked to the shopping bag in my hand. "There's nothing about it, nothing to be afraid of."

What I was afraid of was that she was leaving me. Stalling badly, I said, "When did you stop being afraid of things?"

"I'm afraid of everything."

"No you're not." I chuckled. "Are you on your way to find Fanny?"

"No," she said unequivocally.

This conversation was going nowhere. We were at the peak of the story: sinister Nicky Myer was hunting Fanny and Bender, and I'd been rerouted to a Tudor house surrounded by toilet brush trees.

I anchored the shopping bag under my arm and said, "So what time tomorrow?"

"Not tomorrow."

"We need to work out some—"

"It's fiction."

"I can't—"

"Yes, you can," she said. "You can write anything. That's what writers do. You are a writer, aren't you?"

I put my forearm to my forehead and imitated Clare Assett's southern drawl, "I'm a romance writer in a Charlie Dickens daydream!"

She laughed revealing slightly uneven, baking soda-white teeth. Her laugh had a surprisingly merry resonance, unlike anything I'd heard before. Even the tone of her voice had lightened. This was not Nicky Myer. This was unrehearsed. My Saint was speaking as herself, whoever that was.

Under the streetlight her cheeks were not sunken, but lean with a natural concave curve. No caps, crowns or impactions to change the shape. When she'd picked me up at the canoes, she'd been chewing gum. These slightly uneven baking soda teeth were her real teeth. That's why I'd never seen her eat. Chewing food would have been more trouble than it was worth. Why hadn't I recognized that? Because the breadth of her resolve, her expertise, and her on-going enterprise was beyond anything and everything that I understood.

"I need to know you," I said.

"Consider me the thumbtack in your bonbons."

Not sure what that meant, I said, "Ouch?"

Her silver eyes twinkled. I felt like I was seeing someone I'd never met, but been in correspondence with, like an internet friend. I ached for the link, to split an order of fries, drink coffee — never mind the story, just chat like two friends: Jennifer Allison Sands and … and the girl from the Triangle Bar before Pineapple Daiquiri walked in pale-shady with his epic reinvention saga. We would talk about things, she and I, girlfriend-things, and places we've been and places we'd go. Go together. I'd suggest Miami for the holidays, Christmas Eve at the harness races, Christmas day in Coconut Grove. No Christmas trees. No spiced cider. We'd drink iced rum on the beach. She and I.

I needed her to be my treacherous friend, but I didn't know how to ask that of her. The thought that something might happen to her and that I wouldn't be there, and that I might never see her again, these desperate thoughts flooded my brain: issues I couldn't unload without sounding like somebody's whiny girlfriend.

What I said instead was, "Those are your real eyes, aren't they?"

I commissioned the first cab in line leaving me seventy-five dollars in change. Oh, happy day. I slid into the backseat with my contraband, and we zoomed along the vacant streets while I peered out the window as if somebody was following me. I had no idea who would follow me. If Detective Micks had been lurking around, he'd be following her, not me.

Regardless of how things turned out, I vowed to write her story. I believed she liked and approved of my being a romance writer. A romance writer wouldn't cut such a hard edge. A romance writer could shape a black night into a creamy day in ten words or less. Creamy crime.

At Hennepin and Lake I could no longer stand it. I reached in and pulled out the briefcase. Deep enough to carry two laptops, scabbed and scarred, this leather case had seen tough times. No dial-a-combination or fancy sensor points or tap-a-key from across the room kind of locks. I would need a screwdriver to open the two tarnished snap-down locks. Or the key.

If it was empty, why was it locked?

Because it locked automatically.

Something out of nothing.

I paced my room, peeking through the drapes at the parking lot, at the neighboring rooms, at the traffic, searching for obstacles. At exactly nine o'clock I opened my door and stepped out onto the walkway. All eight cars looked settled in for the night and clean of mischief. Hoping to neuter what surely mimicked the forced nonchalance of Sylvester the Cat, I straightened my shoulders and hummed a junk medley on my way down the stairs and across the parking lot. I unlocked the door, piled in with my shopping bag, and hit the master lock. My strung out behavior had more to do with addled wits than with any speculative fear. I turned the key. The snarl of my engine startled me and I stomped on the brakes without having moved an inch. Several deep breaths later, I successfully exited the parking lot onto Excelsior Boulevard. If someone had been shadowing me, they'd have said into their walky-talky: 'Follow the pigeon.' I was that bad.

Headed towards Lake Calhoun, I turned right at France Avenue and drove to Sunnyside where I took another right winding back into luxury Edina. On my target street, I crept along until I saw the tapered evergreens she'd described. The street was empty except for two vehicles: a Volvo station wagon and a white utility van. The utility van looked out of place. I stayed in my car and watched, then finally admitted that the house behind the evergreen trees was disagreeably dark and I was stalling. Nothing about the place suggested that a visitor was expected. I retied my hair and took a deep breath, grabbed the shopping bag, got out of the car and cantered along the brick sidewalk and up the steps to a great wooden door that was as tall as a goal post. The only available light filtered through the trees from the streetlamps. I double-checked the street number before ringing the bell. The intercom engaged, but nobody spoke. I leaned towards the speaker box and said, "Barbara." Locks disengaged, click-clack-click. The door opened into a dark foyer. It took me a second to realize the old man in the wheelchair. The riddled streetlight distorted his unsmiling face. A blanket covered his lap. His Mukluks rested on the metal foot flaps. I stepped over the threshold and handed him the shopping bag. He handed me an envelope that'd been lying on his lap. I barely had hold of it when his wheelchair rolled back into the unbounded black space behind him and the great wood door began to close. I jumped back over the threshold, shoved out like street debris. Someone had been standing behind the door. The locks engaged, click-clack-click. I hadn't expected tea, but that was flat-out rude. I ran to my car and jumped in.

The Volvo station wagon and the white van hadn't gone anywhere. But whoa! Something moved in the van. There was someone in the driver's seat. I hit the locks and started the engine. Eyes on the van, determined to unmask the villain, I drove towards it only to find the front seat empty. Two seconds from knocking off the van's rear fender, I yanked the steering wheel like a drunk and almost hit the Volvo station wagon. I slammed on the brakes. Get a hold of yourself! If you stare hard enough at things in the dark, they move. I fled the neighborhood. My first full stop was at the red light on Excelsior Boulevard. I felt breathless. The envelope lay on the passenger seat like a party invite. I picked it up, opened the flap, and pulled out a wedge of bills. A horn honked and the money went flying. The white van behind me flashed its lights. I shrieked. What did he want? The van closed in on my bumper. In which direction was the nearest police station? He honked again. Crap. I was stopped at a green light. I cranked out a left turn and raced away down Excelsior Boulevard. In my rearview mirror, a double-cab, white pick-up truck turned right and disappeared over the hill towards Lake Calhoun. He'd probably given me the finger. And rightfully so.

I wasn't good at this.

Safely parked in the motel parking lot, I gathered fifty one-hundred dollar bills off the floor of my car. I counted them twice. Whose money was this?

I started at the sound of rain on the car roof, and it wasn't the good rain I liked to write about in those artsy neon streetscapes with steam swirls and svelte city people in Burberrys. I leaned back in the seat and considered that, with a little less drama, I could be a reliable accomplice.

I peered inside the envelope again, then sealed the flap and shoved it under the seat and stepped out into the rain, locked the door and walked to the curb where I stood and surveyed Excelsior Boulevard. Cars glided along like speedboats, rain sprouting up under their wheels, their windows opaque with rippling water. Across the street each dark store window promised the red glow of a cigarette, the reflection of eyeglasses. I wasn't dumb enough to think I would actually spot Martin Micks or My Saint, but just in case either one of them was out there, I wanted them to know that I wasn't the prairie-girl-come-to-city they both thought I was, each in their own self-serving way. One pale, vague face in a passing car stared at me, the crazy goon out minding the rain without an umbrella. I abandoned my drama.

Head propped on the pillows clasping the envelope of money to my chest, I thought about the antique briefcase and the old mute in the wheelchair. I was fairly certain this transaction had nothing to do with the kidnapping. This was a different contract. I had collected My Saint's paycheck. What kind of job is worth five thousand dollars?

I imagined a scarlet A on my forehead. A for Accomplice. Having no idea what I'd just accomplished, A for Airhead was more like it.

Questions piled up like dirty socks. Two questions dogged me: where was Bentley Ogren? And where was Fanny Graas? Neither of them had shown up for the kidnapping. And My Saint had set me off in a different direction.

I pointed my finger at the lampshade and shut my right eye. Then my left eye. Right, then left again. The lampshade was too close to see a difference. The painting at Lords of the cream-colored classic car circa 1950 had been forty feet across the room. The omelet-colored Plymouth.

Focused without sights, me.

13. Gone Missing
THURSDAY

My Saint was missing. Anything could have happened. Tuesday night as Nicky Myer could have ended badly. How would I know? She hadn't given me her current, pay-as-you-go number. Or any number.

I hung around the motel, edgy and inconsolable, like on the last day of a vacation — done with the fun, but too early to pack up the car. Maybe I should stop fretting and thank my lucky stars I wasn't in jail. I checked my cell phone again. Nothing, not even a telemarketer. On the jumbo TV a perky girl was demonstrating how to cook a meal in thirty minutes. It took me that long to prep the parsley. I punched mute and zipped open my Lancôme bag.

Brigid#2, Clare#1, Toni#1. If not for the tapes, the last few days might have been about too many soylent cocktails in the castle bar, and any minute now, I'd wake up in my four-star hotel room just in time for the Welcome Romance Writers kick-off cocktail party. Angie#3, Clare#2. At the end of Genny's story, Angie had named the street where Genny had met Mr. Dean. I'd been watching her face. Her eyes had flicked to mine, then away. She'd resumed talking as if nothing had been given up. I considered the fact that I hadn't taped Louise Marille or Nicky Myer. True, I had not formally interviewed them; and I'd lacked the presence of mind to have the tape recorder rolling in my pocket. Nor had I thought to photograph her. My misplaced attachment to the protagonist did not a good witness make.

There. Genny#2. FAST FORWARD. PLAY. *Genny latches the bag and stands up from the table.* FAST FORWARD. PLAY. *Wind chimes ... like tangled-up glass...* FAST FORWARD. PLAY. Smiling at her take on the Eukanuba show handler, I registered her description of the cars on the street: *...a van for a locksmith ... a white Infinity behind it, a black SUV with tinted windows.*

"Give me the street."
Genny is miles from Colfax before she starts to breathe.
Colfax.

I shimmied my newfound bankroll to the bottom of my bag, checked for my key card (front pocket), and stepped out into fog so thick I squinted, as if that might help.

Three cars remained in the parking lot: one down on a flat tire, the other two without chicanery. I looked hard. Paranoia had become my anima. My Saint had an uncanny way of knowing my whereabouts. And this detective guy thinks I will lead him to her. His spying on me made sense, but My Saint had no reason to tail me. It wouldn't matter what I said to the police, the priest, or Bartender Bob. She could disappear free and clear, high and dry.

Which appeared to be exactly what she'd done.

The first order of business was gasoline. I turned right and headed towards Hopkins. Before I could say, "I feel like a latte," my left rear tire thumped, followed by a clumping sound that could be either a cluster of jellyfish or a flat tire. Visually challenged by the fog, I almost missed the real live service station with three bays, one of them empty. I wobbled to the empty slot.

I'd never paid attention to rubber, much less changed a tire, but even I could see my tire was beyond repair. The spare, one of those undersized imposters, might get me as far as Anoka. Would my leftover cab fare buy a re-tread?

It got worse. The friendly service man gave me a tour of my tires. Pointing out the severe lack of tread on the remaining three along with the white sprouting threads, he informed me that he wouldn't drive across the street on them. I could not argue the evidence.

When you're low on luck, bad luck follows like mean bees.

The friendly service man could set me up and have me on the road in an hour for $560. Charge card maxed, I could write a bad check. Actually, it wouldn't be all that bad. I could beat the check to the bank and transfer my last dime out of savings. Writing bad checks that you intend to cover wasn't criminal. Not when you had a flat tire. I'd plead with the banker for a mini-loan to cover the remaining balance.

"What's the cash price?"

He knocked off sixty bucks. I hesitated long enough for him to add, "Includes the tax."

Did dipping into the crime funds make me an accessory to something?

I had no choice.

New tires, a full tank of gas, C-notes galore — I celebrated with a large, double-cappuccino-mocha Caribou latte. I cruised up Highway 100 and caught Wayzata Boulevard heading downtown. My plan was to jump off on Hennepin, which would take me to Colfax. I scanned the radio stations in search of sexy lounge music, but Thursday was soprano-girl-music morning up and down the dial. High on mocha foam, I lost myself with Natalie Imbruglia and missed Hennepin and ended up across the river on the University of Minnesota campus. Crap. One-ways, no-ways, all-ways, I dead-ended at a dumpster. While I waited for a break in student traffic, I considered risking LoJack to hunt down the admissions office and verify that My Saint had attended this university. The detective could find out with a phone call. No, he couldn't. Nor could I. Neither of us knew her name. I kept forgetting that. Patience expired, I beeped the horn like a dump truck, backed into the street, and no one died.

I used the Minneapolis skyline, as seen between roiling clouds across the Mississippi, as my marker. Irresistibly close. As a writer of True Crime, I would take a literary look at that rare and antique bookstore, in all possibility, still wrapped in crime tape. The street sign at the corner read Hennepin Avenue. My luck was turning. I crossed the river and set myself up to follow the route Kerby had driven when he'd circled the block five times in his black, right-off-the-rack, ES-300 Lexus, but there was no turning left on Seventh. It was a one-way coming at me. That's not how she'd told the story. Was that an insignificant detail? To some fiction readers, insignificant details were more important than the plot. Pick you to death. Authors were writing disclaimers instead of prologues.

I turned left on Eighth Street. Not only was I traveling in a direction contrary to her story, there was no tobacco shop, coffee shop, or rare and antique bookstore. Flummoxed. Crap, it could have been a grocery store on University Avenue with Sammy and his long fingers picking green beans instead of books.

Maybe I'd keep the money and buy one of those satellite trackers for the dashboard. "Turn right. Abort. Turn left. Abort. Go home." I stayed on Eighth Street, which would take me to the freeway where things made sense.

I had to admit, in spite of the lack of landmarks, material confirmation and hard evidence of any crime having been committed, I'd spent the most interesting five days of my life. I'd dipped into drama that people like me never see. I'd pilfered a warehouse with Louise Marille in her whirly Stevie Nicks coat. I'd been arm-locked in a motel snack room by a detective named Martin Micks, interrogated and given a Snickers bar. I'd driven the get-away car in an attempted kidnapping. I'd delivered a briefcase to a specter in a wheelchair and collected five thousand dollars. I was a drunk just getting started after all the guests had gone home.

I flicked my turn signal to move into the freeway lane, but my fellow roadmeisters were having none of that. Wasn't there a law against tailgating? Same law for jaywalking, I figured, almost nicking a kid who'd darted between the cars. Forced to follow a sign that read Local Streets, I ended up back in the streets and the avenues of outer downtown and dead-ended into Washington Avenue. If the avenues ran parallel with Hennepin Avenue, this would logically be Washington Street.

Get me to the freeway where things made sense.

I turned towards the Metrodome heading into the Metro Hospital zone. The street ended. A car honked. I turned left. Within two blocks that street ended. Left? Right? Honk. But it wasn't my muddled compass that had me stopped. It was the yellow crime tape across the street, yellow like mustard in the fog. Used and Antique Books. To the left was a locksmith shop; to the right, separated by a narrow alleyway, was a drycleaners. The car behind me delivered one last angry blast (to show me what for), pulled around me and roared off.

An inquiry would take less than a dime's worth of meter minutes. Not up for a parallel park, I circled the block and glided into the empty end-space and walked the short half-block to the evidence.

I cupped my hands and peered into the bookstore. The tables with their pedestal signs were exactly as she'd described. GARDENING, GEOGRAPHY, HEALTH. On the wall next to the cashier's counter, a John Sandford poster hung on by one tack. I turned when the door to the locksmith shop banged open, propped with a high top sneaker by a boy in baggy pants and a red flannel shirt as he swept a tide of dried leaves and gum wrappers onto the sidewalk. Littering, another one of those tailgate-jaywalker crimes.

"They're closed for good," he said, focused on his broom.

"What's with the yellow tape?"

The boy stopped sweeping and looked up. The boy was not a boy. He was a weedy, middle-aged man with a puff of black hair. He pointed his broom at the bookstore. "Someone killed the clerk. Broad daylight."

"No. When was that?"

"Tuesday week."

"Tuesday," I repeated. The day My Saint found Sammy in the bookstore.

The little man let his door slam shut and joined me at the window wearing a self-appointed authority on his narrow, furrowed face.

"Did they catch who did it?"

"No, but it sure fanned the smoke around here." We talked to each other's reflections. Up close I could see his puff was a hairpiece.

"Who was he? The bookstore clerk."

"Don't know. Poor sap. Been in the states less than six months."

"From where?" I expected the little man to tell me Germany.

"One of those corrupt half acres in Africa."

"Africa?"

"African-American, yep. My Crohn's flared up so I missed the whole show." He gestured towards the drycleaners. "Those guys had their machines going. Nobody heard nothin'. But the cops still come around. In and out. Over and over with the same darn questions. Like there'd be a different answer the next time. Feds came, too. They don't say much though. It only flows in one direction with those folks. Still don't change the fact no one heard nothin'."

"I guess there wouldn't have been much to hear, the man being strangled and all."

"Strangled," he said, his lips twisted into a pondering pucker.

Strangled. Should I have known that? I inched closer to the window, squinting harder into the bookstore and said, "I read that in the paper."

"I didn't read that." He looked away across the street, his eyes searching the apartments. Or maybe the parked cars.

"Or was it stabbed? No, that was something else. There's so much crime anymore, I can't keep my weapons straight. Ha!" I shook my head at what must be the magnitude of crime, then added in a perky voice, "I'm a bookstore aficionado. These places are magnets. I was on my way home." *Be gone. Pronto.*

"Name's Hank," he said, extending his hand.

I pretended not to see his hand, which looked more like a claw. I blabbered on, desperately perky. "This was a decent bookstore. I hope it opens again. The independents are having a hard time, you know."

"Your name is?"

"Rhoda," I blurted. "My parents named me after a plant. You know, Rhododendron? My mother's a gardener. My sister's name is Daisy." *Shut up.*

"Why don't you come on in here and warm up," he said with sudden cheer. He motioned towards the locksmith shop. "I'll pour you a coffee. Made it fresh."

"Thanks, but I don't drink coffee after ten." I glanced at my watch. "Anyway, I've got to get back to work."

"You said you were on your way home."

"I work at home." *Shut up for real.* "Ciao." I waved and fast-walked in the direction of my car.

Strangled. How'd My Saint know that? Damn her all to hell. I stole a glance back at the bookstore. The locksmith in his red shirt and baggy pants was on his cell phone. He walked after me with a craning posture — to see which car I got into? I anchored my purse under my arm and fast-walked past my car and turned the corner out of sight. I felt clear-headed, invigorated — thank you Caribou Coffee. I jogged across the street and took the next corner, noting landmarks so I could find my way back. Gold Jewelry. Loans. Guitars. The sound of sirens set me running. The little bastard had called the cops. The next street looked like apartment row, except for one sub-level retail sign, Preloved. I almost fell down the steps. I slung open the door and jumped inside. Three seconds later an ambulance roared by.

Not guilty!

Even better, Preloved was a thrift shop.

Small and smelling like rotting drywall, the store held everything a criminal on the run could possibly want. I found a pilled-up, black sweater poncho with hanger-shoulders. It covered my coat. An extra five bucks got me a burgundy scarf. Throw in a tan stocking hat. I should have worn my blonde wig. *My* blonde wig. While waiting for the cashier to write my ticket, I pulled an aluminum cane out of a barrel full of umbrellas and added it to the pile. I inquired about sunglasses. Not this time of year, she said. I stuffed my hair up under the hat and triple-wrapped the scarf around my neck.

Back out on the street, the cane tucked under my arm, I asked myself for the twentieth time what was I doing? None of this involved me. It might not even be the right bookstore. And the guy in the red shirt, strange little man on anybody's meter, had been talking to his mother on his cell phone. Had the bookstore clerk actually been strangled? The locksmith hadn't confirmed that. I'd jumped to a conclusion.

"Abort. Go home," I said to my camouflaged reflection in a Gold/Loans window. I looked ridiculous. My car would be around the next corner. Lucky me, I hadn't parked in front of the bookstore. I rounded the corner twirling my cane like a baton, but rammed it to the sidewalk at the sight of the locksmith outside the bookstore talking to two men in overcoats. The locksmith kept talking, but focused on me. I leaned into my cane with my head bent as if concentrating on my feet and limped to the car, opened the door, and maneuvered myself in like people with canes must do. I dropped the car keys in my lap, picked them up and fumbled them to the floor. *There'll be no proverbial fumbling with the car keys during the get-away.* I'm a fumbler. Key in the ignition, engine full-rich, I accelerated from the curb without so much as a glance in my rearview mirror and near broad-sided a white sedan. Whoa! I weaseled back to the curb. When traffic cleared, I eased out and for a harebrained second contemplated a U-turn. Not up to the challenge, I sped as fast as I could past the locksmith shop. Little man bobbed between the parked cars craning for a look at me. I took the first right turn and saw him skate into the street, but too late to see my license tag. I breathed. It felt good.

Left on Fifteenth would take me past Loring Park where I'd catch Hennepin south to Colfax. Where I would have been a long time ago if not for that business with the flat tire. I passed Convention Hall and crossed both Nicollet and LaSalle before I realized I was on Tuesday night's kidnapping terrain. Jittery, teeth-grinding vagaries from too much caffeine trumped any rational thoughts I might have had. I concluded that it would be foolish not to take a daylight peek at the crime scene. Alleged crime scene. I was here, wasn't I? Dave's Nirvana *Nevermind* CD was still in my glove box. Shifty music played in minor chords brought out the reckless in me. I slipped it into the slot.

For a residential neighborhood, the street was unduly crammed with traffic. Probably detoured from construction somewhere, construction everywhere. No parking, and bumper-to-bumper cars glued to the curb. I pulled into the same no-parking zone where I'd waited Tuesday night with the same clear view of the apartment building, which, in the daylight, turned out to be a favorable, two-story graystone.

The neon A in the Native American Spirit sign in the window of the grocer still flickered. I liked the turquoise awning, under which a faded hero sandwich poster reminded me that, except for two packages of peanut butter crackers at the tire trough, I hadn't eaten. Coffee killed my appetite. You'd think I'd drop a pound or two. I got out of my car and locked the door. While I waited for a break in traffic, a woman in a camel-colored coat exited the apartment building two doors down from the grocer. She wore hide-your-face sunglasses and a colorful, print scarf knotted under her chin in the style of a Russian peasant woman. The scarf looked remarkably like the scarf My Saint had tied around my neck when I was Rose White, Louise Marille's assistant at Heather's warehouse. The woman walked with Alex Edessa's long, fashionable stride. There was something about her.

The dense, moving traffic trapped me on the curb, but my banshee kicked in and I yelled, "Clare!" The woman kept walking, heading towards Nicollet. Louder. "Clare!"

Cataloged by patronage, these glorious martyrs are my identities. It's how I've kept my business organized. It's how I know in any given situation, at any given moment, and without hesitation, who's addressing me.

"Clare Assett!" I could be Fanny Graas calling her name. But the woman didn't turn around. Had she spotted me? "Brigid! Toni! Wait! Angie!" A man exiting the graystone stopped and looked in my direction, probably wondering who was playing the name game, as did the UPS driver in the parking lot. Twenty yards down the sidewalk a collegiate man, key in his car door, craned his head. Everyone heard me. Everyone but the woman behind the hide-your-face glasses.

Who else but Jennifer Allison Sands could say that roster? Stymied by the crawling cars, unable to cross, I trotted along keeping her in sight. At Thirteenth, a transport bus lurched to a stop blocking me. Before I could skirt the bus, the doors folded open and a man bounded to the sidewalk almost knocking me down. Tall, thin, wearing a navy blue pea coat, he muttered something that sounded like 'freaking' and strode away, maneuvering through the crawling cars to cross the street. He slapped the trunk of a black sedan. A car honked. Sammy? Sammy with all the answers? The bus moved off. The woman in the camel-colored coat had vanished. Damn it to hell. I focused on the disappearing pea coat.

"Hey, Sammy!" I yelled. He kept walking. Everybody in denial. Aggressive with the cars this time, I skipped between them and crossed the street. I caught up with the man and grabbed his sleeve. He stopped.

"Sammy?"

Large, dark-framed glasses magnified a pair of eyes the color of blueberries. He stared down at me, then said, "I'm not who you think I am."

I opened my mouth to explain who I was, but he yanked his arm away and skipped up the steps to the same apartment building the woman in the camel coat had exited. "Wait! Please. Just tell me if you know–" I couldn't think what to call her.

He shoved his key in the lock.

"Do you know ... ahmm, a woman? From your high school. Tuesday you helped her with a boy named Bender, Bentley Graas. Do you know Fanny?"

He turned his key and opened the door.

"She came out of this building a minute ago. I don't know her name. She changes it all the time."

He stepped inside and pushed the door shut in my face.

"You can't drop out forever!" I don't know why I said that.

A man was approaching the building, patting his raincoat. I dug in my pockets as if I, too, were hunting keys. He patted a few more pockets before finding his key. I mumbled nonsense about lost keys and followed him into a lobby that was in serious need of rehab with its cracking linoleum and dark, sticky wood. It smelled like old men. Sammy was nowhere in sight. Behind a metal desk at the far end of the room, a bald man with a Sgt. Pepper moustache sat listening to a man wearing a leather jacket and blue jeans. The leather jacket guy ran his hand through his hair. Even with his back to me, I could see that he'd brushed a sheaf of it out of his eyes.

Martin Micks. My Saint had walked right past him. That explained her behavior. Sgt. Pepper behind the desk picked up a snapshot and nodded. I needed to get gone. Try explaining my presence here. I pushed out through the doors and headed back to my car.

The detective who'd arm-locked me in the snack room was standing in the lobby of the apartment building into which the man who could be Sammy had disappeared, the same apartment building where the woman who might be My Saint had exited. Heck, if I hung around long enough I might catch sight of Fanny and Bentley Ogren. A delivery truck honked and I scooted out of the no-parking zone. I searched the streets of Loring Park, car horns up my butt again, but saw no sign of the woman in the camel-colored coat.

...

Houses in south Minneapolis evoked a well-heeled posture with their corniced gables and ornamental turrets and cut-glass windows, their wide front porches as large as the mini front yards that served as playpens, flower patches, and community centers. The old Nordics had built this neighborhood back when it was bad manners to show your business to the neighbors. If they could see it now. I inched along counting front steps. Three to five was the going number, not seven.

I was also hunting for a white Infinity, a black SUV, and a van with a locksmith logo. I stopped in front of a FOR SALE sign. The front porch was only two steps deep. And toys, and a stocked china cabinet visible through the window.

I was running out of Colfax.

Why did I think the vacant house was on Colfax? Because she'd said so? Silly me. I decided to quash this foolishness and almost missed the FOR SALE sign in the empty yard in front of the white two-story with the dark windows. Two SUVs were parked across the street. Although SUVs in these neighborhoods were as common as canoes in the Boundary Waters, one of them was black. And wait ... was that a white Infinity up ahead?

I trolled past the house. It lacked three steps. Pesky detail. But the combination of the FOR SALE sign, the black SUV, and the white Infinity pulled me to the curb. D.O. Realty. Dean Ogren? I punched in the phone number. A live person answered. I told the lady I was interested in a property on Colfax. Could she tell me who owned the house? A retired couple who'd moved to Arizona. It was a wonderful four bedroom, three baths with a finished basement, a great family home. Did I have children? I told her two boys. She told me, "perfect." I'd love the schools. I asked what the D and the O stood for in D.O. Realty. She told me Distinctly Outstanding. No, she had not heard of Dean Ogren.

With mom and pop in Arizona, a quick snoop wouldn't hurt. I climbed the four steps, five if you counted the porch floor. The two steps mid-sidewalk made seven. Was I making something out of nothing again? Nothing was all I had. The porch floor creaked like old wood. I felt like a trespasser on a ghost ship. But with the realtor sign in the front yard, trespassing was expected. At the top of the steps, I faced the street as Genny Ross might have done. I listened hard for wind chimes, but the wind was still, an anomaly in Minnesota. Traffic noise on Hennepin free-sailed through the bare branches. No wind chimes. A door slammed across the street. A girl and her golden retriever raced down the sidewalk, the dog in charge. None of the dogs My Saint had described were on the move. If I hung around until five I might catch the Eukanuba show handler. I turned back to the window and cupped both hands to the glass for a peek. The room was empty. No desk, no cardboard runner on the floor. A lot could change in a week. A wrecking crew could have demolished the house. Mr. Dean could have been nipped by a spider.

On my way down the steps, I noticed that the gate to the back yard was open. What the heck. I followed the stepping stones along the flower bed next to the house. Winter-bare rose bushes and peony bushes alternated with unfamiliar Zone Four perennials. Light from a basement window glowed behind a clipped rose bush. I stepped into the flowerbed and peeked between the thorny branches. Except for a cardboard barrel by the stairwell, the room was empty. I continued along the path, eyes stuck on the windows, which is how I ran into the man with the shovel.

I screamed and stumbled over my own feet. He dropped the shovel and grabbed me by my poncho. I swung at him with both fists, my blows bouncing off his padded jacket. I landed a good one on his jaw. He released me with a shove to the ground.

"Are you crazy?" he said, rubbing his jaw with a camel colored work glove. He was big. Baggy overalls and a down jacket added to his bulk. He wore an Elmer Fudd hat with the earflaps down.

The man was too old to boast a chapter in Ann Rule's book of killers. Because of my knee-jerk reaction, I hadn't realized he'd been trying to keep me from falling. Even so, I kept my eyes on him as I scooted back and up off the ground.

I pulled a clump of wet leaves from my thrift store poncho. "What are you doing here?"

"I saw you peeking around and was about to ask you the same question."

"There's a sign out front. For Sale?"

He nodded. "That's what I suspected, though I wasn't expecting violence."

"Well, you scared the crap out of me."

"And I apologize for that."

"Well, I apologize, too." I touched my head, indicating a moment of hysteria. "I'm not this jumpy. Sorry for the violence. You're ... well, you're a big man."

"I'd a done the same thing if I were you, I reckon." He motioned towards the house. "You looking to buy?"

"I love this neighborhood."

"Been on the market since March."

"It's been empty all that time?"

"'fraid so." He picked up his shovel.

"No one's leased it recently? For a month or a week or anything?"

He looked at me as if wondering why I would ask such a senseless question. "Not that I heard."

"Do you know Dean Ogren?"

He cocked his head, thinking. "Doesn't sound familiar, but that don't mean anything." He tapped his head implying senior moments. "What does this Ogren fellow do?"

"I thought he was the agent."

"Could be for all I know," he said. "I work for a landscape company."

"I don't suppose you saw anybody here inside the house last week? Like when you were landscaping?"

"You looking for somebody?"

"Sorta, but not here, I guess." I wiped the debris from my hands onto my poncho. "Thanks. I'll be on my way."

"You take it easy now." He turned and headed towards the garage.

I called after him. "Sorry I hit you." I didn't think he'd heard me, but seconds later, like a delayed reaction, he held up a gloved hand in acknowledgement, and disappeared around the garage.

On the drive back to the motel, I rehashed the day's events. The bookstore didn't make sense. Was it something else entirely? Nothing else entirely? And the woman in the hide-your-face sunglasses. What about her had made me think she was My Saint? Clare's camel-colored coat? The familiar scarf? Wouldn't hold up in court. What dogged me more than the coat and scarf was the woman's lack of interest when I was shouting roll call. Everyone in the neighborhood exhibited the curiosity gene, including people in passing cars. Or maybe she was somebody simply tired of crazy people, a New Yorker. And maybe the tall, thin man who'd run into me at the bus stop was Sammy's twin brother.

I'm not who you think I am.

Why would he say that to me? Because it's what he said to everybody. And that bruiser detective again. Flashing pictures. Determined, that one.

I'd learned nothing at Colfax. Houses with porches littered the city. The giant gardener had been a nice old man, although he'd scared the crap out of me, what with the shovel and all. Pretty Midwest girls.

It wasn't until I'd passed Lake Calhoun, that I realized the gardener. He'd dropped the shovel and grabbed me with his right hand. He'd released me, then bent over and picked up the shovel with his right hand. His left hand had never left his pocket.

Mr. Dean *crosses his arms, elbows extended, a confident, aggressive pose, nicely done, considering he had a stroke a couple years back that left him with a drooping left side.*

When the yardman walked away, I'd yelled my apology. I'd assumed at first that he hadn't heard me, but it wasn't that at all. He'd transferred the shovel from his right hand into the crook of his left arm, which enabled a right-handed wave.

Mr. Dean dresses like a yardman.

I ripped into the Whole Food's parking lot and slammed on my brakes, flipped open my cell phone and redialed D.O. Realty. The office was closed for the day. I headed back to Colfax.

I half-expected a padlocked gate, but it hung open as I'd left it. I followed the stepping-stones and cut across the backyard to the garage, which was locked. I peeked in the window. No landscaping shovels or rakes, no lawn mower. Empty. So what had Mr. Dean been doing with a shovel? I walked the yard but could find nothing suspicious, as in mounds of fresh dirt or wet leaves, nothing newly buried.

Cripes. The man could be a real gardener hired by the owners, watching me this very minute with his phone in his hand calling the police to report the thief who'd come by earlier and cased the joint. I peeked in the basement again. The cardboard barrel I'd seen by the stairwell had been removed. Or moved. I ran back to my car, started the engine, rammed the heater to full blast, and plastered my hands to the vent while I chewed on the fact that I didn't have a clue what I was doing. The sound of a yapping dog brought me out of my trance. *Across the street a fat man with one of those mop dogs is taking a briefing from a woman tugging on a cocker spaniel…* probably too cold for the woman and the cocker spaniel, but not for the fat man who *…trots away with the dog, one arm extended mid-leash like a Eukanuba show handler.* He turned the corner and disappeared.

"I'll be damned."

When he came back around I'd introduce myself, explain that I was looking for my sister. Had he noticed the woman in black at the top of the steps last week? A Jaguar on the street? I would describe Mr. Dean. He might know him by name. A different name.

I laughed aloud when a woman *in a long coat and sneakers, pulled by a galloping retriever, flies past. She looks exhausted.* One week later, she was still exhausted. I considered following her, but Eukanuba seemed a better bet, nosey in the neighborhood. Across the street a white short-hair with two black spots on his face raced to a patch of ivy and did his business. The owner did not scoop it. Ivy must be exempt.

It was like somebody had turned on a dog faucet. The woman and the galloping retriever raced past in the opposite direction. I was enjoying the show, but too much time had passed, and I was forced to conclude that Eukanuba had taken the alley home. I hadn't noticed which house he'd come out of and did not have the chutzpah to knock on doors.

Maybe I should call that detective.

And tell him what? Some dog walkers over on Colfax might have seen a woman dressed in black come out of a house carrying a Cleo & Patek handbag full of money?

He believed in her.

All and all, it'd been a Charles Dickens kind of day.

I hung around the Cities until Saturday and watched the apartments on Oak Grove. Neither the woman in the camel coat nor Sammy made an appearance. Over on Colfax, the Eukanuba show handler didn't show again, maybe kept on walking, out of the neighborhood, away from the scolding woman and her cocker spaniel, all the way to Arizona and green salsa and red suns and Camelback Mountain. Nor did Mr. Dean return with his shovel. I finally admitted that My Saint was not coming back.

Closing the door to my one-star motel room for the last time, I felt free to show my non-registered-guest face at the front desk. I explained to the college kid behind the counter that my friend had rented the room for me and I needed to pay her back. What was the monthly rate? He told me that my room was a two-week rental. My friend had paid the weekly rate, not the monthly rate, and I had one more week. He added, "We don't do refunds."

She'd rented the room the Saturday she'd shown up as Brigid in her pink headband with her plum colored coat. The same night the detective had shown up at Stonehenge.

PART II

14. Out on the Prairie
DECEMBER

Back home on the prairie, cat-sitting Mystery Cat, I'd written the story into and out of gyrations that would daze a focus group. In the latest version, My Saint had retired to London as Francis de Sales, Patron Saint of Writers, and was serving Pernod and oyster crackers to the literates *a la* Gertrude Stein. I'd changed things up: chop-cropped hair grown long and flowy, colorless eyes under lavender lenses, denim to gossamer, Calvin Kleins to Louboutins. Even more disturbing, I had written her a true love named Quincy, a forever soldier in the IRA. The book was backsliding into a romance novel. Fortunately, TRASH was just a click away.

My new plan focused on criminal cunning. In need of professional blather, I'd called on Penny's dad, available psychologist, and explained my hardened heroine. I'd established up front, emphatically, that My Saint's concealment was for cover only, nothing more. Disguise, the mainstay of her operation, was not the result of some deep-seated psychodrama that sprang from her inability to come to terms with her sins. Frankly, she dealt with her sins rather well.

"She's a curiosity, your saint character," he'd said, pointing out textbook personality traits manifested in unprecedented combinations — the degree of My Saint's commitment to these unprecedented combinations being historically and clinically undocumented. "You might ease up on the multiple personalities. Maybe add some mannerisms that indicate a diminished capacity. Give her social qualities, some nature that regular folks can relate to. And have her live in one place. With no home and no possessions other than costumes, and, at the same time, to blend and function soundly within society ... well, kiddo, that's a stretch. How about a ritzy condo on the Mississippi? People don't normally up and move on a weekly basis."

"Homeless people do," I said. "Gypsies. Itinerants."

"But she's not a gypsy, itinerant, or homeless. She drinks Pernod and eats risotto. If you can't mate her with a brain dysfunction, you might make her flat-out clinically crazy. She could have a frontal lobe disability and lack conscience and judgment. But, then again, you've characterized her possessing ample forethought." He picked up a pen and drew a brain. "You've got her stable in the temporal lobe. Her emotional behavior and understanding of people and her language are above average. You're not communicating pathology from either the parietal or the occipital." He handed me a diagram of five cloud-like lobes, each labeled with a certified pathology. "Focus on the frontal lobe would be my suggestion."

"I didn't realize things were so compartmentalized."

"On paper, yes. In real time, crazy is not always well defined."

"She's not crazy."

"You talk like she's a real person."

"Well, you know writers."

Penny quipped: "It's fiction, for gawd's sake. Make something up and get on with it."

I couldn't. Nor could I fit her into a lobe. Without My Saint in the flesh or knowing anybody even remotely connected to her, I was blocked. I shelved the manuscript and considered myself lucky to have come away unscathed.

Short on inspiration, short on buoy, I rewrote *Love is a French Verb* with a wee bit less swoon. The morning sex on the verandah stayed on the verandah, but the musky toilet soap, the French perfume, the floral bed linens, and the Chateauneuf du Pape got trashed. Both Penny and Dave had volunteered to read and give their opinions, but because I'd logged too many hours for what I had to show, I ignored their offers, afraid their sentiments would fall just short of Mrs. Torrance when she discovered Jack's labor intensive 'all work and no play' manuscript at the Overlook Hotel.

Fact was I hated my new Haut Medoc soul mates on the verandah without any swoon. I'd even tinkered with my handsome hero as a vampire, but couldn't wrap myself around that.

Stalled, I started a new novel. The heroine was a slender, dark-haired piano teacher who'd lost her husband in a car wreck and gotten emotionally involved with the outlaw lawyer for the drunk driver who'd killed her husband. I liked my characters, even the drunk driver.

And there I sat, holed up in my computer cove staring at the screen. I reached over and shut the blinds. Big snow had come early this year and the glare off the banks would blind a polar bear. My heroine and the outlaw lawyer for the drunk driver resisted romantic involvement, but tensions ran high. Face to face on the courthouse steps, my heroine's lovelorn eyes belied her angry voice. The doorbell rang. I typed *the doorbell rang.* On the courthouse steps? I stopped typing. It was my doorbell ringing.

"Cripes." I clicked SAVE. Who was bothering me? Everybody knew my parents had ducked out early this year. Dave quit calling after I'd told him no way was I moving to Fargo. I would have ended up going to nursing school, which would have revealed a math allergy and a debutante's reaction to blood. I would have married Dave, nice man that he was, but so far from the outlaw-lawyer-for-the-drunk-driver type he could have been a priest, not that that held sanctity anymore. I'd told Dave that I was obsessed with a woman I'd met in the Cities and was asking myself some serious questions. He had assumed what wasn't. I'd taken the shirkers way out of our relationship, but I didn't have the energy for the pointless drama of apologia that can be argued into eternity. Some lucky girl in Fargo could name her first-born after me.

So it had to be Penny at my gate.

The hermetically sealed door sucked open leaving one thin aluminum screen separating me from my attacker. I grabbed the door to slam it shut, but curiosity, as usual, trumped common sense. On my doorstep, one eye shaded by a flop of dark hair, stood the one and only connection to My Saint.

Sheepish would best describe the look on Martin Micks' face. "I didn't start on the right foot with you and I apologize for that. I'm not like that. Not at all."

"How'd you find me?" My eyes dropped to the lock that wasn't locked.

"You're easy," he said, still sheepish. It was only noon and his jaw was the color of graphite dust. He patted his gloves together, puffed-up and cold in what looked like a Buzz Rickson parka. I'd never read a William Gibson novel, but purportedly, his heroine would shoot the dog if it meant saving her Buzz Rickson jacket from a barf stain.

I said, "You didn't drive up here to apologize." Sound-minded emotions such as anger and fear were muzzled by my bizarre elation at the sight of this man who'd arm-locked me in the snack room and bought me a Snickers bar. My Saint had come back to me.

"I had the name wrong," he said. "Toni Padua is an alias, same as Brigid. The picture I showed you was a woman named Angela Folly."

Tired Angela Folly with the mousey brown hair. He would never get it right.

"Would you take a look at some photos?" He peeked around me into the house. Behind him the green SUV sparkled in the sunlight. The sidewalk hadn't been shoveled since Dave. Except for a snowplow at the end of the block, the street was empty.

"Photos of what?"

"Your friend." He shivered, making a show of the cold. "And her friends."

He was an officer of the law of sorts. Obviously without a warrant. Just a friendly visit. I pretended to unlock the unlocked door, pushed it open and stepped aside. A whoosh of snowflakes followed him in. His blue jeans were fashionably faded with frayed hems, not the nouveau vintage the boutiques sold to fashion mavens who wouldn't own anything long enough to fade, much less fray. Martin Micks had good old-fashioned wear and tear going. His scuffed, tan hikers were laced (no cheater zippers). Blasé cool. It was too late to kick off my pink rabbit slippers.

"Thanks," he said with a birthday boy grin that surprised me.

I ran my fingers through my hair. Realizing the message I might have just sent, I folded my arms with an air of inconvenience to disguise the joy I was feeling to be talking to somebody other than Mystery Cat. Martin Micks stuffed his gloves into his Buzz Rickson pockets and pulled out an envelope. He anchored it between his teeth and shed his jacket on the side chair where it stuck. He wore a black crewneck sweater over a navy shirt. He saw my eyes drop to his boots and sat down on top of his jacket, set the envelope on the floor, loosened his laces, and wiggled his red woolen feet loose. He snatched the envelope off the floor and stood up. Eye to eye, I had him by an inch. I had a lot of guys by an inch. That's all I had.

He followed me into the living room, talking. "Angela Folly is the name I picked up from a property manager in Anoka where she lived in October."

He tossed the envelope on the coffee table and sat down on the sofa. I remained standing and tried to radiate enough forced patience to establish dominance. He pulled a picture from the envelope and stretched across my mother's gingham flower and ceramic angel Christmas centerpiece and handed it to me. The woman in the photo stepping off a metro bus was not Angela Folly, the yawning, slightly bored Patron Saint of Temptation with her stringy hair and oversized army parka. I tilted the picture towards the light and realized I was handling the photo so as not to leave fingerprints. To put that silliness to rest, I logged a full thumbprint. The bus stop woman didn't look like My Saint in any disguise.

"Don't know her," I said and handed it back.

"If you remember anything, anything at all about this woman, help me here. Please."

Put a Buzz Rickson flight jacket up against a pair of pink rabbit slippers and six ceramic angels floating through a gingham floral arrangement … well, I felt compelled to demonstrate a higher level of *savoir vivre*, an up-sell, so to speak, which was accomplished by flaunting my familiarity with his case — tease a little, suggest a secret knowledge. I said, "Angela Folly slouches. Your bus stop woman has schoolmistress posture."

His reaction was worth the betrayal.

He'll never touch me. With or without your help.

Acknowledging her prescience, my face flushed. Oh, stop, I told myself. My Saint was so well insulated there wasn't anything I could say that would compromise her.

"That's not Angela Folly. I have no idea who it is. Could be the holy saint of the Rose Bowl parade, for all I know."

He gave me a stern look.

"She's that good," I said, realizing he knew nothing about the saints, her filing system, her method of identification. I thought about that a moment. How would he know? How would anybody know? Unless she'd told them. I folded my arms again, feeling superfluously privileged.

He positioned the bus stop woman next to the gingham centerpiece. He wasn't wearing a wedding band, which told me nothing except that he might well be a married man reserving his options. He handed me a photo of a slightly plump blonde in a streetscape. Add a pink headband.

"That could be Brigid Ireland," I said, knowing that Martin Micks already knew that. I handed it back.

"Brigid Ireland worked at a bar back in the seventies called Valentines. The owner disappeared. Brigid Ireland disappeared. They found the guy at the bottom of a lake. I see a connection."

He set the picture next to the bus stop woman and pulled out two more photos. He placed one face down on the coffee table and thrust the other at me, bumping the gingham centerpiece. The angels twirled.

I was looking at Nicky Myer, the most cryptic of the saints. Not only was it Nicky Myer, it was Nicky Myer exiting the apartment building the night she'd gone to kidnap Bentley Ogren. Never mind her shadowed face, the black jacket and baseball cap were unmistakable. The shot was taken about twenty yards out, probably from a passing car, a slow passing car. She'd raced across the street, jumped in next to me and ducked. There had been a flash, like car lights in my wing mirror. I considered the remaining photo that lay face down next to Brigid. I already knew who it was. Best for last. Could this man arrest me? I smeared my fingerprints off the photo. The bus stop woman on the coffee table bore my full thumbprint. I'd need to revisit that.

"How did you get these pictures?" I asked with strained lightness. I pulled at my sweatshirt. It felt like a cocoon.

"Surveillance, eyewitnesses, street talk, cons making deals. I do the math. I am her Captain Hamer."

"Captain who?"

"Bonnie and Clyde, you know. Hamer stayed on it. Finally got 'em."

I curbed a laugh. Who did he think he was? None of these guys had Hamer-time anymore, much less the tenacity to stick with it. This detective's obsession was something else. Somebody important had put him off, brushed him off. Demoted for aggressive tactics would be my guess. Goes off on his own to show 'em all.

Martin Micks nodded towards the photo I held and said, "She looks like the walking dead, huh? Some bad business went down that night." He watched me for a reaction. I would give him nothing, nothing worth the trip. I bent over the coffee table to escape his eyes and dropped Nicky Myer on top of Brigid Ireland.

If you're getting itchy vibes, get the cough going.

I cleared my throat and coughed. "Excuse me," I mumbled, hand to my mouth. "I'm coming down with something."

"Me, too." He pulled a box of cough drops out of his shirt pocket and offered it. I shook my head, not about to open my sweaty palm. He shoved the box around the gingham centerpiece within arms reach and set about positioning Nicky Myer next to Brigid Ireland next to the bus stop woman. He had not said the name Nicky Myer. He did say, "It could be argued that the resemblance between these three women is no more significant than Marilyn Monroe, Jane Mansfield, and Madonna at a distance in the dark."

I coughed and glanced at my wrist where a watch might be, then at the cuckoo clock in the kitchen that my father had discreetly disarmed.

"Am I keeping you from something?"

"I've got a deadline," I lied, curious beyond prudence to know what 'bad business' had gone down that night. The facedown photo was making me crazy.

"We knew that a man named Laddie Ogren was in the states. A suspected arms dealer with chemical connections. He showed the Feds what for when he killed their mole." He tapped on the Nicky Myer photo. "There was a good chance he'd show up at this apartment." He tapped again. "This bonus picture came from our guys working the murder of the bookstore clerk. Laddie Ogren was Fed territory, but fuck 'em; the bookstore clerk was killed on our turf. We investigate."

"Bookstore clerk?"

"The mole, yeah. Worked in a bookstore downtown." He added a derisive snort to that and picked up Nicky Myer's picture. "This woman came out of that apartment, got into a black sports car. Someone else was driving." With his other hand he curled his trump card off the table. I snatched it out of his hand and stared at the white face in the car window. Indistinct, splendidly indistinct. Taken from the distance of a passing car and enlarged to billboard grain. I had looked square into the flash. I tossed the picture on the table as if it were a porn shot and coughed with enough force to warrant my red face.

"Obviously, the police can't afford a real camera," I managed to say and grabbed the box of cough drops. I shook one into my mouth and almost swallowed it. I choked and patted my throat. "Getting worse."

"You don't sound congested."

"It's that first tickle." I coughed again.

He gazed at me impassively.

I averted my eyes to the pictures on the coffee table and ran down a list of names in my head of people who might bail me out of jail. I wondered if Dave was still in town.

"We don't know anything about the driver or what role she played. It might be just a matter of talking to her." He stopped talking, forcing eye contact.

"Talking to her," I repeated, struggling not to appear discombobulated. *Divert the focus*. I spit the cough drop into my hand and eyed it with disgust. "Horehound. That alone will make you cough. Where do you find horehound anymore?"

"The bartender at Stonehenge said you were at the bar on three different occasions."

I choked, for real this time. Bartender Bob? That asshole hadn't acknowledged my presence one time and he'd ratted me out? "Oh, please," I said patting my chest. "I had drinks there with five different writers from the conference. That bartender was a Martian." I considered how I might explain the tape recorder.

"Tight-lipped bastard. I should have laid my handcuffs on the bar. That gets 'em talking."

Bartender Bob hadn't mentioned the tape recorder. He'd noticed it. Could he have forgotten?

"I had to pay your bar tab just to get that morsel. He didn't recognize any of the photos, not even Brigid."

"My bar tab? My bar tabs were on my room."

"Sure they were. Like I said, we could cut her a deal."

I popped the horehound back in my mouth and wiped my hand on my pants. "Not worth much, that picture. Could be Demi Moore in that car. Or Mary Osmond."

"Marie."

"Whatever." We stared at each other. His eyes would dry out of their sockets before he'd blink. I blinked. Where was Mystery Cat when I needed him? Pets and kids, those sweet opportune interruptions, excuses, diversions.

He repositioned my photo next to Nicky Myer. "Interesting coincidence here, don't you think? I see you with this woman and three nights later we have two murders in town."

"Two? The bookstore clerk and who else?"

"Not the bookstore clerk. He was already yesterday's news. Laddie Ogren was the perp in the bookstore kill. Case closed."

Not the bookstore clerk. "So, who got murdered?"

He tapped on Nicky Myer's picture. "What's her connection to Laddie Ogren?"

"I have no idea. Why?"

He opened the envelope again. A bonus photo. A dark-haired man in plaid Bermuda shorts and a pink polo shirt, unaware of the camera, stood next to a food cart squeezing some condiment onto a hotdog, a carnival ride in the background. "Did she ever mention Laddie Ogren to you?"

Hair flat to his head like a Labrador retriever. Even with the downward angle of his face, Laddie Ogren was posh and miles better looking than what she'd described, like someone who owned polo ponies.

"She never mentioned Laddie Ogren. Uh-uh." I handed it back. "What murders?"

"She won't help you. You're on your own, Jennifer Sands."

"On my own? On my own for what? I met her for the first time in my life at that cornball bar. It was a Romance Writers Convention, for gawd's sake. Why don't you answer my question? If not the bookstore clerk, what murders are you freaking talking about?"

"The first hit was at this apartment." He picked up the picture of Nicky Myer crossing the street. "A woman named Fanny Graas." He pronounced it Grass.

Legs no longer reliable, I tottered around the coffee table and dropped to the couch. The detective moved to the center cushion next to me.

"You know Fanny Grass, don't you?"

"Know? No."

Fanny? Dead? Had My Saint killed Fanny to get Bender? While I waited in the car like some barnyard simpleton? Nicky Myer killed Fanny Graas. No, I wouldn't believe that.

"What did Brigid tell you about Fanny Grass?"

His pronunciation of Fanny's name hackled me. I blurted, "It's Graas. Aaah. Graas."

"Aaah," he repeated. "Graas." His eyes were smart. "No ass in Graas, hmm?" He drew a slow victory breath, almost a whistle.

The asshole had set me up for that little show of familiarity. How had he gotten control of the dialogue? In my house: double asshole. Uninvited: triple asshole. I pointed at Brigid's picture. "She said the name. That's all. Graas. That's how she pronounced it. I'm a writer. I remember shit like that." He was sitting too close. I shifted into the armrest. "You said two. That there were two murders at the apartment."

"That's not what I said."

Would he arrest me if I broke his jaw?

"I said there were two murders that night."

I clasped my hands between my legs to keep from smacking him.

He took his time. "The second kill was over in Saint Paul. Laddie Ogren took it in the head."

I choked. Laddie Ogren in the pink polo shirt.

The detective picked up Laddie in the pink polo shirt and gazed at him with an unbefitting admiration. "All the Feds in the world couldn't catch him, couldn't get near the man." He tossed the photo back on the table. "Ogren's connections were zipped up tighter than a rap gangsta. Except for the mole in the bookstore, and you see what happened to him."

"I don't see," I mumbled, trying to process the fact that My Saint had killed Fanny Graas. Impossible. "I don't see anything."

"Fanny Graas…" he enunciated correctly, having known all along, "…was murdered between five and six o'clock. We came on at nine."

"Six o'clock?" I blurted in a voice too loud for the room.

"Forensics narrowed that one down."

At six o'clock Nicky Myer was picking me up at the canoes. She couldn't have killed Fanny. "So these two murders are connected? One in St. Paul. One in Minneapolis."

"Laddie Ogren and Fanny Graas were married. That's no coincidence."

"The same person did both murders?"

"No. Two different guns. One gun is accounted for, retrieved off the kitchen counter in Ogren's apartment. It was wearing a silencer. It was the gun that killed Fanny Graas. She was shot in the chest at close range." He grimaced. "White sweater." He shifted on the couch, quiet for a moment. "Laddie Ogren was standing at his kitchen sink when he took it in the head from about fifteen feet, which put the killer just inside the entry door. Either Ogren didn't know what hit him or he wasn't fast enough going for his gun. A bullet in the head is a contract kill for sure. There's no doubt from ballistics that Laddie Ogren's gun killed Fanny Graas. The gun that killed him is missing."

"Was Laddie Ogren's gun the same gun that killed the bookstore clerk?"

"The bookstore clerk was strangled."

Confirmed.

"Laddie Ogren killed Fanny Graas. Case closed. Who killed Laddie Ogren is where I'm stopped." He picked up Nicky Myer's picture and gazed at it. "Nobody in Ogren's building heard the shot. It's a transient, monthly rental next to the railroad tracks. The Burlington comes through every night same time. Somebody knew that."

We'll get you a cab over by the convention center. I got a train to catch. She'd caught that train. On time. One shot. *I've never triggered anybody in my life.* If she had hit Laddie Ogren bull's-eye, it was a damned lucky shot. Or had she lied about that? She'd shown me my target eye. The detective's hair blocked his right eye. I wondered if he was left eye dominant.

"The Ogren hit," he said, "that was nothing personal."

Nothing personal. My Saint had dropped me at the cabstand. We'd chatted. She'd laughed, unrehearsed. I'd envisioned coffee and fries and Christmas in Miami. She'd been on her way to kill Laddie Ogren.

I'd asked her, *What time tomorrow?* She'd said, *Not tomorrow.*

Not ever. For her, the story had ended. Laddie Ogren killed Fanny Graas. My Saint killed Laddie Ogren. Kerpow!

"His body lay there two days, so the exact hour of death wasn't nailed down. Same time the night train passed through is my guess. We got no stray fingerprints, not one stray hair, fiber, footprint, nothing."

She wouldn't have said a word, My Saint. She would have opened the door with her proprietary lock picks, stepped her rubber garden shoes into the foyer, aimed the gun and fired. Crazy O didn't see it, didn't hear it, train roaring like a tornado. She stepped her rubber garden shoes back out into the hallway and shut the door. I shivered and pulled my sweatshirt tighter.

He pushed my photo and Nicky Myer's towards me. In all seriousness, I was unidentifiable. Nicky Myer was Nicky Myer, whoever that might be. What didn't show in Nicky's picture were her leave-no-fingerprint gloves and her leave-no-footprint rubber shoes with the duct tape on the soles.

The detective said, "No one handled Ogren's gun but Ogren. The bullet in his head came from a second gun." He aimed a finger-gun at Nicky Myer's picture. "This woman triggered Ogren and I don't have a damn thing to prove it."

I own a gun, but never use it. Truth be known, I'm not fierce enough to use it, which might appear to be contraindicated for someone in my trade.

"Might the bullet that killed Laddie Ogren have come from a Kimber 1911?"

"More like a Smith & Wesson. Damn near blew his head off. What do you know about a Kimber 1911?"

"She compared it to a box of chocolates."

His puzzled look turned suspicious. "You two talked quite a bit, Jennifer Sands. You throw me these little bites."

"You forget. I'm a writer. That's what we do. We remember trivia. We remember sounds. Kimber 1911 sounds like a street address. I live at Kimber Nineteen Eleven." I'd regained a modicum of control only because I questioned my position, not in any organized sense, just fleeting notions about unfulfilled and unrealistic expectations, that was then, this is now kind of thoughts. I chewed on the word 'liability.'

He rubbed his hands together. "How about I read your notes? I might see something you may not know is important."

"You can read my notes if I can read your files."

"I can't show you working files. You know that. You also know I can force your notes."

Not liking the sound of that, I said, "I write on cocktail napkins, bus schedules, receipts. I wrote that Kimber thing on a cocktail napkin, a wet cocktail napkin, with the express purpose of checking it on Google."

Fanny Graas was dead. When My Saint had come from the apartment, the only thing she'd said was that Fanny Graas was gone. When I'd asked where she had gone, My Saint had said, *If I knew that…* and, as always, had answered the question, but said nothing at all.

She'd also said: *I fucking told her I'd handle it. Nobody fucking listens. Nobody can follow the simplest goddamn instructions.*

Fanny hadn't listened. She'd come to the hotel searching for Clare Assett. Unable to find Clare, she'd handled things herself. Then Laddie Ogren walked on.

I'd bet the farm it was Sammy who'd hustled Bentley Ogren out of that apartment, hiding him until My Saint guaranteed safety. Forever.

I pointed to Nicky Myer's picture. "Whose apartment was that?"

"It was going out of lease. The prior tenant deceased. Closets empty, refrigerator unplugged, bed linens for show."

I glanced at the bookcase where My Saint's manuscript languished. She'd told me the wrong story. I had written the wrong damn story. That alone should change the way I felt. About everything.

"Jennifer, I need you to tell me what you know." Solicitous.

How much could I say without implicating myself, exposing myself as an accessory? An accessory to what? Laddie Ogren killed Fanny Graas. Case closed. I was delivering a briefcase in Edina when My Saint was playing out the inaudible, anonymous climax. Laddie's murder will be a cold case forever.

So, why was I spooked? Could a case be made that I was an accessory to more than I had accessorized? I envisioned myself in prison with a cellmate named Burly Birdie. Me, a romance writer who'd met a stranger in a faux castle bar. I'd conducted an interview, undertook some research, fieldwork. Was I not under the same protective umbrella as a journalist? Surely to God, I didn't need a lawyer. I couldn't afford snow maintenance, much less a lawyer. Bartender Bob was already on the witness stand embroidering his smug answers to the poorly crafted, worthless questions thrown together at the twelfth hour by my public defender.

Stop it.

I coughed. My throat burned from the strain.

"It's going around." Martin Micks leaned back away from me. His heat evaporated. I hadn't realized just how up-close and friendly he'd been sitting.

I needed to find her. The man on my couch would help me, although he didn't know that yet.

"Could I fix you a sandwich?"

"Call me Micks."

15. Baloney

"To impress a man, cook him dinner" was my mother's "Leave It to Beaver" advice. A baloney sandwich on white bread with mayonnaise and kettle pickles was not what she meant. It was all I had. Not only that, I'd scraped the ice crystals from the frozen bread and thawed it in the microwave, which gave it the consistency of a damp dumpling. Micks chewed like a ruminant. Micks. Nobody called him Martin, he'd said. And never Marty.

He'd lined up his photos between the pickle jar and the butter dish: the bus stop woman, Brigid Ireland, Laddie Ogren, Nicky Myer, and Nicky Myer's driver. Indistinct, forgettable faces. The face that stuck in my mind's eye suffered dyed black hair and a crescent bruise. Beautiful, despairing, dead Fanny Graas. Somebody needed suffering; Laddie Ogren hadn't suffered. One shot in the head, oh, please. The man should have been tied up and blistered.

Micks pointed at Nicky Myer's picture. "The apartment had a live phone. The two calls that mattered prior to the shooting tracked to a Woodbury address and a woman named Gert Nivels. I'm thinking another alias, but Nivels used a traceable phone. Criminals pay-as-you-go, you know."

"So maybe Gert Nivels wasn't a criminal." I bit into my sandwich and chewed. Spongy baloney between dumpling wafers.

"The leasing agent couldn't identify the Nivels woman from any of the photos. Not only that, he thought they were five different women. I got nothing on Gert Nivels."

Gert Nivels, Gertrude of Nivelles, The Patron Saint of Cats. *Gert wears a blonde braid wrapped around her head that agrees with paisley skirts and Birkenstocks.* I wondered if Micks knew Gert's employer, Barney and his boys.

"This Nivels woman signed a one-year lease, paid rent for eight months, paid off the balance and disappeared. Told the leasing agent she was a nun and would be in Africa for three years. She left no forwarding address."

When I've finished with a Barney job, I pack up and move.

"The unit re-leased the next day. Didn't need to clean, the guy said. Their janitorial service couldn't do that good a job. She was a nun. Like that explained it."

"Maybe she really was a nun. And Fanny knew her from church."

Micks snorted.

I plucked the baloney out of my sandwich. Somewhere along the way, My Saint and Fanny Graas had disconnected. Fanny had lost her phone and hadn't memorized My Saint's current pay-as-you-go number. Fanny had come to the hotel looking for Clare Assett. To drop off Bender would be my guess. But My Saint wasn't registered as Clare Assett. Knowing that Laddie Ogren had her in his sights, unlocked and loaded, and unable to find Clare Assett, Fanny had tried to handle it herself. When Nicky Myer and I got to the target apartment, we hadn't picked up Bender. We hadn't picked up anybody. Fanny was already dead. So why hadn't Laddie Ogren grabbed the boy? He couldn't find him? I popped a shard of baloney into my mouth.

He didn't look.

But Nicky Myer had. Under the bed? Under the kitchen sink? Somewhere. She'd found him. She'd called Sammy. Sammy had run with the boy.

She'd denied it. *The place is full of families.*

Detective Micks hadn't mentioned a boy.

"Where's the boy now?" I patted my mouth with my crumpled-up napkin.

"What boy?"

"Bender. Fanny's son."

"You mean Bentley Ogren? How do you know Bentley Ogren? Bender? Nickname, huh?" In the kitchen light his eyes were Teflon brown. And Teflon hard. I looked away.

"Brigid mentioned him. I don't remember in what context, but I remember the unusual name. Wasn't there a grandmother? Brigid mentioned something about them all living together."

"There was no evidence of that. What I'm starting to see here, talking to you, is that Brigid Ireland had racked up a mess of details about Laddie Ogren: his wife, his son, possibly a mother-in-law, and everybody's shoe size in between. She gets the goods on Ogren, then shows up at the wrong address? Doesn't add up."

I'd handed Micks something to chew on considerably more sustaining then a baloney sandwich. My brain hummed with unreleased data. What I should reasonably know versus what I actually knew teetered between fact and fiction, and was changing by the minute. I glanced past the detective into the living room at the manuscript on my bookshelf. Fiction, all of it.

And if Lil was a red herring, who'd claimed Fanny's body?

"Did Fanny Graas have a funeral?"

"One would suppose." He tapped on the picture of Nicky Myer exiting the apartment on her way to the black Saturn and its simpleminded driver. "She came for Laddie Ogren, but found a dead Fanny Graas instead." He picked up Nicky Myer's snapshot and waggled it. "She was a contract killer at the wrong address. Or the wrong time. The wrong something. That, in itself, doesn't track for this woman." He stared at the picture as if it were a trick of the eye. "Somebody put a sheet over Fanny Graas. It wasn't Laddie Ogren."

"How do you know that?"

"The sheet was laid down after the blood dried." Micks swallowed the last bite of his sandwich. The man had good manners. Or no taste buds. He patted his mouth with the napkin, stood up, and carried his plate to the sink, rinsed it off, pulled a plastic glass from the drying rack and filled it with faucet water. He took a long drink, turned and leaned against the counter, one hand in his pocket jiggling the contents; nothing sounds like quarters against a Zippo.

"You can smoke," I said. When he didn't move, I got up and opened the basement door. Mystery Cat scooted out, cranky face. Sorry, buddy. Micks pulled a pack of Marlboros out of his pocket. He offered me one. I declined. I'd liked to have whipped out a plastic bag of exotic tobacco and rolled one of my own, like Genny Ross had done for the benefit of Mr. Dean. Even a cheroot or a spicy bidi. Out on the prairie.

Micks fired up the Zippo. "Anything else you remember? I'll take anything. Anything at all."

He sounded sweet. I couldn't resist. "Sammy knows. Find Sammy."

He blew the smoke at the ceiling. "Sammy?"

I gave a nod at his row of pictures on the table. "A friend of Brigid's. He could be a bookie or a choirboy, for all I know. I got the impression he was a Loring Park kind of guy."

Telling Micks about Sammy and the boy leaving the apartment would put me at the scene of the crime. Nor would I mention that two days later while he interrogated Sgt. Pepper in an apartment building a couple hundred yards from the scene of the crime, the real story had strutted past him in both directions.

Explain my expertise. Nah-uh. "I don't remember why she mentioned him."

"Sammy may not be his real name. I got a trail of convoluted aliases. I lie awake with them."

"Look," I said, biting a nip off my pickle spear, "that woman could, this very minute, arrive at my door wearing a UPS uniform. If I didn't stare at her, and I mean stare, up close as in a study period, I'd sign the receipt, and poof! She'd be gone. She was that good. She did things with her face, her voice, and the way she carried herself. She had teeth that gave her an overbite, teeth that gave her an underbite. She wore devices under her wigs that made her eyes narrow and her cheeks high. She can talk a southern accent, a Boston accent, a Brisbane accent." I picked up the photo of the unidentified bus stop woman. Theater caps on the uppers, that steel band up over the head, muscles tight at the mouth — yeah, it could be My Saint. Then again, if you picked at it long enough, it could be Nora Roberts.

Micks dropped his cigarette in the garbage disposal and sat down at the table again and opened up the pickle jar, pulled one out, took a bite and laid it on my plate. He had a way about him. I wondered why he didn't talk about himself. Most men did so readily. The reticent ones were always married.

"You know a lot," he said.

"I was writing a story about Broadway when I met her. She offered some tips."

"How many aliases did you see?"

"Three."

"What'd you talk about?" He picked the pickle off my plate and took another bite.

"Stuff. The theater, the weather, my career as a romance writer. She said Fanny Graas and Laddie Ogren had a dysfunctional marriage and if I wrote about dysfunctional marriages, everyone would identify and buy my book."

"She might have a point." He picked up Laddie Ogren's picture. "She studied them. She used Fanny Graas to get to Laddie Ogren. Probably got Fanny killed. It was a big payday for Brigid, killing Laddie Ogren, I'll guaran-damn-tee. Nobody got to Ogren."

It'd been a big payday, but not for killing Laddie Ogren. Or was Micks right? Had Laddie been the target all along? If so, where did papa Dean Ogren fit in? If Laddie was the target, she'd made me an accessory to a contract murder. Then abandoned me. I'd been a covered base. That was all I'd been. Why was I protecting her? Micks fished in the jar for another pickle. He took a bite, tossed the hair out of his eyes and gave me a collaborating look.

"You've had no contact with her since October," he said, more a statement than a question.

I shook my head. "I'm telling you, you won't find this woman, and I'm not being a smartass, but you won't find her. You've got non-descript pictures of someone you call Toni Padua, Brigid Ireland, Angela Folly, none of which is her real name. You don't even know what she looks like."

"I'm putting together a computer compilation of the pictures. I should get a fairly good composite." He blew a puff of air in frustration. "But I need her name. If I knew who I was looking for–"

"What good would that do? She probably hasn't used her real name in twenty years. She'll probably never use it again. Why would she?"

"Did she mention any family?"

"Her mother was a nun."

"Cute," he said, gathering the pictures. "I'm serious and you're cute."

I contemplated his syntax while I watched both my photograph and my fingerprint slide back into the envelope. Did he mean cute as a kitten? Or lampoon cute? Crap, it didn't matter. The fact that he had me in his envelope, albeit unrecognizable, unnerved me.

The window over the sink framed a single square of tropical blue: no clouds, no tree limbs, no neighboring rooftops. We could be anywhere. Switch baloney out for pastechi, who's to say we weren't in Aruba? My winter white arm said so. The sound of the pickle jar sliding across wood brought me back to the table. Micks tightened the lid.

"Pickled out," he said.

To come clean was tempting. I was, by accident, innocent. What had started out as a well-engineered, albeit cruel, kidnapping had ended up a rescue. That would make my involvement as the get-away driver benign. Why had she needed a get-away driver? *Six year olds can be soooo difficult.* But Fanny would have instructed Bender to go with the nice lady. Had My Saint foreseen a complication as extreme as Fanny Graas dead in the chair? For what reason would she put herself at risk to kill Laddie Ogren? Exactly what had she been contracted to do?

I didn't believe My Saint used Fanny Graas to get to Laddie Ogren. Nor did My Saint's actions lead to the death of Fanny Graas. Laddie Ogren had Fanny Graas in his sights years before My Saint walked on. The bare, sad fact was that if she hadn't killed Laddie Ogren, he'd have gotten away with murder.

That I might not ever know the truth bedeviled me. That I'd been a dim-witted juvenile smack in the middle of the operation irked me. Duped. When My Saint had told me about the Eddie Valentine murder, she'd said: *Roach said there'd been a back-up plan.* My Saint's back-up plan had been me. Anything could have happened outside that apartment in the dark in the car: men with guns snapping pictures, a determined detective, Laddie Ogren in town. Laddie Ogren could have killed My Saint. Could have killed me. To have been her back-up plan, her crib sheet, some dopey professor's assistant with a cast-off Sony tape recorder was … was what?

Embarrassing, that's what.

My Saint had moved out of the free pass zone.

Here at the table sat Martin Micks, my ticket to privileged information. I opened the pickle jar and slid it towards him. "So what about Bentley Ogren."

Micks told how the police had tracked Fanny Graas to the house in Burnsville, which they'd found empty except for three packed suitcases by the door. Fanny had lived at that address for less than six months, so the neighbors knew nothing. There was no mention of an older woman living there. Fanny Grass had taken Bentley Ogren out of school early October. His records had been forwarded to a private school in New Orleans, but the school had no record of his application, much less his admittance. The boy had not been reported missing.

I did not mention that Bentley Ogren had not been reported missing when Laddie Ogren had stolen him into Canada, nor had he been reported missing when My Saint had stolen him out of Canada. Retrieving stolen merchandise. Something no legal system could do. Something My Saint did do. By way of Lance.

Who the hell was Lance?

There are people who pay taxes who wouldn't think of calling the cops. They handle it.

Lance. Clare Assett's handler.

"Some relative probably has the kid," Martin Micks said with a shrug. "That's not my department. We know who killed his mother. Case closed."

"The boy is registered in school somewhere. Isn't there a school database in your network? Punch a key?"

"He hasn't been reported missing." Micks tapped his pack of Marlboros on the table.

I pushed my empty plate towards him and said, "No one smokes anymore."

He lit up. "I'm scheduled to quit." The way he held the cigarette, there would always be one between his fingers.

I wondered if 'the department' thought My Saint was relevant to the murder investigation of Laddie Ogren or was Martin Micks solo on that? With no evidence, no nothing. An unidentified woman on the street and an unidentified driver in a vehicle does not a crime scene make. How far out of the legal loop was Detective Micks? Investigator Micks. Mr. Micks.

Heck, we were both out of the loop. Even with my proprietary knowledge, I was clueless as to why My Saint would kill Laddie Ogren. Her contract had been with Mr. Dean to kidnap the boy. Or so she said. A clip from me about a mysterious man named Mr. Dean Ogren, who I knew to be Laddie Ogren's father, might inspire additional disclosure. Mr. Dean Ogren did not appear to be on Martin Micks' radar.

If we did collaborate, I'd parcel out my sundry clips. Micks could not be trusted with an information dump. He'd dump me and disappear. That very moment at the kitchen table, the mood seemed right for investigation.

I said, "There're a couple of things I've been wondering about."

"Wonder away."

"You got the room key from my plum-colored coat at the bar and tracked me to that dive out on the freeway. I get that. What I don't get is how–"

"Dive out on the freeway? So that's where that key fit. Never did figure that out."

"The name of the motel wasn't on the key?"

"Just a room number. Which didn't fit the American Inn on Excelsior Boulevard."

"How'd you find me at the American?"

"I wasn't looking for you. You were my consolation prize."

"What brought you there anyway?"

"A book of matches in the pocket of that pink coat."

Leave it. It's not my coat.

She had left the plum-colored coat Saturday night knowing I would bring it back Sunday night. Could she have predicted I would leave it at the bar with the incriminating matchbook in the pocket?

She would have had a back-up plan.

She had put him onto me. Why?

That detective. You have his card?

"How'd you happen to be at the Stonehenge bar in the first place? It's a hotel bar and not a good one."

"I got a phone call, a vague tip. A woman's voice. Said I should get over to Stonehenge. Someone of interest was at the bar." He waved his cigarette in dismissal. "I didn't take you two for outlaws at first, so it took me a minute. Then she hightailed it out…" he eyed me through a cloud of smoke, "…and that left you.

Listening to you talk, I was fairly certain who she was, and I got to thinking that you might have got unwittingly involved in something."

"Unwittingly?"

"You told me she was a writer from Iowa. I figured she'd duped you."

I snorted. I could tell Mr. Duped what I knew about a case or two, throw in a few saints for grins, show him … show him what? All I knew was what she'd told me. I'd been live at Heather's warehouse, but I'd not actually seen Kerby's file in her hands. As her get-away driver at the apartment, I'd not seen her kidnap anybody, much less kill anybody. There was that spider, wiped up and tossed out.

"Did you know a banker named Roland Keach?"

"Roland Keach? What do you know about Roland Keach?"

"She called him and left a message to call her back."

"His name danced on the radar when shit went down. Could never stick anything on him. Steered himself into a retaining wall. Turns out it wasn't so straight and simple. Roland Keach had ambitious competitors. He invented ruthless. The case is still open. What do you know about Roland Keach?"

"Nothing. I remember his name because I wrote a character named Roland Ketch into my first romance novel." My lies were coming easy. "Why is the case still open?"

He shrugged. "It's privileged. They're thinking somebody will trip-up and spill some undisclosed information. Between you and me, the only place that case is going is cold." Micks rubbed his shady chin. "I'm not surprised she knew the Roach."

"The Roach?"

"Street name. He'd have used her kind of service." He stubbed his cigarette out on the plate.

Roland Keach. *Ronnie the Roach.* Well, goddamn. Why hadn't I put that together? Ro-ach. Two names in one. Roach. The man who'd hit Eddie Valentine.

Itsy Bitsy.

She'd walked to his table carrying her drink — Jack and Coke, typically a man's drink, but it'd fit Angela Folly's personality. I'd bet Maggie's Farm that Jack and Coke was Roland Keach's drink of choice, not rum and coke. Roland Keach's drink didn't have a cocktail napkin stuck to it, but Angela Folly's did. She'd handed him *her* drink, spiced up right before my very eyes while I entertained myself with my third-rate, Ann Rule-Barbara Walters impersonation. The damning evidence got loaded into an industrial dishwasher and erased with industrial detergent a half-dozen times before the night was over. She'd filled a contract at Lords. And I'd watched her do it.

To give myself a little credit, I'd been suspicious, but she'd been convincing in her denials. The white cable sweater, the omelet-colored car in the painting, that stretch of the neck, the black menu with the silver Zarathustra letters. I'd been her daughter up from Mankato, and, I admit, touched by that. Touched in the head.

In real time, I'd been nothing more than a dumb prop. Dumb was okay with me. Dumb meant I'd not been part of anybody's crimes. Case closed. Oh, happy day!

I should have stood up right then and there in that fading afternoon sunlight that wasn't Aruba, dismissed this detective, and ducked back into my computer cove, back to my lawyer-for-the-drunk-driver romance, back to my imaginary life. But I couldn't. For some inexplicable reason, I wanted to find her and that meant keeping the detective close.

We both winced at the crunching sound from the living room. I got up to investigate. The gingham centerpiece, its Styrofoam base spiked with a decade's worth of pine needles, lay upended on the floor. Mystery Cat batted at a gingham flower. I snatched up the centerpiece along with a couple stray feathers and headed to the coat closet where I jostled it in underneath the coats and shut the door on it once and for all. My eye caught the Buzz

Rickson jacket. I'd never touched a true Buzz Rickson. I ran my
hand up the super-grade nylon sleeve and pulled it around to check
the famous wing logo. No logo. I arranged the jacket to read the
label. Alpac? B-grade nylon, faux fur? No Buzz Rickson.

That catchy "Oh Happy Days" tune popped into my head,
and I sang it, pink rabbit slippers flapping at my heels. Martin
Micks sat at the table with the look of someone trying not to hear
the bass through the floorboards.

I plunked down, patted his arm and said, "I am a romance
writer. That's all."

"Sure you are."

His brown eyes locked on mine, a provocative draw, a
Cybill Shepherd-Bruce Willis moment. My parents had taped
every episode of "Moonlighting" ever made. I was the only person,
other than Cybill, who could say her lines before she did. Micks
blinked first. I wondered if he danced. He seemed like the kind of
guy who lived to surprise you. Drive you nuts.

There was that bottle of cheap bubbly something or another
under the sink, an anniversary present from somebody who didn't
know my parents. Nothing a couple of ice cubes wouldn't cure. I
slid back my chair ready to fetch two flutes. Peanuts, too, in the
pantry. Buzz Rickson. Ha! Feeling more badly timed humor
coming on, I aborted a laugh and repeated myself: "I'm a romance
writer. That's all."

"This isn't a romance novel." Martin Micks brought an
elbow to the table and propped his chin with his fist in the style of
continuing evaluation. "Laddie Ogren wasn't the only dead guy on
the list, you know."

"Laddie, Daddy. One shot in the pocket, huh?" I sang, "Oh,
happy day."

"That was the Edward Hawkins Singers," he said. "The
sixties."

"Ah! That's why it lives in my head. It's on the jukebox
downstairs." I headed to the sink for the champagne.

He stood up, slid his chair back under the table and said, "I can make it to the Cities by six." He checked his watch against the cuckoo clock. "Weather's still decent." He talked like somebody who'd suddenly lost patience.

Two seconds. That's how close I'd come to confessing that the Roach had bought Angela Folly and Rose White dinner the same night he'd hit the concrete, the same night I'd left Martin Micks at Stonehenge along with Bartender Bob and my bar tab and the plum-colored coat. "She coerced me" teetered on the tip of my tongue.

Martin Micks picked up the envelope and tapped it once on the table. "You're damn lucky, Ms. Sands, that you didn't get in any deeper."

I would have told him about Eddie Valentine. Cheap bubbly something or another on the brain, unable to stop myself and past the point of caring, I would have told him about the briefcase and the old man in the wheelchair and the money, most of it still at the bottom of my Hanky Panky underwear drawer. I'd have slipped away and changed my bed sheets. Maybe even given a nod to the ghost driver in his picture packet.

But he'd dismissed me like some cheap informant.

"And I'll pretend, for now, that I do not have a picture of you in this envelope." He tapped again. "I count on your cooperation."

"Count all you want."

He stepped back, as if sensing a contraction better left alone. "I'll let myself out. Thanks for the sandwich." He headed for the foyer.

I plopped down at the table, opened the pickle jar, and fished a salty slug out of the brine. It took him long enough to lace his boots and zip his jacket. Finally, the front door clicked. The screen door clacked. Silence.

The faux detective in the faux Rickson slipped away, replaced by Fanny Graas and her courage and her lost moments and her sentry son. The dead and the missing breathed again in my alternative world. I bit into the pickle. And the tears came and ran down and caught the corners of my mouth. No more than one hydrogen molecule, I swear, separates pickle juice from tears.

Tears for Fanny Graas. Pickle juice for me.

16. Coffee and Creamers

There are those who suffer an inner self that dictates solitude. This separation from community is not to be confused with the cool dude at the end of the bar polishing his Pynchon imitation all the while drizzling pico de gallo down the front of his Tammany Hall t-shirt. Nor can this detachment be confused with those minutes of ephemeral autonomy that crash in with the waves on an empty beach — won't hold past breakfast. The deep-as-a-well separation I refer to is never spoken of by those who suffer it, because they don't know it's aberrant. Their preference for disengagement is congenital; it's in the DNA strip, *that twisted, double-strand, jokester slideshow of chromosome hell*, most often infecting the Y chromosome. These custodians of seclusion simply assume that the rest of us (seekers of body heat) have been unwittingly coerced into humankind's propinquity. What these custodians of seclusion do not comprehend is that we people of community truly need each other's trash. We seek it.

The literary image of solitude remained seductive; but, unlike the Pynchons and the Garbos, that stretched and spiritless isolation dulled me. And dulled I was. I had not left the house in two weeks. Some nights I didn't make it to bed, zonked out in my computer cove, neck crooked, waking to dancing pixels when Mystery Cat waggled the keyboard. A Pynchon I was not. I flat out needed other people's trash. Separation was not in my DNA. I was *a front-line enthusiast* without the charm.

With Christmas one week away, I experienced a brief, spirited revival and climbed into the attic to gather twinkle lights, wreaths, and reindeer only to discover a tidy stack of taped and neatly numbered cardboard boxes. Somewhere in the house, a spiral-bound notebook connected the numbers to a description of the contents. I climbed down from the attic empty-handed intending to resurrect the gingham and angel centerpiece from the closet where I'd tossed it. I couldn't make that happen.

My parents had offered to fly me to Florida for the holidays. They'd love to take me golfing (like I knew how to do that). Alligators in the rough, twinkle lights on palm trees, roast turkey in the clubhouse — and the best part, my mother informed me, was that my sister and the dentist would be there — which meant three nights on the couch. Holiday tradition being what it was, I almost went for it; but Penny saved me with an invite to their lake home near Brainerd for a storybook Christmas in the woods, which included Penny and her soon-to-be-ex-boyfriend, her mom and dad, one set of grandparents, her two sisters, one husband, and four children under the age of seven.

Even though the house by the lake was Christmas card perfect, I found myself chewing my nails and twirling strands of hair, habits I didn't have. It surprised me at first, my lack of camaraderie. So unlike me, raised to please, coached in protocol. To hide my despair, I swept the floors and washed the dishes and shoveled the sidewalk. I played cards and checkers and talked nonsense. By Christmas Eve, my computer cove didn't look all that bad. By Christmas morning, I had full appreciation of what My Saint had said when I'd gotten sentimental over the Christmas tree in the Miracle Mile store window.

That would depress the hell out of me.

On my last day in the woods, Penny's dad saved me from seppuku. After our first talk at his office, I'd assumed that his sole expertise was in behavioral guesstimates. He surprised me with his solid scholarship in genetics and was more than pleased to find one of his Christmas guests sincerely interested in his solitary avocation. He hunkered down at the kitchen table with pen and paper and mapped out the blue alleles and chromosomes 15 and 19 with the brown-eyed parents and the modifying genes for sparse melanin, and the once-in-a-blue-moon, blue-eyed offspring that two brown-eyed parents could produce. I asked him about once-in-a-silver-moon offspring and described the man I'd seen in the pizza parlor with the silver eyes. He explained that colorless eyes expressed with dark hair and normal skin tones would be Type 3 Albinism, which, so far, had only been documented in dark-skinned people. Because of the lack of melanin, there would be problems such as poor vision, jumpy eyes, sun sensitivity — a myriad of complications. In ocular albinism, blood vessels behind the eye gave the iris a pinkish cast. Even with the Minneapolis streetlamps straight on, that singularity would have been undetectable in the dark. My Saint had claimed perfect vision. Nor had I witnessed squinting or jerking.

The color of melting ice had come down the pike from someone, someone who carried the modifying gene for sparse melanin, which meant there might be a familial link walking around somewhere. Genetically speaking, that could be anyone. I narrowed my search to blue eyes. Not sunshine blue, but aquamarine, that pale Pantone logged in around 2706 in a printer's swatch book, RGB snow 3, 16 on the Martin-Schultz scale, the Boys from Brazil. I never intended this method of research, but eye color was the one and only gemstone in my box of bling.

Did I really think this street search would net me anything?

I am one for the long shots. It's all I had.

My first encounter in color fixation was an old man in the tool aisle in a hardware store in Sauk Center. His eyes were faded blue, close enough for me to go conversational. Yes, he had three daughters and six grandchildren down in the Cities. Yes, one of the daughters had inherited his pale eyes. No, he'd never heard of a convent called Bibiana. His wife had taught school in Parkers.

Long shot. Who ever heard of a short shot?

...

Martin Micks telephoned from The Pancake House out on the freeway. I'd been expecting his call. He'd e-mailed that he had business up in Fergus Falls and would be passing through. Would I look at the compiled drawing he had of My Saint? Would I look? Ha! I'd have driven down to the Cities to look.

Our e-mailing relationship had started New Years Day. Sitting very still in front of my computer with a headache and a mocha coffee, I'd been startled awake by the ding of a new message. RE: Micks Greetings. I'd asked him how he got my e-mail address. He'd told me he could get anything.

Except My Saint. But I didn't say that.

He'd messaged that he'd checked out Fanny Graas's interment, which had been a cremation arranged out of Natchez, Mississippi, by a Mrs. Raymond Nonnatts or Nonnats. He wasn't sure of the spelling. Old lady shakes, he'd said. I paged through my handy pocket guide of saints and stopped at Raymond Nonnatus, the Patron Saint of the Falsely Accused.

...the numbers track to addresses where nobody's home in unfamiliar towns like Moline, Caruthersville, Natchez.

"Keep it coming, Martin Micks," I said from the safety of my computer cove. "You and your puffed-up faux Rickson. I will be your cheap informant."

Micks seemed genuinely glad to see me. We chatted about the weather, slushy for January. How long would he be in Fergus? One night was all. The waitress set down two cups and a pot of coffee. I ordered Swedish lace rollups with blueberry jam and powdered sugar and a glass of orange juice. Micks ordered a toasted bagel. I opened five thumbnail creamers and poured them into my coffee all the while considering how urban I would have looked out here on the prairie if I'd skipped the lace rollups and ordered toast and black coffee instead.

He opened his manila folder and produced two frontals and a profile of what My Saint should look like if she lacked the third dimension. According to the artist, she would look like a medical dummy. Although, I had to admit, the profile was spot on. But so what? If this was what she looked like in the shower, it would not be what she looked like close-up in an elevator. Having never seen

My Saint with Asian eyes or distressed teeth, Micks had no idea as to the depth of her craft.

I pushed the pictures back at him. "He's drawn you a store manikin."

He'd been watching me, hoping for a reaction on the high side of consensus. If not that, he'd have simply e-mailed an attachment. I'd disappointed him.

He exhaled and rubbed his eyes as if he'd been up all night. "You haven't heard from her?"

"I don't expect to."

"Would you tell me if you did?"

"I'll put you on speed dial."

"You're the only person I know who's met her."

I shrugged, not sure what I could add to that.

"If she contacted you, would you wire up?"

"Wire up?"

"Get her to talk on tape."

I laughed so hard I had to cover my mouth.

He frowned. "That's funny?"

After two more sniggles, I sobered. "I can't imagine her telling me anything incriminating, much less contact me at all." The 'contact me at all' part was the truth.

He said, "I guess we just wait then."

We?

He told me that he'd checked around the Loring Park area for this Sammy guy and came up blank, which called into question my brief encounter with the man off the bus. *I'm not who you think I am.* Poor fellow could have been sick and tired of being mistaken for Sammy. Maybe the real Sammy *had* met an untimely death in Iowa back in the day, just like she'd said. And maybe the woman I'd seen in the camel-colored coat with the babushka scarf and the sunglasses was anybody's neighbor, anybody's somebody, but not mine. The tapes in my Lancôme bag suggested that I had, indeed, been through Space Bartender Bob's lab experiment last October.

But four months later, here sat Martin Micks in his Minnesota Gopher sweatshirt drinking urban. I rubbed my finger on the table where the triangle of sunshine spotlighted the pancake syrups. I would write: 'Cheerless as her life had become, she would never forget the sweet smell of berries, the foggy, sweating windows, the ceramic floor tiles tracked with salty footprints.' Somebody needed to take a mop to it. Or the delete key.

Martin Micks in his Gopher sweatshirt talked about the weather. No wife, kids, mortgage, or if he'd purchased Google stock ten years ago kind of talk — nothing personal. And I didn't ask. We were professionals, I told myself, professionals with a common goal. I left the last three bites of Swedish lace on my plate and took a sip of my milky prairie coffee.

Screw professional. "You never talk about yourself. There are people who live just to talk about themselves."

He seemed to have to think about that, then said, "I never liked how I felt when I got done talking, like I'd been caught picking my nose." He took a bite of his bagel. "What do you want to know?"

"Who you are."

"You know who I am."

I fluttered my eyelashes in a lame attempt at humor. "What sign are you?"

"Leo."

"Leo," I repeated. There was no glue between Leo and Pisces. That much I knew. He didn't ask what my sign was. So much for humor. He poured more coffee and offered to top mine off. I shook my head. We were out of creamers. "Are your kids in KinderCare or at university?"

"Do I look old enough to have kids in college?"

Answer that question with a question: you're married.

"Is your wife a police officer?"

"Funny you should say that, but no. She's a doctor."

I stuffed the last three bites of Swedish lace into my mouth. "ER?"

He glanced at his watch. "OB."

"How long have you been married?"

"Eight years." He slid the composites back into his folder.

"That's good," I said. "A job like yours married to a job like hers. When do you see each other?"

"Sundays."

He loved his abstruseness.

I wondered what she looked like. There were subtle ways women asked questions and squeezed out information only a woman would care about. I wouldn't give him that. I nodded as if I understood about couples and Sundays even though I was an artist; artists didn't appreciate Sundays the same way other people did. Sundays could be Tuesdays for all we knew. Maybe I would Google her.

Our waitress asked if there would be anything else. We both declined simultaneously, grateful for the cessation of the circular. She pulled the check from her apron pocket and smiled with her sunshine blue eyes.

"What ever happened with that Faber guy who owned the Mississippi riverfront and got pushed off the Washington Avenue Bridge?"

He scowled. "Faber Elliot. Yeah, well, that took a sour spin. Turns out old Faber had pancreatic cancer. He refused to die like that. One of his insurance policies, a big one, didn't pay out on a suicide. The family came up with their own version of how he went over the rail."

"No mystery woman?"

"Turned into an insurance investigation."

"Faber pulled a Berryman."

"Berryman?"

"The poet John Berryman jumped off that same bridge. He knew about solitude."

While zipping up his faux Buzz Rickson jacket outside in the parking lot, Micks told a Lena and Oli joke he'd heard at the gas station in Osakis. I'd heard it ten times and was tempted to say the punch line, but it didn't cost me anything to *be polite, Jenn*; so I laughed, which netted me an 'ah shucks.'

I'd parked next to his green SUV. We stopped at my back bumper. He patted my shoulder and thanked me for my time. I was grounded enough not to ask if he'd like to meet up again tomorrow on his way back down from Fergus.

At the stop sign, Micks took a right heading towards the freeway. A pickup truck had weaseled in front of me and was waiting to turn left back into town. I recognized the truck. Dennis. Dennis was a man who knew I liked him (I won't explain that), but had no time for me, not even to take advantage. Dennis glanced in his rearview mirror, but did not acknowledge me. The last time I'd run into him was New Year's Eve at the Holiday Inn. He was slow dancing with my antithesis: a petite, blonde, angel-baby sweetie.

No way was I following him into town. I turned right towards the freeway, a minor detour. On the overpass I slowed and scanned up I-94 for the green SUV heading to Fergus. Nothing but a semi hauling logs. Micks must have stopped to use the loo, all that coffee. I made a u-turn back towards town. On the bridge again, I glanced down I-94 just in time to spot the green SUV heading to Minneapolis.

He'd driven all the way up just to show me his composites.
My Saint.
That's all it was.

17. Lawyer Kerby, Kerdy, Corde
JUNE

Valentine's Day in the bar at the Holiday Inn Penny met a cowboy. Three months later Penny's cowboy sent her a roundtrip ticket to Dallas. In an e-mail to Micks, I'd mentioned driving Penny down to catch a plane. He'd taken the hint and invited me to dinner. I hadn't seen him since the breakfast hoax at the pancake house. I'd asked him how things had gone in Fergus Falls. Fine, he'd answered not missing a keystroke. 'Fine' was fine with me. The man had resources and information he was willing to share.

There was nothing between us.

What he'd dug up on Laddie Ogren was not pertinent to finding My Saint, but interesting, nonetheless. Adopted by a couple named Harlan and Hattie Ogren, Laddie had grown up rural in northern Manitoba. There was no evidence of a troubled youth. After high school, young Laddie had traveled south to Winnipeg where he'd worked construction. His job as a back-hoe operator was the last traceable entry.

I'd commented that Laddie had learned the con from someone. Was there a record of Laddie's birth parents? That got me a flat-out "no, not relevant." Crime was not genetic.

Cunning Mr. Dean, you card player, buffalo slayer, backyard beaver, not even a byline.

That Harlan Ogren was Mr. Dean Ogren's brother or cousin or some such thing was obvious. And if Harlan and Hattie had raised Mr. Dean's son, the likelihood that they were now raising Mr. Dean's grandson was both plausible and heartening. The notion of Fanny's sentry son snowed in somewhere far away cheered me. Faraway from My Saint, faraway from Mr. Dean, faraway from the tricks and the devils.

Mr. Dean had to know that his son had killed the boy's mother. Had Mr. Dean been prepared for such collateral damage? No matter how bad the son, how do you explain to the father that you killed the son? And keep the money. Begrudgingly, I had to admit that if I were My Saint, I, too, would have disappeared.

I'm not macabre, but Laddie getting his head blown off gave me fist-pump satisfaction. Whenever Fanny's face with the purple crescent flashed in my mind's eye, I killed Laddie Ogren myself. Different though. I killed him cruel. It wasn't right, his being dead before he hit the floor. Didn't suffer a dime.

After I'd dropped Penny at the airport and found a passable one-star motel, I'd headed downtown to meet Micks. And there I sat, early, of course, sipping chardonnay and wishfully thinking. Even though our dinner was strictly business, the anxiety arcs under my armpits suggested otherwise.

Then someone yelled, "Hey Kerdy! Over here!" Kerdy. Kerby? It was close enough for me to turn and look. A man wearing a navy jacket and khaki pants navigated the tables. He stopped, shed his jacket, talking while he fit it over the chair back. He sat down with the punch line. The men at the table, late-twenties to fifty, and one old guy, all laughed. Kerdy must be a funny guy. *We're driving down Hennepin, Kerdy and me.* Kerdy. Might I have heard correctly? *B's and D's are phonetically muddy.* She'd covered her error by referencing phonetics. I emptied my wineglass in three gulps, ordered another to save my seat, and headed to Kerdy's table.

"Ahmm, excuse me," I said, smiling at eight appraising faces. I focused on the man they'd called Kerdy. "Sorry to interrupt, but I heard your name. Is it Kerby or Kerdy?"

"I'll stick with Kerdy," he said with an easy smile, eyebrows raised, a question mark.

Could this man belong to My Saint? His short, graying hair was fashionably spiked, not from any current fashion sense, but from cowlicks. With more laugh lines than age lines, he could lob a joke at any moment.

"Ahmm," I said. "I'm a linguist and also a genealogy buff. Might I ask how you spell Kerdy?"

"With an E," he said and spelled: "C-O-R-D-E."

"And a C. I'm sure it's mispronounced all the time. We're phonetically fanatical here in Minnesota. It's the German in us."

The old guy said, "All you got to remember is that it rhymes with dirty." The men guffawed. The two young dudes, bored with somebody else's trivia, talked between themselves.

"Well, thank you," I said. "Sorry for the interruption. Thank you." I retreated to the bar. Corde. Kerby? It's hardly even the same name. Why would she change it so radically? She hadn't changed the names of Roland Keach, Laddie Ogren, or Fanny Graas.

And they were all dead.

I glanced back at the table of jolly Joes. They might not even be lawyers. Were lawyers that jolly? Crap. The whole place was yucking it up. Not to look like the ace loser at the Fellowship Awards, I busied myself with my cell phone. The missed-call light blinked. Martin Micks. Tied up. Free at seven. I'd be trashed by seven.

"You're not a linguist."

I turned. "What? Oh, hello." I glanced past Corde to the empty table and said, "You're all married."

"Friday night is spaghetti and meatballs at my house."

"Now there's a ritual to die for. I'm actually a romance writer."

"So you are somewhat of a linguist. Are you published?"

"I stand in the rain, but have never been hit by lightning. I play the lottery, but have never matched three numbers."

And there came that funny little grin, the one My Saint had described. "Experienced with the long shots, are we?"

"I'm drawn to them. What do you do?"

"I'm a lawyer."

"I knew that." I turned full face on my stool. I was word-searching for a way to inquire about My Saint, but, once again, I didn't know what to call her. Toni, Alex, Nicky, Clare, that girl you went to high school with?

"Do I know you from somewhere?" he asked.

"Not yet."

The man seated next to me folded his credit card receipt and slid away, probably a bubbling crockpot waiting in the burbs. I glanced at the empty stool. Corde glanced at his watch. I sensed he'd seen *Fatal Attraction* more than once. He said, "Spaghetti's waiting. Good luck with your romance." He waved two fingers military style and turned towards the exit.

I called after him: "Did you ever find Sammy?"

He walked back to me, clearly surprised. "Sammy from my high school? Did you know Sammy?"

"Yes."

"Are you with the orchestra?"

"The orchestra?"

"The Minnesota Orchestra. He worked there."

Orchestra Hall was walking distance from where the tall, thin man had jumped off the bus, walking distance from where I'd seen the tall, thin man haul the kid out of the apartment. Close enough for coincidence.

"I'm a scribe, not a minstrel."

Corde squinted his eyes at me. "How did you figure I knew Sammy?"

"He told me he knew a lawyer named Corde."

The word 'shock' is a word of extremes, a word I rarely use. But there was no other way to describe it: Corde looked shocked. "You talked to Sammy? And he said he knew me?"

"Weren't you his lawyer?"

Shocked changed to puzzled. He said, "Sammy was a lawyer."

Sammy was a lawyer? Had My Saint said that? "You worked with him?"

"He wasn't practicing that I know of. You actually talked to Sammy?"

"Yes, yes I did."

"None of us had talked to him in over twenty years. A sighting every now and then. A couple of people got close enough for him to make a quick exit. How did my name come up?"

"I don't rightly remember," I said. "Do you know where I might find him?"

He cocked his head, truly puzzled. "Sammy's dead. He died this spring."

It was my turn to be shocked. "That can't be."

"'fraid so."

"You mean he's really dead this time?"

"I'd always suspected he was alive, but he stayed out so long, nobody could believe he was out by choice. Which is why some thought he was dead long before he was."

"How'd he die?"

"Ulcers or something."

"He died with a lot of answers." I gave him a hopeful look. "One trail dies, but now here you are."

His eyebrows jumped.

"I need to find another classmate of yours. She and Sammy were friends. I haven't seen her in awhile. She might not know he died. Unfortunately, I'm short a name."

"You don't know her name?"

"No, but you do. She does work for you. You do work for her. Like bailing her out of jail and stuff."

"Are you sure you got the right lawyer?"

"I believe I do."

"This mystery girl was in touch with Sammy?"

"She's not a girl. She's your age."

"Careful."

"You graduated high school together."

"I haven't seen anyone from high school since the last reunion." He twisted his lips in a thinking man's way.

I added, "She has silver eyes. You'd have to remember that."

His expression indicated that he didn't.

"Okay, I don't know her name and I'm not even sure what she looks like. She changes all the time." There wasn't much he could say to that either. "Do you still have your high school yearbook? Maybe I would recognize her."

He patted his pockets. "Left it at home."

I grinned. "Could you maybe take a peek in the attic? I'll stop by your office Monday. This is important." My parents were home for the summer so I wasn't worried about Mystery Cat. I could stay an extra day or two.

"Even if I could find said yearbook, if you don't know what she looks like now, how will you identify her from a high school yearbook? What'd you say your name was?"

"Jennifer Sands. Jas for short."

"Can I inquire as to why you're looking for this phantom?"

We're all a bunch of phantoms.

"Phantom, yes. That's exactly the way she described the whole lot of you. I write crime novels. This phantom has information critical to my story."

"You're not a romance writer."

I'd forgotten I'd said that. "I've changed genres. There's more interesting crime than there is interesting romance."

"Ahhh," he said, as if that made sense. "Well, Jennifer Jas, I wish I could tell you something interesting, but…"

I lowered my voice. "I helped her steal a file out of a warehouse over in St. Paul last October. It was payback to some lawyer who got her off a breaking and entering charge. We fought off a pack of Swedish guard dogs. Did she tell you that?"

His baffled look did not change, but his demeanor shifted. I might have just assured him that I truly was a loonytoon.

He chuckled, but was no longer amused. "It sounds like something out of a crime novel."

"You drive a brand new, black Lexus ES300."

"I think somebody's fooling with you. '03 was the last year they made that model." He pushed up his sleeve and tapped his watch. "Cold spaghetti, uh-uh. Tell you what, I'll look around for that yearbook." He reissued his two-fingered salute and walked away, faster this time, and no looking back. No phone number. No matter. I knew how to spell his name.

If Corde turned out to be another red herring, who was the real lawyer? Sammy? He'd had neither the appearance nor the demeanor required by the justice system.

Sammy, one time philosopher, defender of liberty, now a short-order cook right here in Minneapolis.

Defender of liberty.

18. A Stillwater Saturday

A skylight? What pervert would install a skylight in a motel room? Add a wall-mounted, billboard sized TV. Not a motel room. Not on my budget. Matter of fact, beige, polyester armrests on either side of my head would make this a fold-out couch. I drew up on my elbows. No books, magazines, nary a knickknack or quilted throw. No photographs. The single artistic element in the room was a wedge of sun stripes on the wall compliments of the blinds. A counter with two barstools separated the kitchen. A wilted philodendron wrapped in foil and a purple florist's bow languished on the countertop. The place was terminally male. Down the hallway a door closed.

Micks. Micks and too much wine.

He hadn't shown up until eight. We'd shared a feed-the-world bowl of spaghetti and meatballs. Spaghetti and meatballs — Lawyer Corde. I had scored. I also had no idea what, after four drinks at the bar and a bottle of Cabernet at the table, I had given up. I remembered the night's pitch and drift, but the details were sketchy.

I peeked beneath the cocoa brown sheet and matching blanket. Except for my shoes, I was fully clothed. The sheets smelled new, itchy crisp with out-of-the-pack sheet creases. Divorce sheets.

One of the stools by the counter creaked. I folded back the covers and said, "Three is my limit. Four max."

"I didn't realize you'd drank so much."

"I had a head start, excuse me."

"Sorry. I know better than to plan ahead. There's always something."

"Where's my car?"

"Downstairs."

I pointed to myself. "I drove?"

He pointed to himself. "I drove." He pointed at me. "Your car."

"Is this your place?"

"We already covered that."

"What'd you say?"

"It is now."

After four glasses and a bottle of wine, newbie-divorced was a subject I'd have tackled. I couldn't tackle again. What I needed was a shower. Hot, pounding water would stimulate recall.

...

Back in my one-star motel room, I'd knocked off my base haze with a shower and a couple of OTCs, but total recall hadn't happened. Micks pulled up in the green SUV and honked his horn. He needed to pick up a package downtown and shepherd it to Stillwater for a signature. I'd agreed to tag along. Given my current condition, there was nothing else I felt like doing. And it would give me an opportunity to figure out what, if anything, I'd given up.

"I need your opinion on something," he said, wrenching out of his jacket. He unbuckled a shoulder holster, rolled it up, gun intact, and stuffed it in the glove compartment. I caught a whiff of copper pennies. He closed the glove box. It fell open. He slammed it shut.

"Opinion on what?"

"Video surveillance."

"It's Saturday."

"Twenty-four-seven."

We cruised off 35W and headed up Third Street into downtown Minneapolis. Micks parked at the curb next to an Official Vehicles sign, pulled a card from the visor, and slapped it on the dashboard. We entered the building through a basement door. A man behind a screened-in counter nodded at Micks. We walked a maze of hallways and stopped at door number B. He flipped the light switch and ushered me into a windowless room about the size of a jail cell. We settled in front of a computer on a desk shoved up against the wall. The sleep light flashed. He tapped it awake, punched past several titles, and stopped at Number 29 Hightower something or another that I didn't catch before it flicked to a dimly lit, wood-paneled hallway. The camera followed a grainy, black and white Santa Claus down a narrow corridor. Santa disappeared through a doorway. The LED read DEC 25 2:49 A.M. Micks punched the keys and Santa reappeared frozen mid-corridor.

"I assume Santa's not bearing gifts."

"You assume correctly."

"Bad Santa."

"Pay attention." Santa moved again down the hallway with a long stride. "That's obviously a mask, so watch and tell me: male or female?" Micks replayed the scene, but nothing in the moves defined gender. The slouchy hat with its trademark puffball along with the bulky costume made gender identification impossible.

"Flip a coin," I said.

The screen flicked to Santa rifling through the drawers of a desk befitting the oval office, then away to a wall painting of geese posing in long grass. Two more seconds, Santa appeared and with a gloved hand pulled on the picture frame, which opened to a wall safe. Just as Santa moved his gloved hand to the combination lock, the camera flicked back to the desk.

Micks said, "This surveillance system has since been upgraded."

"The old closing the barn door after the cows get out?"

"Something like that."

The camera flicked back to the geese just in time to watch Santa close the picture. He was a smart thief, dressed for the camera, not to be made no matter how many times you zoomed in and enlarged the frame. He moved out of the camera's crippled eye.

"That was fast," I said. "He must have known the combination."

Micks shook his head. "Don't think so. Watch."

The camera arrived back at the desk and caught the thief stuffing an envelope inside his fat Santa coat.

"Didn't come from the safe. It was on the desk, although they swear it was in the safe."

"What'd he take?"

"A recipe."

"For what? Fruitcake? Lutefisk loaf? No money? No bearer bonds or compact discs?"

"A disc, yeah. The company is into medical equipment. This technology was breakthrough in heart transplants. Off the computer, it was that proprietary."

I waited for more details. None came. "This was Christmas?"

"Christmas eve, yeah. So it was two days before someone figured out it was missing."

"How'd he get into the building at three in the morning?"

"It's not a building. It's a private residence."

"Protected by a flock of geese."

"The family was home. Asleep. One of the kids got in late. Didn't arm the system, a zone alarm, although he swears he did. If this had been an office building, it would have been an inside job. No question. The same company was hit in their downtown office back in October." Micks looked at me. "About the time you were in town."

I frowned at him, not sure of the implication.

"Somebody waltzed in, snatched a briefcase out of the comptroller's office, waltzed out. Broad daylight. And the briefcase wasn't stock — total retro, old, beat-up. It would have been noticed."

"A beat-up briefcase?"

"Yeah. You know, full-size with the brass locks that open with a key."

I swallowed hard and said, "Maybe it got out in a shopping bag."

"As a matter of fact, it did. Surveillance showed three shopping bags leaving the building. The bag we couldn't track down was carried out by a woman wearing a security guard uniform. Now there's a cliché for you."

...always, always, always stay within the cliché.

"Anyway, it looked like a woman. The hat hid her face. Not to want to admit the company could be raided that easily, they insisted it was an inside-the-building job. That's why they removed the disc over the holiday, brought it home to the geese."

"Why didn't they use a safety deposit box or something other than the geese?"

"Wacko eccentrics don't always process the mundane like you and I would." To my withered look, he added, "Cheerios aren't always kept in the kitchen cupboard. Watch what happens here."

He tapped the keys. We were back in the hallway. Santa emerged from the office doorway. A large, pale-colored dog walked into the frame, tail wagging, and hunkered up to the thief like an old friend. The thief bent over and rubbed the dog's head, a good ten seconds worth, then held up a gloved finger to the dog. Stay? Santa turned and walked towards the camera on his way out the door, issues finalized. Adios, sayonara. The dog stayed sitting in the hallway.

"The dog knew the thief?"

"It looks that way, but it was a Golden. They love everybody including thieves. The only thing we can figure is that the family had a 200 guest Christmas party mid December. Invitation only, checked at the door by security. All the guests have been considered. We've interviewed the security company, the caterers, the florists, the housekeepers, and the yardmen, half of them seasonal with the shelf-life of a fruit fly. We were unable to locate four of them. One of which was our thief. Had to be."

"That makes sense. He could have shown up early with a flower delivery or come in carrying a cleaning basket and a clipboard. He cases the place, learns the dog's name. Or, better yet, just shows up at the party in a waiter's tux and works the room with a tray of pigs in blankets."

Micks' eyes slid to mine.

I shrugged. "Hey, the pigs are back."

Micks tapped the screen.

"Have it your way. Caviar and toast points."

"Do you recognize anything about Santa here, anything at all that might be familiar?"

I snorted. "What's there to recognize? It's a costume. There's nothing that identifies him."

"I don't think it's a him." Micks walked the shadow backwards to the dog. "Look at this." Micks zoomed in on Santa's shoes, visible when he leaned over and rubbed the dog's head. "That's the shine of rubber. See that vague stripe below the ankle? Those are rubber garden shoes. Size nine, I'd guess."

I leaned towards the screen and twirled a strand of hair forward to conceal my flushed face. I managed to say, "Well, isn't that the damndest thing."

Christmas is my busiest season, like retail.

It was hard to keep the smile off my face.

On our way out of downtown with a clear sky, light traffic, and Micks driving, I kept an eye half-open for the bookstore and the locksmith shop. Somewhere between the streets and the avenues, that murder scene existed. Last October there'd been enough fog downtown to lose a school bus, but not today. I wondered if the little locksmith with the broom and the darting eyes would remember me. He'd had that spooky carnival-mechanic thing going on. Pretty Midwest girls. I wanted to ask

Micks if he'd heard anything new about the bookstore murder, but then he'd wonder why I wanted to know. With Laddie Ogren dead, that case was closed. I glanced at him.

He caught my glance and said, "What?"

"I didn't say anything."

"You were going to. I know when somebody's working on something." We flowed into I-94 traffic heading towards St. Paul.

"It's wine withdrawal."

"You're a good drunk, Jas. You don't get all teary-eyed when you talk romance."

"Talk romance," I repeated, searching for memory.

"As of last night, I know more about romance novels than everybody I've ever met all totaled. I now know the difference between Nora Jones and Nora Roberts. And the next time some burly-ass cop mentions Anne Taylor Bradford, I can chime right in. And that Victoria something or another who always kills somebody off."

"Victoria Holt." It was coming back to me. "Did I mention that I'm writing crime?"

"Yeah, and your criminal got himself written out of the story, and you're trying to write him back in."

Him. I'd had the good sense to change the gender.

"You don't remember any of this?" He chuckled at my stupefied look. "The love scenes in your French book would make the French blush. You are an impassioned lady, Jas, under the influence. Maybe you should keep a case of cabernet in the closet. I probably wouldn't read the French thing, but your crime book might be something I'd pick up. Provided you didn't sissy it up."

"Sissy it up?"

"You know, girl stuff. You don't remember this conversation?"

"I can bore myself into a blackout."

Stillwater is an old logging town chiseled into a hillside on the St. Croix River. Twenty years ago it was a place for country living within driving distance of big city living, the best of both worlds. Now it's a suburb of St. Paul, albeit a good one. The only landmark I knew was The Lowell Inn, a comfort food rendezvous since the 30s, fashionably old-fashioned. I'd eaten there once as a child and still remembered the hot, homemade buns. I wondered if they still served them. In this day and age.

We crawled along Main with high hopes for a parking spot. Summertime Stillwater was like the State Fair. We turned around at the Marina and took another run at it. Three cars ahead, a station wagon pulled into traffic vacating a space. The three cars in front of us had other plans. Timing.

"Come on," Micks said. "It's a cool old building."

It was, except for the elevator. Its machinery scraped and creaked like an oilrig. The doors shuddered open. I hesitated. He nudged me. I eased in sideways just in case the rubber jaws reacted negatively to human flesh. Three mirrored walls gave the illusion of more space, but I wasn't soothed. Micks punched TWO and we wobbled up to the second floor. Climbing the stairs on our hands and knees would have been quicker. The elevator stopped with a jerk and the doors opened just wide enough for us to slip out sideways into what looked like the set of a Sam Shepard western. The black and tan linoleum tiles, old and cracking, had been recently buffed. The hallway heading left ended at an opened window with a blue-sky view of a tarred rooftop baking in the sun. The frontward hallway, lit by amber door windows, dead-ended in shadows. Low-shine mahogany woodwork deepened the gloom. Slowly rotating ceiling fans thunked like flat tires. I followed Micks into the gloom. The names of the occupants were stenciled in black on the amber glass. We stopped at a two-partner law office — one name I would not pronounce, the other was Olson. Micks opened the door to a reception area that was lit up like an operating room and just as grim with its windowless, stadium gray walls and one white laminate desk that looked permanently vacated. Micks opened one of the two doors and disappeared. The gray plastic chair behind the empty desk wobbled under my weight. My entertainment choices were *Field and Stream* March and *Field and Stream* April. Just as I was about to discover the secret to reeling in a prize-sized walleye, Micks reappeared, and we were out the door into the Sam Shepard hallway on our way to my favorite elevator.

Jaws wide open, the elevator was waiting for us like it wasn't finished yet, the finale tangled in its ropes and chains. Instead of sitting like a dupe contemplating prize-sized walleyes, I should have searched out the stairwell. Oh, well. A one-floor drop — how bad could that be? I glanced down the hallway to the opened window where a woman and a kid, backlit by the blue sky, exited an office and headed towards the elevator. Micks hustled me into the buggy, but didn't follow. The door quivered. Micks put his hand on the rubber.

"Get in," I said. "They'll take the stairs. Nobody rides this thing."

That barely out of my mouth, a boy leaped through the quivering doors. Cripes. He must have run the hallway just to ride the elevator. He turned to the mirrored wall and examined his teeth. Probably a dentist down the hall. After what seemed like two chapters later, the woman ducked through the doors and stepped to the back of the elevator. Micks followed her in. The door pulsed without closing. Oxygen seemed finite and I breathed deep to claim my share. The boy frowned at himself in the mirror and rubbed his jaw. His hair was black and too long for the times. Neither his jeans nor his aqua-blue tee bore a logo. Was he from another planet? Micks pushed the CLOSE button. The door pulsed.

My skin went damp. "I'll find the stairs," I said.

"Hold on," Micks said. He tapped the button, committed, like a man who's lost and won't ask for directions.

I peeked sideways at the woman in the mirror. Her eyes were on the boy. A brimmed straw hat secured her charcoal gray hair behind her ears. What I could see of her face looked fresh, a little too fresh for the charcoal hair. The dental assistant probably moonlighted as a cosmetologist.

The elevator trembled.

"I'm out of here!" I stepped forward and the doors sucked shut. I jumped back with a yelp.

Micks hooted. "They don't make 'em like this anymore. Vavoom!"

"Vavoom?" I said, fiercely. The boy glanced up at me in the mirror. His eyes were the best of blue skies under thick black lashes. If I had been alone, and not bathed in sweat, I might have made conversation with the woman, a family tree inquiry. Just for grins.

I swiped the sweat off my upper lip. The boy smiled his Novocain mouth at the mirror again. We stopped with a bump. The doors ground open and I jumped out and ran to the exit where I stopped to gulp air and compose myself.

Micks caught up with me. "Do we have small space syndrome?"

"It's the machinery. Machinery has a life of its own and it's always contrary to mine. We could have lost limbs." I glanced back at the woman and the boy to confirm that they'd not been dismembered or bleeding or something. Standing at the elevator, the woman was searching through a large leather bag. I turned back to the door, which Micks pushed open with a bow and a sweep of his manila envelope to usher me through. That's when I heard her speak. It was foreign, so it wasn't what she said. It was a familiarity, a remembrance, that stopped me. I turned again to look. She handed the boy a bottle of water. He grabbed the bottle and took a long drink. She slipped on a pair of sunglasses and adjusted her bag onto her shoulder. Her cream-colored dress looked like a tea party frock, one of those pastel florals gathered at the waist, flattering on thin people.

Out on the sidewalk I stopped, just out of sight, knelt down and fiddled with the strap of my sandal. Micks waited by the SUV with that 'I'm a patient kind of guy' look men know to do. Any minute now she would come out. And out she came. The boy first. He started in my direction, but she grabbed his arm and redirected him. German. She sounded like Angela Folly, Patron Saint of Temptation, imitating the bookstore clerk.

"Hi!" I called out, cheerfully low on the sidewalk, non-threatening. "Excuse me. Do you know where the Lowell Inn is?"

"*Englisch, nein,*" she said and spoke what might have been an apology. I caught the tick of a smile at the corner of her mouth before she took hold of the boy's hand and led him away. I heard what sounded like "be island." From her body language, I'd gamble she'd just told him to hurry up.

"Grandmamma," the boy protested.

Grandmamma? No way. There was a better chance My Saint showing up as a mermaid.

The traffic stopped. My two curios stepped off the curb and crossed the street. I stood up and brushed nonexistent dirt off my jeans while I watched them walk away.

The world has become too small anymore for there not to be coincidence.

A quick breeze fanned off the river. The woman put a hand to her hat. Her skirt swished at the knees like fine material does. She walked young. I added seams down the backs of her nylon stockings, picture perfect for *Love is a French Verb*. She would wear gloves. The year would be 1940 when gloves were fashionable even in the summer heat. I stared after them until they disappeared into the River Exchange building.

My Saint and Bentley Ogren. How likely was that?

Micks was leaning against the SUV fiddling with his keys. Should I ask him to wait a minute? I'd be right back? Or just tear across the street after them? Either way, Micks would follow. Not good.

"What's that all about?" Micks jangled his keys. "I know where The Lowell Inn is."

I slogged to the passenger door, unable to shake the notion that the German woman was My Saint. Now if this were a Charles Dickens novel.... I opened the door and slid in. Micks settled behind the wheel and pried open his key ring with a pocketknife. I chewed my fingernail. *Not all my German is lost*, she'd said on the bookstore tape. This woman spoke German like a first language. And the boy had understood. When she'd touched her triple cream collar, I'd glimpsed a cross. Not Toni Padua's Celtic cross, but a cross all the same.

I needed to dump Micks.

He continued with the keys. "I got to shed some metal." How long would this key thing go on? Micks could be a janitor.

Red herring. Red herring. Let me be daring.

"I'll check out those shops over across the street." I opened the door. "While you do that."

"Wait. I'll come. I got carried away here." He pulled one key off the ring.

I shut the door. Why did I think that woman was My Saint? And Bentley Ogren, too? I'd never seen the boy's face. Did Micks have a photo in his files?

I couldn't contain myself. "Those pictures you've got?"

"What pictures?" He punched the glove box. It fell open. He tossed the key inside, slammed it shut and locked it.

"Toni, Brigid, Alex." That got his attention. "Do you have a picture of Bentley Ogren?"

"Fanny Graas's son? No. Why?"

I shrugged. "Is Graas German?" I hadn't meant to wonder that aloud.

He stared at me a moment. His eyes slid to the Sam Shepard building, then to the River Exchange Building where the woman and the boy had disappeared. "Damn her."

"What? Graas is Dutch. Grass is German."

Micks mumbled, "Same difference," and out the door he flew, wheedled through the moving cars, and almost fell over a waddling toddler before he disappeared into the River Exchange building.

"Ah, shit," was all I could say.

19. Hunting

How'd he jump there so fast? I'd said nothing, not enough for him to go bonkers on me. And double damn, My Saint seeing me with the enemy. *He'll never touch me. With or without your help.* She'd read me like a street sign.

Blame the previous night's overindulgence (I'll never drink again), but I couldn't think what came next. I stared at the River Exchange Building and flinched when Micks blew out the door. He stopped dead on the sidewalk, hands on his hips like a TV cop chasing a perp. Obviously, there'd been no perp. Perps. Kidnapper and kidnapee.

The boy had called her Grandmamma. Mum-Maaa. Foreign.

Grandmamma hadn't looked like either of my grandmas, Mrs. Claus off a Christmas card. Nor had the German lady looked like My Saint in any one defining way. It'd been more like a sense of her, a sleepwalker's déjà vu. My skin prickled.

Traffic stopped. Micks could cross but he didn't — just stood there next to a 'Best Turtles in Minnesota' tent sign. What was he waiting for? Not believing she'd disappeared that fast? He didn't know My Saint. He spun around back inside.

He won't quit. What if he found her? I needed to find her first.

Bullying Main Street traffic into stopping for me was a sure sign of my plummeting blood sugar. One could also argue a lack of basic good sense, which some jerkball in a Mini Cooper succinctly pointed out. Sorry. Across and undamaged, I tore into the Exchange building, but stopped short at the smell of hot caramel and toasted nuts. Desperately in need of food, anything at all, I slipped into Best Turtles in Minnesota. Then Micks grabbed me by the arm and yanked me out.

"Christ, what?" I said twisting loose.

"Take outside, the back door," he ordered and ran up the steps to the St. Croix Crab House. Was I working for him? I peeked back into the candy store. The line to turtle bliss was seven deep. I headed out the back door.

The street smelled like popcorn, an equally agreeable remedy, but I didn't see any red or white circus carts, not even a clown with a basket. My mouth watered, not in a happy way. I crossed the street to the Freight House and walked up the ramp to an outdoor patio summer-flush with diners. I inspected the crowd, fairly certain I wasn't looking for a pastel floral sundress. If she was still in the vicinity for whatever reason, she'd pulled a quick-change. A waiter set three monster salads and a triple-decker cheeseburger on a table close enough to snatch a French fry. The man with the triple-decker cheeseburger caught me ogling. I moved out of his space and wandered towards the river. What I needed was a pair of hide-your-face sunglasses.

Three boys wearing identical baseball caps ran rowdy with a leaping farm dog. Three suspects. But those in charge of suspect boys didn't remotely resemble the German woman. My Saint could not have rendered a complicated fat disguise in five minutes. At the river's edge a woman and a little girl, both Norwegian-blonde, were tossing crumbs or something into the water. Bender had worn a blonde wig out of Canada. The girl's denim shorts and madras shirt and the woman's blue jeans and baggie t-shirt typified quick-change clothes if I ever saw quick-change clothes. A nylon backpack lay on the ground, the kind that fold up like origami, large enough to pack both a costume change and a brown leather bag. It would be just like her to hang around and feed the wildlife knowing I would assume otherwise. I eased towards them, planning my approach, which wasn't necessary because they turned, done with the ducks. The woman was all of seventeen and the little girl was just that, a little girl. I wondered how Micks was doing.

Would Grandmamma and the boy split up? Maybe there was a third person. They had visited someone in the Sam Shepard building. Had there been more than amalgam and Novocain down that hallway? My speculations were growing more obtuse by the minute. Fact was grandmamma and grandson had vanished.

A houseboat puttered by, cozy and inviting with its colorful deckchairs and their homespun pillows. I could live on a river, but never a lake where you went round and around and around and covered the same acreage day in, day out, going nowhere like a gerbil on a wheel. Rivers point away. Keep going if you felt like it, clean and clear of the ridiculous. I imagined myself on the deck of the houseboat with a martini and a laptop, liking the idea until the mother of all motorboats cruised past. The houseboat rocked like a cradle.

Not today.

Up on the street, a true American entrepreneur had set up a hotdog tent. I ran to it and beat out a family of ten on the approach. My transaction took less than a minute. I collapsed on the curb and devoured two shriveled-up dogs and a mini bag of over-salted potato chips. Nothing had ever tasted so good. I kept one eye on the street, just in case, scrutinizing each suspect who strolled past, each milky face an assembly of what even the most uninspired make-up man could pull out of his bag of paints and gels. We weren't ever going to find her. I wiped my chin clean of drifting condiments, stood up and dumped my trash. The family of ten was still ordering.

Lightheadedness on the wane, I meandered back down to the river and stepped up into a stucco gazebo filled with afternoon wayfarers. Suspects came and went. Every one of them a possibility. Smear on those paints and jells, pull on a blonde Clare Assett or a black Genny Ross wig, tack on a mole or two, a wire headband, plumpers at the cheeks, change up the attitude — *voila!* I had Dusty Springfield, Patti Smith, and everybody in between. I abandoned the stucco gazebo.

On down the river at the Stillwater Marina, PD Pappy's patio bar was hyped-up with the motorboat crowd. Five tawny brokerage dudes with rolled-up shirtsleeves and khaki shorts stood at the bar, plastic grocery bags at their feet. Come off the boat for supplies? I wondered where they'd sailed in from: New Orleans? Cancun? The Yucatan? I scanned the slips for what boat that might be and spotted it at the end of the dock. Extreme white fiberglass, windows on three levels, a dinghy perched on top. The big boat had a temporary rift about it, fueling up, stocking up, ticket to ride clean and clear. This was no boat. This was a yacht. I didn't know anybody who knew anybody who owned a yacht.

A little girl wearing white shorts and a red tee, a baseball hat pulled low over her snarly blonde hair, ran along the dock towards the water. The mother, a bleached blonde dressed in a baggy, sea-green, pants outfit, hurried after her. She carried a multi-colored travel bag, the strap diagonal across her chest. Even though she was runway thin, she moved with the arched-back straddle of an overdue pregnant woman. Maybe she was carrying rocks.

I watched them flick in and out between the docked boats. Well, dang it. They were heading for my tawny brokers' yacht. Hijackers. Rich tourists. Rocks in the bag? Hell, no. More like money in the bag. Stillwater afforded nooks and crannies where one could spend an inheritance. Feeling ridiculously disappointed at this reversal of fortunes, I turned back to channel condolences to my tawny broker dudes, but they'd skedaddled, grocery bags and all. Land dwellers.

I wandered down to the river's edge and leaned against the fence. The yacht was heading out, running fast. No cost per gallon worries. Trust fund baby. The depletion of the earth's resources was somebody else's problem. Evaporating ethyl in my frontal lobe had manifested into self-righteous animosity.

I turned away to face a hillside of multi-storied condos and offices and storefronts both old and new and rehabbed — a battery of places to hide. She could be standing in one of those windows this very moment watching me watching her. I waved at the hillside. Just in case. Where was Micks?

What Micks wasn't understanding was that I was not on his side, not to mention payroll. What did he expect me to do, anyway, in the middle of downtown Stillwater? Grab her by the arm and blow my whistle? A citizen's arrest? Buy her coffee, keep her occupied until he showed up?

In the turn-around a man and a woman were packing picnic gear into a station wagon. The woman was twenty pounds overweight wearing blue jeans and a striped t-shirt. Her dark hair was wet as if she'd been swimming. A Jack Russell bounded out of the backseat followed by a dark-haired boy who let go a Frisbee that the dog caught with the ease of an outfielder. The woman yelled at them to get back in the car. They didn't.

And there came Micks trotting across the grass.

I said, "I think that's them," with a nod at the station wagon. "The kid throwing the Frisbee is dead on. The woman's hair is wet. Quick color rinse. Quick change."

He stared at them, interested.

"Go on over there," I coaxed. "Show your moxie."

He shot me an irritated look. "You just don't get it, do you? Nobody gets it." He folded his arms.

It occurred to me that Martin Micks operated in a perpetual warning mode, shaking his proverbial finger. Or was it impatience, that demeanor? I wondered how he acted around other people.

"Ever consider that it might be you who doesn't get it?"

His eyes narrowed.

I met his narrowed eyes and said, "When you see a young person playing the role of an old person in the movies, there's always something not quite right. Watch closely and it's awkwardly transparent, the imposture, like how a tomboy walks in high heels. Or the person wearing the coat they just stole; their posture is weak, their head barely ducked, not a shameful duck, but a stealthy duck. It's not obvious, but if you're paying attention, you know something's up. A woman who's just had her hair done stands taller. You must aggressively hunt to catch these nuances."

He thought about that for a moment. "Yeah. If you know people, you can pick up on it." He snapped his fingers to show how that was done.

I gave it some timing, then said, almost a hiss, "There was no such thing about her. She was that studied. She was that skilled. She has control of her autonomic nervous system, I swear to God."

A whoop from PD Pappy's got our attention. The tawny brokers were back at the bar. They'd exchanged the grocery bags for women. We turned away simultaneously and looked across the water at Wisconsin, fed up with other people's picnics, fed up with each other, fed up with a nowhere day on the riverfront.

Micks said, "You're probably the only person who's ever met her multiple selves."

I leaned into the railing. "Don't take it personal. Those pictures of yours that the apartment manager thought were different women? They could just as well have been different women. Each one has her own handwriting, her own perfume, her own pitch of voice, her own way of walking. Do you get what I'm saying? Hell, she might have figured out a way to change blood types. So what I'm telling you, sir, is that if you don't have her cuffed to the steering wheel, she's gone."

His shady jaw twitched. He said, almost wistfully, "I had a front row seat once. Watched two or three of her parade in and out of an apartment building. I had no idea what I was seeing. And my royal thrashing? She moved out right in front of me."

I was tempted to add 'in your green Toyota,' but that would have upped his ire. He leaned into the railing next to me. I could feel the hairs on his arm touching mine. He had to feel it, too. Pride told me to move my arm, but I couldn't. It was fused there by possibilities.

Would our inimitable relationship be clear to me when examined from the distance of time and space? An impossible dimension when we existed in the here and now in the age of possibilities, ambitions fired by our imaginations. I would write that he leaned closer and whispered something potently personal in my ear, that his lips brushed my hair. But in real time on the St. Croix riverbank, he did no such thing.

What he said, with more admiration than ire, was: "I'd give my left nut for one hour with her."

I was standing in a Mitch Albom novel, for Christ's sake. I moved my arm.

"Amazing," he continued. "The woman is fucking amazing. Think what we could do if she was on our side."

"She'll never be on *your* side," I blurted, no longer fused. "The day Bob Dylan moves back to Hibbing. Those were her exact words. Then she laughed." I hated how I sounded, bitter and punishing. Truth was I was out of my league with his women: his wife, a doctor and My Saint, the Einstein of crime. He, too, was out of league with his women, but, like most men, he didn't know it. I had his full attention: Jennifer Sands, two-penny tipster, his 'rabbit in the hat' when he broke the case and debuted as the world's top detective. The fact that one day I might be called to witness infuriated me. "Give it up, Micks. You have proof of nothing. Otherwise, you'd have cuffed me long ago on some dumbass girl-charge and wrenched it out of me. Give it up. You're embarrassing yourself."

We watched the river in acrimonious silence. Late afternoon the boats converged on Stillwater like picnickers in a park. The St. Croix needed traffic lights. Speaking of traffic lights, the white yacht had reached the bridge. The string of cars, stopped by a drawbridge on the rise, backed up into Wisconsin.

"There should be a charge for that," Micks grumbled.

"That's *The Trust Fund*," I said with equally bad temper.

We walked back to the SUV, not a word between us. He yanked open his door, hopped in, slammed it shut. I opened my door and crawled in, exhausted. He slapped his hands on the steering wheel. "Why didn't you say something? When you were on the sidewalk screwing with your shoe?"

"Say what?"

"You knew that was her."

"Hey, Micks," I said, theatrically enthusiastic. I pointed to an elderly couple holding hands and talking with the devotion of newlyweds. "That woman with the yellow pants outfit is skinny Toni Padua. She's got it going big with the fat pads. That grey fuzz is a wig, for sure. No, wait! It's Cathy Senna, the holy saint of goddamn fire. She's bleached her hair. And for sure she's just been to the dentist." I patted my cheeks.

Micks stared at the elderly couple. "Do you know what thin ice is?"

"Oh, please. The woman in the elevator was too young. Just exactly how old do you think your criminal is?"

"Can't lock it down."

"Our septuagenarian out there on the sidewalk could have killed Jimmy Hoffa back in the Fifties."

"That was the Seventies. And maybe she did."

"Yeah, and maybe she kidnapped the Lindbergh baby. You have no reason to be ill with me. The woman didn't even speak English. Have any of your street punks ever heard her speak German?"

"Nobody's heard her speak anything."

"Well, damn. And what were you going to do anyway? Arrest her? Ask her to follow along to headquarters? She'd jump right on that." I opened the door, but couldn't catch a breeze. I fanned my face.

Micks didn't have a plan. He just wanted to find her. And if Micks couldn't find her with all his resources, how could I? He opened his door and got out.

I yelled, "Where do you think you're going?"

He headed towards the Sam Shepard building. I jumped out and ran after him and caught the door in my face. He passed the cranky elevator and disappeared around the corner. When I caught up with him, he was waiting at a door labeled STAIRWELL. He opened it and said, "After you." He had a way about him.

At the top of the stairs I opened the door and there we were again in that Wild West time warp. A woman reading a newspaper, a wooden cane over one arm, waited for the cranky elevator. If not for her cane, I would have suggested the stairs. We headed down the hall towards the open window passing a law office and a land surveyor. The last door was, indeed, a dentist's office. Two dentists. Don Warner, DDS, and R.L. Ricky, DDS. My teeth tingled at the searing sound of a drill.

"Can I help you?" from a young woman seated behind the L-shaped counter. Her eyes were faded hazel, serious and unwelcoming. Denise, according to her name badge.

Micks said, "The woman who was here about an hour ago with the boy..." he waited. When Denise didn't fill in the blanks, he pulled out his investigator card and placed it on the counter.

"Can I help you?" she said again, ignoring the card.

He leaned into the counter, comfortable in his role as seeker of information. "I need to get a hold of her. She might have information that could help in an investigation."

"And how might I assist you?"

"You could tell me how I might get in touch with her." He pushed his card towards her. He'd have called her Doll if I hadn't been standing there.

She leaned back in her chair and crossed her arms. "And her name is?"

"It could be one of several. She's covered up in aliases."

The phone rang. Denise held a finger to Micks and answered it. After several affirmations while writing on her pink pad, she ripped off the page, tossed it into a tray labeled ISSUES, and said, "We close at noon on Saturdays." It wasn't clear if she was talking to us or into the phone. The clock on the wall read three-fifteen. Denise said, "Good-day, sir," and dropped the receiver into its cradle. She picked up the business card.

"So, Mr. Micks, why do you think our patient is the person you're looking for?" I suspected she got a lot of mileage out of this posture. I was paying attention. Micks tossed his hair out of his eyes and shifted into an even more sociable pose.

"We know what she looks like," he said.

She countered with a parental tone, "I don't give out names. You know that."

"I understand," Micks said. He glared at me — for being there, I was sure. He said to Denise, "I'd like to speak with the boy's dentist."

"It'll be awhile."

Micks said, "We'll wait," and headed for a row of semi-Bauhaus chairs. We plopped down. I snatched the magazine off the top of the stack and slapped it open to a generic color spread of a cityscape. Micks folded his arms for a minute, then picked up *Newsweek*, fanned through it twice, then said to Denise, "About how long?"

She didn't look up when she answered, "About three days. Dr. Ricky is gone for the weekend. You might have passed her by the elevator." I slid the magazine to the bottom of the stack and followed Micks out the door. *Stadtleute*.

. . .

Micks jammed his key into the ignition. "Little bitch."

"Shouldn't you have pulled a fifty off a roll of bills?"

He sent me his all too familiar warning look. "I'll be back Monday and have a talk with Miss Ricky." He started the engine and added, "Alone."

"Give me a basic break. Without me, you'd have nothing."

"I've got a shitload of paper on that woman."

"I don't think you got shit." I stared at the spot where the German woman had stood with the boy and set about designing their lives. They are people who spend summers in Iceland. They own reindeer and employ a chauffeur named Abraham. Afternoons the lone sound in the summerhouse is the soft tat-tat-tat of marbles dropping through a great brass maze followed by a spiral roll down a centrifuge, tat-tat-tat followed by another roll and on into eternity. Evenings Abraham plays the white grand piano while she reads Joan Didion and drinks aquavit. She and Joan know about obsession. So do I. As does Micks. Especially Micks. How many imaginary conversations has he had with her alone at night under the covers? Could Mrs. Micks get his attention? An apartment with a dead philodendron says no.

Micks shoved the transmission into drive and crawled along Main, on-guard, ready to jump, chase down the Frau, arm-lock her. Maybe I would take him out of the novel and add a James Garner detective with a good haircut and a sense of humor, loving the ladies and rare Scotch. I could do that. *Writers can write whatever they want.*

I settled back in the seat and shut my eyes. If I'd been alone in the elevator, would she have spoken to me? Mute point now. I'd signed with the wrong agent.

Micks tapped my leg. I let out a yelp. He said, "That, my dear, is guilty on all counts."

My dear? Oh, he had a way about him. "You startled me, for God's sake."

"How's that? We're the only people in the car."

"I'd dosed off. What?"

"Weird road sign back there."

How do people marry and live together for years on end? I'd spent ten years writing about such nonsense. Maybe that's why I couldn't sell a story. I didn't know what I was talking about. Too much swoon, Jenny moon, you loonytoon.

"You know that was her," Martin Micks said.

"Quit," I said. "It wouldn't make sense."

"I can't figure how I lost them."

"Why didn't you call for back-up? Close down the town."

"I wasn't that far behind," he said, ignoring my sarcasm.

"You're alone on this, aren't you? The real cops don't believe in your phantom. You've taken it upon yourself to prove them wrong." I puffed my cheeks and exhaled. "The boy and the woman were probably huddled behind some Hallmark rack reading greeting cards. Can you even say what they looked like?"

"I know exactly what they looked like. The woman, for sure. I have an eye for detail. As a matter of fact, I can describe everybody in that building and that includes the lady's toilet."

"You raided the lady's toilet?"

"There was one woman standing by the sink. She lived through it."

"You scared the holy crap out of her."

"Hell, she scared the holy crap out of me. Screamed Jesus holy hell. Yelled at someone in the stall to keep the door locked, a pervert was in the toilet. She actually called me that, pervert." Micks waited for my reaction.

I looked away out the window.

"This is what I'm saying," he continued. "I was in there less than ten seconds and I can describe her to a tee. Bleached blonde, skinny, greenish-blue top and matching pants — that slept-in linen look, which I know all too well. My ex had a closet full of it. The lady grabbed a big old flowery bag and was ready to deck me. Got my ass out of there. Flashed my badge at the two woman come running from the candy shop."

Micks interpreted my stare as stupefying fascination with his escapade. In a way it was.

He said, "She'll have a Minnesota experience to brag about."

"A Minnesota experience?"

"She wasn't from here. I figure Georgia. Someplace with a southern drawl."

Her metamorphosis had taken less than five minutes. That might have been a record.

The boy had stayed in the closed stall, not a word. So well-trained. How do you do that with kids nowadays?

Experience.

Don't make a sound, Fanny Graas had told her son, not knowing her life was over. *Hush, my child. Stay secret until Mommy says.* Bentley Ogren had stayed secret. Not a word. Bentley Ogren had experience.

Little sentry.

I'd watched them escape. Both Micks and I had watched the drawbridge release them. I chuckled.

Micks chuckled, too. "Funny, wasn't it? She was ready to deck me."

"Watch the road."

I shut my eyes to shut out Micks and crossed my arms to keep from fidgeting. I needed to think. Even without this unexpected windfall of enlightenment and the resulting agitation, late afternoon was a restless time for me. Some kind of frontal lobe transitioning took place in my head. An unfettered compass point pricked my nerves, and I itched to travel beyond my boundaries down some mother of a river or down some narrow, empty highway to a destination beyond the vanishing point, beyond what I could not see; always west (never east) these roads, these streets of palms, five-o'clock sun-dapples, slim silhouettes carrying silver trays of Blue Curacao. The uneasy side of this unrelenting itch was that if — by some strange quirk of physics — I actually landed on a street of palms one afternoon at five-o'clock with a blue cocktail in hand, it would no longer be beyond my boundary, beyond what I could not see, and I would have to go again. Heading out.

Drove me crazy.

Micks tapped his head. "I got memory for detail."

I squeezed my eyelids tighter, needing to be somewhere, anywhere. Anywhere but here. Micks finally shut up. I sensed his irritation at my lack of admiration for his dexterity. I was tempted to explain why I wasn't impressed. I would enjoy that.

But I needed to think.

The Trust Fund no longer fit. *Laundry Money* might make a better christening. Money laundering. What would it be like having so much money you had to launder it? How did that conversion work exactly? I'd never considered it. Nor did I know how to convert knots into miles per hour. How far would the boat have traveled in an hour? I needed to find her. I wanted to find her. And who was piloting the boat? Mr. Dean? Lance?

Did she think I'd recognized her? I'm the only one who would have. But I hadn't. Nor had I actually seen her board the yacht. The woman and the blonde-haired kid could have boarded any one of the boats tied along the dock or out behind that floating gas station. Could still be there, down the hatch in some minicruiser drinking Pernod, eating oyster crackers ala Gertrude Stein. Right this very minute.

But it didn't feel like it.

When I'd spotted the blonde girl feeding the ducks I'd remembered *the cap with the curls she made him wear*. But having been so ridiculously wrong, I'd overlooked the snarly blonde hair anchored down with the baseball cap running towards *The Trust Fund*. Calculated to eliminate the tipsters.

I needed to get back to Stillwater.

Micks stopped dead center to my room. The motel's utilitarian windows and gray metal doors suggested a one-nighter kind of place. It was what I could afford.

Micks didn't propose anything later, not even a drink, just stared at my shabby digs and said, "How do you find these places?"

20. The Boat

I quick-changed into my Sweet Dream jeans and a tiger-striped tank top, re-tied my Barbie-at-the-beach hair, grabbed my bag, walked into my mules and out the door; slammed it, heard it click.

The world has become too small anymore for there not to be coincidence.

What were the odds? My Saint, Micks, and me on the same elevator? Bonus Bentley Ogren. We'd stood together in that mineshaft with its crawling gears and shimmy-shimmy doors — Micks close enough for handcuffs. It felt like an afterburn, this belated awareness, this stepping in after the fact to realize this woman, the sense of her. That very rhythm I'd fallen in sync with (at the same time she was leaving me) was ineffable and intoxicating.

Driving down the freeway, high on possibilities, I likened myself to a reporter in possession of proprietary information on the whereabouts of solitary Pynchon. What about that? Without the celebrated asterisk, old T.P. would be nothing more than a quirky old man in the neighborhood. The truly curious were those who willfully stepped off the dreamer's treadmill without record, having never considered the asterisk: My Saint, Sammy, BD Cooper before he jumped. Acting the recluse and simultaneously exposing your proprietary self to the pulps was a shameful counterfeit. I meant hypocrite.

The spot-on proprietary fact I possessed was that I didn't have enough proprietary information to write her story as True Crime. However, heavy on the bestseller list, idling between fiction and nonfiction, lay the murky business of Memoirs. As a memoir my accounting would be stringently correct (no dental work without Novocain). The heart of the story would be *my* perception, *my* memory of the five days I'd spent with her seven different selves. Sweet, the politics of Memoirs, the marrying of fact and fiction — perfect for the reality-obsessed, the same people who believe what they read in the newspaper.

Tomorrow was a free day. Micks wouldn't show again, not until he needed something. I'd spend the entire day sorting the facts on recipe cards, spread them out, arrange and rearrange until the story made sense.

What facts? Every scene, including the intermezzos, and every last thread of costume and makeup, Toni, Brigid, Clare — all an act. With Fanny Graas dead and Laddie Ogren dead and Mr. Dean out to pasture (God only knows where), what did I have? My role in her contract had been nothing more than a covered base, Micks the outfielder, Sammy her resurrected catcher's mitt. Then she'd disappeared, done with us.

Eight months later, she's cruising down the St. Croix on a yacht. Eight months later, I'm cruising down I-94 in a rusted Chevy.

By the time I reached the St. Croix Trail, my mood had undermined my determination. Following the river south to Hastings, let alone Red Wing, was over my limit what with the hangover and all. It hadn't looked that far on the map. A small airplane could be there in a dog's bark. I turned north to Stillwater. If it hadn't been for the late-in-the-day irritability from metabolizing alcohol keeping me wired and unable to sleep it off, I would have quit this stalker-biographer mania and headed back to the motel.

I passed a sign. Bayport Marina. Well, hell, I'd come this far. I turned back to it. The marina was small and swept tidy like a stage set, and easily navigated, allowing me to peruse the docks and the water without leaving my car. No vessel, docked or dunked, resembled *The Trust Fund*. I considered asking around, but lacked the energy.

On my way up the St. Croix Trail towards Stillwater, I slowed every so often for a peek through the shrubbery that lined the river. Nary a yacht headed north or south. *The Trust Fund* could be in Iowa by now. My Saint and her pilot ... pilot? My Saint would pilot her own damn boat, barefoot at the wheel in her sea-green linen. My restless thoughts long on the rococo, I saw myself standing on the quarterdeck in a gauzy, yellow dress (I'd never owned a yellow dress in my life), my toenails painted earthen umber, squinting into that low western sun. The water below me folded and unfolded like a busy milliner. Heading out.

Life is like a river. Well, no shit, Sammy!

I reached Highway 36 just south of Stillwater, drained and dismayed, gas tank empty. I pulled into a convenience store where I stood at the pump logging a major debit to my beleaguered VISA. The numbers spun into double digits and suddenly this chase seemed foolish. The yacht was long gone. My Saint long gone. Micks was history. What I needed was sleep.

I got back in my car feeling somewhat relieved at my decision to bail. Crowded, mind-numbing, multi-lane Highway 36 heading west would take me back to Minneapolis to my one-star motel where I'd suffer three more hours of daylight alone in my one-star room without the most far-flung hint of a shadowed palm or a blue cocktail. Having just missed the left-turn arrow, I settled in to wait. I forced a yawn to stop from grinding my teeth. Oh, what the heck. Nobody idling behind me, I made a diagonal right turn with enough yardage to jockey myself into the line of summer cars turning north down the St. Croix Trail into Stillwater. The first right on Nelson got me a parking space. I managed to squeeze in parallel, cockeyed, but good enough. I dug for my phone and checked for R.L. Ricky's number. Unlisted. No afterhours root canals for R.L. I punched in the Warner-Ricky office number. The Monday morning message sounded like the sassy receptionist, which triggered a pinch of glee.

I got out of the car and headed to the River Exchange. Inside the door I stopped to watch the 'Best Turtles in Minnesota' girl pack up a mix of dark and milk chocolate nut caramels big as sunflowers for a skinny chick in running shorts. I swallowed hard and headed down the hallway to the toilet. I stuck my head into the yellow, cellular space, which was clearly not the kind of place you'd pick a splinter or pluck an eyebrow.

No one gets in my daylight space.

Someone flushed a toilet. I shut the door and followed the arrow up the steps to the St. Croix Crab House. One beer might clear my head and enable me to answer questions like what was I doing in Stillwater? I settled on a stool at the bar. No longer anybody's guest, a PBR would do me fine, if somebody would take my order.

"Well, well, Jennifer Sands. Why am I not surprised?"

I twirled around on the stool to find Martin Micks, cell phone to his ear, accompanied by a short, curly blonde wearing red cargo pants and a white t-shirt embroidered with Dala horses. Mrs. Micks? Hardly.

"Just what *are* you doing here?" Micks said to me.

"Fancy meeting you here," I said pointedly. We spoke simultaneously.

"You know what I'm doing here," he said. His tone suggested ownership. The phone remained at his ear.

I made a purposeful glance around the bar and said, "I thought I might catch a glimpse of Sam Shepard."

"He doesn't live here anymore," the woman said.

"Stacy," Micks said. "Meet Jas."

We exchanged greetings. I said to Micks, "Bally up. We can compare notes."

Micks said to Stacy, "Go ahead. I gotta do this call." He walked away, phone to his ear. Stacy hoisted herself onto a stool. I suppressed the urge to ask who Micks was talking to.

"So how long have you known Micks?" I asked instead.

"About five hours. I work at the bookstore down the street. He was in earlier. We're on our way to a party out on the water. The guy who owns the boat needed a caterer. A friend of mine,

Meg, caters and said okay even at this short notice. So I got a party invite. He said to bring a couple friends. Want to come?"

Micks is in Stillwater one hour and gets a party invite.

"He's way good looking," Stacy said.

For a crazy moment I thought she meant Micks.

"He's not from here," she added.

"That's a door buster," I said, wishing I wasn't ten pounds overweight. Okay, fifteen. Even so, the thought of being trapped out on the water on some undulating houseboat in my distressed condition, shoulder to shoulder with strangers wearing polo shirts and Dockers, gave me a shiver.

Micks snapped his phone shut.

I turned. "That was quick."

"Yep." He brushed his flop of hair aside. Clearly we were not comparing notes.

"I invited Jas to the party," Stacy told Micks.

"Good," he said, giving me the once-over. "I thought of you when Stacy pointed out the boat. It's the one you called *The Trust Fund*."

"I'd love to come," I said to Stacy.

She slid off the stool and said, "We'd better go or we'll miss the boat."

Stacy knew everyone onboard. Neither Micks nor I knew anybody. We were leaned against the guardrails sipping beer, waiting for the captain to show. The sun had dropped below the tree line. The colored Christmas lights strung along the railings gave the boat a loopy Vegas feel. I liked the idea of Christmas lights in June. I liked the boat. Whoever owned it was rich. That My Saint was somehow involved would make perfect sense, even though I doubted that she and the boy were onboard; the first thing I'd noticed was that the dinghy on top was missing. Had they been let off downriver? Questions only the captain could answer.

Next to us, a double-decker showboat was pulling away from the dock. People on the decks waved at the shoreline as if they were going out to sea. The minor wake was enough for me to grip the railing. Micks smirked. We both turned around at what sounded like Fran the Nanny on gin. A man in a white polo shirt was helping a tall and way-too-tan-for-June woman in strappy sandals, totally unsuitable for watercraft, step onto the boat. Her legs sparkled. Micks watched. All the men watched. Fine. A couple of strappy-sandaled chicks flitting around, I wouldn't have to concern myself with Micks.

"So, Ms. Sands. Just what *are* you doing in Stillwater?" His eyes stayed on the people boarding the boat.

I didn't like the way he said my name. "I could ask you the same question."

"I'd answer, my job."

"Who's hired you?"

No answer.

I said, "That's what I thought."

A pregnant woman in sneakers, cell phone to her ear, tripped. The man in the white polo caught her. Both cell phones went flying. I considered what the weight limit might be on this boat. I tapped the side. "What exactly is fiberglass?"

"Glass fibers."

I turned and faced Wisconsin. "You need a cigarette."

He leaned in next to me and eyed me from under his hair. "What'd you mean today when you said, the holy saint of fire?"

I kept my eyes on Wisconsin. "Holy saint of fire?"

"In the car. The old lady on the curb. You said she could be the holy saint of fire."

"I think I said *goddamn* fire."

He sucked his lower lip, then said, "You used that phrase when I was up in December. The holy saint of the Rose Bowl parade. What's this saint business?"

"Did I mention I was Catholic?" My lies could come back to bite me. Not if I kept my mouth shut.

"That's you in the photo. You know it and I know it. My advice to you, Miss Sands is to come clean."

I snorted. "What are you talking about?"

"Two people dead and you drove the car. That's what I'm talking about."

"You should write fiction."

Arms resting on the railing, he held his beer bottle by the neck. His eyes stayed on me. "You've turned into one tough cookie, Jennifer Sands."

Being someone who took no for an answer without a fight, most often with a passive resignation, but always eternally hopeful that everybody would do the right thing, I chewed on 'tough cookie.' More like soft cookie, me. Never tough, but I liked the idea of it. Micks took a long pull on his beer.

A shout from shore got everybody's attention. A thirty-something, A-list guy with a Jamaican tan wearing long white pants and a red crew t-shirt strode down the dock and hopped onboard. Bronze roots showed beneath the bleached tips of his hair. Stacy was right: he was not from here.

She joined us, sipping a margarita from a plastic glass that had a two-inch layer of salt around the rim. "That's Rudi," she said, licking salt from her lips.

"So where *is* he from?"

"Don't know. But, like I said, he's not from around here."

"For sure."

Micks scowled. "What's that supposed to mean?"

Stacy and I ignored him.

Rudi greeted everybody as if they were old friends, shaking hands, squeezing shoulders, a touchy-feely kind of guy. I wiped my hand on my pants.

"This is magnificent," he said to Stacy, "your friend and her culinary expertise." I half expected him to sound Jamaican. He didn't. I couldn't put a region to his talk.

Stacy said, "You should see what she can do with a twenty-four hour notice. Meet Micks and Jas."

"Micks and Jas," he said and glanced at Stacy. "I thought for a minute you'd said Drinks and Jazz." Micks and I harrumphed simultaneously, and we all shook hands. Up close his hair didn't looked tipped, but truly sun bleached. His eyes were espresso brown. He jerked his head towards the stairs and announced, "Heading out."

Micks quickly put in to "see the hardware on a boat like this." They walked away chatting like old pals.

Heading out.

Dixieland jazz rambled out of a high-priced sound system. I would have figured him for Reggie. Reggie Rudi. I snatched a beer and took a tour with an eye out for anything that might suggest that two afternoon fugitives had paid a visit. My first stop was the guest quarters below. I stood in one of the bathrooms with my eyes closed, but could not catch the scent of vetiver or geranium. *I have an island connection.* I sniffed for frangipani. What I caught was synthetic with a hint of bleach. The medicine cabinet was locked, which probably had more to do with undulating waves than with secrets. Ditto on the closets, locked up, battened down. The beds smelled fresh with crisp sheets. The only sign of vicissitude was a paisley tie looped around a wall sconce. Polished, shipshape, swept clean.

Rudi's guests roamed the boat with nods of approval and murmurs of admiration at the teak paneling and the beveled-edge mirrors and the marble counter tops and the extraordinary use of space: organized, compact, lean and mean. A woman jangling an armload of bangle bracelets vowed to pare down her lifestyle starting tomorrow. I positioned myself next to three cheery women earnest in conversation on preschool politics. Having nothing to offer, I moved off unnoticed. Up top on the flybridge I learned the difference between grey water and black water. For those who lived on the water, the dumping of crap into the river was a mighty concern. I didn't see myself there anytime soon.

None of the flybridge crowd claimed ownership of a yacht, but two men had experienced much larger sea-faring vessels. The realtor's brother won the "My Dog's Bigger Than Your Dog" contest. He'd been a guest on a private yacht in the Mediterranean with its own helicopter pad. Feeling like a bum at the opera, I headed back down to the bar.

Gold margarita was on the tip of my tongue, but I stopped and reminded myself why I was on the boat and loaded up a plate with crudités and cheese, a roast beef biscuit, a slice of smoked salmon, a half-dozen shrimp, and a caramel brownie off a silver platter. I settled into a corner on the California deck with my plate and silently thanked the gods of serendipity for not sticking me on some fern deck in Red Wing with a basket of fries waiting for a yacht to float past. I could see Micks in the galley, casual against the Miele oven, chatting with the banker and his wife and the Pearsons. I never did get the Pearsons' first names. They introduced themselves to everybody as the Pearsons. "Hi! We're the Pearsons!" The wife-half of the Pearsons pulled a phone from her bag. Competition was fierce.

I made a mental note to add at least four single men to my story, and two of them would be smoking. No one smoked anymore. It made for a sterile scene. Although I'd never smoked in my life, in social settings such as this one, a cigarette would afford me a distracted, imposing panache. But distracted, imposing people didn't smoke anymore. They talked on cell phones. I imagined Marlene Dietrich in *Frenchy* without the cigarette, thumbing her iPhone. Greta Garbo striding down Fifth Avenue, one hand on her pocketbook, one hand to her ear. Ingrid Bergman texting at Rick's.

How many calories in a caramel fudge brownie?

Except for the guy in the LA Lakers t-shirt, and Micks, of course, all the guy guests, including the realtor and his brother, acted responsibly mated. Not only that, there seemed to be a peculiar cliquishness on board that I could not tap. And, as usual, everybody around me was in some stage of good humor. Micks, too. Hearing him laugh had startled me. I had never heard him laugh. I caught his glance and raised my hand to wave, but retied my ponytail instead; he'd pointed two stern fingers at his eyes, then one back at me.

Watch all you want, asshole.

He'd known about this party all the while he was driving me back to Minneapolis to dump me at my one-star motel. Triple asshole.

Over my limit by one beer and ready for dry land, I was tempted to slip over the guardrail and swim to shore. If not for all that blackwater crap talk, I might have.

And I hadn't interviewed Rudi yet.

I dropped my empty plate into a plastic pail on my way to the salon where I had a clear view up the steps into the pilothouse where Rudi was in session. A popular guy, Rudi. It didn't look good, not without forcing my way into somebody's conversation. Just as my patience expired, the tall and way too tan blonde with the strappy sandals, who'd been hanging on Rudi in a style that suggested they'd slept together, pulled herself out of the assistant's seat and headed for the stairs. Her name was not Fran. Her name was Karen. Karen negotiated her sparkly legs down the steps and pulled on the bathroom door, which was occupied. She folded her tan arms, leaned back against the wall, and shut her eyes. I raced up the steps. I figured ten minutes before Legs returned.

"Hey," I said, sliding into the leather seat Karen had just vacated.

"Hey yourself," he said with a Sunday morning grin.

"This is complicated," was all I could think to say about a control panel as mind-numbing as an airplane cockpit. "What happened to the Captain Bly wheel with the spokes?"

"I could learn you in a week."

"Learn me? Are you from the South?"

"I pick up regionalisms. Sunny little things my ears tune in on."

I glanced at the bank of levers and switches and screens and was tempted to pose, show interest in gadgets and machinery, earn the ticket to ride awhile, bored to tears — what women do when they're investing. But I was short on time. Get to the point.

"I saw your boat earlier this afternoon. On the north side of the bridge. Couldn't help but notice."

He patted the console. "She's six years now. Takes me anywhere I want to go."

"Do you hire out?"

He seemed to have to think about that. "Not really. Not for hire. Friends offer to pay the gas." He chuckled. "Until they find out how much she takes. You have someplace you wanna go, little girl?" He did the Groucho Marx thing with the imaginary cigar. His brown eyes twinkled.

"Oh, not me. But I saw two passengers board this afternoon. Then you sailed off." I waved my hand downriver.

He cocked his head, puzzled.

"A woman and a young girl. Or boy. It's hard to tell nowadays. The woman wore a green shirt and pants. Carried a big flowery bag."

"Not on my boat," he said. "Unless they're stowaways holed up in the bilge. There was an Explorer behind me gassed up. They might have boarded that. It took off up river."

"Explorer?"

"A Cuddy Cabin. Twenty feet give an inch."

I'd watched the kid run along the dock. The woman trailed behind. Distracted by the PD Pappy dudes, I'd assumed the two interlopers had absconded with *The Trust Fund*, but I had not actually seen them board.

"She's a friend of mine," I said, feigning disappointment. "I hadn't seen her in awhile. Didn't know she was in town. I was hoping she might be here."

He studied me, thoughtful. "Probably got on that Explorer."

"This afternoon there was a small boat up top."

"On the boatdeck, yeah. Dropped it downriver for repairs. Damn thing's inbred, always something."

He reached towards me, his hand brushed my hair. I surprised myself and didn't flinch. He held up a quarter for me to see. I couldn't help but laugh. That coin-behind-the-ear trick was long worn-out, but no one had ever played it on me. I was momentarily taken by that. He held my gaze and said, "Eye on the quarter," and snapped it high in the air. I lost sight of it and waited for him to reach out and grab it coming down. He didn't. I squinted at the darkened ceiling, half-expecting to see it stuck to the teak. He opened his hand, the quarter exposed, rabbit in the hat.

"Snafued," I said with a grin. "It never went up."

"But it's what you thought you saw." His eyes flicked past me. He said, "How'd it go?"

I jumped out of the chair just in time for Sparkle Legs to topple in. She'd just sprayed perfume. Or air freshener.

"Nice chatting," I said with as much good spirit as I could muster. Rudi nodded with an abbreviated wave. It felt like a job interview gone bad. At the steps I looked once more at the sunny couple. Rudi focused on Karen, who was laughing hard, her thin, tan arms sweeping a wide arc, probably describing her experience in the toilet. One more drink would finish her off. I bumped into the guy with the Lakers t-shirt who was on his way up the steps. Mutual pardons aside, I asked how he knew Rudi. Glassy eyed, he said, "Who?" and stumbled away up the steps. I didn't like him either.

21. River Guides

First off the boat, desperado for dry land, and not to vanish without some kind of thanks-a-million (*be polite, Jenn)*, I waited for Stacy at the top of the steps. The Lakers guy staggered off the boat followed by two of the moms, followed by guests I'd done no more than brush shoulders with. Meg and the bartender rolled their canvas totes through the parking lot. Stacy and Rudi stood together at the Christmas guardrail, probably discussing the next outing. I wondered why Karen, the boat mistress, wasn't bidding everybody adieu. Passed out in the stateroom, was my guess. The real estate agent had latched onto Micks. Like Micks could afford Stillwater. Maybe Mrs. OBGYN paid alimony. The Pearsons stepped off the boat along with Stacy. And, lo and behold, sparkle-legs Karen.

When Stacy and the Pearsons reached the top of the steps, I caught the words 'zebra mussels.' Mrs. Pearson had that gourmet cook look going. Stacy, not so much. Karen, clearly over-quenched and obviously bored with the cooking channel, danced into my energy sphere.

I couldn't help myself: I said to her, "I thought you'd be sailing away with the ship."

"Ya, Rudi, what a guy!" She swept her tan arm towards the boat that was pulling away. "I sold him that very boat down in N'orlins. Now he's trading up. Too bad I'm no longer in the biz. That man would talk boats to a fence post. Boat this. Boat that." She giggled. "Sail away with Rudi. Ha! First I'd have to figure out what to do with Lou and two snot-nosed kids." She waved at a suburban flavored man who was talking with the polo couple from the boat. Karen's wedding rings glittered in the streetlight. How had I missed that? Lou waved back, shook hands with the polo couple, and headed towards us. He hadn't been on the boat. Karen was married. Rudi and Karen had been talking boats. I vowed to give my presumptuous self a rest. It got me nowhere.

"Lou is your husband?" I said to Karen, no longer my enemy.

"Sure, I had a thing for Rudi back when. Everybody did. If I'd wrapped myself around that lamppost, I'd still be waiting on the levee. You know the type. Were you on the boat tonight?"

"Not the entire time. Rudi's not married?"

"That man will never marry. Not for lack of trying. I mean women trying. Except..." Karen puckered her lips as if remembering, then waved a hand in dismissal. "Tomorrow I quit drinking, for sure." She glanced at her husband who had stopped to talk to the banker. "Or cut back a tad."

"Except?" I eased in front of her willing her to focus. "Was he ever married?"

"Rudi?" She strained for recall. "I think ... hmmm. She was pregnant. Oh, for sure. Or was that Murray and that crazy sign painter? Now there's a story. Uff da, fawn."

"Who got pregnant?"

"And then the husband shows up. And that was that." She attempted to snap her fingers. "Gone. The both of them. We all did our share of partying down in N'orlins, let me tell ya."

"Gone? Who?"

"That's what I call it. N'orlins." She did a conga sway. "I was a dancer once. Rudi can dance, and I mean real steps, not just that shaking around thing that men do." She clapped her hands above her head, fast-stepped back and forth and, considering the strappy sandals and the alcohol content, executed several surprisingly complex moves. "Lou can't dance. Won't even shake around. 'Real men don't dance,' he says."

I watched, momentarily entertained by her showgirl talent, while untested possibilities scrambled my brain: Rudi had an affair with Fanny Graas; Laddie Ogren came down from Canada and grabbed his pregnant wife; Bender is Rudi's son. How does My Saint fit in? The boy had called her Grandmamma. Could Rudi be My Saint's son?

Whoa, presumptuous self! Not a thing on that boat suggested that My Saint and Bender had ever been there. What proof did I have that the German woman in the elevator and the southern woman in the River Exchange toilet (whom I had not seen) and the skinny woman on the dock were all one and the same person?

But it fit the sequence, at least from where I'd stood. I stared at the boat that was slipping away.

Micks and the realtor had advanced to property taxes in Stillwater versus Houlton across the river. I inched away from him as far as I could get without losing Karen's half-cocked attention. I lowered my voice: "You don't perhaps remember her name, do you? The woman in New Orleans?"

Karen stopped with the conga, but continued to sway. "What woman?"

"The pregnant woman."

She laughed, loud. "Lordy, schmorty, half the time I can't remember my own name." She stopped swaying and focused on me, nose squinched. "Why do you want to know that?"

Feeling obliged to explain something, I blurted, "I write romance novels. It sounded like a story."

She let out a yelp and clapped her hands. "You're a writer? That is so cool! What have you written?"

"Ahmm..." I talked without moving my lips. "Well, I've got five novels–"

"Five novels? Oh, way wow! I'll buy them all, every last one of them."

She didn't hear the rest of my sentence. "–in the closet."

"Stacy's got them, right? That's why you're here. You did a reading today. Hey Stace! You didn't tell me you had a reading." The remaining party passengers zoned in on me as if seeing me for the first time. I could feel my face go red. Karen pointed at me. "The writer here."

Stacy was clearly surprised, but not thrilled. She probably thought I was going to hit her up for shelf-space. I chuckled and explained to Stacy how I wasn't published yet, and had changed genres, and was writing crime. "You know publishing. As soon as I hear something..." I turned to Karen and said, "...I'll be in touch." But Karen had already lost interest, skinny arm beckoning her husband who was chatting up the banker.

"I swear," Karen said, her smiley eyes unfocused, "that man could talk a pear off an apple tree given half an acre."

"He looks like a keeper," I said, hoping to steer the conversation back to N'orlins. The female-half of the Pearsons pulled at Stacy's sleeve. Saved by the zebra mussels. Maybe the woman had a way to make them taste like chicken. The fascination with those shriveled-up foreskins defied good sense.

"But he doesn't dance," Karen whined and launched into a combination of pas de basque and fandango accompanied by some sexy bitch French song. *Je ne veux pas*. I struggled with the notion that this woman spoke French. Hell, she probably knew Claudine Longet. With a burst of sexy French buzz, *Je ne, Je ne,* she grabbed my wrist and twirled me around.

"Whoa, ho!" I croaked and twirled once more before I was able to extricate myself. Hands up in protest, I said with forced merriment, "I don't dance either."

Karen stopped and cocked her head as if seeing me for the first time. "Look at you. The girl in the tiger tanker." She pointed to my tiger-striped tank top. "Oh, my gawd, I'm so dumb. You're the one. Rudi asked if I knew you."

"Me?"

"I told Rudi 'you're on your own, mon.' I quit fixing that prick up years ago."

"He asked if you knew me?"

"Heartbreaker, dream maker," she sang. "My yoga teacher in Metairie never spoke to me again. Like it was my fault. Oh, he's a heartbreaker, that one." Karen two-stepped left, then right, fingers snapping.

Behind her, mid-lake, the fading Christmas lights promised champagne and dark chocolate, dangling conversations, black water breaking under miles of stars. A fractious longing came over me that I didn't like, an urge on the edge. I swear, if that boat had sounded one of those forlorn horns that ships do in the night, I would have jumped in the water and swam after it, explained how I wasn't the enemy.

"Where's he headed?"

She followed my gaze. "He's here till September, then down to the Caymans. Lucky dog." Karen's husband came up behind and put his arm around her.

"I'm the lucky dog," he said and planted a kiss on her forehead.

She leaned into him and cooed, "Would you have been peeved, hon, if I'd sailed away with Rudi and the boat?"

Lou rolled his eyes. "You'd be leeward just in time for the hurricanes."

"Hi Lou," Stacy said, back with us, the Pearsons headed home. "Where have you been all night?"

"Looks like I got here in the knick a time. My wife's about to hightail it off with Rudi."

"Fat chance."

The man with the Lakers t-shirt slapped Lou on the shoulder. Lou turned to shake hands taking Karen with him.

"Speaking of..." Stacy gave me a devious look, "...Rudi asked if I knew you."

"Me?"

"On the deck after we docked. I told him I'd just met you and the detective. He sounded interested. I was about to wave you back down, but he said he had to sail out."

How did I keep missing the beat? Missing the boat, more like it. The boat that was sailing out of reach with its Christmas lights small as a string of colored beads. Clearly, Captain Rudi had nothing to do with My Saint, Fanny or Bender. He was a cool guy with a yacht. That's all. And he'd asked about me. Me. (And, yes, I was aware that I'd been the only single female onboard.) I should have stayed seated in Karen's chair, where I might still be sitting, instead of standing on dry land with my presumptuous self. I'd be tracking constellations all the way down to the Southern Cross. Micks came up behind me, followed my gaze and said, "That's one big chunk of change out there. What's a guy like that do for a living?"

Annoyed at Micks, I answered, "He's not in law enforcement."

Karen, bored with Lou and the Laker, twirled back to us. "Let me tell you," she said with a wave at the water. "That's a complete and totally lega-gitimate write-off, that boat. Rudi's one-hundred percent." She sang, "Works hard for his honey..." then stopped, focused on me and smacked her forehead. "Oh, man! You two have got the glue. He's a writer, too."

"A writer?" I said. "Rudi?" The writing life being a serious common denominator between people: Joan Didion and John Dunne; Lillian Hellman and Dashiell Hammett. Jennifer Sands and Rudi something or another.

He'd asked Karen about me. He'd asked Stacy about me. Because I'd been focused with my eyes closed, I'd missed the party. A party that neither My Saint nor Bentley Ogren had attended. Rudi was innocent of all aiding and abetting charges. A guy and his boat. I watched it disappear around the bend and decided that very moment to find him down the river. The next marina was Bayport. It was still early enough. For a weekend. I would drive to Bayport. For the first time in forever, or so it seemed, I smiled.

Rudi, a writer. It didn't get any better than that. Prepared to make my exit, I called out to anybody who might give a flip, "Nice meeting everybody. I'm out of here."

Karen waved her arm at me as if I were across the parking lot instead of three feet away.

If I'd made my exit, it would have been a romance novel kind of night. But I niggled for one more affirmation. I asked Karen, "Have you read any of Rudi's books?"

"Heavens, no. Rudi writes river guides."

Micks gave a loud harrumph and said, "He must be the Stephen King of river guides to keep that thing oiled up."

Stacy peered at me. "You okay?"

"You don't look so hot," Micks said and focused in on me too intently for someone who thought I was neutered.

I fanned my face. "Two party nights in a row. Throw in a rocking boat. Uh-uh."

One of Karen's ankles buckled and she tipped into Micks. He caught her by the shoulders and straightened her up.

Stacy pointed at Karen's outrageous sandals and said, "You'll turn an ankle."

I know someone who writes river guides.

"No, I'm serious," Karen said. "Rudi's the best goddamn financial ... finance ... fancy fi-nanc-ier and has the paper to prove it."

Lou leaned towards me and muttered, "Casinos." He nodded with authority. "Couple three we know of."

Karen sang, "Let me tell you, Rudi's tax return—"

"I think we're done here, sweetie." Lou anchored her by the shoulders, turned her around and steered her towards the cars.

Karen stuck an arm in the air with a twirly wave. "That's all for tonight, folks. Dubba dubba do-da-day."

Micks asked if I was okay. Should he walk me to my car? His tone was either solicitous or suspicious. Maybe both. I didn't care. My plans did not include him.

River guides. Casinos. Maybe a couple of Laundromats in Natchez, Mississippi. License plates tracking to *unfamiliar towns like Moline, Caruthersville, Natchez* — river town real estate all the way down the Mississippi. Two plus two equals four.

"Walk Stacy," I said to Micks. "She's down at the bookstore. I'm right out on the street." I started walking and had to concentrate to keep myself from running.

Feeling around underneath the car for the keys I'd fumbled and kicked to God knows where, I was startled to see a pair of Dockers two feet from my nose. I looked up. "Jesus, what?"

"If you know something, Jennifer Sands, that you're not telling me, you could get yourself into more trouble then you know how to handle. Get yourself dropped in the river. Things happen out there."

"What on earth are you talking about?"

Micks squinted down at me.

I pulled myself up and wiped my hands on my pants. "I believe we've already had this conversation, which, if memory serves me, was accompanied by an arm-lock in a motel snack room."

He fixed his thumb and index finger an inch apart and said, "You're only this much too smart, Jennifer Sands. That's dangerous."

Back at him, fingers set a quarter-inch apart, I hissed, "Then that would make you this much too smart."

"Juvenile." He turned away as if to leave, but whipped around and thrust his pinched fingers in my face.

I slapped his hand away, infuriated beyond good sense and squeezed my fingers so tight they showed white and shook them at him. "Before you even got to the woman's toilet, she'd stripped off her flowery dress and yanked on her green wrinkled outfit and bleached blonde wig. The flower print bag of rocks was a brown leather pouch turned inside out." Frustrated with him, frustrated with myself, angry with everybody including myself, I couldn't stop. "Your someone in the toilet stall was a blue-eyed, black-haired boy with a Novocain mouth." I thrust my pinched fingers back at him. "So don't go pinching at me, Martin Moron!"

He grabbed my wrist. His face rippled with both rage and incredulity. "What do you know, little bitch!"

I moved to swing at him with my free hand, but he caught my arm and twisted it behind me shoving me against the car, his lips catching mine. Stunned by both the intensity of the kiss, as unexpected as a freight train on the moon, I stayed with it, unable to move out of it, lips both cold and soft like ice cream all at once. Pressed hard against me for three long moments until the taillights of a police cruiser faded away down Main, he released me, bent over, picked up my keys from God only knows where and handed them to me. He tossed the hair out of his eyes and walked away. My anger found legs, and I bolted after him and slammed into him. He stumbled forward to his knees catching himself with his hands, and he was up and around and grabbed me like a sack of flour, but before he pinned me, I landed a punch to his face, which stunned him for a second. Then he took me to the sidewalk.

"You're one stupid vixen!"

I didn't swear or spit out any other shrieking expletives. I wouldn't give him that. Nor did I fight him. His muscle in the motel snack room was a lesson learned. I caught my breath and emphasized every word: "And-you-are-one-stupid-dumbass-dick." He released me and sprang to his feet. I pulled myself off the sidewalk and brushed down my arms. My butt hurt. Two boys came around the corner and walked past with no more than a glance. No witness.

Micks rubbed his face where I'd hit him and mumbled, "I should have arrested you in the snack room."

I motioned towards my car. "I should have had you arrested two minutes ago." I gave him one last hateful look, spun around and walked away. I felt his eyes on me, but when I turned to reiterate my hateful look, the sidewalk was empty.

Vixen. What an ass. I unlocked the car door, got in and slammed it shut, tabulated damages and rocketed out again. "Vixen was a reindeer!" I yelled down the empty street. I picked a stone out of the gutter and threw it. It didn't reach the curb. My eyes burned with tears. But only for a minute, after which I collected myself and my original plan. How fast was a knot?

I plopped back down in my car and turned the key once, twice, three times. Two deep breaths. Three deep breaths. Six more turns. Freaking dead battery. Freaking flooded engine. As I pondered my options, that shifty patrol car pulled alongside me. The good cops.

Was everything okay?

No. Nothing was okay. I was tempted to report an assault; that embrace they'd witnessed was an attack. But I would have ended up down at some station, photographed and filling out papers, a complication I was not prepared to carry through.

Full-service gas stations were history. Convenience stores sold gasoline and Pepsi, neither of which I needed. Fortunately for me, the nice officers had a towing service at their beck and call.

Fifteen minutes later Pauly in his I LUV FISH t-shirt and Twins cap showed up.

"I think it's a dead battery. And flooded. I'm not good with cars."

Pauly opened the hood and shined his flashlight. He studied the engine for less than three seconds, reached in and plucked up a black wire that, unlike its linked-up sisters, hung like a loose end.

"This wire," he said, "for all practical purposes, should be attached to the distributor cap." He fit the loose end into what was obviously (easy to say in hindsight) its empty slot. I stared at the offending wire. He flicked his flashlight off.

I'd like to think I would have figured it out if I'd had the presence of mind to open the hood. But what with Micks and all...

"You might consider that somebody's messing with you."

This was the same car I'd driven last October. The back bumper sported a distinctive crease by way of that U-haul I'd backed into at the hotel. She knew that. Rudi had called her from the boat. She'd come to town. She and the boy and the missing dinghy were someplace close where a car could be had. Bayport would be my guess. A real sleuth would have driven down there, but no way could I hunt the river at four in the morning. The marina would be closed. They could be all the way to Red Wing by now.

I asked Pauly, was Bayport the closest marina? He asked did I have a boat? I explained that I knew somebody up in Scandia who owned an Explorer, and I'd seen one this afternoon heading upriver. Pauly told me that my Explorer might not have gone far. Boats didn't go up past High Bridge because of the zebra mussels. The St. Croix had an infestation of zebra mussels (a plague on our river, he'd added) from off the boats coming up from the Mississippi. The little cancers clumped like fungus to everything in the water. If you sailed down into mussel-infested water, you didn't sail back up into clean water. You hauled your boat up by land and cleaned it off before putting in again. Anyway, that's what you were supposed to do. He, himself, docked at Bayport. If I'd like to ride the river sometime, he'd be obliged. I told him that was the best offer I'd had in two months. I could have said two years, but I didn't. I asked him how one might find a boat on the river, if one were looking. He told me that if it was important, the sheriff might keep an eye out for it, although they have their hands full with all the drunks out there. Was I looking for the Explorer? No. I described *The Trust Fund*.

"Ah, ya. Everybody knows the *Brendan*."

"Brendan?"

"Got a letter on it, too. S, I think. *S. Brendan*. Been coming up from the gulf four or five years now. Last year people had their boats put up by the time it docked."

"October," I said. It wasn't a question.

"Didn't stay long that time."

"Do you know who owns that boat?"

"Rudi is all I ever heard." Pauly's eyes were measuring. "Yep, there's money on the river. Then, I guess you know that."

Wired as the ice machine that clunked outside the door, my mind shifted from the trick quarter to the ice cream kiss and back to the quarter, back and forth.

In my altered reality, Micks lay next to me naked between my bleach-stink sheets, ice-cream kissing on the edge. But just before I gave it all away, I would save myself; in some hazy peripheral, the red taillights of a police cruiser floated by like two bloodshot eyes.

I won't argue my lack of perspicacity. I should have kicked him in the groin the second he grabbed me, flagged the cruiser down, and got his ass put in jail for assault. Funny thing, what he didn't grasp, was that my white flag unrolled there for a second. He could have had what he wanted.

Nanosecond.

Mind-shift, silly girl, back to the river and the big white boat. I exchanged Micks for the sun-soaked islander with his sun-tipped hair; that quarter soaring, flipping over and over, climbing so high it became the moon.

It's what you thought you saw.

S. Brendan. St. Brendan. The Patron Saint of Sailors.

Explorer, my ass.

Daylight had reached the edge of the curtains before I fell asleep.

DO NOT DISTURB. *No moleste.*

Three o'clock Sunday afternoon I rolled out of bed with a scraped shoulder and a bruised tailbone. Blue fingerprints tracked the backs of both arms. Micks would have a black eye. He'd wear it like a badge. I threw on some clothes and drove back to Bayport knowing full well that the S. Brendan was long gone.

It was a wasted trip.

Back at the motel with two more hours of daylight, I drew the curtains shut and crawled back under the sheets. Not in the mood for recipe cards, I worked the dialogue in my head. I was her mockingbird. I had reached the point where, in my mind, I could say her lines.

22. Lawyer Corde

Corde was easy. Big office. Downtown. I dropped in unannounced, confident he would see me, knowing I'd keep coming if he didn't. Even if he hadn't found his yearbook, I had questions. Would he bill me if I inquired about personal culpability?

Stick with the script.

I'd come prepared to wait all day, but was shown to his office as if I'd had an appointment. Lawyer Corde may well have been interested and just a little concerned about who was throwing his name around with such careless regard. Eye on the governor's chair and all.

He handed me a soft leather-bound book and herded me down the hall into a conference room. I sat down at a table large enough for a Jackson Five family reunion. Happy hunting. The smooth, crisp-edged pages suggested minimal reminiscing. I paged to the graduating seniors and found Corde. He hadn't changed much. *You'd think that twenty-five years in the legal system would have rubbed him wary ... born with front-line DNA.* She'd called that one. Studying the photos, I came up with two possibilities: both women had sainted names and no stand-alone facial features. Ann had freckles and glasses. Freckles? Also, My Saint had claimed perfect vision. Scratch Ann. That left Monica. Her dark lashes and downcast bent shaded her eyes. I opened my handy pocket guide of saints to Monica, the Patron Saint of Mothers and Married Women. Would a disgraced nun name her illegitimate daughter after a June Cleaver saint? I perused the group pictures. Monica in the band holding a flute. Possible. Monica in the choir. Possible. Monica serious in the Latin club. Definitely possible. Monica smiling in the cheerleading squad. Scratch Monica.

I paged through the seniors again, slowly, one by one, and ended at Vance, Yager, and Zigler, three school pals alone on the last page. I wondered if they'd beaten the end-of-the-alphabet odds; or had they been destined to spend their lives at the end of the list, last in line, last to be seated. Yager had possibilities with his congressional smile. Probably sold insurance. I flipped back to the beginning of the alphabet and read the activity specs below each picture and stopped at the clean-cut boy with the guarded smile. Black-framed glasses, dark hair, navy sports coat over a white, button-down shirt and a paisley tie. Sammy. Clearly the collegiate version of the man off the bus. Young and clean and clever and dead.

I'm not who you think I am.

Oh, yes, you are.

So where was My Saint in this musty memory book? Or had she found one at some garage sale and adopted this little school? I had never witnessed My Saint and Sammy together. Nor had I seen her with Corde. I read the hand-written notes. Corde had been a popular guy. Born with the look that women zone in on. A "Boston Legal" kind of lawyer.

I snapped the book shut and headed to his office. Phone to his ear, he motioned to the guest chairs in front of his desk. He finished his conversation with several deadpan affirmations, set the phone in its cradle and steepled his fingers. I'd always wondered what homogeneity compelled people to do that. I'd never once had the inclination to steeple my fingers. Or maybe that cavalier occasion had yet to present itself.

"I can't find her," I said. "It's all been fiction. Every last bit of it."

"As a writer you should appreciate that."

"I found Sammy's picture." I paged to his photo and held up the book.

"Yep. That's Sammy."

"And he just died this year?"

"That is correct."

"Everybody she talked about is either dead or missing." I anchored the book on my lap as if it belonged to me. "But you're still here."

He grinned. "I must be a minor player."

"What part did you play?"

"I wish I could help you there."

"What was your class motto?"

He looked genuinely surprised at the question. "I couldn't tell you if my life depended on it."

I said, "Life is like a river."

"That doesn't sound right."

"She said it was Sammy's idea."

"Sounds like something he would have said. But I don't think our sensibilities would have allowed such a flip summation. Fanatical humor was not recorded."

"What was Sammy like in high school?"

Corde thought a moment. "He played in the band, the clarinet, I think. You know, it's been so long ago." He glanced at a mahogany mantle clock in his bookcase.

I laid the yearbook on his desk, but remembered the end-of-the-alphabet boys and pulled it back. "Just out of curiosity, what ever happened to…" I'd already forgotten their names. I flipped to the last page of seniors. "…Vance, Yager, and Zigler?" Corde re-steepled his fingers.

"Zigler farms south of town. Yager lives in International Falls, something to do with boats. Haven't seen Vance in awhile. Last I heard, he…"

I didn't hear Vance's story. I focused in on Zigler's signature scrawled over two lines of ten point sans serif type. The first line read: Jude Templeton, in absentia. The second line in parenthesis: (No photo available).

"Mother Mary and Joseph!" I stabbed my finger at the legend. "That's her. It has to be. What happened to Jude Templeton? Why isn't she in here?"

"Jude Templeton." He drew out the eu in Jude like a choral note, and noticeably more thoughtful over those steepled fingertips.

"A classmate of yours disappears and you don't remember? There were forty-three of you, for God's sake, forty-four if you count Jude Templeton. I think I'd remember if somebody up and disappeared. You all knew when Sammy disappeared and that was five years later."

You're not missing unless somebody misses you.

His brow furrowed, as if he were thinking harder. "Back in those days if a girl disappeared, pregnancy would have been a good guess."

"Everybody knows everything in those little towns. Pregnant out of wedlock was juicy gossip back in your good old days."

"The world revolves around you when you're in high school. You move on, quickly." He shrugged his eyebrows. "She never came back and explained herself."

"She must have graduated. She went to the U down here."

"GED, probably."

"There are no pictures of this person. How can there be no pictures of a person?" I flipped through the yearbook. "Not even some one-act play? She majored in theater." I read the legends under the class play photos. No Jude Templeton. Not even a token walk-on.

"How about a debate team?"

"That wouldn't have warranted a picture."

"A Philosophy Club? She and Sammy read Nietzsche at the bowling alley."

"There was the bowling alley, but no philosophy club. We read Charles Dickens, not Nietzsche."

"Her least favorite novel was *The Pickwick Papers*." I tapped on the book. "She's here. She has to be."

Corde glanced at the clock again.

"Or she's some kind of anti-matter. I was next to this woman on seven different occasions, and I don't know what she looks like." Frustrated beyond grace, I blurted a laugh and snapped the book shut. "This whole damn school's a blank."

"Look, Miss Sands, and you'll understand this when you get older, but those schooldays, those dear old golden rule days, are not the highlight of people's lives."

"Try this," I said. "Shut your eyes and conjure up Jude Templeton. You've got to remember something."

His grunt was two degrees friendlier than a growl.

"Play along and I'll never bother you again. I promise."

He played along. "Let's see ... hmmm ... dark hair, plain, but not homely. Average height, I think. Thin."

I wondered if my high school memories would grow this dim. "Her eyes were silver."

"I barely remember her face. I wouldn't know her if I passed her on the street."

"Would you know her if you passed her in the Hennepin County Jail? After she'd busted up The Cascade Nine?"

"You lost me there. Listen, what I know, all I know, is that she moved to town in our high school years, freshmen ... or was it sophomore? Many more years ago than you are old." He'd taken on a lawyerly tone. "She was a nice girl. Hardly the type to bust up a bar. They lived across the tracks by the cement works. Now you know what I know."

"What about her parents? Mother? Father?"

"I believe her mother worked at the Boys Home."

"Boys Home?"

"It was a correctional lock-down for delinquent boys. Dubious place. They finally tore it down."

A home for delinquent boys. That made more sense. *Growing up, I spent time at the prison while my mother worked. Prisons weren't as locked down and litigious back then.*

"So it wasn't a real prison?"

If you were under twenty-one it was."

I said, "She told me her mother was a nun." Corde's expression was just short of incredulity. At what surely must be my gullible nature. I shrugged. "It made sense at the time. What about her father?"

"I don't recall the subject ever coming up. I was never invited for dinner. I don't think they had indoor plumbing. Or was it electricity? One of the utilities."

I opened the yearbook to the last page of senior pictures and ran my finger over the two printed lines of black type where Zigler had scripted his signature as if those two scant lines were no more than a copyright. I had found My Saint buried under Zigler's blue ink. I had identified Sammy in his paisley tie. In front of me sat Corde, no longer steepled. I had substance.

Corde stood up. The meeting was over. "You could write to the school. Try Google. Or Connie Classmates."

"Connie cashed in. So when will you be running for office? She said you had your eye on the governor's chair."

He appeared honestly amused. "If you run into our Jude Templeton, tell her hello."

When I got to the lobby, two men in suits who'd been standing at the reception desk followed me into the elevator. Neither of them spoke. Outside the building, I hung around the entrance until they'd disappeared up the street. Who and why someone would be watching me, I didn't know. It just felt like it.

I'm not a writer and you need a story. She should know by now that I'd taken her offer seriously.

Safe in my car with the doors locked, I opened the glove box and fished out my books on saints. I'd acquired three so far. All three of them dubbed St. Jude as the Patron Saint of Desperate Causes; but, as I was discovering in the world of saints, scholars varied in their opinions, tacking on vague monikers with dubious verity to an already dubious identity. The saint guide in my lap feathered back to one of my yellow sticky notes: Saint Brigid. Brigid Ireland, the perky blonde with the pink headband. The real Brigid saint was the Patron Saint of Ireland. There was no mention of fugitives in this guide, although her "charity for those in distress" was noteworthy. Saintliness as a title, as a description, seemed arbitrary. One detail my scholars did agree on and pointedly clarified regarding St. Jude was that Jude, The Patron Saint of Desperate Causes, was not to be confused with Judas of Iscariot, the killer, the traitor, apostle renown. Jude was not to be mistaken for Judas.

Okay.

Despite the obvious ambiguities, I was ninety percent certain Jude Templeton was My Saint. The ornery question being, so what? It's not like I could run to the courthouse and dig up records on Jude Templeton. Corde had taken care of that. Or had he? Maybe it'd been Sammy all along.

I tried to retrace Micks' quick exit route out of downtown. As many times as I'd floundered around on the streets and the avenues, I should have learned something, but I hadn't. I found myself by Metro hospital again, which was where I'd been when I'd stumbled onto the bookstore last October. For some chimerical reason, I thought I could find it again, but the landscape didn't fit the directions in my head. In my case, confusion was the child of poor observation and retention rather than a rebuilding of downtown. A couple more turns and I'd be back on the freeway (freeways were akin to dry land on my mental terrain). And there it was, Preloved, the consignment store where I'd purchased cape and cane. I backtracked the route I'd walked and took an easy right at the very corner where I'd started the limp. A near empty curb allowed me a drive-in spot in front of the bookstore. A realtor's sign hung on the door. I got out of the car.

A tear in the brown paper allowed me to peek inside, which was empty. I don't know what I'd expected. Next door at the locksmith shop a man of Middle-eastern descent stood behind the counter paging through a catalog. I went inside and asked about the bookstore. He shook his head. Where he came from 'here today, gone tomorrow' was a way of life. I described the locksmith, which got me another shake of his head. He'd bought the business at auction.

If last October I'd sidled up to the little locksmith in the red shirt and asked to purchase a *small and very expensive case of proprietary lock picks*, would he have shown me how to use them?

Heading out to my one-star, but still in a sleuthing mode, I revisited the hotel and the Stonehenge Bar. The first clue to the futility of my enterprise was that the green vine carpet had been replaced with royal blue and yellow fleur de leis that reeked of out-gassing polymers. There were no Saxon Swords. Had there ever been Saxon Swords? I pulled open one of the double doors and found myself in a dark auditorium filled with people focused on a luminescent screen that pictured the human digestive tract. Where knights on horses had once ridden into the highlands, bowel obstructions flickered like SciFi aliens. Any minute now, Sigourney Weaver would appear and take charge. I glanced around. The Modigliani ladies in waiting and their Norman Rockwell rose garden had been whitewashed. No dungeon doors. No Ouzo, grappa, or caraway seeds. Operating on air pressure, the door sucked shut with a click. Several heads turned. I focused on the screen. The obstructed bowel changed into a pyramid of fruits and vegetables. The cure? A man with a stick-on name badge approached and asked who was my up-line sponsor? I asked did he know if this room had once been a bar? He stared at me, uncomprehending. I excused myself and exited the planet.

I don't know what I'd expected. Stonehenge had not been a neighborhood bar; it'd been a hotel bar. Transient. Anonymous. A prop.

On my way out, I hesitated at the concierge's desk. Surly Bill had been replaced by a buxom lady in a black pants suit. I asked where was the Stonehenge Bar? She told me the new owners utilized a service bar. She'd be more than happy to call for a cocktail. I imagined Bob pushing a stainless steel housekeeping cart loaded with tiny liquor bottles up and down the fleur de leis, perfect for his churlish self. I asked if Bob managed the cart.

"Bob?"

"He tended bar in Stonehenge. I was here last fall for a convention."

"Bob." She remained puzzled.

"Somber guy with spiky hair." I flicked my hand off my head to illustrate Bob's apocalyptic coif.

"Oh, ya, the deaf guy."

I stared at her.

"He won a scratch-off. The lottery, ya know. Up and walked out. Just like that."

"Deaf?"

"Oh, you'd never know it. The man could read lips across the room."

Deaf.

That I would even give him a second thought in the first place annoyed the crap out of me.

But, maybe not. If Bartender Bob had not stood up in the nightlight at that very moment in my life, I would have gone to my room and tapped the mini-fridge. And everything would be different.

Deaf. She'd known all along.

23. Scheherazade

Determined to leave town with one positive check on my reality meter, I looped back up to St. Paul, certain that the warehouse I'd helped Louise Marille pilfer last October would give me one. There'd be no stopping to chat or anything risky — a quick drive-by would suffice. I turned off Shepard Road, weaseled around a sign that read ROAD CLOSED 3,000 FEET, and bumped along the ruinous ruts willing all car parts to remain attached. The ruts were nothing compared to Heather's warehouse. The shell of blackened brick, broken windows, and churlish graffiti looked like war zone Dresden. How could that have happened so fast? A blast of rocket fuel and a match would be my guess. Ignoring the Absolutely No Admittance Without Permission sign, I got out of the car and waded through brush thick enough to hide a pack of Swedish guard dogs. If not dogs, snakes with fangs up from the river. I peeked around the side of the building. The rickety iron staircase had fallen off the brick wall and lay in pieces in the weeds. Who knew? Off to the right, the long grass rustled. I ran back to my car.

The last possible testament, my last chance for corroboration, was the house on Colfax Avenue. To ignore it would be sloppy sleuthing. I headed back to Minneapolis and was not surprised to find Mr. Dean's quotidian white marker painted *Better Homes & Gardens* blonde with tan trim. White lace curtains billowed out the open windows, tropical palms and pink and white caladiums lushed up the big front porch. Four yellow Adirondack chairs fitted with matching chintz pillows suggested lemonade and snickerdoodles. Two calico kittens wrestled on the steps, tumbled to the sidewalk, and chased off around the house. The D.O. Realty FOR SALE sign had been exchanged for a Big Wheels poised to break your ankles.

In a couple hours the Eukanuba show handler and his little moppet and his stormy woman and her pee-pee dog would walk on, but I didn't have the energy to wait for another dead end.

My cup of tampered evidence runneth over.

Out on the freeway and cruise controlled, I dumped my thoughts into my tape recorder. Considering My Saint's newfound parental status, which Corde had virtually confirmed, the facts and the fictions I'd written so far would need a tune-up. Jude Templeton had gotten pregnant and dropped out of high school. It was reasonable to deduce that she'd given up her baby. Years later she'd reconnected with her adult child and discovered she had a grandson. Grandmamma.

So who was My Saint's illegitimate child?

I could make a case for either Fanny Graas or River Guide Rudi. I liked the idea of My Saint having a daughter. It created a logical nook for Lil in the role of the adoptive mom, which also, in my construction, neatly explained Fanny's maiden name. I considered that My Saint's reaction in the car after she'd found Fanny Graas dead in the apartment (which I hadn't known at the time) had been well below par for a mother who'd just found her daughter murdered; although, having not raised or known Fanny Graas as a child might explain her diminished anguish.

Diminished? What was I thinking? She'd gone on and killed Laddie Ogren.

Obviously, River Guide Rudi and My Saint linked and would make a romantic story if Rudi was My Saint's son and the birth father of Bentley Ogren by way of one quick fling down in New Orleans with an AWOL Fanny Graas. Sparkle-legs Karen had implicated Rudi's involvement with a married woman and an inopportune pregnancy. I hadn't thought to ask Sparkle-legs what was Rudi's surname. He'd had that one-name character about him: Cher, Moby, Rudi.

After careful consideration, I chose to leave Rudi with the boat and write Fanny Graas as My Saint's biological daughter given up at birth. I would take the position that Jude Templeton's truancy from motherhood did not erase her rage. I would niche the 'blood is thicker than water' bromide into a parental exculpatory vengeance premise. My Saint's motive for killing Laddie Ogren demonstrated just how far a mother would go to avenge or protect her offspring. Avenge Fanny Graas; protect Bentley Ogren. It made perfect sense.

That didn't let Rudi off the hook.

Concerning My Saint's criminal career, I didn't buy into her 'it happened that fast' maxim the night Billy Soderholm came to the Triangle Bar with The Party Joke Company card. People don't just pop into crime. I would add discontent and Nietzsche's angst. I would put traction on crazy Mrs. Templeton and ramp up Jude Templeton's absent father. I would fluff over the achromatic — like the break-in at Broder Circle — colorless, pedestrian crime, nothing more than machismo naughtiness. I should have asked Lawyer Corde about the good Judge Wilkerson.

Then there was the bookstore. Micks identified the dead clerk as a mole caught without his cover having nothing to do with My Saint or Sammy, but everything to do with Laddie Ogren. Categorically disconnected to My Saint. I would delete the bookstore and focus on the locksmith shop. People don't buy a proprietary set of lock picking tools at the hardware store and dash out and open doors. My sensibilities dictated that Little Man Locksmith and My Saint translated into Trainer and Trainee.

My Saint had known that the bookstore clerk had been strangled (information that hadn't made the news) because Little Man Locksmith had told her. Confidential information is cheap nowadays, enthusiastic even.

Her telling of the bookstore caper at Lords was background noise to keep me occupied while she set up a hit. She'd planned that dinner with one purpose: to kill Roland Keach. Barely settled in, she'd made a point to introduce me to our waiter. Diners don't introduce themselves to the wait staff. She needed Darren to remember that mother and daughter up from Mankato as an unremarkable duo. Or not remember at all.

After the spider bite (alleged spider bite), she'd needed to monitor Roland Keach, who wasn't moving out as fast as she'd planned for. She'd already killed off her bookstore clerk, Sammy had disappeared, and the omelet-colored Plymouth had driven off. And there was Roland Keach ordering dessert. ...*freaking A's*. My Saint hadn't intended to bring Mr. Dean and Colfax Avenue into the story, but thanks to Roland Keach and his ice cream sundae in the tulip glass, Genny Ross came to life. $400,000 for a kidnapping. Right over the top.

How would I know?

And sneak-peeking at her watch all night long until finally, Roland Keach, a.k.a. The Roach, walked out of Lords to his destiny and we were free to go. And go we did. Right past his dead body. Micks had said that the cops had privileged information on the crash. Ha!

And Sammy, who went from good schoolboy to dead cipher. Nothing more cryptic than a dead cipher. I would add some color to Sammy, put a little Frey on him. Unlike *A Million Little Pieces*, nobody could prove a thing. Sammy was dead. *And lost twenty years ago*.

I'd passed her test at Heather's warehouse. Good-by Louise Marille. Enter Clare Assett, Lance's operator, the cross-link to the kidnapping. The point where the story gums up. And Fanny Graas dies. I turned on the radio to escape the image. The thought of Fanny Graas with her blood red bib made my heart hurt.

Casualties spanned Jude Templeton's thirty-year run. A few would stay privileged in Micks' files, but most of them never having surfaced at all. *Class I crime is so finely orchestrated that nobody knows it happens. It simply and matter-of-factly cannot be seen.* No shit, Sherlock. Everyone she had negatively implicated was either dead or disarmed. Except for Lance, friend of the enigmatic Lil. Who the hell was Lance?

Walk-ons like Pineapple Daiquiri, Zen, Matzo, and Billy Soderholm picked out of the landscape ala Kevin Stacy in *The Usual Suspects*, Keyser Soze stories prompted by bric-a-brac on the bulletin board. White cable sweaters, omelet-colored Plymouths, black books with silver type.

And Trust Fund Rudi, casino magnate, money launderer, my silly regret. If I could just get back to that one. Have a do-over. I'd be makin' for the trades instead of makin' for the prairie.

I told him I'd just met you and the detective. 'The detective.' Thanks, Stillwater Stacy. You capped me there, you chirpy little bitch.

My one and only glee was that My Saint had prided herself on never underestimating people; but she'd underestimated me. She would be anxiously chagrined at what I had uncovered. She hadn't anticipated my finding the bookstore downtown Minneapolis or the house on Colfax, the latter resulting in my running into Mr. Dean and his shovel. Mr. Dean, the gardener, might have hotwired a car once and got his ass thrown into Juvie and gotten sainted by Mrs. Templeton a million years ago, but I don't think he made it to the big time. Mr. Dean Ogren in his baggy overalls and Elmer Fudd hat didn't feel like money. I'll stick with my 'petals in the toilet' theory on rich people. I'm guessing Mr. Dean is still gardening. He will remain in my active file. I might run into him again. Figuratively speaking.

Her characters, all of them, as dreamlike and distorted as the Modigliani knights in their Norman Rockwell landscape. White washed.

Who the hell was Lance?

Whose story did I have here? If there was a parallel story, did it matter? It can't matter, because I can't find it. Why was I so crazy to find the truth? Why was the truth so all fiery important? Truth was nothing more than an after-dinner mint, a fine Port satiety *after* the action, *after* the fact, *after* the damage. At that late date, what did it matter? Other than for my own aggrandized self-satisfaction, knowing the truth wouldn't change a damn thing.

"The truth will set you free." Free from what?

Fact was, truth was narcissistic, a soothing elixir. Having been lied to meant you'd been duped. You'd been had. A stolen wallet was easier to stomach than being lied to.

Made people crazy.

Truth was a reticent leg of Ego.

I slowed at the Sauk Center exit. That's all I did. My last detour of the day would have taken me down Highway 28 to that tiny town that had spawned both a malefactress and a misanthrope in one insanely small graduating class. My Saint and Sammy.

Beat up by altered real estate, dead-ends and dead people, I didn't have the energy to take that road. I wasn't a private eye. Tracking down a bunch of middle-aged Boomers and drilling them on somebody they'd long forgotten was unimaginable. If Corde's assessment was correct, nobody had known the Templetons, much less remember why Jude Templeton went missing so long ago. If they'd ever known at all. Stopping strangers on the street to ask if they remembered the Templetons from thirty years ago was what "Cold Case Files" did.

Just how do they do that with those resurrected cold cases on TV? Blow into town twenty years later and the gas station jockey studies the old snapshot of an unremarkable woman and says, "Yeah, I remember her. Changed her oil. She bought a Hershey bar."

Stop it already.

24. Skiffy's

Midsummer, I'd scored a freelance job writing copy for a swimming pool chemical company in Minnetonka. Having never officially moved out of my parents' house, one load in a pick-up truck was all it took to move me out and down to the Twin Cities. My studio apartment was not much bigger than a no-star motel room. The foldout couch stayed folded down. A lunch counter separated my stopgap bedroom from the kitchen and served as my writing desk. Next to the refrigerator was a foyer-sized bathroom privatized by a plastic accordion door not much better than a curtain.

Two months later my quick brush with fiscal comfort ended. Contract expired. My father, thrilled at my move towards independence, pledged an occasional stimulus check (which he'd just sent last week). It didn't change the fact that I was lucreless again — I shouldn't have bought those Keens, what with my car note due. One more late payment on my previously owned-by-the-plumber and soon-to-be-uninsured automobile, I'd be riding the bus.

Those maintenance checks were also part guilt. My ten-year housesitting gig for Mystery Cat ended when my parents leased our house and moved to Florida. Mayflower had backed up to the front door and swallowed everything including the cat box. I prayed that Mystery would stay clear of the alligators in the rough. The nice, young *married* (my mother's emphasis) couple who leased the house I'd called home for the last thirty years had an option to buy.

The unofficial reason I'd moved down to the Twin Cities was that I believed that's where I'd find her. The Santa Claus video and the Sam Shepard elevator encounter were proof enough that she frequented my climate zone. Still playing the long shots, I set out again to track her down. I needed to track her down. I was writing True Crime. There were details missing that only my protagonist would know. If I tied up those loose ends, I could submit the manuscript with a clear conscience.

Fixated on the truth, me.

That's what I told myself.

In this version of search and find, I narrowed my scope and became a predator of middle-aged women, chasing after anyone who bore a resemblance. Resemblance to what, I wasn't sure. But I was practiced in apology: "I'm sorry, you looked like...." I saw her everywhere. And nowhere. It took a couple weeks for me to calm down and quit tugging at sleeves. Did I, in my heart of hearts, really believe I'd see her again?

I may have already seen her again, walked right past her, brushed shoulders, rode the elevator. The dots on my page were connected by my own ragged reasoning, which, in the end, defaulted back to her one and only defining characteristic: those pale, otherworldly eyes. Hidden with colored lenses.

After settling into my no-star efficiency apartment, I'd made the drive across town to Stillwater to visit Stacy at the bookstore. She hadn't recognized me. I'd explain how we knew each other. She'd acted properly embarrassed. I told her I'd lost weight, which was true — svelte as hell, me. My upswept Barbie-at-the-beach tsunami was chopped short Nicky Myer style.

Stacy hadn't seen Micks since the boat party. He probably went back to his wife, she'd said, and pointed to a rack of comic books and added with a shake of her head, "But maybe not, you know." I asked what did that mean? She was surprised that I didn't know this apocalyptic detail about our man Micks: Micks was a pannapictagraphist. At my dumb look she explained that he collected comic books. He'd started collecting as a kid and had owned several plums including *Captain America*. He'd forgotten his wife's birthday and she'd thrown them in the trash.

Stacy whistled. "No telling what they were worth."

I processed that, then quickly refocused. Did she know Rudi's last name? She thought a moment, then shook her head, not sure it had ever come up. He'd paid Meg, the caterer, cash. But Karen would know. Ah, Sparkle Legs. I asked where was Karen? Karen had moved to Denver, Lou's home office. She'd promised to write, but knowing Karen.... Stacy went on to explain that she and Karen had known each other, but had never been friend-friends. Did Karen have a last name? Johnston, Stacy said, but added that was Karen's maiden name. She didn't remember Lou's last name or his company's name. Something to do with computers.

I told Stacy that Karen had mentioned that Rudi wrote river guides, a perfect birthday gift for my cousin. Stacy said that Rudi's work was academic. He wrote for the trade: research as in universities, government agencies, EPA, FEMA. No tourist guidebooks from Rudi. Uh-uh. She hadn't seen him or his boat since the party back in June, even though he'd planned to spend the summer. Changed his mind, she guessed.

Stacy and I promised lunch. I'd thought that we could become friends, but that friend-thing had eluded me since high school where friends linked to proximity and time spent.

It always tempered me, how people sail in and out of each other's lives, for whatever reasons, having raised nothing more than a breeze in the trees or, in this case, a rustle in the mussels.

Sailing in, sailing out, me.

...

The first week in September Martin Micks showed up on my caller ID. Having not heard from him since the boat party, I knew immediately that My Saint had resurfaced. Screw self-respect. I picked up. The first thing out of his mouth was an apology for acting out in Stillwater. Alcohol was not his strong suit, he said, and complimented me on a good left punch. Would I meet him for coffee? That afternoon I received a bouquet of yellow daises, the kind that grow along roadsides. The erotica at my car door was not mentioned.

I wasn't dumb enough to spin yellow daisies into daydreams. Micks wanted something. And it had killed him to call me, or he'd have done it the day after. I was okay with that, because I, too, was scrounging for information. He'd even thrown in a primer, telling me about visiting the dentist in Stillwater. R.L. Ricky had been most cooperative. Yes, her last appointment that day had been a young boy. She'd pulled the boy's file and Micks had artfully noted the address, which was two blocks up the hill behind the Sam Shepard building. Micks had watched the house on three random occasions. The muscular, mid-thirties lady of the house maintained two fair-haired rowdy boys, who Micks described as bullies. The family bore no resemblance to the German lady and her dark-haired charge.

Which reconfirmed what I suspected: there'd been two sets of woman-boy patients at the dentist office that Saturday. The surly receptionist had assumed it was R.L. Ricky's patient Micks was looking for, when all along, the Don Warner half of the dentist duo had the answer. I didn't share my theory with Micks.

I dug up Angie#2 and listened again to her conversation with the bookstore clerk: *I tell him that I don't speak German. It would be a gift for my dentist.*

Ricky is English, of Saxon origin.

Warner is full-blown German.

As soon as I saved some money, I'd make an appointment with Dentist Warner. I'd explain my familiarity with the magazine *Stadtleute.*

My non-lucrative, fiction-writing career had turned into a hobby. Hobby. That's what I called it. My Word file of form rejections was full, thank you very much. And that didn't include the zero response queries from the agents who'd simply hit the delete key. No one fancied a piano teacher/lawyer for the drunk driver romance.

My unrighteous holdings from the old man in the wheelchair had dwindled to a few hundred dollars, and the righteous universe had not afforded a refill. I lived frugally, but the high-rent competition among landlords kept me checked. Just as I'd talked myself into downsizing to a boardinghouse, I landed a job bartending at Skiffy's, a beer bar out near Glen Lake that had recently acquired a hard liquor license. In anticipation of a new and improved clientele, Skiffy had collected a college-educated, all-star cast: a romance writer (me), a mural painter, a metal sculptor, a jewelry designer, and an art history major.

Our lack of marketable experience enabled lucky Skiffy to staff up for not much more than pocket change. An artist's resume was not a good read. I'd sent resumes to fifteen real companies that had advertised real jobs. Not one hit. Maybe I should have included self-addressed, stamped envelopes. Fact was my history major didn't hold up to the first cut MBAs applying for the same jobs. A decade out of college, my work experience consisted of a Taco Barn, a Moo Goo China Pan, a drugstore breakfast counter, and five unpublished romance novels. Newspapers and magazines were not impressed, white-shirt corporate even less. The minimum wage companies regarded fiction writers as short-term players, never mind that few people could sustain life on those non-sustaining paychecks. Dave once suggested that I take a class and learn the difference between a spreadsheet and a silk sheet. Fargo Dave.

He was right, damn it. At my age I should be able to support myself. Or, like my mother said, marry somebody who could. And birth some grandbabies. If I took her advice, my mother said, I wouldn't have to beat myself up every time I opened my checkbook. I could restart this writing business after the kids were grown. And if it didn't work out then, I'd have an excuse: The kids this, the kids that. No time. Too tired. Blah, blah. Kids, she said, would give me a wide berth, a diaper bag full of excuses, and I'd be looked upon as having contributed largely. It was tempting.

I cleared the crumpled napkin and cheeseburger plate from the bar and pocketed the dollar. I had twelve dollars in tips jingling around in my apron pocket. One hundred dollars was a slow lunch at Lords. I couldn't get an interview there. I lacked platform.

I squeezed a lemon into my water glass and wedged into Skiffy's lone window booth to contemplate the pros and cons of driving without insurance. Across the street a truck pulled up to the green grocer's — Fridley Refrigerated Freight tattooed on the side. I watched the man unload boxes until a car pulled in and blocked my view. Two women got out. The door behind me scraped the linoleum. No need for a jangle bell at Skiffy's. After I'd delivered their beers and fried up an order of onion rings the size of vacuum cleaner belts, I dug the Yellow Pages out of the furnace room. T is for trucking. F is for freight. How many transport companies could there be in the Twin Cities? This wasn't Chicago.

I called down the list. Not one Lance. The seven point Times Roman roster of companies, addresses and phone numbers blurred on the page. My Saint was taking on evanescence like a sinking ship. Search fatigue set in. Even my eye-color inquisition had cooled, although the inclination remained, like with a subject one has knowledge of, but has lost the passion for. The door scraped behind me when the onion ring ladies with their matching brown eyes toddled out, leaving me a fifty-nine cent tip under the onion ring basket. Not having mustered up the enthusiasm to smile, much less chit-chat, I'd become Bartender Bob.

By four o'clock, I had seventeen dollars and forty-nine cents in my apron pocket. At five o'clock the jewelry designer came on duty. She was ecstatic, having just sold a four-hundred and fifty dollar silver and ceramic bead necklace. I cheered her good fortune, but it depressed the hell out of me. The thought of my no-star apartment and the stack of unopened, number nine, cellophane-window envelopes blooming in the faded Easter basket on my countertop depressed the hell out of me. Too early to wallow in the gloom, I drove to the Hopkins library and rustled through the reference section where I unearthed a magazine that listed businesses and their owners. I perused the pages. Not one Lance. Lance must not be on the A-list of boy's names.

Maybe I wasn't looking for Lance. Roland Keach had shortened to Roach. I fingered down the list again, studying each name. One name hung with me. Laurence Vance. Laurence Vance shortened to Lance. Laurence Vance did not own a refrigerated trucking company in Fridley or anywhere else. Laurence Vance owned a concrete company in Burnsville. I thought about that. Among other things. Like what I was going to wear for my coffee date with Micks.

...

I pulled a wobbly stool to my makeshift desk at the kitchen counter and dragged my manuscript out from under the Easter basket. I'd bought a ream of paper and printed it, intending to read from hardcopy, but had set it aside when Micks called. I would wait and see what insight or addendum he might provide. I didn't plan on a big rewrite. I was happy with the way I'd presented Jude Templeton, my unlikely saint. Facts ruled, yes, but I'd plaited them with considerable psychological and emotive prose. My presentation included exposition on the concept that all mothers have a natural, protective nature regarding their children. This protective instinct, mother to child, transcends the law and all rights and wrongs and in betweens; it flies above common sense and reason, as does "but he was such a good boy!" railed by the mothers of sons who'd hacked their wives to death. I had bequeathed Jude Templeton this blind, maternal characteristic because it explained her cold-blooded killing of Laddie Ogren: she'd killed the evil predator and vindicated her daughter.

I'd put the same indulgent spin on My Saint's kidnapping contracts. She had not kidnapped Bentley Ogren. She'd rescued him. Twice. Twice from the clutches of Fanny's dirtball husband. This approach worked with my sensibilities, with my history as a writer of romance. I'd spent many hours finessing this angle. I was happy with my summation. It made perfect sense. I slid the manuscript back under the Easter basket.

Micks didn't recognize me with my boy-cut hair and my new svelte body. His only comment was that I was missing the nose ring. Fine. I hadn't come for him. I ordered my coffee black, straight up urban, and almost wept at the tarry taste, but did not weaken even with a basket of creamers within arm's reach.

I came with high expectations, high hopes that somehow he'd found a current photo of My Saint, a photo that would give her life again, bring her back to me. He brought two new photos, but the photos weren't of My Saint. The first one was the old man in the wheelchair who'd given me five for a beat-up briefcase. I asked who was this man? A person of interest, Micks said. At my stony glare, he'd added, "He's a shipper, the tramp trade, a pirate."

"What does that mean?"

"Just that."

Same old Micks. I shrugged and told him I'd never seen the man before in my life. I'd gotten good with the shrugs: shoulder shrugs, mouth shrugs, eyebrow shrugs — a woman of shrugs wishing she had another beat-up briefcase to deliver to this shipper of interest.

It was the second picture that took me down. A police mug shot of a man with short, black hair, *flat to his head like a Labrador retriever*, an acid curl on his lips. I imagined two rows of mercury fillings inside that snarling mouth. I planted my elbows on the table to keep my hands from shaking.

"Who is it?" I asked, knowing the answer.

"Laddie Ogren," Micks said. "Shot his wife back in October. You remember. Then took it in the head over in St. Paul. Canada sent down what they had. We never had a clean frontal.

Never arrested in the states. I know that your Brigid Ireland — alias noted, all aliases noted — she triggered him. But these two outlaws don't connect, she and him. Brigid Ireland and Laddie Ogren don't add up, which means it was a hit. One clean shot..." he pointed a finger at his head, "...means there's nothing personal. That's a hire, a damn good hire. What I want to know is who hired her? Every good, bad, and ugly shithead out there wanted Ogren, so no one stands out in that tar pit. The case may never be solved, but that's not my problem. Where I'm coming from is, if I knew who contracted the hit on Ogren, it would lead me to her and all her slippery selves. So, Jennifer Sands, I figured I'd run this by you. Maybe when you and Brigid Ireland were bonding, you might have crossed paths with Laddie Ogren, or heard something, saw them together. If you remember anything she might have said. Anything at all."

I was without words. I couldn't take my eyes off the photograph of Laddie Ogren. My throat had tightened into my ears. I couldn't swallow. I coughed.

Micks talked, watching me. "You've seen him before, haven't you?"

"No. Never." I coughed again and patted my chest.

"Think hard."

"No. Uh-uh." I shook my head. "I'd have remembered those eyes."

Eyes like his mother.

She'd picked that lock in South Saint Paul and stepped in fast. Stepped in and shot him in the head before he could turn and look. Not because she was a detached, professional killer. Because she wouldn't see those eyes, those cold and colorless, crystalline eyes.

I tracked him down in Winnipeg ... his cold, crystalline eyes stopped me dead.

PART III

25. Rose White
genus *Rosa*

Even with my new triple-short hair sans tsunami (a glaringly obvious solution), the blonde wig fits tighter than a sausage skin. Feathered bangs conceal my black eyebrows. I lean towards the mirror and coat my lips with the Ruby Spring I'd unearthed from the shoebox where I toss my years-past-sell-date make-up. Out of the box comes a no-name violet eye shadow. Add a dusting of Pink Icing to my cheeks.

I don't look like myself. That's good. I look like a Norwegian call girl. Not good. I wipe off the colored stuff and pat a pale powder over my face. Except for my stained red lips, my face is neutral. Blonde and pale, I could be Genny Ross in reverse, minus the ritzy black. My white sweater and khaki pants combo is hardly ritzy white. It will do. Add a mocha low-rise Hanky Panky. Things go better in lace underwear.

I stare at my blonde self in the mirror. My mother could spot me from the freeway. Skiffy would wonder what I was doing behind the bar.

"Hello, my name is Rose White."

Laddie Ogren's crystalline eyes had changed everything. That staggering correction didn't fit the pages I'd tweaked and nurtured like a proud parent, pages with psychological and emotive blather as to why My Saint had killed Laddie Ogren, unleashing her blind maternal instinct as the mother of Fanny Graas and ridding the world of the evil predator. I'd plugged the holes and tied the knots. I liked my pages, agreeably respectable as True Crime. Obviously, that no longer worked.

What's more, Jude Templeton was too far off the wall to tack on a Fiction sticker. Fiction required a credible character, and that would be a major overhaul. At the same time, incorporating this genetic upset into my polished manuscript would be an equally major overhaul. But without it, the story was no longer true.

The pages stayed dormant under the Easter basket.

Then The Gatekeeper at the swimming pool chemical company called with a new freelance project. Because of budget cuts, would I take less? Hell, if it were any less, I'd be paying them. I said thanks, but no thanks. Two days later I called her back and asked just how low had their rate dropped? But she'd already found a writer off Craigslist. He was in India, but for what he was charging, they'd deal with it. She would call me next time, maybe work something out, because, she'd added, I had superb technical writing skills.

That three-second accolade was all I'd needed. True Crime it was. Write the facts clearly and succinctly (a spirit sorely lacking in my Romance Period), objective in the style of Ann Rule, although I couldn't fathom in what professional category Ann Rule would file My Saint. Halfway between Aleksandr Solonik, Russian assassin extraordinaire, and French 'it was an accident' Claudine Longet would be my guess.

Halfway was no way. A new plan was born.

My new plan was to shift the focus off My Saint's character, who, under the magnifying glass, made cockamamie sense. The seven distinct women I'd met (Toni, Alex, Brigid, Angie, Louise, Clare, and Nicky Myer) were perfectly disconnected — except in their enterprise. The consistency of the characters was in their enterprise; therefore, I would get inside the enterprise.

I'm on my way to visit Laurence Vance.

Many writers do that, you know, go underground to better understand their assignments.

"Hello," I say to the mirror, my voice two tones lower. "I'm Rose White." It sounds like a sex solicitation from an alley. After three more attempts, I decide that my natural voice would be best. I'd be nervous enough meeting Laurence Vance, the man I believe is Lance, business associate of Clare Assett, the Patron Saint of Television, the saint who had, two years earlier at his request, accepted two grand from the inscrutable Lil to rescue Bentley Ogren from his psycho father. The same Lance, who, two years later, petitioned Clare Assett to hide Bentley Ogren from his psycho father. Because the Laddie Ogren, Mr. Dean Ogren, and Jude Templeton trinity is firmly established, I'm linking Lance to the Graas side of the family.

I don't believe a contract ever existed for those kidnapping jobs. They were rescue missions, not contracts. Domestic.

I extend my hand towards the mirror as if to shake it: "Rose White," I say, unlabored this time.

Then what? What will I say to Mr. Laurence Vance, if indeed, he is My Saint's taskmaster? Nothing sounds reasonable except to inquire about employment. But the only job I might be qualified to do is what the owner's wife or some unemployable family member diddles at two days a week (and gets paid for five). And what if Mrs. Larry Vance is already sitting at the front desk?

"Excuse me, Mrs. Vance, I'm writing a research paper on the chemical reaction of cement with bleach and algaecides in swimming pools."

How about that?

"I'm writing a story on how rich businessmen get their arbitrary agendas accomplished." That could get me into a cement mixer. Hoffa-esk.

My soon-to-be-disconnected landline rings. I'd applied for an entry-level job at a start-up insurance company in Bloomington. They'd actually telephoned to verify my address. I listen to the message. It's not a job offer. Nor is it some marketing executive impressed with my prose on Ph balancers and clarifiers. It isn't Penny, prairie girl turned cowgirl. Nor is it Micks, who rings up every now and again to see if I remember anything. It would be contrary to his agenda to concede that nobody hired anybody to do anything.

The caller is Raben Collections. Crap, I sent them a check last month. Why the hell are they bothering me?

"Get in line," I yell.

October is the jewel of the temperate this year in Minnesota. I grab my hoodie off the hook. My cell phone falls out of the pocket. I pick it up and for some hackneyed reason, I speed dial Micks only to hear 'the cell phone user is not available at this time.' I don't know what I'd planned to say. Invite him along?

The first thing out of his mouth is always, 'hear anything?' Not even a programmed hello. Bartender Bob had better manners. If I pressed for conversation about something other than My Saint, like a movie or a concert or an article I'd read on distressed polar bears, he'd act distracted, like he was in the middle of something big. 'Gotta run. If you hear anything.' If anything comes up on his end, he'll call. You betcha.

If not My Saint, he has nothing to say to me except to ask if I'd installed that nose ring yet. Every so often, I think about doing surveillance on him just for grins, see what holes he crawls into. But I don't. I have limits.

The last time I'd called, he'd said, 'Look, I gotta go.'

Look?

I could reel him back in with two words: Jude Templeton. Watch my name fly to the top of the screen. Martin gumshoe Micks. I should be the private eye, Kinsey Millhone move over. Hell-bent on facts, I'd googled Broder Circle. There's no such circle; her business with the Glock and the black party dress — DELETE. I'd also queried Find a Classmate on the University of Minnesota alumnae website. No Jude Templeton. Worthless degree in theater? How about NO degree in theater? Not that Micks would care about these superfluous details.

I finger my cell phone. Truth is, popping in alone at a potentially forbidding and anonymous cement factory makes me uneasy. I'm tempted to leave a message on Micks phone. Instead, I write a note, describe where I'm going, and drop it in the Easter basket on the counter.

I wish I could get him out of my head. Had he ever given me a reason to think there was anything between us? That's what hacks me. It shouldn't. But it does. It is discomfiting to admit that I would rather have been charmed, seduced, and dumped than to have been nothing at all. That phony kiss on the street still unhinges me. I'd been a half step out of pigeon shit.

Sometimes in the dark when I can't sleep, I go there with him again, change things up a bit, reach my own conclusions.

I start the car and am grateful to see I have a half tank of gas. I pop the glove box and file through my CDs looking for shifty music and find Dave's *Nevermind* CD. If I had his new address in Fargo, I'd send it to him. No I wouldn't. He never liked Nirvana. Into the machine it slides, and loud, all the way to Burnsville.

Having never imagined the landscape of sand and gravel eaten up in the production of cement, I am compelled to pull into a roadside clearing and get out of the car and take a look. Down in the crater the semi-truck parked next to the sand pyramid is the size of a toy in some kid's sandbox, it's that far down. I wonder how long before this quarry pit is empty. Centuries it would seem, but probably more like a decade — two max. I get back in the car. Kurt Cobain swears he doesn't have a gun. Heard that before.

A couple roads, no more than tire tracks, lead down into the pit. I imagine navigating one, a slide and a tip into some bedrock crevice, sand blowing over me, never seen again. I stick to the main road, which leads to acres of pavement where trucks lumber around, their mixer bullets rolling. I head towards what looks like headquarters, a one-story outgrowth off a multi-story elevator connected to silos linked by conveyer chutes. It doesn't make sense, the apparent mechanics, moving dirt against gravity. But I can't think about purposelessness right now. I am hunting Laurence Vance.

Parked in front of headquarters are four pick-up trucks the color of dust and two equally camouflaged sedans. I pull in between the sedans, turn off the engine, and study the movement. On a metal scaffold at the far end of the asphalt, a man in a florescent jacket hoses down his rolling bullet. Midway, two men negotiate a giant tractor. They take no notice of me. The whine of distant hydraulics is constant.

How many times had Clare Assett parked in this very spot? That is, if I'm right about Larry Vance. I think I am. I might score a kingpin. A niggling detail regarding this kingpin that I've tried to retrieve, but my memory fails me because I was focused on Zigler's signature scrawled over Jude Templeton's paltry tagline, is that I believe Laurence Vance was one of the end-of-the-alphabet boys in Corde's yearbook; but I can't swear to that. *They lived across the tracks by the cement works.*

For a fraction of a second I consider calling Micks again, tell him where I am. Sit him down over a cup of urban and tell him the whole story. Who am I kidding? He would plagiarize me, 'clean up a bunch of files,' and get back in the good grace of the department. Well, he can take his files and his artist renderings … artist renderings, ha! Render a baseball hat over Laddie Ogren's Labrador retriever haircut and you've got Nicky Myer.

Eyes like his mother.

I'm stalling. It's not too late to start the car, drive away, sink back into Skiffy's world. And what if there is a job opening here? Could this square, gray bunker be my destiny? Two years ago I would have argued the possibility. Then again, if I got employed here, I would be embedded. Keep an eye on Lance. I might find Lil, enigmatic Lil, penciled in as the birth mother of

Fanny Graas. If Lil is, indeed, the birthmother of Fanny Graas, I wonder if Grandma Lil was ever properly introduced to Grandma Jude Templeton. Grandmammas.

My characters are culminating at an industrial cement plant. Where's the romance?

All my characters except for Riverboat Rudi.

With the absolute certainty that Laddie Ogren was My Saint's son and married to Fanny Graas, Rudi may be no more than an unrelated ally of Jude Templeton, a priceless accomplice and laundry machine. A "strictly business" relationship works in True Crime. Nor am I one-hundred percent convinced on the true source of blue-eyed Bentley Ogren's Y chromosome. Laddie Ogren seems most probable. Brown-eyed Rudi carrying the modifying gene for sparse melanin is a long shot.

I'd wanted Rudi to be more than a criminal scullion. Rudi intrigued me. I liked his tack. I liked his sun-tipped hair. If I'd known what for back in June when I was aboard *The Trust Fund*, a.k.a. *S Brendan*, I would not be sitting in this dirt bowl. I would be down in the Caymans in time for the hurricanes. Riverboat Rudi would not have misinterpreted my intentions.

Walk on, walk off, rustle in the mussels.

Speaking of walk-ons, Penny married hers. Ministered by a J.O.P. on some beach south of Houston. Spur of the moment, she'd said, otherwise I'd have been her maid of honor. They'd worn cowboy hats. The last time we'd talked she was lovin' Dallas.

No one's gone in or out of the bunker and I'm still stalling.

My conclusion on how Mr. Dean Ogren and Jude Templeton met and conceived Laddie Ogren is reasonable and most probable. There is no new information. The information was there all along. In defense of myself, she'd had a circuitous way of talking. She'd told stories, reported untraceable entries, customer service commentary — seemingly trifled at the time.

I am not a freaking mind reader.

That very first day at the Stonehenge Bar Toni Padua had said: *Like my mother ... I got a miscue.* All the times I'd listened to that tape, I'd missed the catch in her voice, that elliptical pause, the million miles between the dot dot dot. *Like my mother ... I got a miscue.* In that one sentence, she had told her story. I'd assumed she'd meant Pineapple Daiquiri and the police pageant. I was wrong.

Mr. Dean was in prison once. But that was 36 years ago.

I would bet the stack that Dean Ogren and Jude Templeton met on her mother's watch at what Corde called 'a correctional lock-down for delinquent boys.'

There was an incident.

The incident adds up to Laddie Ogren.

Like my mother...

Unlike her mother, Jude Templeton had not kept her baby. But mean Dean Ogren had. Papa Dean had arranged for his son. I wonder who'd named the boy Laddie? Such a happy name.

She was a storyteller, that one. Better than I will ever be. I am embarrassed at having thought that she had actually wanted me to write her story. Double embarrassed at having conjured up a minimum of five (I admit, not-so-logical) reasons why a criminal outside the walls would want her story written. She no more cared about her story than I cared about nursing school. She'd needed help. And I'd pulled up a stool.

All the while, a parallel story had been playing out, the real story, a situation malignant enough to involve Sammy, myself, and, in a way I don't even try to articulate, Micks. Micks, my substantiated marker. If I hadn't met Micks, or if he'd walked off early, I would conclude that everything she'd told me was fiction. Not one accessible character remained to be compromised, not one accessible character who could verify one damn true crime fact.

Except for Laurence Vance.

She never dreamt I'd find him. The look on her face as I introduce myself to Lance would be worth a thousand manuscripts. A trucking company in Fridley. Ha! Try a cement company in Burnsville.

Yeah, I'm pleased with myself. I am about to get face time with an accessible character.

I truly appreciate the fact that most people are smarter than I am. Consequently, I underestimate no one.

Jude Templeton, in absentia, no photo available, had underestimated her biographer. I roll that around in my head. It warrants a smile, and I feel the tension in my face and consider backing up, driving away, shaking her off once and for all. She's forgotten me like a bug in the mortar. "Lithium" tracks again. Kurt Cobain won't crack, and I'm out of the car. Now is neither the time nor the place for the long view. I push and the gray metal door swings wide and hits the wall. I step inside and slam it hard enough to wake up anyone who might be napping. My cheery hello yields nothing. I won't crack.

Cracked are the plaster walls up into the ceiling. One small window faces the light but is too dusty for much light. No matter, the ceiling florescent is bright enough for a blind tailor. A Fifties retro, metal desk freighted with file folders and envelopes heaped beyond credible balance butts the wall. Barely audible static buzzes from a dusty, plastic radio on the desk. Beyond the desk, a door leads into a scruffy, rooms-to-let hallway. A hammered tin crucifix hangs above the door, its bruised and pitted Jesus face promising nothing. I step to the desk and peer at the day's mail bound with a rubber band. The postcard on top announces The World of Asphalt conference. Las Vegas would be my guess. I peek under the bundle at a magazine called *Aggregates Manager*. Cement is enough commerce to warrant a magazine? Who knew? No less interesting than swimming pool chemicals. Industries that exist outside my literary vacuum always startle me. I don't recall careers in these abstruse industries highlighted as employment opportunities in my high school career guide.

I pick up a pack of spearmint gum and quickly put it down. *Don't touch anything. It's hideous, this human compulsion to touch everything.* I remind myself that I have nothing to hide and snatch up the pack of gum and roll it boldly between my fingerprints while I imagine what Jude Templeton would say if she could see me now. Frankly, what would please me more than anything would be for her to walk through the door this very minute with her rosy Clare Assett cheeks and true blue eyeshadow and flippy blonde wig. Her irritating manner of amused unconcern would change in a hurry. Change to what? Dread? At the very least, to an unamused concern at my having found her.

"I will call you Jas," I chirp ala Toni Padua. "Jas didn't stick, ma'am." I unwrap a stick of gum and deposit it in my mouth, wrapper to the wastebasket.

So who tends this dirt bowl? No one, from the looks of it. Five MBAs work out of some tree-lined business park. This cement block is headquarters for the dirt operations. And they don't employ receptionists.

Plan B? *This is improv. Unrehearsed.* Prowl around. I tiptoe across the cement floor to the tin crucifix and peek down the scruffy hallway with its marred walls and thin, worn carpet curled at the edges.

"Excuse me. Anybody? Are you hiring?" I touch my wig to make sure it's not cockeyed. A second hello yields nothing. I step gingerly into the corridor. The first two rooms mirror each other with metal files and desks and cardboard boxes shoved against the walls. Nothing lethal. Laurence Vance may be nothing more than some nice guy who negotiated operating expenses in an overwrought, child custody battle. And here I am, ready to convict. Cement man Laurence Vance in Burnsville might have nothing at all to do with trucking company Lance in Fridley. My cell phone is in the car. "Hey," I would say to Micks, if he picked up. "I'm out here in Burnsville at this cement company. Not far from where Fanny lived and..." And what? I jiggle the car keys in my pocket. *If your data is undefined, stick with the plan.* I move down the hallway, my hellos barely audible. Door number three yields a broom closet, door number four a male-dominate toilet needing Clorox. I catch a glimpse of my pale face with the blonde wig in the mirror and it stops me. That's not me. That's Rose White. Rose White spits her gum into the wastebasket, lets the door bang shut and marches to the open door at the end of the hallway.

Which gives up the prize.

...the smallest office an owner of a large trucking company could possibly have and still do business. It's also the messiest office an owner of a large trucking company could have and still do business. Papers, receipt books, accounting books, tablets, white envelopes, brown envelopes, stacks of envelopes bound with rubber bands piled everywhere... The stale doughnut on the stack of ledger books is missing. She hadn't mentioned the top-of-the-line Mac. I'd kill for one of those.

He's got six TVs mounted to the wall so he can watch CNN, Fox, and the networks... I count three flat-screen, high definition ... screw the details. What's priggishly delicious is *the straight-back, worn velour, what might have once been a fiery red chair...* where Clare Assett sat. On which I now sit.

"Hello, Lance," I say to the empty room. My eyes take in the window. *It faces a cinderblock wall. A gray, muted light is all the window will allow. It's depressing light that steals the color from your eyes.*

"Steals the color. What color?"

I lean back in the red chair smiling, and, I admit, more than a little pleased with myself — 'thrilled' being a better word, an emotion unlike anything ever typed into a manuscript. Words won't get me where I am now. I like it. I try to catch the scent of Clare Assett's geranium, but ascertain only dry impalpable dust. I focus on a brushed steel display cabinet jammed full of trophies and framed photographs. Sports teams, it looks like. I abandon the red chair and tiptoe around the desk to see what sport is so zealously represented. The trophies both silver and cut glass are etched in foreign languages. *Fútbol*. Football? Looks like soccer, but what do I know? Laurence Vance probably owns the team. If what My Saint said was true, he'd be too short to play the game. I spot a floral, ceramic frame wedged behind a crystal bowl and squint for clarity. It's a headshot of a woman, professionally posed. The latch lifts easily. I ease out the frame.

She's Eva Braun with a Renaissance smile, hard to age-label, but I'm guessing mid-twenties, which syncs with the gold-etched date at the bottom. The woman would be in her mid-sixties now. The photo is signed *Regards, Lili*. Lil?

"My missing Lil. You've always been here, haven't you, Lili Graas."

For some uncharted reason the old woman, first spotted in the doorway at Stonehenge, then the next night at the bar with a cup of coffee, flashes in my mind's eye. Because of the woman's age, she'd been of little interest, and I'd not registered her face. *…the older a woman gets, the less visible she is.* Lil. Her presence would explain My Saint's omniscience.

What is Lil's relationship to Laurence Vance? My Saint never said. The photo is signed *Regards*. Regards suggests friendship, not romance. Photo still in his trophy case? Old friends. Old *good* friends. Something's loose on the back of the frame, a second photo anchored under the easel joint. I pry it loose. It's a studio shot of a boy and a girl, both blonde and about four or five years old, seated on a concrete garden bench. Hands folded on their laps, they're smiling like children do when they're confident in their world of possibilities, safe and unafraid, as if they will make it out there with the tricks and the devils. One of them did. The photo is signed, *Love from the twins, Fanny and Rudi.*

I stare at the boy who grew up to be Riverboat Rudi. Fanny's brother. Fanny's twin brother who would one day help extricate his sister's son from the devil and his almighty hell. Images flash through my head faster than a flipbook. I press the frame to my chest as if I might gather these people and make them safe, kill the wretched bastards who come calling with their self-serving reckonings.

A door slams. I fumble the frame, but catch it before it crashes to the floor. Me, the sloppy, unchecked savior, half-blind with tears, come to save you all with my witless intentions — can't save myself. I shove the photo behind the easel and slip it back into the cabinet and leap from the office with a long-step and a light-toe down the hall. I blow through the doorway and freeze.

He hasn't heard me. He stands at the desk with his back to me, sorting the mail. Concrete dust lends a faded chic to his denim jeans and jacket. A baseball cap covers his salt and pepper hair. I probably weigh more than he does.

Lance is as small as Mr. Dean is big.

The radio has been adjusted and a sing-song phone number for furnace repair repeats itself silly. Laurence Vance tosses the colored stuff in the wastebasket and gathers the white envelopes.

I wipe my sweaty palms on my pants, clear my throat and say, "Ahm, excuse me?"

He whirls around so fast I jump back to Jesus with a yelp. "I'm sorry," I say, one hand to my chest, one hand on the doorframe. "I-I thought somebody was down the hall, so I took a peek." No way could I have pulled off the two-tones-lower voice. Two-tones higher more like it.

"Can I help you?" he says, holding his frown, holding his mail, holding me in rough regard.

I strain for a good-natured look and walk towards him, hand extended. In one breath I say, "My name is Rose White are you hiring?"

It is all I can think to do.

He tosses the mail back on the desk and grabs my hand with both of his.

"Ah, yes. Rose White," he says and looks straight to the backs of my eyes. "Clare said you'd be coming by. What took you so long?"

THE END

Summer 2012
MY *Unlikely* WITNESS
ACT I, BOOK 2

cccarlquist.tumblr.com

Made in the USA
Charleston, SC
18 February 2012